Fathers and Sons

Otis Thorne Series Book One
Arla Jones

Acknowledgements

I would like to thank my editor Kate Seger and TMT Book Cover Design.

I would like to dedicate this book to my husband who has always encouraged me to do what I love to do.

What Readers Say

"A riveting political thriller... If political intrigue, secret organizations, treachery at every turn, and emotional stakes are your jam, this book is for you."

"Amazing story! This story is non-stop action and wonders from the first page through the last!"

Contents

1

Prologue: Otis Thorne

January 2023, CIA Headquarters, Langley, Virginia

Otis Thorne's fist connected with the desk in a satisfying thud. His supervisor froze, eyes widening, and then, almost mechanically, reached for the intercom. "Thorne... this is unacceptable!"

"I'm done with your games," Otis said coolly. "I've followed orders for years. I've saved lives you'll never know about. But enough is enough."

Minutes later, his career as a field operative ended. Permanent leave. No mission debrief, no warm farewell. Just a letter in a manila envelope, a new contact number, and the tacit dismissal of a man who had once been one of the agency's finest.

Three months later, Otis sat at a small desk in a sunlit classroom at Georgetown University, lecturing on security studies. The adrenaline of the field had been replaced with the hum of fluorescent lights and the scratching of pens on paper. He enjoyed it, most days. Quiet. Safe. Predictable. However, life wasn't that easy: the memory of unfinished business, of threats he hadn't stopped, haunted him like a shadow he could never shake.

And some problems... had a way of finding him.

2

Shadows in the Capital

King Street, Arlington, Virginia

On a cold, crisp night in the waning winter days of 2026, a lonely doorman stood in front of a dimly lit restaurant on King Street, Arlington, Virginia. It was past midnight. Most restaurants in the area had closed hours ago, but the lingering glow from earlier crowds still painted the pavement with faint shadows and muted reflections.

Inside, a secret meeting was underway—unbeknownst to Otis Thorne or the President of the United States. Men in tailored suits spoke in hushed tones over a polished oak table, their faces lit by the flickering candlelight, the air thick with tension and hidden agendas. Outside, the city slept, unaware that the first moves of a deadly conspiracy were being set in motion.

Three years earlier, Otis Thorne had been a CIA operative at the top of his game until one impulsive act put him on permanent leave. Now, as a visiting professor at Georgetown University, he thought he'd left the shadows behind. Little did he know, the shadows had already begun to reach for him again.

If there had been an observer, he would have noticed a line of limousines arriving. In each one of the limousines was a single passenger. After the passengers got out of their luxurious limousines and walked up the few marble steps to the heavy iron door, the limousines drove quietly away. Each passenger showed his right wrist to the burly-looking doorman, who then opened the door and let the passenger inside after checking it.

An exclusive group of rich and powerful men had gathered for a clandestine meeting. This was their first gathering in person. The men had talked several times on the phone and held video conferences, but they had never met in person. Only Hydra, their leader, had met the participants individually on a few selected occasions. But those meetings had been kept discreet and in remote locations, like his well-guarded dacha, his luxury holiday country home by the Black Sea.

These men wanted to shape the global economy and international politics for the benefit of their homeland and themselves. Operation Pobeda had brought them together. Pobeda means a victory or a coup in the Russian language. The operation had started over seventy years ago and had required lots of money and time to prepare. But the most important thing was that they needed one man on their side who could fulfill their demands and get them what they wanted, namely the president of the United States.

The group called themselves Septem, the Seven. The name, Septem, referred to the number of participants in the group—seven—even though not all of them participated in person in the meetings. The Septem needed one day to start a successful execution of all the activities in Operation Pobeda that would change the world and threaten the stability of the world order.

The ages of the Septem ranged from mid-forties to seventies. Each man had a different tattoo on their right wrist: Phoenix, Hydra, Werewolf, Hippogriff, Cyborg, Nachtkrapp, and Basilisk. Each tattoo represented a mythical or a sci-fi creature. They used their tattoos both as an identity check as well as code names because they did not want to be heard communicating with each other by their real names and talking about their secret operation. Their faces and businesses were too familiar to everyone following the news. If their collaboration had been known, someone might have started asking questions. These men were too clever and too careful to let any outsiders know about Operation Pobeda. They knew that knowledge was both leverage and power. The stakes were high.

When the Septem group members entered the restaurant, they glanced around to ensure it was as private and secure as their leader, Hydra, had promised. The place was empty except for these men who had arrived.

The color scheme inside was of cool grays and blues, with metallic touches on the walls. The tiny lights on the ceiling bathed the room in a soft glow. The thick blue curtains were drawn over the windows so no one would see inside the restaurant. One wooden table was placed in the center of the room. A few flower arrangements of white Callas and purple anemones in tall vases on the pedestals were arranged around the dining room.

The table was set for seven men with as many tablet computers on it. In the middle of the table, a set of glasses and bottles of sparkling water, house wine, brandy, and vodka bottles were ready. However, none of the participants considered this visit a social one.

One seat was empty, but there was a tablet computer because this participant joined the meeting via video call. He had covered his face with a black bird mask called il dottore. The mask had glass openings in the eyes and a long, curved black beak. The bird mask was fitting because his tattoo represented a mythological bird—a Nachtkrapp, a scary night raven, inked inside his right wrist. Just like all the other participants, he showed his wrist to the others for identification purposes. He used voice-altering software that gave his voice a deep metallic sound to make sure that nobody recognized him.

They could have had all the meetings online via video conference call, but none wanted to do that because someone could still be listening, monitoring, and might discover their plans. The man with the Hippogriff tattoo on his wrist owned the restaurant, and no outsider could have planted listening devices there without him knowing it. He also provided limousines for the participants. The most important thing was to keep Operation Pobeda secret. The other reason was that if they had to make difficult decisions, it was always better to do it face-to-face, for example, if they had to sacrifice a member of this group to ensure the operation's success.

"Is everyone in order?" Hydra, the spokesman, asked with a thick Russian accent. He glanced at the computer screen in front of him. They were all there. The operation was ready to launch.

Hydra was in his early seventies. He was a tall, slender, white-haired man with eyes as friendly as a shark's. The many-headed serpentine monster, Hydra, was tattooed on the inside of his right wrist. He was one of the oligarchs that had emerged in Russia after its transition from socialism to capitalism, and he was well-connected to the Russian mob and the government. He knew how and who to bribe to get things done in the new Russia. His billions had come from owning media companies in Russia and transferring his investments to Swiss bank accounts before the economic sanctions sank the ruble.

"Yes, Hydra, Operation Pobeda will be set in motion today as agreed," an elderly man with salt and pepper hair replied. "The doppelganger is ready to play his part." He had a Basilisk tattoo, a legendary reptile that can kill with a single glance.

"Any new developments?" Hydra asked. His icy gaze went around the table. Some of the participants faced his stare with blank, brave looks, and some turned their eyes toward the tablets in front of them. Everyone feared Hydra, their government ally, their strategist, not just because of his fortune but because of his influence and his high-level allies in Russia.

"Everything is going as planned. No delays, no changes. My men are in place and ready to go to the airport," a man wearing a black leather vest and pants replied. He had a huge, fiery-looking Werewolf with flaming eyes tattooed on his right wrist. He looked like a member of a motorcycle gang. He was in his mid-forties and had earned his fortune in drugs, sex, collecting debts, and later setting up legal shell companies to hide his more illicit businesses.

"Thank you for the update, Werewolf," Hydra replied and asked the one person participating via video conference, "Do you have anything else to share with the rest of us, Nachtkrapp?"

"The President won't have a clue what hit him," Nachtkrapp replied with a metallic voice, but you could still hear a slight Bostonian accent.

"Everything seems to be in order. "If there is nothing else, then we will meet again after the first phase of Operation Pobeda is over," Hydra said, ending the clandestine meeting.

It had started raining, and the raindrops glinted in the streetlights like silver silk. The doorman held a large umbrella for each man until they got into their limousines. Then he went back for the next one. Hydra was the first to leave, and Werewolf was the last. Each man left the same way they came, alone and in a dark limousine with tinted windows. The doorman closed the restaurant doors and turned off the lights.

CODE NAMES

HYDRA

CYBORG

WEREWOLF

BASILISK

PHOENIX

NACHTKRAPP

HIPPOGRIFF

3

The Technician

6:00 a.m., Jack's Home, Essex County, New Jersey

Launch day of Operation Pobeda

The morning sunlight had barely breached the horizon when the first noises sounded. Jack's wife, Mary, was at the stove, frying eggs for the kids' breakfast. Her curly blonde hair caught the faint light, and the aroma of toast filled the small kitchen. She hummed a little tune, unaware of the danger lurking just beyond the locked kitchen door.

A sudden crash tore through the quiet. The door splintered, hinges groaning as it gave way. Four masked figures in black leather stormed inside, moving with precision that made her heart seize.

"Who are you?" Mary shrieked, instinctively moving to shield the children.

Two of the intruders seized the kids and dragged them toward the living room. The others grabbed her arms, pinning her to the spot. Fear tightened its grip around her chest.

Jack, upstairs in the bathroom, heard the muffled screams. He rushed down, only half-dressed, razor still in hand, foam on his face. His heart pounded as he saw the intruders.

"Stop! What do you want?" he demanded, trying to sound calm.

One man, tall, muscular, with a dark stare that chilled him, pressed a hand to Jack's shoulder. On his vest, a nametag read: Dentist. Jack caught glimpses of tattoos: a crown below the ear, a cross on knuckles, the devil on the top of a hand. Prison tattoos, maybe.

Dentist's voice was low and firm. "If you want your family to live, do exactly as we say."

Jack swallowed hard, trying to memorize the men, their size, their marks—anything for the police. He saw the names Snake, Typhoon, and Alien on their vests. Each man was tall, bulky, like wrestlers or bodybuilders.

"Call your work," Dentist instructed. "Say you're sick. Tomorrow, forget this happened."

Hands trembling, Jack grabbed his phone, dialing his supervisor. His voice wavered. "Hey, Al... I've got the stomach flu." He hung up, hoping it sounded convincing.

Dentist nodded, retrieving the phone. "Good. Everything is on schedule."

Outside, the black-masked men moved with mechanical efficiency. Dentist mounted a motorcycle and drove to a white van near the airport. Jack's ID badge, keys, and phone were handed to the next operative. Jack's life and his job were now instruments in a larger, invisible operation.

The real Derek, the man who had been scheduled to take Jack's shift, lay in a hospital bed, injured in a "hit-and-run" that was anything but accidental.

The abduction had set the first domino in motion.

4

The Crash

6:00 p.m. EST, Press Briefing Room, the White House

"Good evening. Thank you for coming on such short notice," Press Secretary Brad Buchanan greeted the press. His face was grave when he looked over the Press Briefing Room and continued reading his statement: "Today, at 3 p.m., we received the news that the helicopter carrying President's eldest son, Zachary, and his son-in-law, Dan Wheeler, had crashed into the Potomac River. Only Dan Wheeler was recovered alive at the crash site, and he has been taken to George Washington University Hospital."

His voice trembled as he struggled to continue. "The search is still ongoing for the president's son and the pilot. The Sikorsky S-76B helicopter departed from Essex County Airport in Fairfield, New Jersey, and was headed towards Washington, D.C., Reagan Airport. The flight conditions were such that the fog was obscuring the visible landmarks, but an experienced pilot should have been able to make this flight without any problems."

As the questions started firing from the reporters, the Press Secretary held out his hand and said: "Please, no questions at this time. We only ask you to pray for the president and his family. Good night." His clear blue eyes were usually bright with enthusiasm, but now he was holding back tears as he walked out of the room.

Brad Buchanan was a muscular man of twenty-eight with the golden good looks of the wealthy New England family he'd sprung from.

After the briefing, he headed towards the exit. His emotional distress was obvious because he was Zachary's best friend, Dan's best man at his wedding, and a close friend to Dan Wheeler, too. The three of them had been like the Three Musketeers ever since they met at the Harvard University campus in Boston. He knew that only family members were allowed visitation at the hospital, but he had received permission to visit Dan.

It was cloudy outside. The cherry trees on the White House ground were blooming pink, but Brad did not pay attention to their springtime beauty. He was too occupied with the helicopter crash. He took his car and drove directly to the hospital. The media vans had gathered outside the building, and when they saw his car approaching, they tried to gesture for him to stop and ask for more details from him, but he just waved them off without any comments and drove to the underground parking lot. He took the elevator to the ER.

The elevator's door slid open silently when Brad entered the hallway. He smelled the familiar antiseptic scent of the hospital. He heard the intercom paging doctors, calling out names, codes, and directions. The nurses passed by him carrying trays with bandages, bottles, and medicines. His footsteps echoed on the linoleum floor when he walked along the hallway looking for directions and where to find Dan. He saw nurses and paramedics hurrying past him. Several patients were waiting for their turn, sitting in the lobby area and some were lying on the temporary hospital beds waiting for treatment or surgery.

Busy day for the hospital staff even without the accident, he thought. He looked around to find someone there to guide him to Dan. He found the information desk, and there was also Irene, the president's daughter, pacing in the hallway impatiently, her arms crossed, her lips tight, and her face tense with concern. Her outfit was plain, no makeup or high heels, no designer clothes, and her eyes were puffy and red from crying.

Dan must be here, Brad thought and approached her.

When Irene saw Brad, she ran into his arms, and the tears ran down her cheeks when she sobbed, "He's alive. His face is all covered in bandages. He is sedated now. The doctors allowed me to see him only for a minute." She wiped her cheeks. "They will transfer him to the third floor to a private room when they have checked his vitals and know what's going on with him."

Brad held her in his arms and squeezed her gently to comfort her. She leaned on his shoulder.

"How's your dad?" Brad asked. He had not seen the president since the helicopter crash news broke.

She wiped the tears off her cheeks before answering. "He is worried sick for Zachary. He was here and then he hurried back to the White House. He told me that the search and rescue teams of the local police, the Coast

Guard, the Port Authority, and the Secret Service are going through the crash site searching for Zachary and the pilot and to determine if this was a terrorist attack or an accident."

Brad checked on Dan from the doorway. Several patients were treated in the same ER room separated by curtains. Irene whispered, "The first bed is Dan. You can barely recognize him because his head is so bandaged."

"At least he is alive," Brad replied quietly. "That accident was bad, and I would not want to lose him too."

Brad could smell the antiseptic liquids and the scent of blood in the air, and he heard the monitors beeping steadily and saw the EKG monitor's lights blinking and showing the heart activity and the pulse. Dan didn't move. Brad assumed he was unconscious due to the accident, or the doctor had given him something to stay asleep due to the pain.

Brad returned to the hallway to be with Irene. She needed all the support she could get.

5

Zachary

7 P. M. Unknown location

Zachary Burr woke up to silence. He was in a dark room where the only light came from under the doorway. Nothing was moving. He assumed he was alone.

He tried to move, but he noticed that his arms were tied up behind his back and his legs were tied up around his ankles. He was sitting on a metal chair in the middle of the floor. He tried to call for help, but his mouth was taped over. He couldn't get words out, just an incomprehensible mumble.

What's going on? Where am I? Why am I here?

He could smell the garlic and grilled meat. His belly grumbled. He realized he was starving.

It must have been hours since I ate last time. What time is it? How many hours have passed? Where am I? Why am I tied up like this? Did someone kidnap me?

He had a splitting headache, and he winced when he tried to turn his head.

I can't move. I've been kidnapped. I'm a prisoner! Zachary thought, panicking. His breathing became rapid, and the fear churned his stomach.

Loud footsteps echoed from behind the door, a lock clicked, and the metal door opened with a clank. The harsh fluorescent light flickered before the room was lit.

Zachary blinked several times and squinted to see better. His eyes were not adjusted to the light.

Two biker guys entered and glanced at him, then went to sit by the doorway.

Guards! Zachary realized. They are the kidnappers! His heart pounded fast as he tried to figure out what had happened. He had no memory of how he had gotten here and who these guys were. The only sure thing was that he was a prisoner.

As Zachary's eyes adjusted, he scanned the room where he was held: a cellar or a basement with a wooden floor.

The brick walls looked worn, and no windows. Wooden and plastic crates were piled up against the wall. There was some metal, industrial shelving by the walls filled with boxes, packages, and bottles. He noted neatly stacked wine bottles against the wall and a television.

This place could be a storage room of a grocery store or a restaurant, Zachary thought. *Why did they bring me here, whoever these guys are?*

The guards kept their eyes on him but did not say a word. They wore black leather vests, black leather pants, worn T-shirts, and unruly hairdos. Both were tall and bulky, like wrestlers or bodybuilders, with huge bulging muscles in their arms. The other biker had a black handlebar mustache, and the other was bald.

Zachary's memory was coming back: He remembered flashes of the airport and the helicopter pad. Nothing made sense.

They must have given me some drug to make me unconscious, he thought. He tried to remember the details because he knew they would be important if he ever got out of this mess.

Zachary struggled to get his memories in order. He recalled he was on his way to meet his father at the White House.

I was with Dan. We took the company sedan to the airport with the driver. We parked at the airport near the helipad. There was an SUV parked, too. A guy dressed as an airport security guard came from inside the helipad and asked us to follow him. He said there had been some incident at the airport, and he wanted to make sure that we were safe and would not have any delays in departure. We followed him to the hangar area and there it happened: two other men came from out of nowhere, dressed like motorcycle gang members with leather vests, helmets, and leather pants, and they pointed guns at us. I was forced inside a black van that was waiting for us outside. They made me sit between the two huge guys in the back seat. Then I remember I felt a prick on my neck. They must have injected some drug in my neck intravenously to make me lose consciousness.

Zachary did not remember anything after that. The next memory was when he woke up in this place. Then his eyes widened as he remembered his friend Dan.

What happened to him? Maybe he is in a different room.

Zachary noticed that his guards were armed and dressed the same way as his airport kidnappers.

One of the biker guards came closer and removed the tape from his mouth. Zachary inhaled a few times, coughed, and swallowed hard.

Both bikers had their gang's name written on the right side of the vest: The Werewolves, their rank in the gang, and their nicknames. The one who had removed the tape from his mouth had a handlebar mustache and was called Sniper. His rank was a soldier.

"Where am I?" Zachary asked. His voice sounded gravelly, and he tried to clear his throat. He looked at the guard who had taken the tape away, but he ignored him and went back to sit.

No reply. The two men just stared at him.

"Can I have some water, please?" Zachary pleaded. His throat felt so dry like he had not had a drink for hours.

Zachary heard the two men exchange a few words. Zachary recognized the language: Russian!

He guessed he was kidnapped because of his father, but he did not know why. He wondered what the Russians wanted from his father.

After the short exchange of words in Russian, the bald biker got up, took a bottle of water from the table, and walked toward Zachary. He held the bottle against Zachary's lips and poured the water into his mouth but did not release him.

Zachary wrinkled his nose: he could smell the sour, sulfuric scent of the foot sweat and dirty clothes.

Zachary guessed Spider had gotten his nickname because of the cobweb with a spider tattoo on his neck. He had never seen or heard of these gang members before.

New footsteps approached the room. Spider and Sniper turned towards the door to see who was coming in. The metal door opened with a clang, and its hinges creaked, echoing in the room.

A third biker marched into the room. "Snake, long time no see," one of the other bikers greeted him.

Snake glanced at the two bikers, nodded approval, and then approached their prisoner with long strides. He looked him over to see if he was okay, then returned to exchange a few words with the guards.

The newcomer was called Snake. He was a Werewolf lieutenant based on his vest, a higher ranking than the two other bikers. He smelled like old sweat and onions.

Zachary tried to memorize Snake's appearance. *If I ever get out of this place, the police might want me to describe my kidnappers to a police composite artist.* Snake had a goatee, mean, beady black eyes, Slavic high cheekbones, a high-browed nose, a crew cut, and a cleft chin. His outfit was the same as the others: a black vest and pants.

Snake talked with the two guards in Russian, probably hoping Zachary didn't understand him, but Zachary was fluent in that language. "Is he okay? Any side effects of the anesthetic?"

Sniper, the biker with the handlebar mustache, replied in Russian, "No, he looks okay. He was a bit disoriented at first."

"Good," Snake said and turned to look at their prisoner, Zachary. "We did not want him to experience serious side effects or die from the anesthetic. He is the most valuable prisoner we could imagine and vital to our operation. That's why we didn't use ether or chloroform; instead, we used intravenous anesthetic."

Snake approached Zachary and opened the hand ties. Zachary rubbed his wrists to get his blood circulating. Snake waited for a moment and then handed a cell phone to him. "You need to send your father a text message," Snake spoke English with a thick Russian accent. He told Zachary exactly what to write. "Don't press send yet. I want to read it before you send it."

After Zachary had written the text message, Snake took the phone back.

Snake viewed the screen and read aloud, "Dad, I'm alive. I've been kidnapped. No one else knows I'm alive. Do as they say. Please. Watch the video link."

Snake nodded, satisfied, "Good. Now we'll send it." Zachary watched him press the send button on the phone. After it was done, he pocketed the cell phone and tied Zachary's arms behind the back of his chair.

Snake turned the chair and made sure the television was behind Zachary, explaining, "I will also make a video for your father."

Snake said a few words in Russian to Spider, who got up, walked to the television, and turned it on.

Snake had positioned Zachary so that the television was behind Zachary, showing the recent White House press briefing.

Zachary understood that the video would assure his father that he was still alive. No other reason to make it. He looked straight to the camera to convey to his father that he was still fighting and doing okay for the moment, although he had no idea what he looked like.

Snake pointed the cell phone toward Zachary and checked that the television broadcast was visible behind him, then he shot a short video, which he posted to Zachary's father. When he finished it, he left the room, leaving the prisoner with his guards.

6

The President

7 p.m. (EST), The Oval Office

The man whose angular face with his short, blond hair and vivid blue eyes was among the most recognized in the nation, sat behind the Resolution Desk and stared at the text message he had received on his personal cell phone from Zachary, his missing son's cell phone: "Dad, I'm alive. I've been kidnapped. No one else knows I'm alive. Do as they say. Please. Watch the video link."

A couple of hours earlier, the president of the United States, Andrew Burr, had been informed of the helicopter crash. He had thought his son was dead and his son-in-law, Dan, severely injured. However, after receiving the message, nothing was the same as before; everything seemed unreal.

How could it be possible to kidnap a sitting president's son? It should not be conceivable. *At least, not without help from inside,* he thought.

Andrew's eyes went from frigid cold to blazing anger. This was planned all along. *Nothing happens by accident, especially in politics,* he thought.

President Burr had asked his security detail to wait outside and give him a moment alone. He did not want anyone to hear or see his son's message. He stared at the link on his phone and finally pressed to view it. The video showed his son sitting in a chair with hands bound behind his back, looking frightened but in good condition. Behind his son, a television showed Brad Buchanan giving the press briefing on the helicopter crash.

The president sighed in relief. *The press briefing confirmed that Zachary was alive after the crash,* Andrew Burr thought. An endless stream of questions ran through his mind: *what do these kidnappers want? Why such an elaborate scheme to get his attention? How much time does my son have? Are these kidnappers Americans or from a hostile country? They could be members of a homegrown terrorist group supporting ISIS or Al Qaida.*

He knew he was not the most popular president this country had seen. He had faced multiple demonstrations and riots against his political campaign and his rise in power. Many had opposed his hard nationalist and populist views, but more had also supported him and got him elected. But his enthusiastic ethnic-nationalist comments during the presidential campaign had fueled the formation of dozens of new grassroots resistance groups who did not want to see him in office. Could any of those groups participate in this kind of criminal activity? He wasn't sure. How far would someone go to change the political leadership for their own liking?

If the kidnappers were from a hostile, foreign country, he was in trouble. A foreign power controlling the president and the executive branch of the government! That would be a catastrophe. A new kind of fear swept through his mind when he considered what the kidnappers could ask of him, the president of the United States of America.

When the recorded message ended, he replayed it to see if he had missed anything or any clues about who the kidnappers were. No visual sign of the kidnappers. No idea of what their demands were going to be.

His phone chimed. Another message arrived from his son's cell phone number: "If you want to see your son alive, don't tell anyone. Our contact will use the code: Postmaster."

President Andrew Burr sat at his desk, his mind racing after a failed attempt to reach his son on his cell phone. He slowly placed his phone down, swiveled his chair around, and gazed out the window towards the Rose Garden. His thoughts turned to the events of the past few hours, weighing his options carefully.

As a leader known for his unwavering stance, he now faced a dilemma: his son's life was at risk. He needed a strategic plan, one that required expertise he couldn't find within his immediate circle. His estranged wife and daughter couldn't be informed, not yet.

There was one person he could trust: Otis Thorne, a visiting professor at Georgetown University's Security Studies Program. A former CIA operative with experience in Eastern Europe and Russia, Otis was the perfect ally. Their friendship and infrequent meetings made him an unlikely suspect.

To avoid raising suspicion, Andrew decided on a discreet approach. He would invite Otis to play golf at the Congressional Country Club, despite the unfavorable weather. This casual meeting would allow them to discuss the situation without arousing attention.

He hoped that Otis was not on their radar. Otis was his old friend but not a regular visitor to the White House. Sometimes, they grabbed a drink or had dinner together, but it had been months since the last time.

7

Otis

7:30 p.m. (EST), At Otis Thorne's apartment

Otis Thorne had just returned home from the university. He'd had a long day with lectures and papers to correct. He tossed his keys on the hallway table and placed his takeaway food bags beside them.

His apartment was small but modern and functional. Simple glass table, nice comfortable chairs in the living room, a wide-screen television, and a soft wool carpet. His office had a desk with a computer, and multiple volumes of books stashed on piles and filling the bookshelves spoke of the owner's occupation.

Otis was obsessed with his family background. His father's family originated from New England, and his family had been among the original families that left Great Britain to seek freedom of religion. Considering his family, he probably inherited his curiosity about new things and his forward-thinking nature from his ancestors.

His mother's family could be traced back to the Civil War black scout, Orville Turnbull, who served under Frederick Douglass during President Lincoln's administration after the Emancipation Proclamation was announced. He had joined the army when the previous slaves of the southern states were allowed to enlist in the U.S. military and form the first authorized black regiments.

Otis's mother, Estelle, was born in 1954 in Mississippi and went to Tennessee State University to study communications. After the university, she moved to Washington, D.C., to be a news reporter in a local newspaper. In Washington, D.C., she met her future husband, Reginald Thorne, while doing one of her news reports. They had several dates, and one thing led to another, and they got married in 1982. Otis was born two years later and grew up to be a handsome man with honey-colored skin. Otis Thorne was a 6'3" tall, lean guy, physically well-built with slightly outward protruding ears. He had deep brown eyes and dark brown hair that was flat on the top. He had a precisely cut goatee and kept his hands and fingernails meticulously neat.

Otis was a quick thinker, and his killer charms had helped him get out of a lot of trouble when he was younger. His intelligence and ability to think and act fast were the qualities that earned him an academic scholarship. His mother had always encouraged him to study harder and be the best he could at whatever he decided to do with his life. One Christmas, his mother Estelle gave him a framed quote:

"We may explain success mainly by one word, and that word is WORK! WORK!! WORK!!! WORK!!!!"

– Frederick Douglass

He kept it above his desk at home.

Otis was an Ivy League graduate who had studied political science at Princeton University. He chose the Political Economy track because of its cross-disciplinary studies of individual behavior and social phenomena. He had aced his class in game theory and microeconomics and impressed his supervising professor with his thesis of a thorough analysis of the decline of the Soviet Union.

His father, Reginald Thorne, had studied at the same university and later chose to become a spy in the CIA during the Cold War era. He was killed in the late 1980s in East Germany just before the Berlin Wall was torn down. His killer had never been revealed, although Otis thought the agency knew his identity.

He had decided to follow his father's career path in the CIA, secretly hoping to find out who killed his father. He had his own suspicions: maybe someone in the agency gave up his father's identity to the enemy, and he was executed, or perhaps his father made a mistake and got himself killed. Otis had always thought the first choice was more believable than the latter because he didn't believe his father would have made such a fatal mistake.

Otis's academic and linguistic skills gave him an advantage, and he could decide where he wanted to serve. He had chosen Eastern Europe and Russia. His linguistic skills were remarkable: he could pick up a dialect in any conversation, mimic it in his speech, and he was able to tell from which part of the world and even from which part of the city the person was originally from. He learned new languages with uncanny ease.

Even though he no longer worked for the agency, he still automatically used his spy skills: checking out if any vehicles were following him in the traffic and memorizing faces, looking for recurring patterns. He had learned to operate under surveillance on the enemy ground. But that was all past.

As a visiting professor in the Security Studies Program at Georgetown University, all the counterespionage and analysis were behind. He had seen his colleagues going on a downward spiral using drugs and alcohol because they could not take the stress, lying about their jobs to their friends and family—if they ever had any—and being on alert every minute of the day.

Otis admitted that he had wanted out because he felt he had nothing left to give to the agency. His superiors had agreed with him because they did not want a burnout operative on their team.

Otis stood by the hallway table, browsed through his mail, mostly bills and advertisements, and threw them on the table next to his keys.

I can open these later, he thought. His stomach was growling. He had gotten two takeaway paper bags from a nearby Chinese restaurant, which he had left on the table when he got home. Now, he grabbed them and ambled to the living room. He reached for the remote control, pressed it to turn on the television, and went to the kitchen to get a glass of water. When he returned, he saw more blue and red emergency lights flashing on the screen than he could even count. His first thought was that another terrorist attack had happened. He sat down on the couch and turned the volume up.

He was just about to put the first bite of the dinner in his mouth, but his hand froze in midair when he heard the news reporter's first words, "There is no sign of the president's son yet. The rescue team, the Coast Guard, the police, and the FBI have all joined their forces to find him and what happened to the helicopter."

Otis was dumbstruck. *The president's son is missing? That's not possible or even likely. They have the Secret Service to watch out for them. Not unless someone inside was involved in this...*

He sat staring at the television screen and forgot to eat dinner. He had known Zachary his whole life. He had been at every major family event with the Burr family. They had fallen apart when he was elected to office, but they were still friends even if they had not seen each other for a long time.

He turned to another television channel which showed the White House fence surrounded by media, law enforcement officers, and onlookers holding candles and lights and bringing flowers and cards to the fence. Another scene showed a large crowd of FBI agents, police officers, and Coast Guard people all in their easily identifiable windbreakers over their suits. In both scenes, the onlookers and the media people outnumbered the agents and police. You could see cameramen and reporters wearing their different television station windbreakers and holding their microphones everywhere you looked. There was also a huge trailer-size news satellite van broadcasting the national and international news events.

Otis turned the volume higher to hear what had happened.

"This is CBX Evening News." A somber-looking reporter stood in front of several police cars and other media reporters near the crash site. "... Dan Wheeler is found alive but injured, and the Coast Guard is looking for the president's son, Zachary Burr, and the pilot who is still missing." Another news reporter behind him was about to start her show, and the assistant was giving her a last-minute touch-up with the makeup. She was prepared to interview a man beside her.

Otis changed the channel to hear what her interview was all about. "This is Max news," the same female reporter said. She had blond hair and wore the Max Channel's windbreaker. She introduced the man beside her as an eyewitness, Mr. Marco Smith. He was a pale, dark-haired with a stubble bearded chin, a vaguely rugged-looking guy wearing a plain gray windbreaker, a black sweatshirt, black jeans, and a baseball cap on his head.

"I heard some loud noise, and I looked up and saw this helicopter fall through the fog. It was coming down fast, and I saw it crashing over there." The eyewitness pointed towards the Potomac River. "The helicopter was not on fire. Its propellers stopped moving. It just fell from the sky."

Otis noticed that the eyewitness had a strong accent and placed it as an Eastern European, probably of Russian origin. *But his last name is not Russian,* he thought. *Odd. Smith is usually used as an anonymous name if someone does not want to be identified.*

Otis had read his share of fiction novels featuring the names of Smith and Jones, the most common last names in the United States.

Why wouldn't the eyewitness want to be identified? Otis pondered. He did not believe the name he had given was his real one.

The female reporter turned to the camera and explained, "The eyewitness, Mr. Marco Smith, just described the moment he saw the helicopter carrying the president's son and his son-in-law fall through the fog into the Potomac River." She turned and pointed to the policemen and the onlookers around the scene. "As you can see, the media, the police, and hundreds of citizens are gathered around the White House. This is a sad day for the president and our country. We don't know yet if it was a terrorist attack or just an accident."

The eyewitness, Mr. Marco Smith, quietly stepped back and disappeared into the crowd. He had no plans to stick around. Nobody paid any attention to him.

When Otis had heard enough of the news to put together what had happened, he picked up his phone and placed a call to President Andrew Burr. While listening to the ringing tone, he surfed to another channel to see if any more details were reported. The president did not answer, and Otis left him a message to express his condolences and told him, "If you need anything, anything at all, just call me."

After leaving the message, Otis continued watching the latest news.

"I'm here with the airport security," the XBX news reporter said, and beside him stood a tall man with a serious look. "Mr. George Stockton, you are responsible for airport security."

The man beside the reporter nodded. He had a modern-looking, chest-strapped radio that was on and voicing some of the security team's reports and static noise. George Stockton ignored the radio voices while being interviewed.

"Were the flight conditions so difficult that this accident could have been caused by the weather?" the female reported inquired, trying to look concerned while asking questions.

George Stockton frowned. "No, I don't think so. Any experienced pilot should have been able to navigate safely here."

"What do you think was the reason for the crash?" the reporter asked. This was the important question! Who would be responsible if the president's son was dead? Would it be the weather, the pilot, or a technical malfunction?

"I can't say for sure. We need to find the crashed helicopter. It could have been a pilot's error, or maybe somebody overrode the helicopter controls, and the pilot could not complete the flight. Anything is possible." George Stockton looked concerned. He didn't want to give any clues to the reporter at this time. All the information had to be gathered and analyzed.

"I heard that the Coast Guard is considering the possibility that the pilot's failure could have caused the accident to maintain control of the helicopter during a descent over water because of spatial disorientation. What do you think? Could this be true?" the reporter pushed the microphone almost too close to George Stockton's face.

"I can't comment on that. As I told you before, anything is possible. Our investigation has just begun," George Stockton replied, frustrated.

"Could this have been a terrorist attack?"

"We can't rule that out yet. First, we need to determine what caused the crash," George Stockton replied calmly, adding, "As you might know, the black box is not mandatory in all helicopters. We don't know if this model had it or not."

The reporter pushed the microphone closer and asked, "Do you know where the helicopter's wreck is located?"

"I think the Coast Guard has a pretty good idea where it is." George Stockton pointed toward the Coast Guard representatives on the scene.

8

The Eyewitness

8 P.M. Somewhere downtown in Washington, D.C.

Marco Smith, the interviewed eyewitness, drove downtown, and after twenty minutes of driving, he arrived at a warehouse turned into a lofty, trendy Russian restaurant called Troika. The restaurant was busy, with cheerful Russian balalaika music echoing through the windows. The front side of the old warehouse building was turned into a parking lot, and it was packed with customers' cars.

Marco drove to the employee parking on the side of the building and turned off the engine. Before stepping out of his car, he viewed the alley to ensure no one followed him or saw him coming there.

The alley was empty. There were only some stray cats and rats and trash dumpsters full of discarded restaurant food and food packaging.

He quickly walked towards the backside of the restaurant and walked through the employee entrance. He passed the kitchen area and the dining room and walked directly towards the staircase to the office on the second floor, where he knocked on the door and waited for permission to go inside. He heard the answer almost immediately and opened the door.

A man was sitting in a large leather chair behind the desk at the office when Marco stepped inside. Marco knew him. He was the owner of the Restaurant Troika: Maksim Liskin. He was a pudgy man with a round, doughy face, and shark-looking, pale, cold eyes. He had a tailored black suit with a peach-colored silk shirt. The top buttons of his silk shirt were open, showing two thick gold necklaces around his neck and a part of an old tattoo on his chest.

Marco sat in the empty chair in front of the desk. That chair was not a comfortable leather chair like Maksim's own was. Maksim Liskin did not want his guests to stay a long time in his office, so the visitor's chair was made of steel, hard and narrow. A steel chair also had other benefits, like blood would not stain it if the visitors were bleeding, and it was easy to clean.

Marco observed that the carpet under his chair was covered with thick black plastic. A cold sweat ran down his back, and he felt uneasy and nervous. He moved a little to find a comfortable position on the hard chair. He knew the high stakes of Operation Pobeda and that his role was important. He realized that his failure would have cost him his life, which was why the plastic was placed under his chair. Luckily for him, he had not failed.

"Dobryj vyechyer, Maksim!" Marco greeted the restaurant owner in Russian.

"How did it go?" Maksim Liskin asked. He was impatient to hear all the details. He was expected to report to his superiors after meeting Marco. Everything else in this covert plot depended on Marco's eyewitness story. The authorities needed to believe that the helicopter had crashed. There couldn't be any doubt.

"I was the first one there, and the reporters were eager to interview me," Marco replied. He relaxed a little bit.

"Tell me more," Maksim Liskin urged him and leaned forward, crossing his hands on the table in front of him.

"The helicopter wreck that we dragged and sank into the Potomac River was the same model as the one the president's son, Zachary, and his son-in-law, Dan, were supposed to have flown. Nobody saw our team there by the river. We used the local chapter of the Werewolves in this part of the operation. The foggy weather was a good cover. We had the barge ready with the wreck and drove towards the area where we considered the helicopter could have gone down underwater, and we sunk the wreck there. We left our passenger, Dan, by the riverbank," Marco described. "Dan Wheeler had superficial wounds which bled a lot, especially on his head, and his clothes were wet and torn, and his shoes missing. He looked like he had been in an accident. Everything went as planned."

"And explain your part next," Maksim Liskin requested.

"I went to the shoreline towards the nearest road and called 911. I told them that I had seen a helicopter falling and told them the place. Then I just waited there. They had not figured out who was supposed to be in the helicopter yet. They contacted the nearby airports and the FAA to determine the authorized flights."

"Did someone take care of the helicopter at the Essex County Airport?"

"Yes, one of our members flew it towards the Potomac River and then flew low, under the radar, and landed it outside Washington D.C. No one will find it," Marco assured.

"When did the authorities suspect the crashed helicopter in the river was the helicopter carrying the president's son and his son-in-law?"

"Only when they found our passenger by the riverbank. He was able to tell them his name before the ambulance took him to the hospital," Marco explained.

"And the press?" Maksim Liskin leaned back on his chair. So far, everything sounded excellent.

"They arrived soon after our passenger had been taken into the hospital. I think someone at the police had leaked the information. One by one, the media arrived. But before they interviewed anyone, I went around and talked about the accident with the other passersby. All the major news channels arrived quite fast. A satellite television truck for national and international news reports came almost immediately after the local media representatives," Marco explained. He had relaxed now. "Three channels interviewed me. When I explained how I saw the helicopter crashing down from the sky in the fog, they all believed in my version of the story." Marco recalled how he had conveyed false information to the press. "Besides, you know how the eyewitnesses are: there are as many versions of the truth as there are witnesses. When the other 'witnesses' heard my story, they started imagining they had heard or seen something. It is so easy to influence people to believe they witnessed something when they couldn't have."

"So, you are telling me everything went as planned," Maksim Liskin summarized.

"Da!" Marco replied, agreeing.

Maksim Liskin walked to his wall safe, keyed in its passcode, and opened it. He took out a wad of one-hundred-dollar bills and threw them on the table in front of Marco. Marco grabbed them and stuffed the wad in his pocket inside his jacket.

"Spasibo!" Marco thanked him in Russian and stood up to leave.

"Remember to disappear now," Maksim Liskin reminded him.

Marco replied, "I have a hideout place down south. I'll be like a bear in a cave during the long and cold Siberian winter: I will stay there and not move or say a word. I will wait for the springtime to come out."

"Excellent!" Maksim agreed and sat back in his chair.

"Do svidaniya!" Marco said goodbye and left the office promptly.

Maksim Liskin leaned back in his leather chair and picked up the handset of his black desktop phone and dialed a number he had memorized. He did not prefer cell phones. He believed the new technology was too easy to hack and eavesdrop on. He was like a sly old fox, more careful than the hot-tempered young men working for him, but that's why he had survived and stayed in the business for almost three decades.

"The eyewitness did his job. Everything is on schedule." Maksim reported the status of the covert operation. Then he hung up.

Short calls were better. Nobody would be able to trace their receiver; just a precaution in case somebody was tracking and listening in.

Maksim had a shady background involving suspected extortion and drug deals but had not been convicted. The law enforcement had been after him for a while, but they had not succeeded in pinning anything on him, and he didn't plan to give them anything any time soon.

He smiled smugly and replayed the conversation with Marco again. He was satisfied with his answers. He would still watch the evening news to make sure he had not lied.

The news he'd seen earlier had confirmed Marco's account of the event, but he'd better be sure that the storyline did not change. So far, the operation had gone as planned. Hopefully, the next parts will go just as well.

9

The President

8 p.m. (EST), The Oval Office

President Burr had given considerable thought to how to approach Otis without alerting his enemy, his son's kidnappers. He was not sure how he could do that. He picked up his phone and browsed through his visual voicemail. He saw a familiar number halfway down the list. Otis had called. Andrew Burr's angular face showed relief. He should have known Otis would call him immediately when he heard the news.

Andrew Burr did not even bother to hear the message but called him directly back.

When Otis saw who was calling him, he turned down the television volume.

"Good evening, Mr. President," Otis answered formally, but Andrew interrupted him and said, "Otis, how many times have I told you to call me Andrew?"

"Many, many times," Otis replied, smiling. He realized something was wrong. Andrew would sound sad or devastated if his son were dead, but he was not. His voice was more stressed or irritated.

"I guess you heard the news?" Andrew asked. "I saw you had left a message, but I did not listen to it. I wanted to talk to you immediately."

"Yes, and I'm sorry—" Otis started, but Andrew interrupted him again. "Can we meet tomorrow and play some golf? I have something to run by with you?"

"Sure." Otis raised his eyebrows in surprise. "I'll have an evening lecture, but I'm available any time before that."

"Let's meet at 11 a.m. at the Congressional Country Club," Andrew decided. That was one of the places he favored for golfing. It was not too far away, and the Secret Service protective team knew the area well and was able to accommodate the president's wishes on short notice. Many previous presidents of the United States had enjoyed playing there, including Gerald Ford, Dwight

D. Eisenhower, Woodrow Wilson, and Calvin Coolidge. The place had a high initiation fee, six figures if Otis remembered correctly. It was not a public golfing place.

Andrew's voice sounded too calm. Otis analyzed it quickly in his mind. *He might be in shock after hearing about his son's helicopter crash. Unless something else is going on?*

"I'll see you then," Otis replied, and the call ended.

Otis placed his cell phone on the table by his now-cold Chinese dinner.

Something is not right, he thought. Andrew possibly lost his son; his son-in-law was at the hospital, and he wanted to play golf tomorrow! Otis frowned. He was no longer hungry. He thought about the conversation he had just had with the president. *The winter is barely over. It's early spring and not even golf season yet. This must mean that he has something else to talk about,* he thought.

Otis turned the television volume back on. The news reporters continued repeating the crash news. No bodies had been found yet. They had the approximate location of the helicopter's wreck, and the Coast Guard and the rescue team with divers had been out there for a couple of hours now, looking for survivors and salvaging anything from the wreckage.

The XBS news reporter was in front of George Washington University Hospital's main entrance. "This is the hospital where Dan Wheeler, the president's son-in-law, Dan Wheeler, was taken to after he was found near the crash site. The hospital has announced that Dan Wheeler is in fairly good condition and that he might be suffering from hypothermia due to cold water and possibly trauma after the crash. He also had some lacerations on his face and his head. The doctors are checking if he has a concussion."

The view changed to an earlier video clip showing the president and his daughter entering the hospital's main entrance surrounded by Secret Service agents and media representatives. The reporter continued, "The president visited the hospital earlier today. His daughter, Irene, is still at the hospital with her husband, Dan Wheeler. All our prayers are with the First Family tonight."

The reporter pointed towards the front entrance of the hospital, where several people had gathered with signs saying, "Get well soon, Dan." They held candles in their hands and seemed to be praying. Some had left flowers by the hospital entrance.

10

At the Crash Site

8 p.m. (EST), At the crash site

"We would like to speak with the eyewitness you interviewed tonight," two FBI Special Agents asked the female reporter. She had long blond hair and wore the Max Channel's dark blue windbreaker.

"He was just here," the reporter said and looked around. "Did you see where he went?" she asked her cameraman.

"No, I'm sorry, I didn't. I was following you and the crowd," the cameraman replied, shaking his head and pushing back his cap from his forehead.

FBI Special Agents Luis Rochas and Nat Griffin approached the XBS news channel's van and asked the same question, and they got the same reply.

The FBI agents tried to find other eyewitnesses, but even though there were dozens of onlookers around, no one had seen the helicopter crashing down as that one witness had described. Only a handful of people identified themselves as eyewitnesses, and when the agents interviewed them, they gave completely different versions of what they had seen and if they actually had seen anything. Most of them were probably there for the fame and television interview possibilities. The only common thing was that they all referred to this Marco Smith, who had told them about the helicopter's fall. The agents could not find this eyewitness to interview him.

"It is strange that only that one man was able to describe the helicopter's fall. It was foggy. The visibility was not so good. But there were still many people out. There should have been more witnesses," Special Agent Rochas said to his partner, Nat Griffin, and shook his head.

Luis Rochas was the one with seniority and had taken the lead in this case. He was in his forties, a plain-looking man, whereas his partner, Griffin, was blond-haired thirtysomething and had a round face that made him look younger than he was.

"We got his name from the interview: Marco Smith," Nat Griffin replied. He picked up his cell phone and called his office. "Run the eyewitness's name." After ten minutes of waiting, his phone chirped, and he viewed the message. He had received a list of people with the same name as the eyewitness but of different ages. As he browsed the images, his partner looked at them too.

None of the pictures sent to them looked like the eyewitness that had been interviewed earlier that night. Griffin shook his head. "No luck."

The eyewitness's last name, Smith, was one of the most common last names in the United States, but his first name was not that common. However, their office had found over a hundred Marco Smiths in the Washington D.C. area.

Griffin sighed. "We'll have to check them all just in case the photos in the FBI files were old or incorrect."

"Yes, just in case we find him." Agent Rochas nodded. He was not pleased. Something else bothered him with this witness's description, "Did you notice that this eyewitness never mentioned any sounds? Usually, when you see a crash, you hear the sound first, like the blades or the motor sputtering or when the helicopter splashed into the river."

"Yes, I noticed that. I remember when I saw my first helicopter, the noise was louder and different than an airplane's sound; the rotors whined, and the motor roared. I'm quite sure there should have been some crash sound. But, strangely, no one heard anything."

"Yes, it is weird. So is the fact that the key eyewitness has disappeared, and we can't even verify his identity." Rochas shook his head.

"We can get a team to go door-to-door in the nearby area and find out if there were any other witnesses," Nat Griffin suggested.

"Yes, the team will spend countless hours knocking on doors and taking notes." Rochas sighed.

"First, we'll need to contact all the media companies and ask them to deliver us all the media footage of the scene. It's a good way to develop a timeline and recover the details, even insignificant ones, that somebody might have said or seen," Griffin commented.

"We'll have to set up a hotline. There might be somebody out there who knows or has seen something," Rochas commented dryly and glanced at his partner as they surveyed the scene. "Even if most of the calls will be irrelevant. We'll probably get our usual callers: the lunatics, the fame seekers, and the psychics."

"Well, let's get started then." Griffin thrust his hands into his pocket and gave a last look at the riverside. The same media circus with the rescue team was still there. Nothing had changed.

They walked back to their unmarked sedan and drove away, leaving the scene to the media, the local law enforcement, and the rescue teams.

11

At Jack's Home

8 p.m. (EST), Jack's home, the evening of the helicopter crash

Three of the intruders were guarding Jack Brewer's family. They watched the news of the helicopter crash with the hostages. Jack and his family huddled together on the sofa.

When the news anchor informed that only one person was found alive and taken to the hospital, the three men got up and left the room without saying a word.

The nightmare is over, Jack thought, relieved. He got up, went to the broken kitchen door, and glanced outside. Two of the intruders climbed on their motorcycles and drove away. He could not identify them. He had not seen their faces, but he had seen their vests with their names: Werewolves. Each one had a different name on their leather cutoff vest: Dentist, Alien, Typhoon, and Snake. Dentist was their leader, or so Jack assumed. He had left earlier. He was the one with the werewolf tattoo on his right wrist.

Then Jack realized he had only seen two men leaving with the motorcycles. A shiver ran down his back. They were not alone. One of the intruders was left behind.

Jack turned around and faced the barrel of a Glock, pointed straight at him. He felt the color draining from his face.

No, not this, he thought. He opened his mouth to scream, but the man in front of him pushed the gun into his face, he took a deep breath and didn't utter a word.

"Close the door," Snake said quietly. He was the one with a goatee and mean beady eyes.

Jack closed it. "Please, don't do this. Please, let my family go," Jack begged in vain.

Snake looked cold and determined. Without another word, he pointed towards the living room with his gun.

Jack ambled back to the living room. His eyes revealed to his family the horror that was about to happen.

His children pressed tightly against their mother and tried to find comfort in each other.

Jack feared what would happen next.

"We can't leave any witnesses," Snake said, looking back at him with an ice-cold expression like a professional killer would have. He pulled out a silencer from his pocket, tightened it on his gun, and calmly pointed the gun from one family member to another and shot them. Jack was the last one to go. He had to watch his family die in front of his eyes.

Snake's work was fast and efficient as if he had done this before. After the kills, he trashed the room, throwing papers, frames, CDs, and books on the floor and pushing the television over. It would look like a robbery gone bad.

He glanced around to make sure he had not left anything untouched. On his way out, he turned over the kitchen table, pulled out the drawers, and emptied them on the floor. The kitchen door already looked the part, broken and hanging on its hinges. He decided to view the upstairs. The police might be suspicious if the robbers did not check those rooms. He went through the bedrooms, pulled out drawers, and threw items on the floor. He grabbed a handful of jewelry from the jewelry box. He left the children's room untouched. *No need to do anything there. No robber would grab anything from the kids*, he thought.

He left the same way he had entered the house, through the kitchen door. He strolled across the front yard and checked out to see if any neighbors were watching. No one was out.

No more loose ends, he thought as he strolled to his motorcycle and left the house. *No witnesses.*

12

The Press Briefing

8 a.m. (EST), The Press Briefing Room in the White House

The news of the helicopter crash hit every news channel around the globe with the speed of lightning. The Press Briefing Room was packed full of reporters from different national and international news organizations. The room fell silent when Press Secretary Brad Buchanan entered the room with three other persons. Brad walked to the podium, and his guests positioned themselves behind him, waiting for their turn to answer questions.

"Good morning. Thank you for coming." Press Secretary Brad Buchanan greeted the press. He viewed the notes he had with him and then started reading with a solemn voice. "The search and rescue team has informed that they have not found the bodies of the president's son, Zachary, and the pilot. The rescue team also informed that it was too late to find anyone alive if they had been caught in the wreck underwater. The rescue will continue, and we will find the bodies and the reason for the crash."

"Was this a terrorist attack?" An XBS news reporter in the audience shouted the question to Brad.

"We neither deny nor confirm that yet. I have here with me the Chief of Police of the Metropolitan Police Department of the District of Columbia, Carol Lang, to answer your questions related to the possible terrorism, and Mayor Margaret Brennan." Brad pointed to his left at the two ladies standing behind the podium." He pointed to his right and added, "Lieutenant Commander Peter Hale from the Coast Guard is also here to answer some of your questions about the rescue efforts."

"Is the president going to give us a statement? How is he?" a female reporter from BSN news in the front row asked. More hands raised. More unanswered questions.

Press Secretary Brad Buchanan held out his hand to stop questioning. "Please, I have no comment from the president yet. He will address the nation later when he is ready. We only ask you to pray for the president and his family. Thank you. I will now let Mayor Brennan say a few words, and then you can ask her your questions, or the Chief of Police or the Coast Guard." He then turned over the podium to the Mayor, the Chief of Police, and the Lieutenant Commander of the Coast Guard. He didn't reply to any random questions shouted at him but slunk out of the press room, looking defeated and sad.

Everyone expected him to be worried over the loss of the president's son, who was also his friend. His other friend, Dan, was in the hospital.

Brad quickly walked to his office and closed the door behind him. Giving the press release wasn't easy. *Too many questions, too few answers,* he thought as he sat down by his desk. He had a list of tasks on his calendar, but he pushed it away and instead called his assistant and asked to cancel all of them. He didn't want to attend meetings today because his thoughts would be elsewhere.

The reporters received no new details in the Press Briefing Room. The facts were that no bodies were found.

The rescue team had found the helicopter wreckage, but there was no news of why the helicopter had crashed.

The media representatives tried to press for more information, but with no luck.

The Mayor and the Chief of the Police gave the standard statement. "The investigation is still ongoing, and we are currently pursuing multiple leads in this investigation."

13

The White House

9 a.m. (EST), the next morning after the crash

The fence around the White House had been filled with flowers, teddy bears, signs, and notes from the citizens. Zachary had been liked because of his outgoing, easy-smiling, and handsome demeanor. Law enforcement had placed barricades around the crash site so that they could investigate the crash scene without disturbances. They did not want any reporters or onlookers to interfere with the ongoing investigation.

Law enforcement had placed barricades around the crash site so that they could investigate the crash scene without disturbances. They did not want reporters or onlookers to interfere with the ongoing investigation, especially when it involved the first family.

The whole nation mourned, along with President Burr and his family. The president had been quiet, and he had not given any statements or given any interviews with the press.

The news reporters had pestered the White House press secretary for interviews but with no luck. Some of them suggested that the president was traumatized by the loss of his son. Some opposing politicians had requested that he should temporarily resign and let the Vice President take the lead because "losing a child can be devastating and can interfere with your concentration on the nation's tasks," they had argued. There was nothing to counter-argue that claim. It was true. Andrew Burr was devastated, not because of the loss of his child, but because of the kidnapping, which he could not reveal to anyone.

The first lady, Brooke Burr, was interviewed for the morning show on CBX News. She was dressed immaculately in a black dress, the latest fashion statement by her favorite top designer. Her long blond hair was styled in a bun. Her diamond brooch and earrings sparkled in the studio lights. She often wiped her eyes with a lacy handkerchief during the interview.

The president's daughter, Irene, was also interviewed when she left the hospital that same morning, her husband being the only survivor of the deadly crash.

President Andrew Burr watched the press briefing and the morning shows on television in the Private Quarters of the White House. He saw the stress on his estranged wife's face, but he was sure part of it was also acting. Zachary had always been closer to his father than his mother. He was not even sure how often she and Zachary had talked during the past three years. He turned off the television.

Andrew got up from his chair wearily and strolled to his bedroom to check out his appearance. What he saw in the mirror was not what he had used to see in the mirror. His eyes had bags under them and had lost the vividness. He looked like he had not had a good night's sleep for a while, and his skin was pale, almost pallid, but otherwise, he had the appearance of a handsome businessman in a black suit.

Andrew Burr quickly brushed his flaxen-colored hair with his left hand. He had to get ready to perform his part in public.

His blue eyes turned icy cold when he thought about the kidnappers and what they had done to his family.

He could not reveal to anyone his predicament except perhaps Otis. He could not tell his wife and his daughter that Zachary was alive. He had to play along to show that he was agreeing to the kidnappers' demands. His face turned somber as he thought about the possibility that they might kill his son even if he did what they asked. Moreover, the kidnappers could keep Zachary and ask for more favors, money, or whatever they wanted. He had no control over what they did and when. He took a deep breath and let it out slowly. He took a last look in the mirror, straightened his tie, and then ambled outside. He was ready to play the role of the president again.

14

At the Hospital

9 a.m. (EST), George Washington University Hospital

At George Washington University Hospital, Dan Wheeler, the president's son-in-law, woke up from the medicine-induced sleep. The monitors were placed beside his bed monitoring his heart rate, pulse, and breathing. While unconscious, he was transferred from the ER to the third floor, to room 314. It was a private room. Privacy in this situation was important, especially because the president's son was still missing.

The doctor entered the hospital room with a nurse. "Good morning. How are we doing this morning?" the doctor asked while viewing Dan's chart. He had an ID card hanging on his white coat label on his left side. It identified him as Dr. Mikkelson. He was a tall, elderly man with a receding hairline and metal-framed glasses.

The nurse stood by, waiting for instructions for medication or more tests.

"Where am I?" Dan asked, looking confused. His head was bandaged, and he had bandages on his arms and legs. He looked around as if trying to remember where he was.

"This is George Washington University Hospital. You were brought to the ER yesterday," Dr. Mikkelson replied. "Then, later last night, we transferred you to this room."

Dan looked around, seemingly disoriented. "What happened?"

"You had an accident. Do you remember anything?" Dr. Mikkelson asked.

Dan shook his head, winced, and closed his eyes. "No, I don't remember. I've got a splitting headache," Dan replied, lifting his right hand over his eyes as if shielding them from the bright daylight.

"The nurse can close the shades. The bright light sometimes bothers you if you have a concussion," Dr. Mikkelson explained. "What is the last thing you remember?"

"I was at work. And after that, I don't remember anything." Dan shook his head but stopped it and cringed. It seemed to hurt his head.

"It could be temporary amnesia. Sometimes it happens in accidents. We will monitor you here for a couple of days."

There was a knock at the door. Two FBI special agents came in. "Good morning," they greeted.

They showed their credentials to Dr. Mikkelson, who viewed them and frowned. "This patient needs rest, no visitors."

Special Agent Rochas asked the doctor, "Can Mr. Wheeler answer a few questions?"

Doctor frowned. "He's awake, but it looks like he has temporary amnesia. I'm not sure if the interview will reveal anything. You might have to wait until his memory returns," Dr. Mikkelson replied. "I'll give you a couple of minutes now, no longer than that. He needs to rest."

The agents nodded and turned towards Dan Wheeler, who glanced at them curiously.

"I'm Special Agent Rochas from the FBI, and this is my partner, Special Agent Griffin," Agent Rochas introduced, then continued, "Mr. Wheeler, can you please tell us anything you can remember about yesterday?"

"I don't remember much," Dan replied weakly.

"Try to remember what happened yesterday," Agent Rochas encouraged him.

"I was with Zachary Burr. We had a meeting in New Jersey. After the meeting ended, we headed back to the airport, and then..." Dan furrowed his brow. "I think we were in the helicopter, and... and something happened."

"You took the helicopter, and what happened then?" Agent Rochas pressed, hoping that Dan would remember more details. Anything would help to solve the crash.

"There was something wrong with the helicopter. I can't remember what. I'm sorry," Dan replied, frowning. He glanced at the agents and said apologetically, "I'm sorry. It's all blank after that."

"I think that's enough. This type of head injury can take some time to heal. He might be able to give you some answers later, maybe tomorrow," Dr. Mikkelson interrupted.

Sure, we understand," Agent Rochas replied. "We'll come back tomorrow."

15

Irene

9:15 a.m. (EST), George Washington University Hospital

After the FBI agents left, the president's daughter, Irene Wheeler, entered the hospital to see her husband, Dan. She knew the agents had been there because they had called her before going to see her husband, and she didn't want to meet them now.

The strong smell of disinfectant always made her feel sick, which was why she would not have come to this big hospital voluntarily, but this time she had to because Dan was being treated there. She had always preferred private doctors and clinics to large facilities.

When Irene saw Dr. Mikkelson outside Dan's room in the hallway, she strode straight to him and waited for him to be available to answer questions. The doctor was giving some orders to the nurses, but when he saw Irene, he interrupted it, and the nurses walked away.

Irene introduced herself, "Dr. Mikkelson, I'm Irene Wheeler. Dan is my husband. How is he doing?"

Dr. Mikkelson looked through his notes one more time before giving her any reply. "He has amnesia." He saw how worried Irene looked and considered how to tell her more gently what her husband was going through after the crash. "It's too early to say anything for certain. I just ordered a CT scan, an x-ray, and some more bloodwork."

"Is he going to be okay?" Irene frowned, grabbing her bag tightly.

"We don't know how fast he will recover yet. We can hope for a full recovery," the doctor replied, trying to sound convincing. "Amnesia is always difficult. Some people heal fast, and some never get their memories back. We'll just have to wait and see."

Irene nodded. "Thank you. Can I see him now?"

"Yes, of course. Keep the visit short. He needs rest."

Irene strolled slowly along the corridor to her husband's hospital room. She wore a long trench coat, black pencil skirt with a gray top, and pointed-toe stilettos with a large black bag and looked like she was on her way to work. Her light brown hair was straight and loose, hanging on her shoulders.

When Irene entered the room, she saw that his IV was still attached. The monitors in Dan's room were turned off. He had some medicine pills in small plastic cups on the table. *Probably pain medication*, she thought.

She rushed to the bedside. "Dan, you are awake!" she said happily. "You look so pale. Are you feeling well?"

"Yes, I'm okay," Dan replied faintly.

Irene fluffed his pillow, then bent over to kiss him.

Dan turned his face away, which he never usually did. He had always told her and everyone else that Irene was the love of his life.

Irene's face showed surprise and uncertainty.

Dan rushed to explain, "I have a really bad headache, and my face is so sore and bruised that I don't want anyone to touch it now."

"I understand. Just rest now. I'll come back later," she replied, patted his hand gently, and left the hospital room.

Dan sighed and stretched his arms. He was feeling surprisingly good. His superficial wounds did not bother him at all, and he had faked the headache and amnesia.

After Dan was sure Irene, the nurse, or the doctor wasn't returning, he pushed away his blanket and sat at the bedside momentarily before standing up. He walked towards the window and peeked outside through the blinds. The media vans were parked outside the hospital entrance.

He smiled and looked amused. Everything was going as planned.

He slowly returned to his bed, laid down, and pulled the blanket back over him. He wanted it to look like he had been there all this time.

Dan was sure that President Andrew Burr would come soon. He would like to see his son-in-law and also because he had been on the same flight with his son. Dan had gotten injured, but Zachary was missing.

16

Dan Wheeler

9:50 a.m. (EST), George Washington University Hospital

Dan heard a knock on the hospital door and opened his eyes. He turned his head towards the doorway and saw two Secret Service agents looking inside the room before they let President Burr enter the room alone and closed the door behind him while they stayed on guard in the hallway.

The reason for the visit was that President Burr hoped Dan would remember something useful about what happened the day before, especially about the kidnapping – if Dan even knew anything about it.

"Good morning, Dan. How are you?" Andrew Burr asked, looking at his son-in-law. Of course, he was concerned about how he was doing after the crash. He noticed that Dan had bandages on his head and arms.

"Good morning, Mr. President," Dan replied weakly. "I'm okay. A headache, some cuts and bruises, but I will heal."

"Good, good." Andrew nodded. He wasn't sure how to start asking questions about the crash because the doctor and Irene had both warned him that Dan had amnesia. He pushed his hands deep into his pockets. "Do you remember anything about the helicopter crash?"

"No, the doctor said I have temporary amnesia." Dan shook his head. He lifted himself a little on the bed to be in a half-sitting position. "I'm sorry about your son. Zachary was my friend, too. My best friend." His voice was earnest, and his eyes showed empathy.

"Yes, well, I'm still hopeful that he is alive. You don't remember anything about what happened to Zachary?"

"No, I'm sorry. It feels like there is a wall in my mind when I try to access the memories of the past days." Dan looked apologetically at the president.

President Burr did not want to reveal the kidnapping to Dan. He was a bit disappointed with Dan's answers.

He grabbed Dan's hand, squeezed it, and then let it go. "I must go now. Try to get better soon. And if you remember anything about the crash or what happened to Zachary, call me, or ask Irene to call."

Dan nodded. "Sure. I will do that."

When the president was about to leave the room, Dan loudly said one word—the code word, "Postmaster."

Dan's voice had the faintest trace of humor when the president turned to face him, and Dan saw the surprise, and next, the realization dawned on Andrew's face.

For a moment, Andrew Burr didn't know what to do: leave or stay.

Andrew Burr was surprised, even shocked, to hear the kidnapper's code name used by his son-in-law. When he returned to stand by the end of the hospital bed to face Dan, Dan addressed the president with a foreign accent, "Mr. President, I'm your watcher, your contact. You will get Zachary back if you do as we say."

"Who are you?" Andrew Burr whispered. "You can't be Dan!" He could not believe that this man was Dan. He looked exactly like Dan, like a twin but had a different accent.

"Who I am is not important. What's important is that I operate on behalf of Russia," the man pretending to be Dan told him. His eyes were serious now, and he had changed his friendly voice to a strange professional one.

He is not Dan. This man must have been made to look like Dan with a series of plastic surgeries. It'd have required money and resources, Andrew Burr thought, horrified. His eyes turned cold as ice when he watched this doppelganger, looking for differences in his face that would reveal he was not Dan.

The man everyone thought was Dan gestured towards the chair beside the bed, but Andrew Burr shook his head. He did not want to sit beside the doppelganger. He felt sick even being so close to this man who was part of the kidnapping.

The doppelganger-Dan continued to explain the kidnappers' demands. "We want you to undo all the economic sanctions against Russia. We also need the United States to use its veto in the United Nations to vote against continuing the economic sanctions against Russia. We want all the frozen assets to be returned to the Russian businesses and to lift all the travel bans against Russian nationals in the United States."

"Is that all?" Andrew Burr scoffed. He balled his hands into a fist and held them at his sides. "Just tell me why."

"These are not all our demands, but that's a start." Dan studied the president's face, but Andrew Burr was a seasoned politician, not revealing any emotions when negotiating deals.

"Why?" Andrew Burr asked calmly. When he realized the man wasn't his son-in-law, it was easy to treat him as an enemy, a stranger.

"Do you remember when the Soviet Union collapsed in 1991?" Dan asked the president.

Andrew Burr nodded.

"Gorbachev was the last General Secretary of the USSR. He acknowledged the independence of the former USSR states and gave power to the new Russian President Boris Yeltsin. President Reagan was responsible for the downfall of the former Soviet Union."

"Yes, I know the history and how the USSR collapsed," Andrew replied. "Why do you lecture me on ancient history?"

"You need to know the history to understand the present," Doppelganger-Dan snapped. "Because President Yeltsin could not oversee the transformation from a communist society to the independent states and the societal and economic change in the market economy. His inability to manage state affairs, his drinking, and his health problems gave other parties easy access to our nation's vast wealth. The Russian mobs emerged from the ashes of the former USSR and took over our country and operated behind the curtains. They had the real power. A handful of oligarchs became billionaires. Some were former mobsters who had gained their fortune in illegal business: drugs, human trafficking, and prostitution. Some new oligarchs were clever enough to invest in finance, oil, and gas. However, when Vladimir Putin became President, he wanted the former glory of Russia and the USSR to return. His imperialistic views acquired him the Crimean Peninsula, but also enemies like the freedom fighters of the former USSR states. However, he did not have time to finish his goals when he was replaced by the current President Vladislav Ruskin after Putin's assassination."

The doppelganger kept his eyes on the president to make sure he was following his political history lesson. When Andrew didn't comment, the doppelganger nodded and continued, "The new Russian President understood the needs of the businessmen better than the previous President, Putin. He made a pact with the oligarchs and offered to support them when the decision was made to execute this kidnapping operation. His support was mandatory because otherwise, we would not have been able to use the vast resources of the Ministry of State Security (MGB) and get everything done on time."

Dan paused, looked at the president, and asked, "Do you see why we want revenge? Ronald Reagan started this process, and Vladislav Ruskin will end it. You are the downfall of the United States. When the executive office obeys Russia's orders, it will be the best revenge of all. Russia will make the United States behave as their puppet on a string – all because of you. You'll have to follow our orders because you don't want your son to die."

If what this man says is true, this kidnapping was sanctioned at the highest level of the Russian government, Andrew Burr realized. *Even if it was, I might not be able to prove it. Just his word would not be enough, he thought. This doppelganger might be just telling me stories to impress me. He might be working for a Russian mob, for all I know. There's no proof that the Russian government and President Ruskin are behind any of this. He has not given me any proof of that.*

"Who are you working for? Who is responsible for this kidnapping?" Andrew Burr asked. He wanted to know the names of who exactly was behind the kidnapping and blackmailing. He needed these names to connect the dots directly with the Russian government and President Ruskin.

"Who? I can't tell you that. Let's just say that there is a group of resolute men who want to see a different power structure in this world," Dan replied cryptically and added, "Remember what our previous President Vladimir Putin once said: 'There is something that I have in common with every citizen of Russia – the love for our motherland...'"

President Burr shook his head in disbelief. No direct answer to his question. The demands were ridiculous, but what could he do? He did not want his son to die for political reasons.

Dan watched the emotions on President Burr's face change from disgust to anger and finally to disgruntled acceptance. He was acting like a father now, not like a politician. President Burr realized he could not do anything but agree with the kidnappers' demands.

"I understand this is a lot to digest. Please remember, the clock is ticking," Dan commented. "Tick, tock, tick, tock." Dan laughed when he saw the veiled disgust flicker on the president's face before he turned around and left the hospital room.

Andrew stopped behind the door and leaned against the wall to stop shaking. His legs felt like boiled spaghetti as if no bones were left to keep him standing. He ran his hands over his face to calm down.

What can I do? What are my choices? Zachary has to be saved, but saving my son will destroy my political goals and my image. The United States will probably turn their current allies into enemies and lose their support in the global political arena, he thought.

Andrew Burr had a lot to consider. *Dan is not the real Dan, my son-in-law, but a doppelganger, and the Russian demands were political, just as he had feared. I must contact Otis to inform him about this doppelganger.*

Doppelganger-Dan pumped his fist in the air after Andrew Burr left. Operation Pobeda was successful! They had the president of the United States in their pocket. The president knew he had no choice.

17

Andrew Burr

10:30 a.m. (EST), The White House

When President Burr returned to the White House, he greeted his staff members, and they offered him condolences for the loss of his son. He tried to function as if he was mourning and hurried to the Oval Office. The president's secretary, Esme Santiago, waited for him there, and he nodded to her as she offered condolences and then asked, "Can you please ask Conrad, Lawrence, and John to meet me at the Oval Office now, please?" They were Vice President John Rossi, Chief of Staff Lawrence Conklin, and Conrad Kelly, the political adviser to the president.

Esme Santiago was a petite woman originally from Puerto Rico. She had tears in her eyes as she watched her boss try to act normally. She had huddled around the television with the other White House workers following the news reports of the helicopter crash. She blurted out, "Mr. President, this is so horrible... your son..." she started, but the president interrupted her.

"That's all right, Esme. His body has not been found. We'll have to wait and see. Just make the calls. I'll have to leave before eleven. And please, clear my schedule for today, too."

After giving his orders to his secretary, Andrew Burr marched to the Oval Office.

It took only ten minutes before there was a knock on the door, and Esme let the two gentlemen enter the room. Conrad Kelly, the political adviser to the president, was an elderly Southern gentleman with a shock of white hair. Lawrence Conklin, the Chief of Staff, was a tired-looking blond-haired man in his fifties. They both wore black suits and black ties when they entered.

"The vice president is out of the country. He is visiting Germany and will be back tonight," Esme replied.

"Call him after the meeting," Andrew replied.

Esme nodded and left the room, closing the door behind her.

Andrew Burr sat behind the Resolute Desk, and his guests sat in the chairs in front of him. He nervously pulled down his shirt sleeves from the cuffs and straightened his tie. His hands did not shake.

Lawrence studied his gestures and noticed how Andrew straightened the items on the desk meticulously.

Andrew doesn't show any sorrow, but he isn't the same, not the calm politician I've known for years. This crash had taken him off balance, Lawrence thought. *It might be better if the Vice President takes over.*

"Mr. President, please let us offer our deepest condolences," Lawrence Conklin said somberly.

"Thank you. As you know, this helicopter crash incident has been hard for me. I will have to ask John Rossi to take care of my meetings for the next couple of days. I will try to get some rest and maybe play a round of golf, too."

He saw relief in Lawrence Conklin's eyes. He noticed how Conrad Kelly and Lawrence Conklin exchanged a glance. They were not surprised by canceling the meetings and letting the VP take over, but it was surprising that the president was going to play golf now that his son was missing and probably dead. *He should be mourning and preparing for a memorial or the funeral for his son, but now he wants to go golfing. What would the country think of this?*

President Andrew Burr saw suspicion and question in their eyes and decided to explain. "I just can't believe that Zachary is dead. It is not right for any parent to lose their child. You always expect your child to live longer than you." When the two men nodded in agreement, Andrew added, "I just have to be alone for a while and clear my thoughts." His hands did not seem to rest at all. Now they were opening and closing into fists, repeating the movement over and over again.

Lawrence cleared his throat. "Mr. President, taking a few days off to mourn is a great idea. I'll talk with John about the topics on the table, and he can take over."

The president had not shown any emotion after the rescue crew informed them that there were no signs of either of the other bodies and that they were not expecting to find anyone alive. But now that the president was telling them how difficult it was to accept the loss of his son and asked that the vice president take over his meetings for the next couple of days, it all seemed like a normal grief process. Lawrence was relieved because he wanted to believe Andrew was coping with the loss his own way.

Just before his staff members left the Oval Office, President Andrew Burr added, "I will attend the United Nations meeting. But can you ask if the vice president can take care of any other meetings before that?"

Conrad and Lawrence assured him that everything would be taken care of.

Conrad stopped by the door and let Lawrence leave before saying, "Mr. President, you need to address the nation. It doesn't look good to lock yourself inside the White House and hide from everyone."

"I know. I can't think about it right now." Andrew sighed. "I'll address the nation later." He knew he would never do that.

Conrad nodded and left the president alone.

Andrew Burr turned around in his chair and stared outside at the garden. *I don't like to lie to my staff, but what else can I do? I can't tell them that his son was kidnapped. How can I get out of this mess and save Zachary?*

Then he checked the time: He had less than half an hour to get ready for the golf and to meet Otis. He got up and went to the Private Quarters of the White House to change his outfit for golf.

When Andrew Burr walked outside, he saw his helicopter ready on the South Lawn of the White House.

Its engine's whir was so loud that it was almost deafening when he approached it accompanied by two Secret Service agents.

The Secret Service had pre-checked the golf course and placed some agents along the route to make sure that POTUS was safe there while golfing.

The helicopter's rotors whine rapidly increased in pitch, and they ascended from the White House and zoomed towards the Congressional Country Club. When the helicopter approached the perimeter, Andrew peeked down to see if he could see Otis. He was not there yet.

18

Otis Thorne

10.15 A.M, Otis Thorne's apartment

Otis Thorne was at home preparing for his lecture on the topic of Russian relations with the European Union and the United States during the past decade. He had taken a Sabbatical year from the CIA, and he was offered a teaching job at Georgetown University as a visiting professor teaching the Security Studies Program. The university staff had been excited to get him because of his firsthand knowledge of Russia and the European Union countries, especially because he had analyzed those countries, their politicians, their leadership qualities, and their economic situation. He had visited and lived in many of the countries he now lectured on. This week's topics discussed Russia and Russia's rise from the ashes of the Soviet Union.

He was not married, and he had no children. Because of his professional history, it had been hard to keep any long-term relationships. After Otis's father had died, his mother, Estelle, had gotten interested in gambling in casinos, having short-term relationships, and living like there was no tomorrow. Sometimes, Otis was worried for her because she never seemed to settle down with any man she met.

When his phone rang, he glanced at the screen of his smartphone. Mother! He considered not answering, but he knew she would call back soon.

"Good morning, mother. How are you?" Otis asked politely.

"Otis, I need you to help me to get rid of Paul."

Otis sighed. Mother again. Straight to the point, and again: her men.

He listened as his mother suggested an elaborate plan to make Paul jealous, and Otis should play the role of a secret lover. "Mom, first, he has probably seen my pictures all over your apartment. He would know who I am. And secondly, why do you have to make it so difficult? Just tell him you are no longer interested in him!"

His mother sounded flustered. "No, I don't want to do that. Don't you see: I want him to see that other men desire me, too? I don't want him to consider me as a sure thing."

Otis sighed. "Do you want him to go?"

"I met this other guy at the poker club—" his mother started to say when Otis interrupted, "Mother, we agreed that you wouldn't go to play poker! I had to pay several thousand of your debts last time!"

His mother laughed. "Oh dear, I did not lose any money. I won! Besides, it was just a local game here at the casino. And that's where I met Stan."

Otis frowned. "Stan is your new lover?"

"I would hope so. I invited him over for lunch. He is right here if you want to talk to him."

The phone call ended abruptly. Otis raised his eyebrows. My mother does not usually end calls like that. Something must have happened, or someone had interrupted her.

Otis's phone beeped again. He viewed the screen: it was his alarm. It was time to get ready to meet the president.

He did not have time to check back with his mother. That had to wait. He thought about the short conversation he'd had with Andrew and frowned. He could not figure out what was going on with Andrew. After he became president, he was never available for a spur-of-the-moment golf game or anything else on short notice. Everything had to be planned weeks ahead of time.

Otis surely had not expected the president to go golfing the day after his son's helicopter crash. He took his golf bag by the door, opened his apartment door, and walked out to the hallway. He headed towards his car, a black Buick Cascada, and he went through all the necessary motions in deep thought: he opened his trunk, placed his golf bag inside it, closed the trunk, walked to the driver's side, opened the door, and started the car. He was still thinking about his mother's call and the next meeting with President Burr. He scoped out his surroundings automatically due to his background and his training in the agency.

Otis noticed a motorcycle and his driver idly sitting in front of the apartment building. *He's not anyone living in this building.* Otis was sure of that. He made a mental note of the motorcycle guy but let it be for now because he had a meeting. Heading towards George Washington Memorial Pkwy, he estimated it would take him about twenty minutes to get to the Congressional Country Club to meet the president.

What he did not know was that the motorcycle guy was placed there to observe and follow Otis. He waited for Otis to leave, started his motorcycle, and drove after him. His long hair flew behind him in the air; he wore an army helmet, black leather jacket, and pants. He kept his distance so that Otis would not get alerted.

19

Otis and Andrew

11 A. M. Congressional Country Club, Bethesda, MD

The President arrived at the Congressional Country Club with his security detail. Special agents of the U.S. Secret Service rode their golf cart behind the president and Otis while on duty protecting the president.

The Secret Service Counter Assault Team had searched the country club's surroundings ahead of President Andrew Burr before and watched over him the whole time while he was at the country club's premises. They had rifles with high-power scopes and binoculars to survey the fairway ahead.

Otis was not even sure the golf course would normally be open this early. Andrew must have pulled some strings to get the game going this early.

The sunny spring weather offers beautiful settings for a game, except for the wind, Otis thought as he approached the president. He spotted a couple of Secret Service agents. *Andrew must be close by.* The Secret Service checked him and then let him pass.

Andrew did not usually go golfing this early in the season when it was still chilly weather and even some snow piled up on the roadside. There had to be something else he wanted to talk about, and he rather talk about it in an open area and not inside the White House or anywhere else where somebody could listen to them, Otis pondered. "Where can I find Mr. President?" Otis asked.

One of the agents pointed to the main building, and Otis headed in that direction.

Andrew stood near a golf cart in front of the main building waiting for his guest. His flaxen-colored hair was covered by a red baseball cap, and he wore sunglasses.

Otis waved at him. He walked toward the president. He stopped in front of him and extended his hand, and they shook. But when Otis tried to offer condolences for the loss of Zachary, President Andrew Burr just gestured with his hand, signaling to drop the topic.

"Hop in, Otis," Andrew said. "Thanks for coming on such short notice."

Otis nodded, "No problem, Mr. President."

"Drop the formalities. Call me Andrew," he replied.

Otis tossed his golf bag into the cart and sat next to the president.

Andrew Burr did not say anything else but just started driving.

Otis sensed that something was wrong and decided to wait for Andrew to tell him.

They drove forward in silence. Otis's thoughts ran wild. He kept thinking and guessing what was wrong. Why had Andrew asked him to come here on such short notice? He glanced sideways. Andrew's face was carved in a stone, revealing no emotion as he started at the golf field ahead without saying a word.

Andrew is afraid of telling me, or something else has scared him, Otis realized. *He's trying to figure out how to tell me. He does not want anyone to hear what he has to say, not even the Secret Service agents. That's why he's acting like this.*

Andrew Burr needed a place where no one could listen to their conversation. He waited until they were away from the prying eyes, then blurted out, "My son is not dead. He is kidnapped."

"What?!" Otis uttered. That was not what he had expected to hear. "Are you sure?"

Maybe this was just a father's desperation, his wish that his son was still alive, Otis thought.

"Yes, I'm sure. I have a video to prove it." Andrew's face was stern, and his blue eyes showed anger and determination. "They told me not to tell anyone. I'm telling you. Help me."

President Andrew Burr pulled out his cell phone from his pocket and showed Otis the text message and video.

Otis read the short message and watched the short video over and over again. He handed the phone back to Andrew.

"It looks real and professional. Do you know their demands?"

The President explained what he knew.

Otis's expression turned steely. "The Russians. That accounted for the precision of the crash and the abduction. "Have you been contacted after these messages?"

"Yes, I know who the Postmaster is," Andrew replied angrily, "It's my son-in-law, Dan, who is not my son-in-law, but someone who looks exactly like him. His accent is Russian. He must be a doppelganger. They must have used plastic surgeries to make him look like my son-in-law."

Otis whistled between his teeth. "That would require a considerable amount of money and resources. They had to have a private hospital to keep that operation secret; only a few people could have known about it. Dan Wheeler's face is known all over the world. He has traveled with you and with his wife."

"I agree," Andrew Burr replied.

Otis's cell phone chimed. "Excuse me, Mr. President. I have to take this. It's my mother calling." Otis viewed his cell phone screen.

She has the worst timing. Of all times, he thought. "I have been trying to reach her, but she has not answered all morning." Otis excused himself and answered the phone, but it was not his mother.

"Don't get involved. We have your mother." A strange voice threatened him, then hung up. His phone chimed a second time for a multimedia message. Otis viewed it. It was an image: his mother, Estelle Thorne, was tied up in a chair.

What Otis did not know was that the motorcycle guy who had watched him had alerted his gang members about where Otis went and who he met there. That initiated the call and the multimedia message.

"Now I'm involved, whether I wanted to be or not," he muttered, turning back to the president. "My mother has been kidnapped. I don't have children like you, but they took away my only relative. I guess they have been following you or me, or you have a spy at the White House."

"Or you are just about the only one I could tell: I can't go to the police or tell the Secret Service. You are my oldest friend. Everyone knows that. It is easy to guess that you are the one I would contact if I was desperate enough," Andrew replied. "But you are right. I can't rule out that there might be a mole inside the White House. I have to be careful."

"First of all, your son-in-law is part of the first family and is staying on a floor that is not open to the public. The Secret Service agents are guarding his hospital room. You can call and ask them to only allow him to use the hospital phone. I don't want him using any other phones.

One phone is easy to track, and we might be able to find the White House informant, the mole among us. You can just pretend you are worried someone might listen to his cell phone messages and calls because you can't be sure this was not a terrorist attack against your family. The hospital phones are landline phones. We can get the records from the hospital for all the calls made from the room."

"Okay, I can do that. Let me tell the Secret Service to beef up the security at the hospital. They can do it right away," Andrew commented. He made a call and talked to a Secret Service agent in charge.

"Okay, that's done," Andrew Burr said after his call. "They will make sure Dan will not be disturbed by anyone and that his room has only one phone, no cell phones."

"Andrew, tell me anything you remember of the days before this accident. Did anything special happen? Did your son meet any new Russian business contacts? How did they get to your son-in-law? Who could know his daily routines and his travel plans?"

"I don't remember anything special, but I can check with Irene," Andrew Burr replied, frowning.

"No, better not. Please, don't start asking questions," Otis commented. "Your doppelganger might get suspicious if you ask or say anything to your daughter."

Otis kept thinking about what to do next, adding, "I might need some additional help. I'm just an ex-CIA agent, currently a low-paid assistant professor. My credentials might not be enough if I need to get some answers and f ast."

"I will leave a permanent order in my office that my staff will assist you in any way they can. That will help you get into places where your word is insufficient. Also, if somebody checks your credentials, I will ask them to tell that person that you work for me," Andrew Burr replied.

"Thank you, Andrew, and don't worry. We will find your son and get him back," Otis replied.

Andrew glanced at him and said, "I hope so. I don't know what to do, and you're my only hope."

"Well, we are in this together. My mother is in their hands, too. That makes me involved." *I can't let them hurt my mother or Zachary. I have to find the kidnappers*, Otis thought grimly.

20

Otis

Otis Thorne's residence

After leaving the golf course, Otis drove directly back to his residence, a beautiful brownstone building near the Georgetown campus, to get his Glock pistol. He didn't know if he'd need it but wanted to be sure he had one, just in case. He opened his safe and retrieved his Glock. He checked the Glock's chamber and the magazine to make sure it was in order.

The spring weather was sunny, with just a few clouds passing by the blue sky. Even if the weather looked nice, the wind was still chilling, reminding us that the winter was still not completely over.

Otis knew exactly how to find his mother. During his spy years, he had given her a watch with a GPS tracker. She always wore it. He checked the tracker transmitter, and it showed a precise location where his mother was: near the renovated warehouses on S Street, NW. He was sure that this new guy his mother had been seeing, Stan, was behind his mother's capture. His mother had ended the call so abruptly after saying Stan was there beside her. It was not like her.

Otis drove along S Street, NW, prepared for a fight. He did not know what was waiting for him there. While driving, he pondered over the kidnapping case the president had given him. He had not received much information except that the president's son had been kidnapped, his son-in-law at the hospital was a doppelganger, and his real son-in-law was missing. Andrew had explained that he was not allowed to tell anyone about the kidnapping or the doppelganger. Otis realized that there had been a major strategist behind this operation involving plastic surgery, funding, travel documents, and time to do it.

Somebody must have started to plan this operation right after the first Ukrainian war in 2015. The time would make sense if Russia wanted to get back their frozen funds and their global business relationships back to normal. They had to plan who would be the next president and then prepare for this kidnapping. But how could they know who would win the next election? The 2016 election had been too close. They were just able to use troll factories and fake social media accounts to influence the voters. 2016 was not a success. They had not gotten anyone in the White House to work for them. President Putin could have started this long-term operation, but he would not have had time to finish it. His successor, President Ruskin, must have known about and sanctioned this operation. So, 2016 had been too close for them to do anything significant, and then the next election was also too soon. This time they had had enough time to get their ducks in order and proceed with their operation.

The next presidential election has given them more time to plan this, Otis thought. *But they could not have planned something for all the candidates. How did they know who would win?* Otis frowned. Unless they had several candidates planned and one of them won. But could they have made several doppelgangers? It was possible but not likely. Pieces were missing in this puzzle.

He checked his mother's tracker one more time. The GPS pointed towards Arlington. He kept driving.

He just could not get that one question off his mind: *How could the Russians plan this? How could they plan for a doppelganger? How could the Russians know who was going to win... Unless they had hacked the voting systems and made sure this president was the winner. Andrew had been one of the favorites from the beginning. But in presidential elections, you can never be sure who will win. The favorites don't always do so well in the debates; however, it is possible,* he thought.

Otis recollected the meetings with the Russian Presidents. He had met President Vladimir Putin on several occasions while stationed in Moscow at the U.S. Embassy. He had also had to pleasure of meeting the new president Vladislav Ruskin once at the White House dinner party.

Russian President Vladislav Ruskin had offered him some insight into the future Russian state, his imperialistic views of making Russia as great as it once was during the Tsars and the Soviet Union: a leader, a major player in world politics. His views sounded much like President Putin's views, Otis remembered. But he was never Putin's opponent but instead supported his imperialistic views. He had gotten his chance when Putin was suddenly assassinated.

It would not surprise me if Ruskin were behind Putin's assassination, Otis thought. *He might have been the key player even before Putin's premature death. This Russian operation might all be his handiwork. If the Russian President was behind the attack, the kidnappers had an abundance of funds and other assets available,* Otis thought.

Otis was familiar with Russian politics and current sanctions. Just the economic threats would not make sense for this kind of elaborate plan. Otis was sure the kidnappers wanted more. Something else was going on. The President was not yet aware of the bigger picture, but Otis was sure there was more to this operation than the two kidnappings.

When Otis arrived at his mother's GPS location in Arlington, he noticed that it was one of the old warehouses turned into a trendy bar-restaurant called Troika. He remembered reading about its opening ceremony with the city's most prominent public figures, politicians, and local actors visiting it.

The restaurant was not open yet because it usually opened after 4 p.m. Otis circled the back of the warehouse and saw a kitchen door.

He parked in the back alley and went to check out the door. It was unlocked. He opened it quietly, entered, and looked around. No restaurant workers were there yet, which was unusual for a restaurant getting ready to open that same evening.

Somebody should have been there to prepare the salads and the meals beforehand, Otis thought. Today's menu items were posted on the wall: Chicken Kyiv, Grilled Wild Boar, Borsch soup, and blinis. Otis would have loved to dine there in any other circumstances, but now he was worried for his mother.

When he approached the door between the kitchen and the restaurant, he heard a distant but loud conversation. He decided it was an argument as they were fiercely firing replies and forth. He pushed the kitchen door open quietly, stepped into the main restaurant area, and saw a man standing back towards him, talking to his mother.

"Stan, what's going on? Let me go!" Otis heard his mother plead.

So, that was Stan, her new boyfriend, Otis thought grimly, his face turned somber.

Otis looked around the room. His mother was tied in a chair, and neither she nor Stan seemed to hear him approach.

His mother saw him first, and her eyes lit up with recognition.

Stan noticed the change on her face and turned quickly around. He had a gun in his hand, but Otis was faster and shot him in the right shoulder, making his opponent drop his gun and grimace in pain.

"You didn't have to shoot him!" his mother, Estelle, complained. "Oh, there is so much blood!"

"Mom! He had you tied up! He had a gun! He threatened you," Otis replied, annoyed.

Otis picked up Stan's gun. It was a GSH-18, he noticed, a standard sidearm for all Russian armed forces.

Where did Stan get a gun like that? It's not the usual weapon here, Otis wondered. He put Stan's gun in his pocket.

Otis turned to his opponent, pressed his knee on the right shoulder where he had shot him, and made Stan almost faint in pain.

Stan clenched his teeth and did not make a sound. He was pale as a sheet.

Otis knew that the pain and pressure would work. He had done this kind of interrogation before as an agent.

If you are in a hurry, you'll do what you must to get the information, Otis thought coldly.

"Listen, I need to know what you know and fast. We can do this the easy way or the hard way. If you know me and my background as you do, then you know I'm not kidding around. You know what I'm capable of," Otis explained to Stan, watching his face pale further, and beads of sweat gather on his forehead.

Stan nodded as he grimaced in pain, and perspiration streamed down from his forehead.

"Good, let's start." Otis crouched down beside him.

Stan looked at him and uttered, "I don't know much. I was sent to keep an eye on your mother, Estelle. I was told that I would receive a call if she was to be captured and held hostage. That call came about two hours ago. I did as I was told. I don't know anything else. I was paid twenty thousand to do this job."

"Who paid?" Otis asked.

"The owner of this place. He paid!" Stan told him. "He asked me to get to know Estelle." Stan's face was twisted in pain.

Otis said stone-faced, "Don't show your face near my mother again. You know it is not healthy for you."

Otis decided to let him go. He was just a small fish, not the brains behind this operation.

"Mom, we have to go now," Otis said as he untied her. He helped his mother, grabbed her by the arm, and swiftly walked her outside. When they were back in his car, he told her, "I need you to pack some clothes with you. You can't stay in your place now. It is not safe. I will take you to a hotel. "

"But I don't want to—" Estelle started but stopped when he saw the fierce look on her son's face.

"Don't argue. This is a life-and-death situation. You must go to a hotel for a few days. I can't risk your life. I need to be able to help Andrew and not be distracted."

"Are you working for Andrew now?" Estelle raised her eyebrows and glanced at her son.

"Not exactly. His son is missing. There was a helicopter crash, and Andrew asked me to check up on that," Otis explained.

He could not reveal the truth to his mother about what had happened. Not yet, Otis thought. His mouth was set in a hard line.

Otis drove his mother to her residence and told her, "Please, pack fast. I have made a room reservation, and I need to take you to the hotel now."

"Okay, okay. I will be fast. What's the rush anyway?" Estelle asked, pouting. "Stan won't bother me now. He's gone."

"Stan was just a pawn in this chess game. There are other players more dangerous than Stan. Believe me. You'll be safer if you are somewhere else for a few days. Stan's employers will come after us both if you're around."

Estelle nodded to acknowledge her son and swiftly hurried to her bedroom to pack.

Otis waited impatiently. Too restless to sit down, he paced around the living room. "Can you hurry, please?" He waited a couple of minutes and called her, "Mom? Do you need any help?"

"I'm fine. I'm almost done," Estelle replied from the bedroom.

Otis sat down on the couch. He checked his phone, but there were no new messages or calls from the president. He was not sure if it was good news or bad news.

Finally, Estelle emerged from the bedroom, dragging a large piece of luggage behind her.

"Let's go," Otis said, grabbing the luggage from her hand, opening the front door, and letting Estelle go out first. He locked the door behind him and set the alarm. He did not want intruders snooping around when his mother was away, not after the attempted kidnapping.

Otis and Estelle did not notice a motorcycle parked around the corner. The driver had an army helmet with small horns and a black leather outfit. He stayed out of sight when Otis and Estelle came out.

When he saw Otis and Estelle drive away in the opposite direction of where he waited, he started his motorcycle and quickly turned to follow Otis's car from a distance. He stayed two or three cars behind, trying to remain behind bigger vehicles so that he would not be so easily noticed. His orders were to follow but not be seen, then report back where they went. The motorcycle driver could not know if Otis expected someone to follow him, but he did not want to alert Otis.

Otis viewed his mirrors to check the flow of cars following him. He did not see the motorcycle because the driver kept a safe distance and made sure he was behind a large truck, which blocked Otis's view of him. At every corner and exit, he checked that Otis's vehicle had not made a turn. Once, the motorcycle driver almost lost Otis but then quickly made a turn and got back to his tail. Finally, he saw where Otis was going, the new casino hotel.

21

Andrew

2 p.m. (EST), The Executive Residence

After talking with Otis, Andrew Burr had returned to the White House private quarters directly from Congressional Country Club. He hoped the private residence would allow him to escape the pressure of the office and the kidnapper's demands for a short while.

He took a quick shower, got dressed, and was ready to go to the family dining room for lunch. He wished Otis would contact or come to see him soon. He wanted to hear what had happened after the meeting.

Did he find his mother? Maybe it had been a false alarm, Andrew thought, concerned.

Andrew was about to go downstairs when his phone rang.

Andrew frowned, and his heart skipped a beat when he saw his son's caller ID on the screen. He pressed the answering button. "Zachary? Is that you?"

It was him. Andrew sighed in relief.

He is still alive, he thought.

The kidnappers made Zachary call his father to ensure he would do as instructed. They suspected he might do something they would not approve of or tell him to do.

Andrew Burr was not stupid. He knew that this call and hearing his son's voice were just reminders of what was at stake. He didn't want to risk his son's life for anything.

Zachary's voice was unsteady when he asked, "You didn't tell Otis, did you? You know these guys are serious. Please, help me."

His father heard the fear in his voice. The whole situation was breaking his heart.

Another voice came on the line. An angry man with a strange accent. Russian, Andrew thought and gripped his phone tight. The Russian man said, "You know what to do if you want to see your son again – alive!" The call ended abruptly. Andrew stared at the screen and wished he could have had a chance to talk with his son for a longer time, but he knew the kidnappers would not let him.

Andrew Burr placed his phone back in his pocket. He suspected he was being watched. He had not seen or noticed anyone, but his son had mentioned Otis. That meant somebody had seen him going golfing with Otis. Or were they just being thorough and knew all the friends he might contact? Andrew did not know what to think. He remembered Otis receiving a call at the golf club. After the call, Otis mentioned that he was part of this mess now. His mother had been kidnapped. Maybe he was not being watched, Andrew thought. Maybe the kidnappers had predicted his possible moves, and Otis, with his background in different government agencies, was a viable choice for Andrew to contact. The kidnappers had tried to make sure that he could not do anything, and they had kidnapped Otis's mother as an extra assurance. But it also meant that somebody close to Andrew had given the kidnappers information, or how else could they have known where he was and when to call him? Andrew was deep in his thoughts when he walked to the dining room.

His White House staff had asked him if he wanted a proper lunch, but he told them he would just make a sandwich for himself. He saw a couple of delicious-looking cheese, tomato, and turkey sandwiches waiting for him on a plate. He smiled. The staff had made sure he would eat something. He sat down by the kitchen table and pulled the plate closer to him. He took a bite and realized he was not hungry at all. His mind was too occupied with the kidnapping, and he was too worried for Zachary.

Andrew's thoughts circled the helicopter crash. Somebody had to know the helicopter route and when and where Zachary was going to board the helicopter. That information was not given just to anyone. There had to be a Mole, a traitor, inside Zachary's and Dan's business or in the circle of their friends and associates. Dan was working for the president as a Senior Advisor dealing with business development at the national level, whereas Zachary was running their family business, a string of high-end department stores and golf courses nationwide. His daughter, Irene, was responsible for international business, including new development projects abroad.

A troubling thought flashed through his mind: The traitor could be in his office in the White House. Anyone on his staff could have heard or known that Zachary and Dan were supposed to meet him the day the helicopter crashed. If a real Russian mole had penetrated the White House, and been working there, then the kidnapping would not have been the only thing that this mole could have done, he thought. He considered it for a moment but decided it was not likely. The White House staff had a high-level security clearance. How could a Russian mole slip through the security checks?

He considered contacting the Secret Service and his closest advisors to tell them about the kidnapping situation. He picked up the phone but hesitated before dialing because it was Zachary's life at stake. He placed his phone back in his pocket. He decided to wait for Otis and see what he had to say. It was a hard thing to do to choose between national security and your son. *A little extra time might help*, he thought. *Otis could figure out something!*

22

Andrew and E.T.

3 p.m. (EST), The Yellow Oval Office, the Executive Residence

President Andrew Burr was watching the recent news on the television when he heard a knock on the door, "Come in," he said, and one of the Secret Service agents stepped in.

"Mr. President, the Director of the FBI is here and has asked to speak with you. It is urgent."

"Okay, show him in," Andrew replied, frowning. His blue eyes turned cloudy in worry. *Something must have happened if E.T. is here this time of the day and wants an audience*, he thought.

The Yellow Oval Office had mustard-colored walls with thick silk curtains, and the large chandelier in the middle made the room look more like a dining room than a library. President Burr had added some bookshelves along the walls and filled them with his favorite fiction and non-fiction novels. This office had American impressionists' paintings hanging, including Mary Stevenson Cassatt, who had painted the private and social lives of women and their children, and Childe Hassam, who had painted the flag draped on Fifth Avenue during the WW I and winter images of the Union Square. First Lady Burr had included in the collection a large Jackson Pollock abstract drip-painting with a collage of colors splattered on a canvas that created masterful shapes and lines. The painting was a loan from the Guggenheim Museum for the term of this presidency, but Andrew enjoyed seeing it daily on the wall of the Yellow Ova l Office.

Since President Eisenhower, the Yellow Oval Office has been used as a formal reception room to meet dignitaries before formal dinners and meetings. The office had a door to the Treaty Room in the southeast corner of the Second Floor. One of President Burr's first moves was to open the access to the old passage built right after the Civil War ended in 1865. This passage led from behind the Treaty Room to the presidential Office. The passage had been closed for decades, but Andrew thought it would create easier access to his office when needed.

E. Thomas Ruckert, the Director of the FBI, E.T. as most called him, entered in a hurry. He quickly shook the president's hand and said, "Mr. President, I'm sorry to interrupt you. I heard you have taken a few days off and asked the Vice President to take over your meetings. I just discussed it with him, and he thought, like I do, that you need to know this. It concerns National Security," he added.

President Burr noticed his slightly disheveled appearance as if E.T. had rushed to see him and had forgotten to polish his shoes and comb his hair. His normally well-ironed suit was wrinkled like he had been wearing it for more than a day. E.T.'s shiny jet-black hair was not neatly brushed backward as usual. A few strands of hair hung over his forehead, and he brushed them away with his hand when he faced the president.

"Please, E.T., sit down. Tell me what's going on," Andrew replied, raising his eyebrows.

He used the director's nickname, which referred to the film E.T. and the director's interest in UFOs.

This must be something serious if both the Vice President and the Director of the FBI wanted him to know about it, Andrew thought.

"We have received extremely credible threat information from one of our Russian informants. He has always provided us with reliable information. He said that a hit is going down now," E.T. commented with a slight Hispanic accent and added, "It involves the highest levels of the government. He said it might involve you, Mr. President." E.T.'s eyes were bright, like two shiny black buttons, as he looked at Andrew, and his olive skin looked dull in the room light as if he were stressed, tired, and had not been sleeping well.

Andrew sat still. The blood drained from his face, and he looked unnaturally pale, like a dead body. He thought: *They know. Zachary is gone. I can't help him.* He asked aloud, "A threat?" His voice was barely audible.

E.T. looked at his reaction and thought, *This is bad timing: first, the helicopter crash, and now this. Maybe I shouldn't have come here and told him. This was too soon. Then when would be a good time? The President must know. I had to come and tell him. It's my duty.*

After considering his choices, E.T. replied, "We think the Russian government and the current Russian

President, Vladislav Ruskin, are behind this. We are not sure if it is an assassination or some other type of hit against our government."

Andrew was relieved. The informant's information was so vague that the FBI didn't have much to go on. "That's serious news," President Burr replied.

"We also heard a name: Dentist. That's just his gang's name. He got it because he used to be a dentist and likes to pull out teeth from those who can't pay their debts. He started his career as a hitman and a debt collector. Today he is the leader of a gang: the Werewolves. They have chapters in the United States, Poland, and Germany. It's a new MC club overtaking the drug and gun trafficking business from the older MC clubs and crime organizations. Dentist is a rich mobster and a friend of the Russian President. Close friend, not just a casual acquaintance. Our informant suggested that Dentist had arrived in Washington, D.C. We are currently checking on that. It takes some time to get information through the TSA and NSA," E.T. explained.

Andrew did not recognize the Russian name but committed the name Dentist in his memory. *Otis has different sources, and he could find out about this man. If he is behind the kidnapping, then we might be closer to finding out Zachary's location*, Andrew thought.

"I think we need to wait and see if we get any other information," Andrew said. "We all know President Vladislav Ruskin wants Russia to get back its previous borders and become the number one global power in the world. You know I can't show any weakness because that would be disastrous. Vladislav respects strong leadership and courage. You will just have to protect me and the members of Congress. I don't want anyone to risk their lives. But there is not enough information to go on at this point."

Andrew did not talk about the real threat. He did not want the FBI to know yet. They had gotten this hint that something was going on and Russia was behind it, but they did not know that the worst had already happened. They were too late. Andrew wanted to discuss this with Otis first to see what their options were.

E.T. nodded. He understood the president's point of view. "This was just to inform you. We'll continue to gather more information. If we get anything else, I'll brief you again," E.T. assured. "We'll have a task force ready by the Capitol. There is not much else we can do right now. We don't know when and where the hit will happen." E.T. stood up, paused as if unsure how or what to say, then he looked straight into the president's eyes and said solemnly,

"Let me just offer my condolences on your son's accident. We are still going through the crash site and the wreck. If we hear anything else, we'll inform you immediately."

E.T. shook the president's hand and left.

"When and where," Andrew repeated to himself. He knew when and where. It had already happened. The FBI was too late with their information. He picked up his private cellphone, called Otis, and left him a message: "E.T. was here. He just told me that Dentist, a gang leader from Russia, is in this country, and they are checking on that lead right now. He leads a violent MC club called the Werewolves."

23

At The Casino

4 p.m. (EST), Golden Coastal Casino

While Andrew was meeting E.T. and watching the news, Otis drove his mother, Estelle, to Golden Coastal Casino. It was not too far from Washington, D.C., just about ten miles, situated near Interstate 495 and north of National Harbor's waterfront district. When Otis drove closer, its tall, shiny building reflected the blue sky with white clouds. Estelle pointed out the aluminum artwork in the middle of the entranceway and sighed, "That's so beautiful." She raised her eyebrows in question. "Metal ro ses?"

"No, it describes the Potomac and the water's dynamic movement. I think it's called the Rapids," Otis commented and kept his eyes on the slowly curving road that led to the front of the hotel entrance.

He had studied the artwork when the casino hotel opened, and it was presented in the Washington Post. Otis parked in front of the doorway and got out of the car. He stretched his arms and looked around, admiring the new metal sculptures in front of the building: the three stainless steel figures rotated slowly around their space. He had heard about this artwork before but had not had a chance to see it before this visit.

He glanced back when he heard his mother's voice. "Thank you, dear. My luggage is in the trunk."

The young, handsome valet had already opened the car door for Estelle, and she gave him a wide smile.

Otis pressed the button to open the trunk and then tossed the keys to the valet for parking. The valet grabbed Estelle's luggage out of the trunk, set it aside, and then drove away with the car. Otis took the luggage and walked with Estelle inside the casino hotel. They walked through the archway to the hotel's lobby and saw the shiny floors and modern-looking lobby area with muted black, white, and brown colors.

"You'll have to stay here for a few days until the case I'm on is solved," Otis reminded her. He could not tell his mother about Zachary's kidnapping. He would rather let her enjoy all the fancy games at the casino without any worries. She could play Blackjack, Roulette, Poker, and slot machines while he would have to try to find Zachary and his kidnappers.

Estelle sighed and brushed her black, curly hair, styled shoulder level with trendy red highlights. "Yes, I know. And you can't tell me about the case because it is top secret and involves the president."

"That's right," Otis replied, placing his arm over her shoulder. "I can't tell you now, but I will tell you when it's over."

"I have known Andrew and his family for a long time. We were neighbors. I would not do anything to jeopardize your case or his career!" Estelle shrugged and glanced around the lobby.

"I know that. I just can't tell you how important it is that you don't leave this place. Don't tell anyone that you know Andrew. Don't mention me and my job either. Don't tell anyone that I work for Andrew," Otis explained. "Stick to the weather and small talk."

Estelle almost laughed. "Safe topics: No politics, no spy stuff."

"That's right, mom." Otis nodded and led her to the check-in counter.

She sighed. "Okay, I won't tell anyone."

A couple of businessmen ahead of them were getting their room keys. Otis saw a large, almost wall-size artwork on the wall behind the check-in counter. At first, he thought it represented a world map, but after looking at it for a moment, he decided, he did not know what it was. The color of the artwork was brown, tan, and creamy white.

The front-desk concierge was now ready to check them in, and Otis gave Estelle's real name. He did not believe Estelle would have to be there for more than a few days, and there was no reason to fake her check-in reservation. Otis was sure the casino would be safe. He didn't think there was any danger in using Estelle's real name at check-in. The casino was monitored 24/7. He did not even consider that the Russians would go after her again after the failed kidnapping attempt.

The reservation was fast and professional. It only took a couple of minutes for Otis and Estelle to be ready.

Otis pointed toward the large artwork and asked, "Can you tell me about that artwork? It's interesting."

The front-desk concierge smiled and commented, "It's one of our recent acquisitions. Made by an anonymous street artist. It's called the Map of the Universe. It's made of different materials, like clay, dried leaves, roots, cotton rope, and steel. The red clay came from this area when the excavation of the hotel started. If you like, we have an art tour for our guests..."

"No, not right now. Thank you for suggesting that. That artwork just seems perfect for this lobby," Otis replied, smiling.

After getting the room keycard, Otis was ready to leave. He hugged Estelle and gave her the room key. A young and eager bellhop took Estelle's luggage. Otis handed him a tip.

"I'll swing by to collect you for dinner," Otis declared, maintaining an unwavering gaze on his mother. He was determined to ensure her full attention, having sensed her occasional habit of feigning interest to expedite their conversations. However, this instance seemed different; his mother regarded him with a focused and genuine expression, indicating a sincere acknowledgment of his words. *Maybe the kidnapping and disappointment with Stan has something to do with it*, Otis thought.

"Great. Where are we going?" Estelle asked.

"The same place where I picked you up today, at the Restaurant Troika. I thought you might want to help Andrew and me," Otis said and added, "You can also stay here if you're afraid to go back there?" Otis lifted an eyebrow.

"No, I don't want to stay here. I'll be ready," Estelle replied, and her eyes glinted defiantly. She was not going to just hide when his friend Andrew needed help. "If you think the dinner will help you and Andrew, I'll do it. Besides, if the owner was behind my kidnapping, I want to show him I'm no shy wallflower. I'm not afraid of him." Estelle was now feisty and ready to fight back.

After leaving his mother at the casino, Otis headed back to his residence near the university campus. He was concerned by the news he had received from Stan, his mother's ex-boyfriend and kidnapper.

Stan had told that the owner of the Restaurant Troika had paid him to befriend Otis's mother, then capture her.

He decided it was best to visit the Restaurant Troika when it opened that same evening. His mother would be a perfect cover. A family dinner: A son taking his mother to a nice restaurant. Nothing suspicious.

He could also scope out the owner and maybe find out something about this kidnapping case. He checked his messages and noticed that Andrew had left him one message. He listened to it.

Werewolves and their leader Dentist here in the United States. Interesting, he thought. *How did he get through the TSA checkpoint? He is a known criminal. He must have had a different passport ID or even a diplomatic passport.*

He checked his watch. It was about 5 p.m. *Time to go to see Andrew*, he thought.

24

Andrew and Otis

6 P.M, The Executive Residence, The White House

On his way back to the White House, Otis bought two burner phones: one for him and one for Andrew. It was better if nobody knew their numbers and what they talked about. Cheap prepaid burner phones were easily disposable and replaceable if their data was breached.

He did not know who was behind the kidnapping, but if Doppelganger-Dan or any of his friends were watching and listening to Andrew's calls, Zachary's life would be in imminent danger. He could not be sure who else was behind the kidnapping and the conspiracy behind the blackmailing besides Doppelganger-Dan. He was the only one they knew for certain was involved in this scheme. *Where is real Dan? Was he killed? Was he imprisoned like Zachary?* Otis had no idea. There had not been any clues as to what had happened to him.

Who could be trusted? He was not sure. *No one at the White House. No one who had access to the flight schedule the day when the crash happened*, he thought grimly as he drove forward, heading to the White House.

Any agency could have Russian moles or sleepers. Who and where was the problem? They did not have time to find out who to trust.

When Otis arrived at the private quarters of the White House, the Secret Service agents greeted him and cleared him to go to meet the president.

Andrew impatiently paced the hallway and greeted Otis the minute he showed up and led him directly to the Yellow Oval Office. He did not want any of the White House servants or the Secret Service agents listening to their conversation.

"How are you holding up?" Otis asked, concerned.

Andrew looked tired and stressed. He shrugged. "As well as can be expected." His voice was frail.

"Did you hear from the kidnappers?" Otis asked.

Andrew nodded and said, "Yes. I received a second call. They know you are in on this."

"Yes, they knew it before you even contacted me. They had a man befriending my mother, and they captured her, but I got her back," Otis explained.

"Is she all right?" President Burr had known the Thorne family for decades. He was very fond of Otis's mother, Estelle. They had been neighbors before his election to the Senate and then the presidency.

"Yes, she is fine. Pissed, angry, upset, maybe," Otis said with a laugh. "She knows I'm working for you."

Andrew replied, "That's good." His face turned somber. "What's your plan? What can we do? I want Zachary back alive."

"I plan to take my mother out to a late dinner tonight, to the Restaurant Troika, the same restaurant where she was held hostage. The restaurant is the only clue we have to find the kidnappers," Otis said casually.

"Would she go with you there?" Andrew furrowed his brows. "Isn't she afraid to go back to that restaurant?"

Otis chuckled. "No, she is not afraid. You know my mother. She is ready to help you. You know she likes you, and she voted for you. She's angry that Stan, her ex-boyfriend, pretended to like her then kidnapped her for money. And believe me, angry does not adequately describe how she feels now."

Andrew smiled. "Good. Then I'll hear more after your dinner tonight. What time are you meeting her?"

"At ten o'clock. And yes, I will tell you if I find out anything," Otis assured and checked his watch. He had to hurry. His tight schedule with his university lectures had gotten even tighter with this unexpected meeting with the president. He looked apologetically at the president and held out his hand to shake his hand, "Andrew, I'm sorry, but I need to leave. I have a lecture in half an hour. I can't stay longer. We will find Zach and whoever is behind this kidnapping."

Andrew gripped his hand and gave it a firm two-hand shake. "Sure, I understand. This whole kidnapping and their demands are just so overwhelming. I had to speak with you. It helps me keep balanced when I bounce thoughts and ideas with you."

Otis remembered his purchase. "One more thing: take this burner phone for secure conversations." He pulled the two phones from his pocket and gave the other one to Andrew, who took it and pocketed it. "Please, use only this phone in our communications."

Andrew Burr gave him a quizzical look and then realized what the new burner phone meant. "You don't want anyone to track our calls or your movements," he commented. "You don't know if someone is monitoring our calls."

"Yes. That's correct. If the kidnappers don't know what we discuss and what I plan to do, it's better for us and safer for your son," Otis replied and then, soon after that, left the building.

Andrew, the man whose face was probably the most recognized in global politics, sat down alone. He took out his private cell phone and played the short video clip from his son over and over again. He missed him and hearing his voice. He hoped to keep him alive, no matter the costs. He would do anything to save his son's life, even sacrifice his career. He realized that the stakes might still be too high. He might have to sacrifice his country and destabilize the global political arena to save his son's life.

25

Russia

Georgetown Campus

After leaving the White House, Otis drove towards the Georgetown campus, where he taught Security Studies at the university.

When he arrived at the college, he went directly to his study and reviewed his notes for today's lecture. Several topics were worth mentioning, and he had written down some incidents of the recent past: the Ukrainian crisis, the crash of an airplane containing mostly citizens of the Netherlands, and the crash site proving that it was a Russian missile that took the commercial flight down, the economic sanctions against Russia, the freezing of the assets of the Russian businessmen, the hacking and the trolling in social media websites against the current Western leaders and their politics, dozens of Russian diplomats expelled from the United States as punishment for hacking and using ransomware against the hospitals and the American companies, Russia's alleged interference in the 2016 presidential election, and the Ukraine crisis where Russia supported the rebels and in turn, acquired Crimean as part of the imperialistic goals and now the recent war with Ukraine.

He analyzed in his mind that the decisions or undecidedness of the leaders of the European Union and the previous presidents of the United States of America had caused a vacuum in the international political arena and allowed the Russian Presidents, former President Vladimir Putin, and the current President Vladislav Ruskin, to become more powerful.

Vladislav Ruskin's rise to power could not be attributed to one event but a mixture of factors, including events happening outside Russia like the Brexit vote, namely Great Britain's exit from the European Union, the populist parties, and leaders gaining power in the United States, and in several European Union countries, like for example, in France, Netherlands, Germany, Greece, Sweden, and Finland.

The rise of ISIS and the growth of terrorism around the world have caused world leaders to secure their borders and concentrate more on their internal security instead of on the global political situation. Russia was left to invade and conquer its weaker, neighboring countries.

Internal factors leading to the rise of a new strong Russian president were the strength of the United Russia party that had been in power for more than fifteen years, along with weak opposition due to purges within Russia, not to mention the immense power of the oligarchs.

The previous Russian President, Putin, had secretly attacked and purged the opposition, taken control of the media, and made sure that his political opponents were silenced – either killed or sent to a labor camp in Siberia just like Stalin had done for decades before his death in 1991.

President Putin had missed three components in his power structure: Putin underestimated the enormous power of a certain group of oligarchs, who had made fortunes in the state reforms designed to lead the Soviet Union's transformation from socialism into capitalism. He had also trusted the army leaders without knowing they were secretly working for the oligarchs and the man they wanted to become the next leader of their country, namely Vladislav Ruskin.

The third component in Ruskin's power structure was the young voters: They had not been alive during the Soviet Union and when the new Russia was established. They only knew the Soviet Union from the history books. Vladimir Putin ignored the younger generation's power and the importance of gaining their votes. The young voters wanted change instead of a stable political climate. Many older politicians had dismissed Ruskin as a nonentity and a political figure of no real substance because he was younger than Putin and he had not experienced the Soviet Union and its decline. Ruskin began advocating "Neo-Imperialism," which meant that Russia should focus on building its footholds in surrounding countries and spreading its influence globally instead of just in the territory it already controlled, like the Crimean Peninsula. He had been silent about the recent war in Ukraine but secretly spoke about it as the start of the new Russian regime.

The opposition had secretly tried to assassinate President Putin in 2017 when the nation celebrated the 100th anniversary of the Bolshevik revolution, but they failed. The attempt had been kept secret from the media. The International media noticed that President Putin had canceled several meetings and was unavailable for any comments for weeks. The official comment was that he had injured his back and was resting. President Putin's location was unknown, and no one could verify what had happened.

Vladislav Ruskin had been clever enough to distance himself from the assassination attempt and thus was able to continue his political career. The next assassination attempt succeeded, and President Putin died in a car bombing before his last presidential term ended. Vladislav Ruskin outmaneuvered his rivals for party control and became the new president.

26

Restaurant Troika

8.30 p.m. (EST), The Troika restaurant

Otis picked up his mother later that evening and took her to the Restaurant Troika, the same place the kidnappers had used previously to hide her. She was pumped up with adrenaline: She was ready to play her part to help his son find these bad guys who had paid Stan to kidnap her and help Otis find Zachary.

The restaurant had a queue of wealthy-looking customers in front of it, but the White House had done its magic, reserving a table for Otis and his mother. They walked past the line receiving jealous glances along the way.

Estelle was in a chatty mood even though she had been rescued earlier that day. The new casino had made her cheerful and she was full of life. She wore a striking black stylish jacket with pink and white floral embroidered tulle and a black pencil skirt and high heels – the perfect looking-forward-to-spring-but-still-weather-appropriate outlook for dinner in a fashionable restaurant. She had purchased it in one of the casino hotel's designer boutiques.

Otis wore his usual dark gray suit with a new pink silk tie, also purchased from the casino's store. Their outlook fit the guests inside the restaurant, Otis noticed, as most of the restaurant visitors' faces were well-known from the gossip magazines or the political arena.

The waitress escorted them directly to their table.

Otis browsed the surroundings as they were seated near the kitchen. While his mother was reading the menu, he was more occupied watching the customers and the restaurant employees. Most of them looked slavish, and their waitress had a thick Russian accent. Otis was not sure if the accent was real or just acting to fit the restaurant's image and ambiance.

Otis ordered caramelized onion soup for appetizers, Stroganoff, a red wine braised beef with noodles, for entrées, and the black caviar with warm buckwheat blinis for dessert for both of them. After they had enjoyed their soup and their main course, Otis asked the waitress, "Where is the owner? We would like to congratulate him for the fine dinner we had here."

The waitress smiled pleased, and replied, "Maksim Liskin is the owner." She looked around to see if the owner was anywhere nearby. Her face brightened as she saw him talking to some other customers and gestured to Otis's table and he nodded back. The owner looked towards their table and held up his forefinger as if to ask for a moment. The waitress turned towards her table and said, "He will be here soon. He usually likes to greet new customers if he is here."

It did not take long before the owner approached their table. He stopped by to exchange a few words with the waitress who had signaled him, then he headed towards Otis's table, stopped next to him, and smiled widely. "Maksim Liskin. I'm the owner of the Troika. The waitress expressed your wish to see me" His accent was thick, Russian, Otis noted.

Maxim Liskin was a medium-sized man in his sixties with sharp, black eyes that reminded him of shark eyes: cold but deadly. He had a white silk shirt and no tie showing the heavy gold chains around his neck and hairy chest. His sleeves were rolled up to his elbows. Otis noticed that his right arm had a tattoo of a werewolf with a snake.

Otis held out his hand, and Maxim shook it with a tight grip. Otis gestured to their table and the empty plates and told him, "Congratulations on your restaurant. The menu items were supreme."

The owner smiled and thanked him in the Russian language. "Spasibo, spasibo." His smile was so wide that his golden canine tooth blinked in the light.

Otis remembered that the Russians liked to have gold in their mouth to show their wealth. The poor families had their teeth pulled, but if you had enough money, you would have golden crowns in your molars and canines.

A gang or a prison tattoo, Otis thought as he viewed the arm tattoo. A snake was a common tattoo in Russian prisons. He had studied them when he was stationed in Moscow. A snake tattoo could symbolize a temptation to steal, to take something that someone else owns, or even an addiction to drugs.

If I remember correctly, that can also be an old thief's tattoo. A werewolf tattoo means a transformation from a human into a wolf. Wolves kill dogs. Interesting, he thought. This was the second time today werewolves had come up. The first time was the message from Andrew about the Russian MC club, and now this tattoo. Maybe they were connected. There was an inscription under the tattoo. Otis quickly read it: "беспредел" (bespredel). It was one of the Russian words that did not have an exact translation in English. *The word literally translates to: "without limits or boundaries," but it also includes lawlessness, leaving other persons at the mercy of anarchy,* Otis recalled.

The tattoo clashed with the wealthy restaurant owner—a look that Maksim Liskin tried to fashion. It was not a fashion statement but made to show loyalty to a gang.

Otis quickly assessed the owner and considered him to be a dangerous opponent. He did not believe this man could not know what was going on in his restaurant at any time of the day. *He must know something of this helicopter crash and the kidnappings because Stan had taken Estelle here to be questioned and held hostage,* Otis thought but didn't reveal his thoughts. Instead, he smiled and glanced towards his mother, who fiddled with her wineglass and smiled as if she had nothing else in mind. Otis knew his mother better: she was angry for being held as a hostage and being betrayed by her boyfriend-to-be, and she wanted to pay back whoever was responsible for her kidnapping.

Maksim Liskin looked at them but did not seem to recognize either one. His face showed no emotion except the pleasure of meeting his guest. Otis had hoped that the sight of Estelle would shake him if he was part of the kidnapping plan. Otis was sure that Maksim knew something. But as he did not reveal anything, Otis played along and only expressed his thanks for the fine dinner and the nice atmosphere of the restaurant.

After Otis and his mother left the restaurant, Maksim Liskin went to his office and made a quick call. "Eto ya, Maksim. Mne nuzhna Hydra (It's me, Maksim. I need to speak with Hydra)." He waited, nervously drumming the table with his fingers. When someone came on the phone, he said quickly, "He was here, the man you asked to watch out for."

Maksim listened to the responses on the other end of the phone without saying a word, then he ended the call speaking Russian, "Khorosho (Okay)"

He hung up and stayed quiet, staring at the phone. He felt a sudden cold shiver and thought of the old wives' tale saying that an uncontrollable, sudden shudder is caused by someone walking over your own grave. Something bad was going to happen; Maksim was sure of that. Hydra was not a man to cross. He was sure Hydra was not pleased to hear the news he had just told him.

Otis Thorne and his mother were bold and reckless to show up here tonight, he thought.

The Troika restaurant was compromised; Hydra had told him that. Hydra had also said that he would take care of the loose ends.

Am I one of them? Maxim worried and leaned back on his chair. He believed his services were still needed. Perhaps there was no need to panic, at least not yet.

27

Restaurant Nevskij

The second night after the helicopter crash

Five limousines drove slowly through the dark, tree-lined King Street in Arlington, Virginia. They parked in front of the restaurant Nevskij. King Street's old architecture, brick-lined streets, and a canopy of twinkling streetlights gave a romantic atmosphere for this clandestine meeting.

It was past midnight, and the restaurant was closed for customers – except for the five guests in limousines. One of the participants of this covert group did not attend this meeting.

The limousines were reserved through various companies, and the drivers did not know the identity of the passengers. The drivers had received orders to pick them up at the airport and drive them to this specific address. The passengers did not want any observers in their meeting.

The passengers entered the restaurant one at a time. They were stopped by the doorway, where the burly-looking doorman checked their tattooed wrist and let them in each one at a time.

Heavy curtains on the windows concealed this secret meeting from the outside viewers. The restaurant was empty except for the doorman.

It was the same place where the secret group had met before. The restaurant's flower arrangements around the dining room had been changed from white to orange lilies since the previous meeting. The tiny, round lights on the ceiling gave soft lighting to the cool gray and blue walls and carpets.

The same wooden table was placed in the center of the room as during the previous clandestine gathering. The participants went inside and sat around the table in the same order as before. They had tablets prearranged for each seat.

When each of them had sat down, they opened their tablet and viewed the progress of their covert "Operation Pobeda" presented on the tablet.

Two chairs remained empty, but the seats had the tablets open because two members could not attend in person. They planned to participate online. One of them was Nachtkrapp, the White House contact, and the other was Cyborg, who had urgent work-related issues and could not travel to this meeting.

This was the meeting of Russia's richest men and their American allies, the oligarchs of the future, unknown to most of the world because they liked to stay behind the scenes like puppet masters. Their business arrangements were made under different international conglomerates with so many shell companies and subsidiaries that the real owners, these six men, were almost impossible to trace.

Only one participant was an American with blood ties to Russia. These were the leaders of Operation Pobeda.

They did not count Dan Wheeler as part of their elitist group. He was just a tool to be used and discarded.

The secret meeting was arranged so that these powerful men could discuss Operation Pobeda, initiated three years ago during the U.S. presidential campaign. The Ministry of State Security (MGB) had asked them to meet in the

Kremlin, where they were given the top-secret dossier of Operation Pobeda. The operation was an ancient one. Few knew about it. The origin of Operation Pobeda had been presented to the higher-ups in the Soviet Union after WWII. The elaborate operation required technological and scientific advancements not available at that time. Operation Pobeda was put on hold until such advancements were made. The Soviet Union collapsed in 1991, but the new Russian leaders got interested in Operation Pobeda. A quarter of a decade ago, it was physically and technologically possible to advance with Operation Pobeda. Finally, approximately two days ago, the operation was successfully launched.

A little over two years ago, the U.S. presidential campaign with several different outcomes was ongoing. Fifteen months ago, the winner was chosen. But during the campaign, these six men had secretly funded other powerful entities within the United States to push the presidential campaign toward the candidate they wanted in power. Because these six men were Russian oligarchs, they were not allowed to fund these candidates directly, but what they could do was leak out unflattering information about the candidates they did not want to win. They could also fund their subsidiaries within the United States, and these American companies and their employees were allowed to fund the presidential candidate's campaign as private donors.

The media were ready to publish any information regardless of where they got it. Many good candidates were disgraced or ridiculed with unsubstantiated claims, old photos of them being drunk, or attending demonstrations on their campus.

These six powerful men knew how to find information and use it in their favor. They hired the best hackers to find more secret and compromising information to leak out.

Moreover, they used the troll factories in Russia to leak out even more unsubstantiated news, rumors, and opinions of other candidates to demonize and discredit them. Their own chosen candidate was spared from this rumor mill.

Now it was time to assess the operation and how it was proceeding. The men viewed the contents provided to them on the tablet, which contained short video footage of their prisoner, Zachary. He was in good health, tied to his chair. He did not know he was monitored and videotaped 24/7 in his prison. If they needed to send the president of the United States a video of Zachary, they could use any of the footage they had now. This was to guarantee the president's cooperation. The Werewolves guarded the valuable prisoner 24/7.

Phoenix informed the others, "Dan Wheeler, the only survivor of the crash, our Postmaster, and our associate, has already made his contact with the president." Phoenix brushed his finger over the knot of his red tie. He wore an impeccable black suit with a white silk shirt. He looked fit for his age, closer to his forties, with short, dark hair and a small diamond glistening in his right earlobe.

"Why did we use this gang, the Werewolves, in this kidnapping?" Hippogriff asked. He saw the icy look in the Werewolf's eyes, and he quickly added, "I mean, we could have hired some men to do the kidnapping. I'm concerned that your gang members are too easy to identify."

"Even if they are identified, captured, or tortured, they would not give any information. They are all loyal to Mother Russia and especially to our leader, President Ruskin. He is an honorary member of my club. Besides, I'm their leader, and our president is my close friend. I have often visited his luxurious dacha on the Black Sea." Werewolf, the leader of the Werewolves, bragged.

"Is this the same MC club he rode with when he was running for president?" Hippogriff said, "I remember seeing some photos and videos of him showing off his driving skills."

"Yes, President Ruskin enjoyed parading with us," the Werewolf-tattooed participant boasted.

"How did you get the nickname 'Dentist'?" Hippogriff asked.

"Because I have pulled the teeth from my enemies. I studied to be a dentist but never really got into that business. This gang life is more interesting, especially with special projects like this one we have ongoing now," Dentist replied, grinning. He was the one with the werewolf tattoo.

The next subject was the president and his friend Otis. He had contacted Otis as they had suspected.

The file of Otis was received from the Ministry of State Security (MGB). It was thin but filled with information about his past position as a CIA agent, his current position as a visiting professor, his one previous meeting with President Putin, and his only meeting with the current Russian President Ruskin.

Dentist explained, "The Werewolves have been divided into cells with different tasks. One was a surveillance cell following Otis since day one of Operation Pobeda. This cell is separate from the ones guarding the president's son.

If the enemy captured any members of the surveillance cell, the members could not offer any vital information about the other Werewolf cells. They are all separate. I'm the only one who knows their tasks, where they are assigned, and their part in Operation Pobeda."

The next step was a video call with their secret White House contact, Nachtkrapp. He was a Russian Mole inside the White House. He was one of the Russian kids adopted in the USA and part of the former KGB's program to plant young kids as sleepers in the USA. Nachtkrapp had risen to a powerful position and was now part of the secret group. He wanted to be unknown, unseen. Even in the video call, he did not show his face. He did not want to be identified even by any of these rich men. Only Hydra knew who he was because Hydra had connections within the Ministry of State Security (MGB) agency.

"Good evening," Nachtkrapp started. He used voice-altering software that gave his voice a metallic sound. "I'm pleased with the successful start. I want to congratulate the Werewolves for the effective execution of the kidnapping of Zachary Burr."

Nachtkrapp paused and cleared his throat. "I am concerned about the president's actions and his friend

Otis. They failed to kidnap his only relative, his mother. That was a big mistake. It made Otis interested and personally involved in the kidnapping case. Otis is eager to find out who is behind it."

Hydra interrupted, "Otis knows about this kidnapping and is determined to help the president." He viewed the group in the room and added, "I already talked to Maksim Liskin and told him we will take care of it. Otis Thorne and his mother visited the Troika restaurant. That place is compromised. I would suggest that the Werewolves take care of the restaurant and all loose ends." He turned his icy gaze towards Dentist, the Werewolf gang leader, who nodded, agreeing with the decision.

He looked around the table, saw nods of agreement, and heard murmurs of acceptance.

Hippogriff looked downwards. He had hired Maxim Liskin to run his Restaurant Troika, but now he had to find someone else. It was hard to find good employees, especially those connected to the Russian mob, who were ready to do their bidding.

"It seems that everyone agrees. Do as you consider best," Nachtkrapp replied.

Hydra wondered if the other group members ever contemplated who Nachtkrapp was in real life. He knew him, but he would have never guessed. When he listened to Nachtkrapp, he could not hear his accent. No one would know if he was an American or a Russian.

The voice-altering software makes him sound like a robot, Hydra thought.

Nachtkrapp asked, "Have you been following the news?"

Hydra pointed out that using the fake witness was a brilliant idea. "It is easy to manipulate the media. Nobody suspected the phony witness. Everyone believed him."

Hydra looked around. Again, the other participants agreed. Hydra announced, "The next step is the United Nations General Assembly in New York."

Everyone around the table clapped their hands in unison. It was the next step of Operation Pobeda.

"Our next meeting will be held a day after the United Nations General Assembly. " We will find out if the president has agreed to our demands," Hydra said, concluding the meeting. "That's all for today. Have a safe trip. Our meeting is concluded."

The men exited in the same order as they had arrived. Secretly and alone.

28

At the Hospital

George Washington University Hospital, the second day after the helicopter crash

At the hospital, the doctor on the day shift, Mike Warner, visited Dan around noon. It was the second day after the crash. He viewed his chart and said, "Mr. Wheeler, I think you should stay here for a couple more days for observation."

Dan tried to rise in his hospital bed. "Why?"

"Oh, we just want to make sure that the accident did not cause a concussion. Sometimes, it might take a day or two before the concussion shows. We are also running some more blood tests." The doctor pointed out his chart and said, "You also complain about amnesia and some headaches. We have not found any cause for those yet. Finding the cause for them is important because we would not want you to suffer any setbacks. We'll take an MRI and some x-rays, too, to make sure there are no underlying reasons for these symptoms."

He closed Dan's chart and walked to the door. Dan saw the doctor holding the door open for someone else and heard them exchange a few words with someone, then saw his wife, Irene, coming in.

She smiled. "Hi, sweetheart!" Her eyes turned darker in worry as she observed all his bandages.

Dan was secretly pleased that he had to stay at the hospital. Now, the president knew his contacts with the kidnappers and Russia and didn't know if the president had mentioned anything to Irene. He hoped not because that would cause more trouble.

"How are you feeling?" Irene walked closer, leaned over, and kissed him.

He turned his head away so that the kiss landed on his cheek. He explained, "My head and the entire body still hurt from the crash."

"Oh, I'm sorry." Irene got a worried look on her face. "What did the doctor say?"

"I'm staying here for a few more days. They are taking more tests to determine what's causing the headaches and amnesia. They suspect a concussion."

He grabbed Irene's hand and added, "I'm sorry I can't come home with you. Doctor's orders, you know." He sighed.

"I hope they can find out what is going on," Irene replied. She sat down on the visitor's chair by the bed. "I brought you some reading material and some fruit."

"Thank you, Irene. You are so thoughtful," Dan replied politely. He did not realize he was acting distant and that Irene had noticed something was wrong. "I'll be fine. Don't worry," Dan said and gave her a thin smile.

Irene smiled back, but in her mind, Dan's actions shifted her worry to suspicion. She was concerned that Dan had some sort of post-traumatic stress disorder: He did not like to be touched. She still blamed the accident, but deep inside, she was not sure. It was as if her husband was a stranger. He talked to her as if she were a business partner or an acquaintance, not as a husband. She decided to talk with his doctor and ask could this amnesia and his headache could have caused her husband to change this much. She did not want to show her concern to her husband. She knew Dan was still recovering from the accident. She decided to push the troubling thoughts back, concentrate on Dan's recovery, and help him regain his memories and full physical health.

Dan studied her face and tried to deduce if Irene suspected anything. He had tried to act normally, but he noticed that the kiss had caused concern. He had just turned his head without thinking. Dan decided to be more careful in the future. No one else was supposed to know about the kidnapping and his role in Operation Pobeda. Irene was a perfect cover, but only if she believed in him. *I need to act more like a loving husband,* he thought.

29

The Mole at the White House

The Oval Office, the second day after the crash

The mole in the White House checked out the president's schedule. He was part of the White House staff. He was entitled to the most secret details of the president's daily schedule. He frowned. He did not like what he saw in the president's daily planner: The President had contacted Otis twice. Twice is too much, he thought. He did not want Otis to be in touch with the president while the plan was in progress.

When the president walked in to start his day, the mole straightened up and mechanically fell back on the standard line. He said, "Please, may I offer my deepest condolences for the loss of your son." His voice did not reflect any real emotions, as he knew Zachary was still alive. He also knew he had to say that to keep up his appearance as a loyal staff member.

The president just nodded and said, "Thank you." It felt awkward for President Burr to pretend that his son was dead. He had to remind himself that he was supposed to be a grieving father and act accordingly.

They stood in the middle of the Oval Office for a short moment in awkward silence.

The mole cleared his throat and said, "I'm sure anyone will understand if you want to postpone some meetings. It is hard to lose a son. Your position as a leader of this country makes it even harder because you already carry the burden of making decisions that affect millions of U.S. citizens." The mole presented a genuine concern about how the president was coping with the situation. He knew that the president was more stressed because he was being extorted.

"I just can't believe I won't be able to see him again," the president replied, walking to his Resolution Desk and sitting down. He sat straight, his jaw set, deadpan, and motioned to the mahogany chair placed in front of the Resolution Desk, "Please, sit down."

The mole pulled up his pant legs before sitting down, then opened the leather folder he had carried. A stack of documents was inside the folder. His brows drew together when he browsed through the papers looking for the right one. He looked up to see if the president was ready to discuss business and his schedule.

The large windows behind the Resolution desk illuminated the President's flaxen-colored hair. The heavy mustard-colored curtains were pulled aside, and you could see the early spring weather outside: the trees were still bare, with no snow on the ground, just yellowish-brown grass and dead leaves.

On both sides of the south-facing windows, the president displayed the battle flags of the five branches of service: Army, Navy, Marine Corps, Coast Guard, and Air Force. The star-and-stripes American flag and the blue flag bearing the presidential seal were placed right behind him.

This is hard, this lying, President Burr thought. He had to learn to be a good actor because he was not allowed to reveal his son's kidnapping. He decided to share a memory,

"I still remember like yesterday when he was born, when we took the First Family pictures together when he grew up to be the man he is now, when he went into Harvard, when I announced my candidacy for the presidency, and he stood right by me with the rest of my family. Zachary was always there, supporting, standing by, and assisting me in my political goals. I can't accept I have lost him," the president said. "In my heart, he is still alive," he added. For everyone else, this sounded like a father's futile hope, not giving up the son and trying to hide the sorrow, but the Mole knew Zachary was alive just like the president did.

The mole took the president's words as an act of professing to be a normal father. The mole nodded sympathetically.

"I'm not ready to talk about politics, not now." President Burr continued, "If there is nothing urgent, can we continue this meeting some other time."

The mole raised his hand to stop him from saying no more. "I can discuss these topics in my agenda with the Vice President. I'm sure he will step in." The mole hesitated, then said, "Mr. President, the United Nations General Assembly is taking place soon. It is a tradition for the president of the United States to give a speech there. Do you want me to cancel it?"

The mole awaited the president's answer, his heart pounding with anxiety. This was a critical moment because if the president said no, the Septem group would know that the president would not surrender to extortion. It would also mean the death sentence for Zachary, his son.

President Andrew Burr was silent for a long time, thirty seconds or so, before answering. His eyes were looking at the desktop as he considered his choices. Andrew did not want to go to that United Nations General Assembly but knew he had to go because of the kidnappers' demands. But he did not want to give up and agree to their demands immediately without absolute assurances that Zachary would be freed, uninjured.

Maybe something will come up before that. Maybe Otis will find out something. Maybe... But for now, I must attend that meeting because that's what the Doppelganger insisted. That was the first demand, President Burr thought. Raising his eyes back to his visitor's, he replied, "No, don't cancel. I will go there. I will give a speech."

The mole had been holding his breath for the president's answer and replied anxiously. "Great. I have also got a confirmation that the Russian President will attend it, too. I'm sure he would like to address the economic sanctions." The mole closed the folder in his hand, got up, and shook President Burr's hand.

"Yes, I'm sure. I will say something about those sanctions in my opening speech." Andrew Burr replied. The President had no idea that he had talked with his son's kidnapper, his adversary, a Russian mole in his closest circle.

When the mole walked out of the Oval Office, he had difficulty hiding his satisfaction. He smoothed his fingers over his hair. Soon, their grand operation would progress to its next phase: the removal of all the economic sanctions harming Russia's global expansion.

30

The Oval Office

President Andrew Burr had just ended his previous meeting in the Oval Office when he felt the phone in his pocket vibrate. It was the burner phone Otis had given him. "Good morning, Otis," he answered.

Andrew Burr heard the strong, familiar voice come on the line. "Mr. President," Otis began, "We need to know who that person is in the hospital. You suspect he is not Dan, even if he looks like him. If we get his fingerprints and his DNA, we can run them through our intelligence agencies' databases."

Andrew Burr wavered an instant before replying, "Yes, you are right. I did not even think about that. But who can we use? I can't order the doctors to run the DNA and take his fingerprints for testing, and I can't turn to the FBI or the Secret Service to do that. They would suspect that something is wrong. I don't want Irene to know we suspect her husband Dan."

"You're absolutely right: Irene has to act normally. If she acts any differently, the doppelganger might also figure out that she knows. You were told not to tell anyone about the kidnapping," Otis reminded him.

"I know. Zachary's life is at stake here," Andrew Burr said.

"I can take the fingerprints if he is sedated and unconscious, but I can't if he is awake. He would inform his co-conspirators, and Zachary would be harmed or killed," Otis explained. "One hair would be enough for the DNA sample," he told Andrew and continued, "I don't have access to his hospital room because I'm not a relative, but I could go there with you. We just need to make sure he is unconscious when I enter his hospital room. Someone must administer a sedative to get him to sleep before I go there. I don't want him to recognize me."

"I can't ask the doctors to give him a sedative. They would suspect something is wrong. Do you have a sedative that you could use?" Andrew Burr asked. He did not know drugs well, but he was sure Otis did.

"Yes, I do," Otis replied. "We could use Irene without her knowing about it. Is she still visiting him daily?"

"Yes, she goes there after work," Andrew replied. "Because she is a manager in her own fashion business, she usually works late, but after the helicopter crash, she has only worked for six hours a day and spent the afternoons with Dan at the hospital."

"We could dissolve the sedative in a coffee cup. The coffee would hide the bitter aftertaste of the drug. If I remember correctly, the real Dan loves coffee. The doppelganger must do and act like the real one. He would not refuse a cup of his favorite flavored coffee. You could take the coffee cup to the hospital, give it to Irene, and explain that you had an urgent meeting and wanted Dan to have a cup of his favorite coffee. She could take it to his room. He would not suspect it," Otis said.

"That could work," the president considered.

Otis replied, "We'll meet at the hospital, and I'll bring the sedative. You must go to a coffee shop and buy the coffee for him. Then we must wait until it is safe for us to go to his room and take the DNA sample and fingerprints.

I can't enter the room without you, and my name cannot be added to the visitors' list."

Otis ended the call. He still reconsidered the possibilities of how to administer the sedatives, but he could not see any other choice. They needed to find out who the person was if he was not Dan Wheeler. He was their only lead now. They could not ask anyone at the hospital to take the DNA and bloodwork because they would have to ask for the patient's approval. The DNA tests would reveal to the Russians that Otis and President Burr wanted to find out who this doppelganger was, and Zachary would be as good as dead. They could not ask the doctor or the nurses to administer more sedatives because of the concussion; they did not want to risk the Russians finding out about that.

31

At the Hospital

George Washington University Hospital, the second day after the helicopter crash

A ndrew Burr arrived with two Secret Service agents at George Washington University Hospital the same afternoon. The rest of his protective team was left in the cars waiting for the president when he was ready to leave the hospital. This was not the normally scheduled visit known by the public and the media, so he traveled 'light' with only a couple of Secret Service agents. When he got out of the Beast, his official vehicle, he heard the other Secret Service agent mumble to his radio, "POTUS is out of the car, going to the hospital entrance now."

Andrew Burr wore a Navy jacket and a dark blue ball cap with the seal of the president of the United States in front of it. He stopped by the coffee shop downstairs, and the scents of caramel, chocolate, and freshly ground coffee greeted him. The Secret Service agents led him directly to the front desk, and he was let ahead of the line to order. He smiled, greeted the customers and the servers, and asked for a large hazelnut mocha coconut milk macchiato.

It's good that the real Dan liked flavored coffees, Andrew thought. *That will hide the taste of sedatives as Otis suggested.*

The two agents waited by his side until he was done shopping and ready to take the elevator upstairs.

It's not easy to be discreet and visit a hospital when everyone recognizes you and knows who you are, Andrew thought when he waited for the elevator and saw the curious glimpses of the passing-by hospital visitors and nurses. He smiled and greeted them with a slight nod.

When Andrew entered the floor where his son-in-law was, he first saw a couple of nurses by the desk and two other Secret Service agents on guard watching who entered and exited the floor.

Andrew was relieved to see Otis waiting by the nurse's desk, his hands in his pockets, leaning against the counter.

Otis noticed him immediately and nodded discretely. He wanted Andrew to approach alone, not with his protective detail agents. He did not want witnesses to what he wanted to say and do, and Andrew understood that.

Andrew turned toward the agents and asked, "Please, can you wait over there in the waiting room? I need to see my son-in-law in private." He did not even mention Otis, though he knew the agents saw him waiting by the desk.

When Otis saw the exchange of words, he waited until the agents had strolled further away, then approached Andrew. He reached into his pocket and took out two tiny white pills, the sedatives, and Andrew palmed them quickly.

Andrew looked at him and said, "Irene is already here with... that doppelganger." It was still difficult for him to talk about him because the man in the bed looked exactly like Dan, but he was not the real Dan, his son-in-law.

The president had the coffee mug that he had just purchased downstairs in his hand. He turned his back to the nurses' desk, and Otis covered the view to the agents. He opened the lid and dropped the pills in the steaming coffee. He stirred the coffee with a plastic straw until the pills were dissolved and closed the lid pressing it tightly.

Nobody would notice that there was something extra added to the coffee, Andrew thought.

"I'll wait for you in the conference room," Otis said quietly and walked briskly around the corner towards the conference room. He wore a cap to cover his dark hair and sunglasses to hide his eyes. He had a tan-colored jacket, a white T-shirt, and black jeans. *Inconspicuous clothing was what made the surveillance and secret missions possible,* Otis thought. He had not considered his clothing so much since he left the CIA, but now it all came back to him, what he had learned. *Wear nothing that will make the staff or other observers remember you,* he thought. He preferred comfortable and nondescript, worn and used-looking jeans and jackets. He tried to blend into the neighborhood where he did his surveillance. In a hospital, he did not need any fancy outfit; plain clothing was the best. All kinds of people came to the hospital, from the professional staff to patients and their relatives and friends. In his current outfit, he fit in perfectly.

President Burr waited until Otis had gone and then walked towards the hospital room where Doppelganger-Dan was. He paused behind the door and took a deep breath readying himself to face his daughter and the doppelganger, trying to act naturally. He did not like to lie or hide things from his daughter, but he could not avoid it, not this time when his son's life was in danger. He knocked at the door to draw attention to himself quietly and entered.

Irene sat on the chair by the bed. She held hands with Doppelganger-Dan, turned to see who came in, and smiled when she saw her father.

Andrew stepped forward and stopped beside the bed. He put his hand on his daughter's shoulder and said, "Irene, can I see you outside for a moment."

"I'll be right back," Irene said to Dan, leaving the room with her father.

Outside, the president turned to his daughter and said, "I don't have much time. I have an urgent meeting at the White House. I just got the message."

"I understand." Irene knew these meetings could come any time of the day, and she was not surprised at all.

He handed her the coffee mug and asked, "Please, can you give Dan this coffee? I know how much he likes it. It's his favorite."

"Sure, I will do that. He will love it." Irene took the coffee mug from him and hugged him. "Thank you so much, dad. You are so thoughtful. I'll let you go. I will tell Dan that you had to go to take care of the safety of our country," Irene added with a smile, then turned around and returned to Dan's hospital room.

Andrew watched her go. He wished he could tell her the truth about the man in the hospital bed but knew he couldn't. He walked to the waiting room area where the two Secret Service agents waited for him. When the agents saw the president, they got up and followed him to the conference room to meet Otis.

"We'll have to wait here for a while," Andrew told the Secret Service agents. "Can you please make sure the Beast is not in front of the hospital? I don't want my daughter to see it. I told her I would be gone, but I will remain here waiting room until she is gone."

One of the agents contacted the president's vehicle and asked it to drive around the block.

Andrew Burr addressed one of the Secret Service agents with a stern voice. "Can you please ask your colleague in the hallway guarding my son-in-law to inform us when my daughter leaves?"

"Sure, copy that," the agent replied. He immediately made a call on his phone to the floor agents, saying, "POTUS will be in the hospital for a little bit more. He wants to know when the daughter leaves the room?" He listened to the answer and said, "Copy that."

The Secret Service agents went outside the conference room to wait for the president to leave and to make sure nobody else tried to enter the room unnoticed.

Otis and Andrew waited impatiently.

Otis sat down, picked up a magazine, and opened it to read it, while Andrew paced around the room and waited for his daughter to leave. His eyes wandered to the muted, yellow-colored walls where the hospital had hung prints of abstract artwork.

Outside the conference room, the second Secret Service agent got a call on his earphone. He listened to the responses on the other end of the line for a couple of minutes, then knocked on the door. He waited for the president to respond, and permit him to enter, opened the door, and addressed the president, "Mr. President, your daughter has left the room and is currently waiting for the elevator."

"Thank you," Andrew replied.

The agent closed the door again.

Andrew glanced anxiously at Otis. "We can go now."

Otis shook his head. "Let's wait for a couple of minutes. What if she forgot something? What if she decides to come back? I would just wait a little bit longer and let the pills work. He will be in a deep sleep for several hours with those pills, but we don't know if he drank the whole mug."

Andrew nodded. "Yes, you're right."

They waited for a few minutes before returning to the hallway, and Andrew went in first to ensure that Doppelganger-Dan was asleep.

Andrew saw the doppelganger sleeping on his back.

He glanced around and saw the coffee mug on the bed table.

Andrew stopped by the bed and took his wrist in his hand. "Dan, it's me," Andrew said quietly.

Dan did not wake up.

Andrew walked back towards the door, opened it, and gestured for Otis to come in.

Otis walked briskly to the bedside, took his cell phone out, and used it to photograph Dan's fingerprints. Then he took out a small syringe from his pocket, drew some blood, put it back in his pocket, and then used small scissors to cut hair samples from the sleeping Doppelganger-Dan's head. He repeated this process to make a copy of the hair and blood samples. He wanted to have two samples, and a backup, just in case something went wrong during the test.

They exited the hospital room as quickly and quietly as they could without drawing too much attention to themselves.

In the hallway, the president said to his protective team agents, "We are ready to go."

They replied, "Yes, Mr. President."

One of the agents contacted the Beast and the decoy car to be ready in front of the hospital.

They left the hospital as fast as possible.

The president returned to his car. The decoy car and the Beast followed behind the lead car and headed to the White House.

Otis pulled his cap over his forehead, walked through the front doors, and continued to the next corner, moving towards the parking area where he had parked his car. He had avoided the hospital's parking lot because he suspected the kidnappers might be somewhere around the hospital since their contact person, Dan, was there. Before leaving the parking lot, Otis surveyed the area to see if anyone was waiting for him or following him. When he was sure no one was, he drove to the university campus.

The less I am seen with the president in public places, the better, he thought.

Otis needed someone who could help him with the blood and the DNA samples because the samples had to be compared with the existing ones in the federal intelligence databases. He had a person in mind who could do it if she was available and willing to help him. He knew she had the capability and resources.

32

At The School of Medicine

Georgetown, the School of Medicine

Otis knew his close friend, not yet a girlfriend, Dr. Deena Donovan, at Georgetown School of Medicine, could analyze the samples. They lived in the same apartment building near the campus and had met accidentally when he moved in. Deena had brought him a welcoming present: a Chinese takeout dinner for two. They had a nice evening but did not have time to do it again as both were busy professionals.

Otis parked near the School of Medicine main building in the visitors' parking lot. He jogged to the building and up the stairs, opened the door, and stepped into the hallway. He was not sure where Deena's working space was, but he saw a couple of students approaching. He stopped them and asked, "Do you know where I can find Dr. Deena Donovan?"

"Yes, her office is that way." The student pointed towards the hallway where he just came from and said, "It's the second door on the left."

"Thanks." Otis waved goodbye and then walked in the direction the students had pointed. He saw a row of doors, but only the second one was wide open. Approaching the door and heard a familiar voice: Deena's. She was a tall woman with short dark brown hair with blond highlights and was with a male student explaining something. He knocked on the door. Deena turned her head and saw him. She lifted her right hand and held up her forefinger to wait for a moment. Otis leaned by the door and waited for Deena to finish her mentoring. She was obviously enthusiastic about her work and determined to get her students to learn. When the student left, Deena turned to him and smiled. "What brings you here?"

"I've been meaning to come to see you. Thank you for the last time. The welcoming dinner was great."

"You did not come all the way here to tell me that, did you?"

"No, I have a favor to ask," Otis replied.

"What is it?" Deena frowned.

Otis pulled out the syringe and said, "Can you run this for me? I need to know who this man is." Before Deena could ask or say anything, he continued. "Please, read this paper first." He handed out the note that the president's office had written, asking everyone to assist him.

Deena glanced through the document and raised her eyebrows. "Is this for real? You work for the president?"

"Temporarily. He is an old friend of mine and needed my help." Otis shrugged. He did not want to reveal more.

"Okay. I will do the DNA analysis on the blood. It's not a fast process. The DNA test will take closer to 48 hours, but that's just a basic ethnicity test."

"Thanks for helping," Otis replied. "I'll have the DNA checked against the national databases, too. I want to know if we can find a match there."

Deena looked curious and asked, "Is this related to the helicopter accident and the death of the president's son?"

"I can't tell you now. I can tell you later when this is all over," Otis said. "I have to go now. I have other places to be and things to do."

Otis turned around one more time from the door and said, "Let's do a rain check. I want to buy you dinner when this job is over."

"It's a date." Deena smiled and waved goodbye.

33

Otis

Two days had gone by since the fatal crash. Otis had made no progress in finding Zachary. He hoped identifying Doppelganger-Dan would help, but he worried it would not be fast enough. Andrew needed results. Otherwise, the Russians would get what they wanted, and the president of the United States would be just their puppet on a string.

One place might have more clues, Otis thought. *The restaurant. It is time to go back there and check it out. Maybe the kidnappers left something there that will lead to where they are hiding or their identities.*

Otis dressed in a black leather jacket, a black hoodie under it, and black jeans. He did not want to have any bright colors to be more invisible in shadows and darks. He took his favorite carpet knife, his Glock, and his small flashlight with him. He did not intend to start a shooting contest with anyone but wanted to be ready for everything.

Getting killed would not help Andrew or Zachary, he thought grimly.

Around 2 a.m. Otis drove back to the restaurant and parked in an empty alley a block away. He exited the car and looked around to ensure nobody saw him, checking for surveillance cameras to make sure there weren't any. He did not want to leave any sign he was there because he did not know what he would have to do in the Restaurant Troika tonight.

No witnesses needed, he thought.

The alley was dark, and only a dim streetlight shone from King Street to the alley. He saw the cracked pavements, used Styrofoam cups, cigarette buts, and scraps of paper littering the alley. Stopping on the corner, Otis viewed the street in front of him. He did not see anyone following or watching him and thought it was time to go. He turned left and walked towards Restaurant

Troika. The wind slid a plastic bag across the pavement in front of him.

It took him a couple of minutes of brisk walking to get to the corner of Restaurant Troika's building. He stopped and watched his surroundings. Still no sign of anyone. He was alone. He scooped his hand through his thick hair, wondering how he could get in. The front door had a security camera, and he did not want to be seen. He decided to break in and try to find some clues about what was going on.

He pulled up his hoodie. Stifling a shiver from the cold wind, Otis walked around the building, looked for the restaurant's back door, and was surprised when he found it wide open. He frowned. Something was wrong. It was either a trap or something else was going on in a restaurant. *Could be an inventory night*, he thought, *but more likely something illegal happened*, he decided, as he did not see or hear any employees walking and talking inside or coming outside. The lights were out.

Nobody would leave the restaurant's back door open on a normal night, not even during an inventory, he thought. They would not want rats and mice to run inside the restaurant. The Health Department would warn them of food safety violations or even take away their license due to carelessness in restaurant practice.

It's time to go in, he thought. He put on thin gloves, pulled out his Glock, walked towards the open door, and stepped inside as softly as he could. When he entered the kitchen area, he saw a pair of legs on the floor behind a kitchen working table.

This is not good, he thought.

Otis moved around the table to see who it was and if the man on the floor was alive. The man was one of the employees he had seen earlier that day at the restaurant. Otis kneeled beside him and checked his pulse to ensure he was dead. A pool of dark blood was forming under the dead body, and his skin was still warm.

A recent kill, he thought, and observed two gunshot wounds in his chest. *That means that the killer or killers could still be here. I better watch out.*

Otis stood up, approached the restaurant doorway, and peeked through the narrow window in the door.

The restaurant's dining area was dimly lit, but he saw no movement. Otis did not hear any sounds, but when he viewed the room, he noticed more bodies on the floor: Five of the male workers of the restaurant had been shot, just like the one in the kitchen. Lots of blood was on the floor and sprayed on the walls and over the counters.

Otis entered the dining room, carefully walked around the bodies, and avoided stepping on the blood. He did not want to leave any footprints behind. He kneeled beside each body and checked their pulse but felt nothing.

No pulse. All dead, he thought and frowned. *Who could have done this? Why would someone kill the restaurant workers?*

Still no sign of the shooter.

Otis stayed in the shadows, near the walls, and looked around. *Nothing. No movement. No sounds. The place looks empty.* He walked around the dining area and finally approached the door leading to the private quarters of the restaurant.

He spotted Stan in the hallway outside his office. He was dead as a doornail. He had been shot in the forehead. No doubt he had died immediately.

Stan did not survive long after failing to kidnap my mother. His failure cost him his life. Otis shook his head in disbelief. *These kidnappers are serious*, he thought. *These guys, whoever they were, made sure there were no loose ends and left no trace. I bet I will find the owner dead upstairs,* he thought. *Unless he was part of the cover-up and got away before this shooting happened.*

Otis moved toward the office door and saw it half open. He pushed the door open quietly and peeked inside. The first thing he saw was the restaurant owner shot in the head, sitting in his chair behind the desk.

Somebody's making sure, I don't have a chance to interrogate these guys, Otis thought. *This looks like the work of a Russian mafia. It would fit because this was a Russian restaurant.*

Otis walked around the desk to check the dead restaurant owner. His skin was still warm. *The hit must have happened within half an hour before I arrived*, Otis thought, furrowing his brows.

Otis narrowed his eyes as his gaze circled the office area. *Could there be something that the killers left behind? Maybe they missed something.*

Step by step, he ordered himself. *Every drawer, every shelf, trash, papers, no matter how long it will take*, he thought. He had to find something here.

Otis noticed that the safe had been opened and emptied. *The police would consider this a break-in. Just a burglary gone wrong*, Otis thought.

These guys did not kill just to get the money from the safe, Otis reasoned and kept looking around the room.

He tried to analyze the owner. *What kind of a guy had he been? How would he act?* He did not see any modern computers, MP3 players, or videos in the office. *He was an old-fashioned guy,* Otis deducted. *He had his power position before the new technology. He did not store his valuable items in cyberspace or flash drives. This guy would have used some concrete methods to store information. He would have used paper, letters, and tapes.*

Otis was sure that the killers were younger guys who only looked in the rooms and hiding places for items that they would have used in their own lives: computers, external hard drives, MP3 players, and flash drives. They had not considered what kind of a guy this restaurant owner was. The killers had checked the safe as an obvious hiding place for valuables.

The killers might have missed something. They had been in a hurry. Their main reason had been to tie up loose ends and search the restaurant for any clues related to the kidnapping case. However, they would not have known what to look for specifically. They had just tried to make it look like burglary by breaking and throwing things on the floor.

Otis reviewed the room again, keeping in mind what kind of a guy the owner had been. He noticed that the desk drawers had been pulled open and ransacked. He pushed the drawers closed, but one did not close properly. He opened it again. He reached inside but could not get to what was blocking the drawer. He pulled the whole drawer out and found something taped behind it. He took it out and found it was a cassette tape. An old-fashioned cassette tape that required an old-fashioned player.

His intuition about the owner was right on the spot. He put the cassette tape in his pocket. He checked the answering machine on the table by the landline phone. One of its lights was blinking. He pressed the button to listen to the message: "You are compromised," a strange, muffled voice said. "Your man did not do his work as agreed. You'll pay the price." The message ended.

The kidnappers! The restaurant owner was a lower-level thug in this kidnapping scheme, he concluded. *He had failed, and he was ordered to be killed. But he had not received the message in time because the message was blinking. His execution must have come as a surprise to him.*

Otis reached into his pocket, took out his cell phone, and recorded the message. Then he checked the last dialed number on the telephone. The old-fashioned telephone had the last dialed number on record and showed it on the screen. Otis took an image of the last number with his cell phone's camera and then dialed it to hear who answered. The other end rang thrice, and then an answering machine turned on: "This is Restaurant Nevskij. We are currently closed. Our hours of operation are…" Otis hung up. Another restaurant? This could be a working partner, a subsidiary, or somebody behind the kidnapping.

Otis could not find anything else interesting in the office and decided it was time to go. He expected that the police would show up there in the morning. Either an employee coming in early in the morning or someone else would report the incident. Otis didn't plan to. He decided to call Andrew and tell him. Otis walked away from the restaurant as quietly as he got in, leaving everything as he had found it.

34

Andrew

It was the third day after the fatal helicopter crash. The crash site was deserted. The rescue team, the police, and the media had all left. Some debris was on the ground, but otherwise, it looked as if nothing had happened.

The media's interest had not faded. They still reported in their Washington, D.C. studios, but all their news was just to repeat what everyone already knew: There was no hope left. Three days and no more bodies were found. The president's son and the pilot were assumed to be dead. It was a tragedy. A nation was mourning together with its president. And yet, the president had not given any statement about his son's death. The First Family's privacy was accepted and respected. However, it was also a major topic on talk shows. They all asked: How is the president coping with the loss of his son? Is he dealing with the tragedy on his own? He had not talked with his wife, the first lady, or his daughter about his son's loss.

The rumors in the White House and around the town suggested that the president was in denial, refusing to accept the fact that his son was dead.

The talk show's main topic was: "How to deal with the loss of your loved one" and "How different people cope with the loss differently." They suggested that the president needed to talk openly about the loss and realize that he was not alone. He still had family and friends.

The talk show hosts had guests who had suffered the loss of a loved one, and they all suggested that the president and the First Family needed a grief counselor to help them deal with Zachary's death.

Many of the guests on the shows said that their first feeling was anger: why him, why not me? That they had wished they had died instead or with their loved ones. They also said they blamed themselves for being unable to be there and preventing the death. The guests repeatedly said they understood why the president was acting the way he was. They said he was probably feeling disconnected from the real world and could not believe that his son was gone forever, but they consoled that it was only a phase. Eventually, when the president was ready to deal with the loss, he would come out and talk about it.

The more religious and conservative shows suggested that the president needed to turn to God, pray, and talk to Him. They said it would help him to deal with his loss.

Andrew Burr sat in front of the television in the White House's private quarters. He had the remote control in his hand, flipped from channel to channel to view the early morning shows, and noticed that he and the crash were still the main topics and his behavior after this crash. He felt annoyed, devastated, and helpless to hear how total strangers talked about his son as if he were dead

He understood that a kidnapping had only two outcomes. The first was that the kidnapped person would return alive, which could mean they let Zachary go unharmed, or they could harm or mutilate him, but he would still be alive. The second choice was worse: Zachary would be found dead.

Andrew stood up and walked to the window. It was dark outside.

He saw a crowd gathering around the gates surrounding the White House perimeters. They left notes, teddy bears, flowers, and candles by the gate.

Andrew mourned, not for the death of his son, but for his country because of what he had to do to save his son. He had all the power, but it was not enough to keep his family safe.

35

At the Oval Office

President Andrew Burr had an early morning meeting with the Chief of Staff, Lawrence Conklin, and his secretary Esme.

Andrew sat behind the Revolution desk when Lawrence and Esme entered. He barely glanced up when they came in.

The Oval Office furniture had been renewed when Andrew was inaugurated. His wife considered her duty and pleasure to change the colorings of the walls and the couches in the Oval Office. She liked to see her handiwork in various news as they displayed the president signing laws.

His personal secretary Esme sat on the blue and white striped couch. She was ready to take notes to make sure she got all the details written down.

The Chief of Staff, Lawrence Conklin, sat on the couch in front of Esme and got directly to the point. "Mr. President. We must address the nation. Your son's memorial. We need to organize it." Lawrence Conklin was in his fifties, and he looked like he needed to sleep for at least eight to ten hours and had not gotten a good night's sleep for a long time.

"Sure, what do you have in mind?" Andrew replied, not showing much interest in the topic. He just viewed the papers in front of him on the desk and did not even look up.

Lawrence frowned. This wasn't going as he expected. "We could have the Mass at St. Matthew's Cathedral. We can't do any burial until we find your son's body."

"I just don't know if I want to do that yet. Can we postpone the decision?" Andrew could not and would not tell them his son was not dead. Talking about a Requiem when Zachary was still alive felt like a sacrilege. It would be like inviting the devil to make it happen.

Esme and the Chief of Staff look puzzled. They did not expect that. His son had died, and the president did not want to address the country or have the Requiem for his memory. "But, Mr. President. the Requiem is meant to ask the Lord to grant your son's soul to have eternal peace. You can't deny that for your son? What would your voters and your family say?!"

"I'm sorry," Andrew Burr noticed their surprise. He realized he was not acting like a father who had just lost his son. He thought fast and said, "I can't believe it has happened. Can you put together a memorial or the Requiem plan and date when I need to address the nation?" He covered his face with his hands as if he were still mourning his loss.

Both Esme and the Chief of Staff looked at each other and agreed, "Yes, Mr. President. We'll assist you in that matter."

They both looked relieved. The president was acting like a grieving father.

"Can you please leave me alone? I'm not ready to take care of daily business right now," Andrew Burr asked. His staff members stood up. They understood. Everyone had to grieve in their own way. This was the president's way: Alone, hiding his pain inside him.

After they closed the door, Andrew called to Doppelganger-Dan. When he answered, Andrew informed him, "I'll do what you asked."

Andrew knew he needed to play for time. Otis needed more time to dig deeper and find out who was behind the kidnapping and find his son and his son-in-law.

Doppelganger-Dan replied, "Come and meet me." Then he hung up. It was more of a command than a request.

Andrew considered stalling the meeting, but maybe that was not such a good idea. *It would be better to face the enemy and know what they want and maybe get some new clues on how to find Zachary*, he thought.

36

The Demands

President Andrew Burr met Dan at the hospital. He had made sure Irene was not there when he went to see the doppelganger. Irene had gone to work, but she would return later that evening.

Dan saw the icy look in the man who was supposedly his father-in-law's eyes when he entered the room.

Andrew walked directly towards the bedside and stayed standing.

This is not going to be a cordial meeting, Dan thought. *Well, so be it.* He raised himself to a more upright position in the bed and started their conversation formally. "Mr. President, nice to see you again."

"I want to know that my son is still alive and Dan, too," Andrew demanded. Nobody had heard anything of the real Dan.

"You will get a call from your son. Dan is not available right now," Doppelganger-Dan replied calmly.

"No, I want to speak with them both," Andrew insisted.

Dan shrugged his shoulders. "I'll see what I can do." He took a deep breath and ordered, "Sit, Mr. President. We must talk about our demands."

Andrew Burr scowled at the doppelganger but sat down beside the bed.

"These are our demands and I will repeat them now so that you won't forget," Dan started. "The United Nations meeting is in New York in four days. We want you to be there. You will oppose any new sanctions against Russia and propose that all the previous sanctions will be revoked, and all the frozen assets owned by the Russian businesses will be returned to their owners. These sanctions have been imposed by countries who want to make Russia dance their tune. But Russia is strong and resilient. There will be no more weakness. Russia will be the puppeteer, and the United States will do whatever we want."

"That's all you ask?!" Andrew Burr was shocked and appalled. "I cannot do that! It is against what we have agreed with the EU leaders. I cannot change my foreign policy just like that. I must discuss this with my advisors! We just stated at the last U.N. General Assembly that our country strongly disapproves of Russia's actions in eastern Ukraine. We warned that Ukraine-related sanctions against Russia will not be lifted until Crimea is returned to Ukraine. We also demanded an immediate end to the Russian occupation of Crimea. We also supported Great Britain and the EU in their sanctions regarding that Salisbury poisoning incident."

"You can change your foreign policy and write an executive order just like President Barack Obama did in 2014," Doppelganger assured. "Obama signed an executive order for sanctions, including travel bans and freezing their assets in the United States, against not-yet-specified individuals," Dan replied. "You just have to repeal that order." He kept his eyes locked on the president when he continued, "This is just the start. We will have some other demands." He saw how the initial shock in Andrew's face turned to disbelief and finally to anger.

Andrew Burr felt hopeless. He knew that this doppelganger was right. He could do the executive order, but without negotiating with the State Department and conveying his U.N. Ambassador, he would be acting like a rogue president, like one working for a foreign government, not for his own country.

"Two days," Dan repeated.

Andrew didn't want to say anything to this doppelganger. His eyes had gone from icy to fierce. He got up, turned his back to the hospital bed, and left the room.

Dan threw his head back and laughed. Seeing the most powerful man struggle to obey someone else's orders was fun.

Two days, Andrew Burr thought and wiped his forehead with his hand. He feared that either he would never see his son and his real son-in-law again, or he would throw his career away and possibly face a media storm, accusations of using his power illegally, and he would lose his political influence among the other leaders of the world.

It will not be hard for anyone to guess that the Russians have gotten leverage over me, Andrew thought. *I must pretend to obey them and agree to their requirements regardless of how incredible they are.*

Andrew Burr was worried about the other demands the doppelganger had mentioned. The doppelganger had not specified what they would be. He would have to lie to everyone and make excuses because if he revealed the real situation, he would be immediately removed from his position and replaced by the Vice President. Then his son and his son-in-law would be executed. He shuddered. His only hope was Otis.

37

Otis

Otis's mother, Estelle, called him. "Did you know that this hotel has a casino? And guess who is performing tonight? Tony Bennett!" She sounded like a teenage girl swooning over her idol, her voice high with enthusiasm.

Otis smiled. He could have guessed that his mother would like Golden Coastal Casino for its entertainment. He also liked the casino because it was huge and it had invested money in an excellent surveillance and security system. It was a perfect place for his mother to hide. He did not believe that the Russians would attack and kidnap his mother while she was staying as a guest there.

"I've heard the casino is pretty good," Otis agreed.

Otis had contacted the casino security, asking that they would keep an eye on his mother. He had told them a simplified version of the truth: he had just rescued her from the hands of her violent boyfriend, who might be coming after her. It was partly true because Stan had kidnapped her, and the kidnappers seemed violent, considering the Restaurant Troika massacre.

Otis's new burner phone vibrated. "I've got to go now, Mom. The president is on the other line," he said and hung up.

"I met the doppelganger at the hospital. I found out the demands. Doppelganger-Dan told me I should undo all the sanctions against the Russians. I must free their assets, lift all the travel bans, and announce this policy change in the next United Nations conference, which is in two days in New York City," Andrew explained hastily.

"We don't have much time," Otis concluded and then, after thinking for a few seconds, added, "If you do what the Russians want, everyone will suspect that Russians have bought you or are blackmailing you. We must find Zachary and your son-in-law, Dan, before the next United Nations meeting. Their lives are not worth much after you announce the policy changes. There is no reason the kidnappers would return Zachary and Dan alive. The outside world already believes that your son is dead and that the doppelganger is the real Dan."

"These are not the only demands, I'm afraid. It sounded like there's going to be more," Andrew replied, sounding frightened.

"Yes, the blackmailing can continue as long as they want and as long as you do as they tell you to do." Otis frowned. There was nothing he could do yet. He did not have any new information from Noah.

"Now I must pretend that this imposter at the hospital is Dan. I cannot even tell Irene! This doppelganger-Dan is like a cold, slimy snake that has slithered into my life and my daughter's home uninvited." The sudden anger in the president's voice caused a jolt of adrenaline to course through Otis. He tried to calm Andrew the best he could and finished the call assuring the president that he would do his best to find Zachary and Dan before the next conference.

It was time to visit that other Russian restaurant tonight, the one mentioned in the telephone recording: Restaurant Nevskij. *Perhaps, I can find some clues there,* Otis thought after the call ended.

The one thing that puzzled him was how the kidnappers had created the doppelganger. How could they have known Andrew would be the president? How long had they planned this kidnapping? Changing someone's look completely would take months or years. He had not spotted any additional cosmetic surgery scars on the doppelganger's face, and he was sure he had been close enough to the doppelganger to notice them. No scars would suggest he already looked like Dan, the president's son-in-law. How was that possible? Otis had no answer to any of these questions.

38

Restaurant Nevskij

That same evening, Otis dressed up in a gray suit, a white silk shirt, and a black tie with thin blue stripes for his visit to the Russian restaurant.

Restaurant Nevskij was a popular restaurant with months of queuing for a table. He couldn't get a reservation through normal channels; thus, he asked the president to help him and got a table in the usually busy, trendy restaurant. He drove to the Restaurant Nevskij and parked on the street. He didn't hurry to get inside. Instead, he observed the restaurant outside: The windows had heavy curtains drawn aside to show soft light shining from the dining room.

Nothing suspicious outside and no hints of this place being a hideout for the Russian mob, Otis thought and walked slowly to the main door passing the queue of hopeful customers who wanted to eat there that night. The doorman checked Otis's reservation status, then welcomed him courteously, holding the door open for him.

Inside, the staff wore long dark blue aprons and white shirts. The employees looked the same as in any other restaurant: busy, taking orders and carrying dishes to the table or clearing the empty plates off the tables. Everything looked normal.

A young Russian waitress escorted Otis to the small table by the window. He could view the whole dining room from there, which was exactly what he wanted.

The dining room had smooth blue and gray coloring with several flower arrangements around the room. Most of the tables were occupied. It looked like a high-end, hip restaurant.

Nothing out of the ordinary, Otis thought. He would not have believed this was run by a Russian mob if it weren't for that recording. The link to the kidnappers was here. He just had to find it.

When the waitress arrived to take his order, Otis asked for the summer vegetable salad and the main course pelmenis, dumplings filled with vegetables and meat and covered in a thin dough. He had eaten that often when stationed in Moscow in his CIA days. He ordered bottled water to drink with his dinner because he wanted to stay sharp in case something happened.

The service was impeccable. The food tasted fabulous and spicy but not too hot.

After finishing the dinner, Otis asked for his bill and paid it with cash to the waitress. He did not want to use his credit card. If anyone on the staff was part of the kidnappings, he would recognize Otis's name. He left the restaurant, walked outside, and surveyed the street both ways. It looked like a normal night, with customers arriving and leaving the various restaurants in that area with no suspicious-looking vehicles or mobsters in view.

On the other side of the street, in front of the Nevskij Restaurant, Otis recognized a bank building with security cameras and got an idea. He knew when the call was made from Restaurant Nevskij to Restaurant Troika, where he found the dead owner, Maksim Liskin, and his answering machine. That call on Maxim's answering machine had revealed Maxim's connection to this other restaurant and the kidnapping; however, Maxim had not received the call, and Otis was the one who had listened to it after he found Maxim dead in his office.

That call was made after midnight, Otis thought and glanced once more to the bank building. *It should be easy to find out who left the restaurant after that. I would need some help to get the surveillance records.*

39

Otis and Noah

The fourth day after the crash

It was a cool morning, and it looked as if it would soon start to rain. Otis walked out of his apartment building in Georgetown and headed toward the parking lot. It was the fourth day after the helicopter crash, and the United Nations General Assembly meeting was scheduled to start the day after tomorrow.

Time is running out, he thought grimly. *How do I find Zachary and Dan before the meeting?*

Otis had decided to pay a visit to his old friend, Noah S. Pye. Noah was one of the best hackers he had ever known, but he was not just a hacker. He was simply a genius with any technology. Noah had worked for the FBI and the CIA as an analyst and a programmer since he was fifteen years old. He had hacked unknown numbers of databases, video surveillance, and security systems in his job with the agencies.

Noah was a prodigy, but he did not want fame. He had worked for all the other cryptic government agencies, some of which most had never even heard of. Noah was currently self-employed, and his employers included the private sector and the government's top-secret agencies.

Otis had met Noah when he was a CIA operative. Back then, he needed some quick information on people he met while working undercover as a foreign trade attaché at the U.S. Embassy in Moscow. Noah was able to pull that information out of the databases in the blink of an eye. Otis knew Noah could have made a lot of money transferring other people's monies to his account, but he was not that kind of a person. Noah enjoyed technological challenges, and the different countries gave him new perspectives on what could be done with technology and security.

Noah lived in a yellow-brick house in the east village of Georgetown. He had inherited the house from his parents after their sudden death in the airplane crash on 9/11. Noah's technological intelligence made him rich and allowed him to enjoy a nice, comfortable lifestyle. He owned several technologies and mobile device-related patents that both government agencies and private technology companies used.

Noah had made sure his own home was protected and secure. An iron-wrought steel fence with surveillance cameras surrounded his house so nobody would come unannounced and steal any of his technology innovations and secrets, including the unfinished ones.

Otis called Noah on the way to see him. He hoped Noah was at home and ready to meet with him. "Noah, it's me, Otis. I need to see you. I have a job for you."

"Sure. You know where I live," Noah replied.

"See you in a few," Otis ended the call.

When Otis arrived at the old-fashioned-looking brick house where Noah resided, he saw Noah standing outside with his new project, a robot dog. It was the size of a Rottweiler. The dog had four legs like any other dog. His body was covered with patches of different materials, including metal, plastic, fabric, and some sort of elastomer material. His tail was a tiny stub of metal.

"Thanks for seeing me today. I need your help," Otis said, viewing the robot dog. The dog turned his head from side to side, facing Otis.

"He is memorizing your voice for the next visit," Noah explained. "He only needs to hear you once, and he can match up your voice with the previous recordings in his memory bank."

"What or who is it?" Otis asked, peering at the robodog.

"This is Elmo. He's my improved version of the robot dog used in the military. He is a new project I'm working on. He is designed for indoor and outdoor military operations. He is electrically powered and hydraulically actuated, and he has a battery that lasts seventy-two hours. He has a sensor that remembers commands, faces, voices, and scents. It can easily navigate any terrain with its inbuilt GPS, except water. The water is still a challenge. I have tried different materials to make him waterproof, but his joints remain weak."

"Why is he still looking at me?" Otis said, viewing Elmo suspiciously.

"Besides memorizing your voice, he also memorizes your movements and your scent," Noah explained. "I told him you are a friend to be remembered and that you will often visit us."

"What does Elmo do when he does not like someone or if he meets a stranger?" Otis asked.

"Elmo is trained to attack, to bite on any extremities of a human body. His teeth are made of titanium which makes them incredibly strong and durable. You don't want to be bitten by him." Noah looked proudly at his new creation.

"Nice," Otis muttered.

"Come in," Noah said. "You, too, Elmo."

Elmo turned his head towards his maker and followed him inside.

Otis closed the door behind him. He assessed Noah as he had not seen him for a long time. Noah looked just about the same as five years ago in Russia. His black hair had been shorter, and now it had grown to be shoulder length. His almond-shaped eyes gave a hint of Asian heritage that was a counterpoint to his height, 6'9".

Noah was taller than an average Asian. Otis knew Noah had inherited his tall, lanky body from his father, whereas his Asian heritage came from his mother.

Noah had three small diamond studs on his right ear lobe, and they reflected a ray of bright rainbow colors when the light hit them. He was almost too skinny, and his gray Camo patterned T-shirt looked like it was purchased from an army surplus store. He wore tan-colored baggy work pants and sneakers. He looked like a teenager, except Otis knew Noah's real age. Noah was twenty-two years old.

Otis recalled Noah's file: Noah's teenage years had been spent developing software, and now he was a technology consultant. He had not lived a normal life since his gift for technology had been discovered. Otis was sure Noah was lonely. He had always been younger than the other workers at the Embassy. He was called "kid," "boy," and "babyface" behind his back. Otis had befriended him then and stayed in touch with Noah after they both left Moscow.

"I've only seen these clumsy-looking robot dogs with four legs and no heads. Why haven't you shown Elmo in public yet? He looks more like a dog than what I've seen." Otis knelt and studied the robot dog more closely, holding his head between his palms.

"The earlier models, like the Alpha robot dog that the Defense Advanced Research Projects Agency developed a few years ago, were too loud in their movements. Due to its clumsiness and loudness, the military leaders decided it was not useful in a real war zone because it would reveal their position. Did you hear any noise when Elmo moved?"

"No, I didn't," Otis replied.

"I tried to make him as quiet as possible; no barks, no claw sounds, no breathing, no machine sounds at all," Noah said, pleased. "Elmo is a newer version of the old project. The military leaders are still considering if robot animals are the right way to go in the future. The leaders talk about robot mules that can carry twenty times more load than any human or normal mule. There are advantages in robot animals." Noah brushed a lock of his shoulder-long hair behind his ear when he bent down to pat his pet project, Elmo. "Elmo is more intelligent because of his memory, and he can be used as a guard dog. He can recognize friends and foes just by the way people walk, move, talk, and their accents. He is silent, so he can be sent before the troops to view and send feedback on the terrain ahead. Elmo can also be used as a household guard dog like I'm using him. "

"That's incredible," Otis replied.

Noah grinned. "I have trained him to recognize uniforms, too, so he does not attack the police officers and the mailman. I can't adjust him to recognize the mailman in person because the mailmen can be different, especially if they don't have a regular route. I don't want Elmo to attack anyone."

"Why does he have all these patches?" Otis asked.

Noah sighed. "I have not been able to decide the right material to cover him. Now he looks more like a patchwork because of the different materials used on the outside. There is more work to be done with him, but I like the challenges." Noah glanced at Otis and said, "But you didn't come here to talk about my new projects. Let's go to the living room, and you can tell me about your problem." Noah walked from the hallway to the living room, and Otis followed him.

The spacious living room had shiny hardwood floors, white walls, and abstract paintings anywhere the walls weren't filled with computer screens. Otis thought he recognized a Jackson Pollock painting. He was sure Noah could afford his paintings because he had earned a lot of money with his patents.

Otis brushed his hair with his right hand and asked, "Is this place secure? Can I talk to you about something no one knows except the president and me?"

"Sure. This house is soundproof and bug-proof, and no one can hack my computers, monitor my calls, or listen to what we discuss here. I have a complete blockage in this building," Noah assured Otis.

Otis showed the document he had received from the president's office, telling everyone to assist Otis by any means possible. Noah read it and gave it back. "I would have helped you even without that document. I liked you even when you worked in the embassy in Russia. You were always one of the nice guys."

"Thanks. I could use your help." Otis viewed the room with all the screens showing maps and stock market reports. "Have you followed the news lately?"

"Which one?" Noah grinned and pressed a remote control. The screens flickered, and Otis saw the different world news transmitted on the screens.

"The helicopter crash," Otis replied.

Noah tapped a few buttons on the portable, foldable keyboard that he pulled out of his pocket. The keyboard was as small as a mobile phone. A couple of seconds later, the screens showed different channels displaying the helicopter crash site and the reporters explaining the fatal accident.

"That's the one. The president has asked me to investigate it, and it's off the record. No one can know about it," Otis warned.

"The crash... His son was in the helicopter," Noah said. "Or was he?"

"No, he wasn't," Otis replied slowly. "How did you guess?"

"No one found his body. Then there was only one eyewitness. That does not make any sense in a city this size. These facts do not match up. Something is off. Furthermore, nobody has seen or heard of the eyewitness since that initial interview. He disappeared. The FBI wanted to interview him, but they couldn't find him. It's as if he has vanished from the face of the earth." Noah stared at Otis, waiting for explanations.

"I did not know that." Otis raised his eyebrows. Noah always managed to surprise him. Even now, he knew things that Otis didn't know. "How do you know that?"

"I follow everything: All the news all the time." Noah shrugged. "Tell me about your problem."

Otis knew Noah had time and an excellent memory. He was a genius who could pick up facts that nobody else did. *This was the right move to come here,* Otis thought.

Otis explained what had happened so far: his mother's kidnapping, Zachary's kidnapping, and how they were linked together. "I went into Restaurant Troika. I didn't have to break in. The back door was wide open. All the employees were killed. Stan, my mother's kidnapper, was killed. So was the owner of the restaurant. I guess that someone wanted to tie up loose ends."

Noah stared at him. "You found something. You wouldn't be here otherwise?"

Noah sat down by a glass computer table on the right side of the room, and instead of using his portable keyboard, he typed with the regular one. His searches included the Restaurant Troika and its owners and their business connections.

Otis went to sit by him. "There was a message on the answering machine. I called that number. It was a restaurant called Nevskij."

"Nevskij Restaurant, another Russian restaurant," Noah murmured and typed it in. "Yes, it is owned by the same business corporation as Restaurant Troika. The owner of that corporation is Boris Kryukov. He has made his fortune in restaurants and car rentals. Several restaurant locations in New York City, Washington D.C., and West Virginia."

Otis took out his notebook and wrote down Boris Kryukov. "He is probably connected with the kidnappings. He would not let anyone use his restaurants as a cover unless he knew about it," Otis deducted.

Noah nodded. "What do you want me to do?" Noah asked, a line appearing between his brows.

"Can you check the nearby security cameras? I need to find out if there are any recordings of the night when Troika's manager was killed. Maybe the cameras have picked up something in the past three days at that restaurant or Nevskij. If these two restaurants are connected, and a call was made from Restaurant Troika to Nevskij, then I'm sure someone was there to make decisions. I need to find out who," Otis said.

Noah beamed and said, "Sure, I can do that. It might take a few hours. I must locate the cameras and get access to their recordings. Perhaps, I can find out who killed all the employees at Troika."

"Yes, that would be useful. The bodies were still warm. I think I had just missed them," Otis replied.

"I'll call you when I find something," Noah said, turning to his computer to start work.

Otis smiled. "Let me give you my burner phone number. I only use it in this case." Otis wrote down his number and gave it to Noah, and then he got up from the chair. "I better get going. I still have my lecturing job at the university. I need to read and grade some student papers and prepare another lecture."

"Do you like it, teaching, lecturing, I mean?" Noah asked and turned to stare at Otis.

"Yes, for now, I guess. I have not thought about it so much. I just wanted a change after the agency," Otis replied.

"I always thought you were good at what you did. The intelligence business and finding answers," Noah said. "I never would have believed you wanted to leave the agency."

"I just wanted a break. I don't know if I will go back," Otis replied and frowned as he noticed a flush of sadness in Noah's voice.

Could it be that he had missed me and thought he would never see me again? Otis thought. *I always thought he just liked to help me and find me the information. He probably thought I would never contact him again after leaving the agency.*

"It was nice seeing you. I don't get so many visitors," Noah said, and he got up and walked Otis to the door. He sounded lonely.

"I'll come by and visit you more now that I'm working here," Otis promised and saw a wide grin flash on Noah's face.

Noah stopped and asked, "I never asked you, why your name is Otis?"

Otis looked at him, a little embarrassed, and brushed his hand through his hair. He didn't like to tell his story to anyone, but Noah was an exception. "Washington, D.C., had a power plant failure when I was born. It struck down the electricity from millions of people. My mother got stuck in the elevator with strangers. She went into labor while they waited for the electricity to come back on. It took several hours. She had nothing else to do but stare at the name Otis on the wall while delivering me, and she thought, 'That's the right name for my baby.'"

Noah smiled. "It's a nice story. Otis is not a bad name. You'll hear from me in a couple of hours, tops."

Otis left Noah and drove home. He took a stack of papers on the table, viewed his notes for his upcoming lecture, and then started reviewing his students' papers. It was a gruesome task. Some were excellent reports, and some showed only minimal interest in the topics Otis had lectured at the university.

40

Noah at Work

Noah started working as soon as he had closed the door after Otis. He liked new challenges, and this one was especially challenging: The president's son was kidnapped, and the president was being extorted.

Noah considered himself patriotic, and his duty was to help his country. It was a privilege and an honor to be able to assist the president. Moreover, Noah was also pleased that Otis had come to him for help.

With a quick tapping of the keyboard, Noah gained access to the banks' ATM cameras and the security cameras on every single building on King Street. It only took him a couple of minutes. The difficulty was not accessing these cameras; the more challenging part was ahead. It was also the most boring part: watching hours of low-pixeled, grainy videos.

Because he knew the timeline of the kidnapping, he decided to check the day before the kidnapping first, and secondly, the night of the massacre at Restaurant Troika. He left the King Street videos run while he went to the kitchen and got himself a cup of cappuccino. He thought nothing would be in the videos during the nighttime when the restaurant was closed. When he returned, he glanced at the screens displaying the night view of King Street in Arlington, Virginia, and what he saw almost made him knock his coffee cup over. He stopped the video, rewound it, and started over. At approximately two a.m., the doorman appeared in front of Restaurant Nevskij. He looked like he was waiting for someone. Soon after that, limousines arrived.

Noah counted five limousines, and each one had only one passenger inside. The passengers showed something to the doorman before he let them in.

Noah's other screens showed the limousines arriving and leaving, but the only camera was in front of the Restaurant Nevskij and showed him a better view of the passengers entering the restaurant. He started working on that video. The first step was to make it clearer. He needed to add more pixels to create more recognizable images of the men entering the restaurant.

It took him closer to thirty minutes to perfect the first image. His cappuccino had gone cold, but he drank it anyway. He stared at the figure in the trim black suit entering the restaurant. He froze the image. He enhanced the section of his face, and then enhanced and enlarged the section of his wrist before printing the image to study it further. It looked like something out of Greek mythology.

He proceeded with the same methodology with every one of the passengers. Finally, he got five faces with different wrist tattoos. *Not all the faces are recognizable,* he thought. The camera view and quality were not good enough.

He ran a different search to find out what the tattoos represented. He easily identified the Phoenix bird rising from the fire and ashes, the many-headed Hydra from Greek mythology was easy to recognize. *The snake tattoo was large and looked more like a wingless dragon than a rattlesnake,* he thought. *Maybe the snake was not a snake but a Basilisk if the characters are all supposed to be mythological creatures.* One tattoo represented a Hippogriff, a half-eagle, and a half-horse creature.

To him, the most interesting tattoo was the Werewolf, a large, scary-looking half-wolf and half-man image with bloody, fiery eyes. The werewolf search also gave him a motorcycle gang with the same name and the same Werewolf tattoo on their vests. Noah did not believe it was a coincidence. Otis had also mentioned Dentist, the leader of the Werewolves MC might be in town, according to the FBI.

The Werewolves were a Russian motorcycle gang like Bandidos and Hells Angels in the United States. His search revealed the connection between these bikers with higher-level Russian politicians and the two Russian Presidents: Putin and Ruskin.

He launched facial recognition software to scan the images of the meeting participants in all the federal databases. He was unsure if that search would provide anything because these participants were likely Russians. He decided to start a parallel search with the Interpol databases and online major newspapers and magazines in case he would get a hit with the faces.

If these participants were not criminals, their faces would not necessarily be in federal databases.

If these guys are Russian embassy workers, I can find them, he thought.

Noah played the video again, trying to get a better image of the limousines and their license plates because then he would find out who rented them.

Only one of the license plates showed clearly enough for him to check it against the DMV database. He got a hit with a Russian-owned car rental company owned by Maxim Liskin.

The Werewolf tattoo made him think that maybe he should directly check the current members of the motorcycle gang. He might get a hit. *If that tattoo marks the gang members, then it would be safe to assume that a person having that tattoo is a member of that biker gang.* He was right; his search with the tattoo and the facial image produced a hit within a couple of seconds. It was Dentist, the leader of the Werewolves.

The FBI said he might be in the United States, and this confirms it, Noah thought.

Why is he called a Dentist? Noah wondered and searched for more information about this gang leader.

The information he retrieved from the federal databases told him that Dentist was a dangerous opponent and not only because he was a criminal but also because of his connections.

Dentist is involved in this kidnapping, but if he is in on this, then the Russian government is also involved, and not just the lower level of the government, but the top.

Noah continued accessing the data and considered checking out Dentist's tattoos. With a few clicks, he was in the Russian MGB database, which had the information of the Russians and international people of interest. That did not mean they were all criminals or spies; there were also important politicians, wealthy businessmen, and prominent newcomers.

Noah thought a Russian database would give him more information about the Russians involved in this case. He compared the images of the Dentist's tattoos to other tattoos in the FBI and Russian MGB databases to find their symbolic meaning: a ring tattoo on his left ring finger described his conviction as a juvenile. The grinning devil tattoo on his left hand symbolized a hatred of authority and disregard for the legal system. The forefinger ring tattoo meant trust no one but yourself. The crown tattooed on his neck below his left ear symbolized that he was a kingpin, a leader, and a mob boss. Noah put down the tattoo images and assessed the man himself:

a tall, muscular man, 6'5" tall, with dark brown hair, chestnut brown eyes, and a French Fork cut beard, like Jack Sparrows had, extending past the chin and splitting down the middle into two segments.

If Dentist arrived here, it must have happened recently, before the kidnapping, he thought. *The FBI and the TSA must have some information about his arrival. Otis said that the FBI had a hint that there was going to be a hit and that they were still looking for more information. They are too slow to confirm the facts,* Noah thought.

Moreover, something else bothered him: *Dentist is a known thug, a violent criminal, a leader of a Russian motorcycle gang, and part of a Russian mob. Why would they allow him to enter this country?* He checked first the airports near Washington, D.C. If he was in Arlington, Virginia, he most likely had arrived at one of the airports near the capital city. He got a hit at the TSA checkpoint, but it was not just the Dentist, but also several other Werewolves arriving in Washington D.C.

It was time to call Otis and tell him what he had found out.

41

Andrew

When Noah called, Otis heard the excitement in his voice, "I've got something. Do you want me to send this to your computer, or do you come to visit me?"

Otis considered the choices. *It is better if I don't visit Noah twice on the same day. Noah could be in danger if I'm being watched and followed.*

"Can you send it to my burner phone?" Otis asked.

"I will only send you a short clip of the surveillance video across the street. This is the night before the kidnapping," Noah said, and Otis heard the sound of the keyboard tapping in the background.

Otis opened the video link on his phone and watched the enhanced video. He kept his eyes glued to the small screen on his phone as the video images flicked on. At first, the street looked lifeless and empty as it should be after restaurant closing hours. Then he saw the doorman appearing in front of the Restaurant Nevskij. He looked like he was waiting for someone. Suddenly, the street was no longer empty. He watched five luxury limousines pull in, and each time one passenger stepped out and walked to the door. Each passenger showed their right wrist to the doorman before he opened the door.

"What day is this?" Otis asked.

"It's the second night after the helicopter crash," Noah replied.

"And they had a meeting there," Otis murmured more to himself than Noah.

Tight security, Otis thought. Nobody would enter past the doorman without showing him something on their right hand or wrist. What did these men show to the doorman? Some secret passcodes? What was this meeting all about? The timing of the meeting was interesting. Five men in limousines... A secret meeting. It had to be connected to the kidnapping and the blackmailing of the president.

Otis stopped viewing the video clip and asked, "Can you enhance their right hands? What do they show to the doorman?"

"Tattoos. They show their tattoos," Noah said smugly. "Everyone has a different tattoo on their wrist. I have identified the tattoos: Hydra, Phoenix, Basilisk, Hippogriff, and Werewolf."

"Can you enhance these men's faces so we can identify them? Or maybe the license plates? I could ask the limousine services who had rented these limousines," Otis asked.

"I have the facial recognition software running as we speak. I'll tell you when it matches any of them," Noah replied.

"How about the license plates?" Otis repeated.

"I already checked that. I managed to pull out one license plate. It belonged to Blackline Limousine Rental Company, owned by Maksim Liskin," Noah said and added, "A Russian-owned company."

Otis whistled. "He was the manager in the Restaurant Troika. I met him the other day."

"And he is dead. You told me that," Noah retorted.

"Yeah, it's a dead end," Otis said, frowning.

"About the tattoos: one of them was interesting. The Werewolf is also a mark of a Russian motorcycle gang. Quite a dangerous one. The gang leader is called Dentist. It has connections with the high-level members of the Russian government, even with the two Presidents. I think that the man entering the restaurant is Dentist. His body and tattoos match the information on databases," Noah explained.

"Werewolves. Yes, the FBI had mentioned Dentist to the president. They said he might be here in the United States, and now you just confirmed it," Otis replied, excited.

"That's not all. I'll send you another video clip. It shows several gang members entering Dulles airport," Noah said, and Otis heard the keyboard keys clicking in the background. He heard a beep when the second video clip came through to his phone. Otis viewed it and cursed.

"Yes, it looks like this whole kidnapping was preplanned. Even the muscle men were brought in from Russia," Noah said.

Noah was right. The Russian biker gang was in the airport images. They even had their infamous outfit: leather jackets and pants, carrying their strange helmets in their hands, Otis thought.

Otis ran his fingers through his hair. "How did they get through the TSA checkpoint?"

"It seems that they had Russian diplomat passports. " The TSA officers could not do anything," Noah said, adding, "The Russian government has orchestrated the kidnapping and extortion. They are the only ones that can give out diplomat passports."

"I check the other databases to see if I can identify any other members. I'll add the airport feed around the same timeline as when the Werewolves arrived. I might be able to find the men who met at Restaurant Nevskij too. They might have arrived from Russia around the same timeframe as these Werewolves."

"Thank you, Noah. You've helped a lot. It's possible the men of that Nevskij meeting were already here," Otis said. "I'll talk to you soon. I must inform the president of this news. He'll be happy to hear that we are making some progress."

After letting Noah go back to his work, Otis sat at his desk and considered the information he had just received. Then he picked up the phone and called the president.

"Good morning Mr. President," Otis greeted when he heard Andrew answering the phone.

"Good morning. Do you have any news?" Andrew asked. His voice sounded distressed. "Please call me Andrew. I told you that several times."

Otis was concerned that Andrew would not manage this kind of stress for much longer. "Okay, Andrew. I have some news, but it might not be good news."

Andrew felt the color drain out of his face. He felt his knees buckle and was glad he was sitting when he received the call. "Please, don't tell me that... that Zachary is—" He could not even say the thing he feared the most.

"No, this is not about Zachary. I have news about the kidnappers," Otis interrupted quickly.

"Oh, thank God." Andrew sighed. He rubbed his hands over his face.

Otis could hear Andrew's relief through the phone line.

"Are you alone? Can you speak freely?" Otis asked.

"Yes, I had just one meeting earlier today but returned to the private quarters after that. I can't concentrate on anything now. I'm so worried for Zachary."

"I understand." Otis paused and spoke. "Have you ever heard of the Werewolves?"

"No, I don't think so," Andrew said. "Oh, wait. Yes, I have." Andrew frowned and continued, "You remember I told you that E.T., the Director of the FBI, visited me the other night?"

"Yes, I remember him, although I have not met him," Otis replied.

"E.T. said they had received credible threat information from one of their informants of a hit involving the highest levels of the government. He said the Werewolves were involved in some Russian organized crime here in the U.S., and he mentioned a hit going on. He also said Dentist, a member of this gang, was here. He said they would check to verify that fact, but I have not heard back yet."

"The Werewolves and Dentist are here, and I have the airport video to prove it. They arrived just before the kidnapping happened," Otis commented.

"Are you sure?" Andrew asked, his voice turning chilly.

"Yes, a friend checked the airport video surveillance and sent me a video clip. Let me forward it to you." Otis sent the video of the Werewolves to Andrew, who viewed it silently. *These are my son's kidnappers,* he thought grimly.

"Can you contact E.T. and ask if they have heard anything more from this informant?" Otis asked.

"I'll call him right away," Andrew replied. He was happy to do anything that would help to find out where his son was. "I'll call you back after that."

His call to E.T. was a disappointment.

"Our informant is dead. There was a massacre at Restaurant Troika. He was one of the employees found dead in the restaurant. We haven't heard anything else about the threat involving you or the government," E.T. replied. "We are still checking the crash. The eyewitness has disappeared. We wanted to re-interview him."

Andrew did not want to give him his news about the TSA checkpoint and the Werewolves.

It will not do any good now. Better keep the information just between me and Otis, Andrew thought.

"Keep me updated, E.T." Andrew hung up and dialed Otis's number. His stomach was in tight knots.

The informant was killed. Are these the same people who have my son? Andrew thought and felt a cold shiver going up his spine.

When Otis answered, Andrew said, "Otis? I just spoke with E.T. Their informant was killed in a massacre at Restaurant Troika. Isn't that the same restaurant where your mother was being held?"

"Yes, it's the same place. I must tell you something," Otis replied and sighed. He had not told Andrew yet about the massacre at the restaurant. "I went back there to find some clues. I saw the dead bodies on the floor. The killers must have just left before I got there. The bodies were still warm. I did not want to tell you because it would have worried you more. I followed the lead that I found there to another Russian restaurant. That's how I found out about the Werewolves. And there is something else. "Otis revealed the information he had received about the tattoos and the secret meeting at Restaurant Nevskij.

"A secret business meeting after midnight. A group with tattoos?" Andrew raised his eyebrows. It all sounded like a spy story.

"My friend scans the federal databases for a possible hit. It might take some hours. He will contact if he can identify anyone in that group besides Dentist. If we can identify the participants, then maybe we can get a clue where your son is," Otis explained.

After Otis ended the call, Andrew stared dully at the burner phone.

His other cell phone rang. He checked the number. It was the hospital. *The doppelganger wants to talk to me,* he thought.

"Yes," he answered, his voice clipped and brisk. He wanted the doppelganger to know he was talking as a president of this country, not as a devastated father.

"It's time for us to talk about our other demands," Doppelganger-Dan said. His voice flowed out with a hint of charm and excitement.

Andrew tensed when he heard his voice. His knuckles turned white as he clutched the phone tighter.

"I'll come to visit you later today after Irene has visited you," he said and hung up before Doppelganger-Dan could reply.

Behind the table, his hands fisted on his knees when he thought about the doppelganger and the new demands. He took a deep breath to calm down. He knew emotions could cloud his thinking and did not want that. He had to be clear-headed to get information out of the doppelganger. Maybe some hints about where Zachary could be. He decided to ask to talk with him and with the real Dan.

Nobody knows anything about Dan, he thought, worried. They must grant him that much if he agrees to their demands, or so he hoped. He knew nothing was guaranteed. The kidnappers had all the power now. All he could do was stall and try to get more time so Otis could find out Zachary's location.

42

More News

There was a knock on the door, and President's secretary Esme Jordan opened the door and said, "Excuse me, Mr. President."

"Yes, Esme, what is it?" Andrew asked. He sat by the desk and viewed the papers in front of him. He had done some new drafts for the United Nations General Assembly but was not satisfied with the results. His political counselor Conrad Kelly had made the rough drafts, but Andrew liked to overview and make a personal touch in all his speeches. His problem this time was that he could not just do that. He had to redo the whole speech because of the kidnappers' demands.

"Mr. President, the Director of the FBI is here and has asked to speak with you. He said it is about the helicopter accident."

"Okay, show him in," Andrew said, frowning. He leaned back on his chair and waited a couple of minutes before the Director of the FBI, E. Thomas Ruckert, walked inside. Esme closed the door behind him.

Andrew got up behind his desk and walked around it to greet him. He had just spoken with him earlier this morning. Did he have some new information?

When they shook hands, E.T. burst out, "Mr. President, I'm sorry to interrupt you..."

Andrew interrupted, "Let's sit down first." He pointed towards the sofa.

"Mr. President, I need to tell you something about the helicopter crash," E.T. started.

Andrew straightened his back and said, "Yes, what about it?"

"There was only one eyewitness. That is unusual. A city this size usually has dozens of viewers and many eyewitnesses on any crash site. Usually, we'll have cell phone videos or photographs taken by the passers-by." E.T.

paused and assessed Andrew as a father himself. This is going to be tough for him to hear, E.T. thought. "We think the crash was no accident. We have not found any bodies. We think it is possible, just maybe, that your son was not in the helicopter when it crashed."

Andrew dropped his gaze. It was hard for him to pretend to be surprised.

E.T. noticed that he failed to express hope. "Mr. President, are you all right?"

"Yes, yes. You just surprised me," Andrew replied.

"Your son might be alive," E.T. said. He observed Andrew and noticed that he took a deep breath as if to calm himself down.

"Are you sure?" Andrew asked. "Where is he?"

"We think the Russians might be behind this. Remember we discussed the informant we had. He died, but he left a voice message behind. He said the Werewolves, the Russian biker gang, are here in the United States. The informant said they had a plan, a hit, which has something to do with you. We have a TSA checkpoint confirmation that these gang members entered our country. They had diplomatic passports. We got the notice that they entered our country, but we can't do anything because of the diplomatic cover." E.T. paused and kept his eyes on

Andrew when he said, "We think the hit was the crash, or it was part of the plan. We don't know what else is going on. Your son and his disappearance are part of this plan."

Andrew knew all of that, but he could not reveal it. Otis was much faster than the whole FBI organization. He had this information hours ago.

Andrew got up and said, "Thank you, E.T. Keep me in the loop. I want to know if you find out anything else."

"Yes, Mr. President." E.T. frowned but got up and shook his hand before exiting. Now, he was sure the president knew something.

Andrew walked behind his desk and sat down. He sighed. The FBI was too late with their information.

He called Otis to tell him what the FBI knew or suspected. They were running out of time to keep this kidnapping hidden.

After Andrew's call, Otis did not have time to do much before his phone rang again. It was his burner phone, but this time it was Noah calling.

"I ran a facial recognition program that analyzed the Ronald Reagan National Airport video stream. I got an 88% match with one of the limousine passengers. Alexei Petrov. He's a Russian oligarch. He represents the new money and new wealth."

"The Russians..." Otis murmured. They had money to plan this kidnapping, but they must have had some help from the Russian government to get the flight plan details and Zachary's schedule.

"Aleksei Petrov had the Phoenix bird tattooed on his wrist. He made his fortune in the media business. I'll send his image to you. The airport image is sharper than the one I had from the doorway."

Otis heard a beep when his phone received a message. He viewed it. Aleksei looked fit for his age, closer to his forties, with short, dark hair and a small diamond blinking in his right earlobe.

"The other one, Boris Kryukov, I found him through his business connections here in the United States and his global corporation. He is the owner of both restaurants, Nevskij and Troika," Noah explained.

"Let me write this down," Otis replied, and when he was ready, he added, "Okay, go on."

"Boris Kryukov also owns the limousine rental company. These men used his limousine company for their ride to the Restaurant Nevskij for their secret meeting. It was probably the safest way to get the transportation to use one of their own companies to provide the vehicles." Noah sent his image to Otis. "He had a Hippogriff tattooed on his wrist. I don't know if these tattoos mean anything. Maybe they are just the way they identify themselves to each other," Noah added.

Maksim Liskin, the dead restaurant manager, was one of his employees, Otis thought, and looked like a fox in a henhouse. All these men were connected to the kidnapping and extortion. Finally, he had concrete clues about the persons behind the kidnapping scheme and their faces, not just suspicions.

43

The Kidnappers' Hiding Place

The kidnappers brought Zachary some vegetable-meat pasties and a water bottle. The previous day they had brought him some borsch soup and garlic bread. He suspected they were keeping him in the basement of a restaurant because the food was always steaming hot, and he could smell onions cooking and other scents flowing in the air when his kidnappers opened and closed the door of his prison.

The gang members opened Zachary's ties so that he could eat and go to the bathroom. The kidnappers surveyed his every move. Zachary could not roam around and check out his prison.

The only thing he could assess was his guards and what they looked like and wore. His guards always wore leather vests and pants. He read their ranks on their vests. They were soldiers in the biker group.

"How long have I been here?" Zachary asked. He had no idea what time it was or how long he had been there. He did not know how many days had gone by or how long he had been unconscious before waking up in this basement. He did not know how far away the kidnappers had taken him or if he was in the United States. They could have taken him to another country for all he knew.

The guards let him walk around the room four or six times a day, then they tied him up again. He tried to doze off in the chair but could not sleep.

One of them had an ugly red birthmark on his face right under his left eye, which looked like a rash, so Zachary called him Rash.

The bald guy was Spider. He had heard the other guy calling him that. They didn't know he knew a few words in Russian. They probably didn't want him to know their names.

"Have you heard anything of my dad? Is he going to do what you asked?" Zachary asked and looked at his guards.

The kidnappers just stared at him, but they did not answer. It was as if he was invisible.

"Where is Dan?" Zachary asked. He had not seen his sister's husband since the kidnapping at the airport. "Is he alive? Did you kill him?"

No reply. His kidnappers just gazed at him like he was a fly on the wall.

"I want to see the man behind this kidnapping! I can convince my father to do what you want," Zachary said. He had tried to be convincing but failed. He sounded more pleading and desperate than anything else.

After he had finished eating, his kidnappers tied him up again.

Nobody said a word to Zachary.

Zachary did not know that all that he said had been recorded.

The mole in the White House supervised the kidnapping and monitored every aspect of it. He smiled when he heard Zachary's words. He hoped Zachary was right, that his father would do anything for him. He hoped that Zachary was convincing. It was his life at stake.

One of the gang members returned and handed Zach a cell phone. "Call your father. He wants to know that you're alive."

Zachary sighed. Finally, he can talk to his father. "Hello, dad? It's me, Zachary."

"How are you? Are you okay?" Zachary heard his father's anxious voice on the line.

"Yes, I'm fine. Please do what they ask. I don't want to die."

"Can you tell me where you are?"

"This is a basement..." Zach started, but the phone was taken away from his hand.

"Your son is alive, and that's all you need to know." The same gang member who had given Zachary the cell phone took it away and ended the call.

Andrew called Otis right after the call. "Otis, Zachary called. He is okay. He said they were holding him in a basement. He could not say anything else."

Otis could feel the excitement and relief in his voice.

"That's excellent news. We still have time to find him."

"I don't know if Dan is alive," Andrew added, worrying.

"Maybe he is being kept in a different location," Otis replied. He didn't know if that was true or not.

44

Georgetown University

O tis sat by his desk in his office at the university, thinking about the situation he had been drawn into. The Russians planned to blackmail Andrew.

Because of their old friendship, Otis was ready to help Andrew, but he also realized that if Andrew did what the Russians asked, he would be committing treason.

Otis could be considered an accessory to his crime, or could he?

Many times in history, a foreign power tried to influence or manipulate another sovereign country, like the colonial expansion of the European powers in Africa and Asia or the WII when the Nazis expanded their area to the neighboring countries in Europe. He had hoped these times were gone, but this was a new era with new methods to influence other countries. He didn't know of any cases where a head of the state had been blackmailed by another country.

Otis rubbed his face with his hands. This was a difficult situation. He considered the concept of state autonomy and what it meant: One state, in this case, Russia, could not demand that another state, in this case, the United States, take any internal action. A state's autonomy also granted each sovereign state complete control over its region, and no other state was allowed to influence its internal decisions.

A sphere of influence, that's what this is all about, isn't it? he thought. The assertion of spheres of influence had long roots in history; even the Romans conquered neighboring territories in wars. The European countries exerted their influence in colonial expansion in Africa and Asia in the 1900s.

This was a new kind of imperialistic game: who would control this country, and how much control would the Russians gain through the president?

Otis's problem was that he was loyal to his country and not just to his friend. Should he betray his friend and tell someone in the government that the president was compromised and should not be in the executive office and the commander of the army? The most horrifying thought was that the president held the keys to the nuclear weapons, and the Russians held his son. Could the Russians order Andrew to use nuclear weapons? Would Andrew do that?

Otis had known Andrew for decades. He knew he was loyal, a true patriot, but he loved his son. What would he do? Would he betray his country, and how far would he go to save his son? He did not have an answer to that question.

He pulled a copy of the Constitution of the United States from the bookshelf and read. In Section 110 of Article III of the Constitution of the United States, it is declared that:

"Treason against the United States shall consist only in levying war against them, or in adhering to their enemies, giving them aid and comfort. No person shall be convicted of treason unless on the testimony of two witnesses to the same overt act, or confession in open Court. The Congress shall have the power to declare the punishment of treason."

He read the conclusion that the president of the United States would be removed from Office on impeachment for, and conviction of, treason.

Otis browsed through his files on his computer for examples of persons who committed treason. He found a few of them. For example, John Brown was convicted and executed for attempting to organize armed resistance to slavery in the Commonwealth of Virginia in 1859. Another more recent example was Robert Henry Best, who supported and distributed Nazi propaganda during WWII and was sentenced in 1948 to life in prison.

Otis leaned back in his chair and closed his file. He brushed his hair with his right hand. The outlook for the impeachment and sentencing did not look good.

I should tell the Vice President or someone else about this Russian blackmail, he thought. *Except, I don't know whom to trust.*

He suspected that there had to be a mole in the White House. Someone close to the president had gotten access to his son's travel plans beforehand, and someone knew about his schedule and meetings with the president. Someone was leaking information to Russia. He had to reveal the mole before he could disclose this Russian kidnapping and blackmailing game to anyone.

His thoughts were interrupted by a ringing cell phone. It was his usual work phone, and Deena was calling.

"Hello, Deena," Otis answered the phone.

Deena went directly to the business. "The lab results are ready. Come and pick them up when you have time."

"I'll be there soon. Thank you, Deena." Otis hung up. He got up, walked to the door, and went outside. He was pleased with the call and distraction. He did not want to think more about the impeachment, treason, and possible convictions.

He walked across the campus to Deena's office and knocked at the door. When Otis entered, Deena wore her white lab coat and was sitting at her desk reading some student papers. She heard the knock, raised her head, and turned towards the door to see who it was. A wide smile brightened her face when she recognized Otis.

"You were fast," Dena said, leaning back on her chair and turning it slightly towards the door.

"When a girl calls, you have to be fast." Otis smiled back.

Deena blushed. She took something from the pile on her desk and handed it over to him. "Your sample and your results back."

Otis viewed the blood type report and the DNA analysis describing the sample's genetic ethnicity. Russian? Jewish? He was surprised. "Are you sure this is correct?"

"Yes, I'm sure," Deena replied. "Is something wrong?"

"No, I was just surprised by the results: Russian and Jewish background."

"You never told me whose blood sample this was," Deena reminded him.

"I know. That's just to protect you. Only the president and I know whose blood sample and DNA test this is. It is safer for you if you don't know," Otis replied.

It would be safer for me, too, if I did not know, Otis thought.

"When this is all over, I will tell you what I can," Otis assured Deena.

"Over dinner, I hope," Deena said, fluttering her eyelashes.

"It's a deal," Otis smiled. "How come you don't have a boyfriend?"

"You know you have to kiss a few toads before you find the prince, and I have not found my prince yet," Deena replied, flirting.

Otis kissed her on the cheek. "See you soon."

When he got outside the building, he called Noah. "I have a DNA sample for you to check. Can I quickly visit and give it to you now?"

"Sure," Noah replied. "I'm still running the facial recognition programs with the images of the guys in that secret meeting. I have nothing new yet," he added.

The DNA test was the one taken from the doppelganger. He had Russian and Jewish genetic profiles. The Russian part, I can understand, but a Jewish, too? Otis pondered as he drove to Noah's apartment and left him the DNA results and the blood sample. Deena had used the other one, but Otis still had the backup one to give to Noah. He wanted to see if they could find a DNA match on any criminal databases.

Deena's blood type analysis had shown that the doppelganger had a blood type A.

It's not an uncommon blood type. Over 30% of the population has that blood type, Otis thought.

45

The Yellow Oval Office

A ndrew could not concentrate. He tried to read while sitting on one of the upholstered sofas, but he was unable to do that. He opened his television to catch up with the latest news, but he could only think of his son and the kidnappers' demands.

He had asked for a couple of days off to grieve his missing son, but he could not tell anyone that his son was alive. It made him feel like a liar, and he had never been a good liar, even if he had dealt with the politicians and their white lies and half-truths ever since he chose to run for the presidency. He was sure the people he worked closely were already suspected of something. Esme, his secretary, had given him curious glances whenever Zachary was mentioned. He knew he hadn't behaved like a father who had lost his only son.

Vice President John Rossi had taken over his tasks. John was a good politician and had stepped in when Andrew needed him the most. He wished he could tell John what had happened to Zachary, but he couldn't.

Andrew had spoken briefly with Irene after his talk with Doppelganger-Dan at the hospital.

Irene was worried for her husband. She thought Dan might have PTSD after the crash because he was acting strangely.

Andrew could not tell her what was wrong. He just tried to calm her down.

Andrew Burr was distraught and angry because this Doppelganger-Dan was like a spider weaving a net around him and his family, imprisoning them.

Andrew was not sure what to do. He wanted to tell Irene what was going on, but he couldn't. If he did, he didn't know if the Russians would harm or kill Zachary and Dan. He hoped Dan was still alive. That would be Irene's first question if he revealed anything to her. *Fortunately, Irene is busy with business decisions, so maybe she won't have to deal with this doppelganger at their home,* he thought.

Andrew needed something to do with his hands, so he walked over to the liquor cabinet and poured a brandy. He stood for a moment, swirling the liquid in his crystal glass, and then lifted it, smelled the familiar scent, and sipped it. He hoped it would calm his nerves. He walked towards the window and looked outside. It was early spring. Still chilly outside, but the days were getting longer. He could see the white and pink buds on the cherry trees. Soon they would be blooming.

He drained the rest of the brandy, walked back to the table, and set the glass down on the wooden surface of the side table.

Andrew hoped Otis would find the kidnappers soon. His time was running out.

The United Nations meeting was scheduled in New York in a couple of days. What would he do if Zachary were not found before that meeting? He couldn't betray his country! Andrew walked back to his desk, buried his face in his hands, and sat still for a long time. He had no idea what he would do. He had to consider all the choices but didn't have any. He had to save his son. Andrew loved Zachary and didn't care if he would go to prison after that. He knew it would be treason if he did anything the Russians demanded. He also hoped he had not caused problems for Otis and didn't want him to be charged with anything.

46

Restaurant Nevskij

3 a.m. (EST), Septem

The temperature had fallen, and a pale moon shone through the clouds. A row of limousines arrived at their next meeting at Restaurant Nevskij. It was their third meeting on U.S. soil. The front of the restaurant was lit, and it was the only building on the street with any lights.

The thick blue curtains were drawn over the windows so that no one would see inside the restaurant. One wooden table was placed in the center of the room. The flower arrangements of white lilies with pine branches were scattered around the dining room. The table was set for seven, and two seats were empty. Nachtkrapp participated via video conference call. This time Cyborg had also informed the group that he would join the meeting via video call from his current location.

The tablets on the table included video footage of their prisoner, Zachary. He was tied up, and two of the soldiers of the Werewolves were guarding him.

"Let's start the meeting," Hydra said with a thick Russian accent and looked around the table. He was the spokesman for this group. When he saw nods, he continued explaining. "Our prisoner is alert, but he is not aware of where he is. He can't see outside. All the windows are covered, the walls are soundproofed, and the heavy metal door blocks any sound and attempts to break them. Besides, the sheer look of the Werewolf members will make him think twice about crossing them or fighting. They have automatic weapons. They will not go to see the prisoner alone. The boy always has two guards, and if he is smart, he won't do anything stupid like try to escape." He looked around at the other members, and as they didn't have any comments, he added, "We are on schedule. We have informed the president of our demands and what he needs to announce at the U.N. General Assembly," Hydra told the Septem participants. "I got this information directly from the Postmaster whom you know is still in the hospital. He has done an excellent job, by the way."

The other Septem members clapped their hands and murmured compliments on that fact.

Hydra smiled, pleased. "Let's hear about your progress. Let's start with you, Basilisk."

Basilisk nodded. He was an elderly man with salt and pepper hair. "The Ministry of State Security has continued its support by offering the use of the troll factory in St. Petersburg or Moscow. They have been active in promoting our cause to support the lifting of the sanctions and claiming that these sanctions are based on lies made by the enemies of the state of Russia. They have also provided fake news regarding the situation in Ukraine, saying that ninety percent of the citizens of Ukraine support the Russian leadership."

"That sounds excellent," Hydra commented.

Basilisk nodded and added, "In addition, they have supported extra funding up to one hundred million dollars in case we need some extra money to fulfill this mission. The money is deposited in a bank account in Switzerland, which is untraceable. We don't want anyone to know that the Russian government and the Ministry of State Security are behind this operation."

The other participants clapped their hands and cheered.

Hydra raised his right hand and gestured for them to calm down. He had more to say. "Nachtkrapp has more news from the White House."

The members turned their eyes to the screen where the person wearing a black bird mask, il dottore, faced them. The mask had glass openings in the eyes and a long, curved black beak. It was impossible to recognize the man behind the mask.

Nachtkrapp started, "The president is under severe stress and is not acting normally. He has not told anyone about the kidnapping and that his son is alive. Now, his Chief of Staff has requested him to address the nation and have the Requiem Mass at St. Matthew's Cathedral for his son's memory." Nachtkrapp's voice was metallic due to the voice-altering app he used to disguise his real voice. His video image with his il dottore -mask, a black bird mask, gave his message an eerie sense of doom.

"Can we use the troll factory to leak out fake news that the president of the United States is incapacitated and not responsible enough to deal with state affairs?" Hydra asked.

"No, I don't think that is wise. If Congress decides that the president is unable to perform his duties, the vice president will become the acting president. It is better if we let the plan go forward as planned and let President Burr announce the removal of all the sanctions against our motherland. What happens to him after that is not that important. We must make sure that the United Nations meeting goes as planned," Nachtkrapp replied.

Hydra viewed his audience. "As you all well know, we have other demands after the United Nations General Assembly is over. We need to keep the president in his position. Otherwise, he is useless to us, and we have no use for his son."

"But we can create fake international pressure with the trolls to lift the bans and sanctions. They can flood pro-Russia news and comments all over social media. That would help our cause." Hippogriff insisted. He was the restaurant owner.

"Sure. You are right," Hydra agreed. "Now, we still have the other matter to discuss: Otis Thorne. What do we do with him? We tried to blackmail him by kidnapping his mother, but that failed. We corrected that failure. The Werewolves eliminated the persons responsible for it. The police and the FBI are currently looking at the Restaurant Troika massacre; however, I've heard that they have no clues. Any suggestions on what we should do with Otis

Thorne?" He pointed toward the tablets in front of each participant. "You will find the basic information about Otis, his work, and his family history on the tablets. The information is accurate because it was provided by the Ministry of State Security."

The meeting participants reviewed the information gathered by the Ministry of State Security.

Sitting on Hydra's right side, Phoenix cleared his throat and said, "We could go back to our first plan and abduct his mother again. She is the only person in his life that he cares for. He is unmarried and has no children, so there is no other leverage. His mother is his weak point."

"You are right. He might not suspect another kidnapping right away, especially because the first one failed," Hydra agreed. "It would be so much easier if he had a wife or children."

"Yes, I completely understand your point, but just like the famous American scientist Randolph Bush once said: 'we cannot change the cards we are dealt, just how we play the hand.' Do we know where his mother is now?" Phoenix commented. "We might find a suitable time and place where we can kidnap her if she follows routines," he added.

"Yes, we had one of the Werewolves follow him 24/7. Otis took his mother to a casino," Werewolf commented. "The casino is about ten miles from Washington, D.C. We checked the front desk, and she is checked in under her own name and staying for three days."

"Anyone of us could easily go to that casino. We are wealthy businessmen. They would gladly take our reservations. Nobody would suspect anything," Phoenix suggested. "If we manage to lure her to an area where there are no security cameras and security personnel present, then one of the Werewolves could take her where we keep our other prisoner."

"We never considered dirtying our own hands, not directly," Hydra said disapprovingly.

"But we should consider it now. We cannot let Operation Pobeda fail just because this one guy was better than our first team," Phoenix reminded. "This is still a question of our businesses, the future of Russia, the world dominance, and controlling the United States."

The other participants nodded approvingly.

"We can't all go to the casino. Maybe just one... Because if we fail again, we won't jeopardize the whole operation and the confidentiality of this group," Hydra said. "Do you all agree?"

He glanced around the table, and he saw the silent nods.

"Who will go to the casino?" Werewolf asked.

"I think it should be someone closer to his mother's age. " Only two of us with that age range," Hydra replied. "Me and Basilisk," he pointed to Basilisk, who had an angular face and was ruggedly handsome with salt and pepper hair.

"I'll offer my services. I can do it," Basilisk replied. "I have no plans for tomorrow. I can always woo a woman to a secluded place. Besides, Estelle Thorne does not look bad at all," he added, smiling.

"Basilisk, you know now you're a crucial part of the operation's success. Our Operation Pobeda must continue as scheduled. You must remember: If you get caught, you know what to do," Hydra said.

"I know, I know. Do not reveal our plans or the timetable. Besides, even if I get caught, the officials cannot hold me in custody because I have a diplomatic passport," Basilisk replied.

Hydra nodded. "Okay, let's proceed." He turned his eyes to the tablet and said, "Let's go on. Cyborg next. Your part is essential to the future."

Cyborg answered via video conference call. "Dear friends, I cannot stress how important my ultimate goals are for the benefit of society, even for mankind. They are our goals. I could not have reached where I am today without the help of our government's support and you all. If the president of the United States does what we have requested, we will proceed to the next phase, which will help our homeland to operate more freely around its borders. The final stage of our Operation Pobeda is the most revolutionary one and the most important for me personally."

"Thank you, Cyborg," Hydra replied, adding, "The Ministry of State Security has been a good ally in this plot. The diplomatic passports let us in and out of the country without checking our luggage. We were able to bring in the weaponry needed for the Werewolves."

"Do we still keep following Otis?" Werewolf asked.

"Yes, I think the same Werewolf cell should keep following him. We need to separate the Werewolf cells: One cell is guarding our prisoner, and the other does the grunt work like surveillance, following the president and Otis," Hydra replied. He viewed the faces around the table and did not see any disagreement. "That is all for tonight. We'll meet next time after the United Nations General Assembly meeting is over, and we have heard what the president of the United States has said in his speech."

The private meeting ended, and each participant left one after another the same way they had arrived.

The doorman turned off the lights after the last visitor had left with his limousine. He locked the doors and walked away.

Hydra sat in the backseat of his limousine. He took his cell phone from his pocket and searched for a secret number he only knew. He had to make a call.

47

Noah

Noah was ready when the luxury limousines parked again in front of Restaurant Nevskij. As the passengers walked inside, they were unaware that Noah was following them via the security cameras on the other side of the street. This time only five men arrived with the limousines.

Noah managed to get better facial images of the passengers. When he ran the facial recognition program against government databases, he was able to identify the meeting participants.

The one with Basilisk tattooed on the inside of his right wrist was Sergei Stolyar. Noah got a hit with his face and found out he owned the largest private bank in Russia and was a billionaire.

The next one he was able to identify was the one that had Hydra tattooed on his wrist. He was Orel Andruchenko. He was a slender, white-haired man with eyes as friendly as sharks. He was from an old Cossack family with a long military history.

When Noah dug deeper, he learned some trivial information about Hydra. Hydra's first name, Orel, meant eagle. His parents wanted him to fly high, to reach the sky. He had done that. He was part of the oligarchs that had emerged in Russia after its transition from socialism to capitalism. He was well-connected to the Russian mob. He knew how and whom to bribe to get things done in the new Russia. He was close to the previous and the current Russian presidents. He had worked as an advisor of the previous President Putin in the reorganization process of the Ministry of State Security (MGB) in Russia. MGB was an intelligence and security service organization. It was created when the previous President, Putin, reorganized domestic security, foreign espionage, and counterintelligence agencies, the Federal Security Service (FSB), the Foreign Intelligence Service (SVR), and the Federal Guard Service (FSO).

These agencies were equivalent to the American FBI, CIA, and Secret Service, respectively.

Now Russia had gathered them all under one administrative umbrella called the MGB. The new superagency covered everything from espionage abroad to suppressing opposition in Russia and was only responsible for Russia's president. The FSB was the former notorious KGB, Komitet Gosudarstvennoy Bezopasnosti. The KGB, the Russian security agency, was the opponent of the CIA. The KGB was established after the Second World War and ended after the dissolution of the Soviet Union.

The newly elected Russian President Vladislav Ruskin had reorganized the MGB and strengthened its role while making it a more secretive organization than ever before. The old phrase of the Cold War time fits the description of the MGB today: "Its doors are shut tightly to the public." The new KGB within the superagency was powerful and secretive, spying on everything and everyone by any possible means. President Ruskin had increased the power of the FSB within the superagency. He wanted the global superpower position in Russia and to re-establish the former borders of the old Soviet Union and the great Russia of the 19th Century.

Hydra had been instrumental in the formation of the MGBs from the previously separate entities, namely the FSB, FSO, and SVR. He was entitled to the intimate secrets of every single person in Russia and the secrets collected from the international community.

Hydra had unlimited power in secrets within his reach, although his vast fortune was based on his shrewd business knowledge. He had made his fortune by investing in energy and oil. His billions were safe as he had transferred his investments to Swiss bank accounts before the economic sanctions sank the ruble.

President Ruskin appointed him as the head of the MGB which gave him almost unlimited power in Russia, even over Russia's president. He had access to all the internal and global security secrets available in any databases in Russia.

Interesting, Noah thought as he waited for his facial recognition programs to finish processing. He might recognize someone else besides Hydra and Basilisk.

The secretive meeting was between political and financial tycoons of Russia. *Why did they meet here in the United States, and what was their ultimate goal?* Noah was sure there had to be something else behind the kidnapping of the president's son. *What was going on?*

48

Otis

It was pitch dark when Otis woke up to an annoying ringing that did not seem to stop. *It can't be morning yet,* he thought. It was not his alarm clock. It was his cell phone ringing.

He checked his alarm clock by the bedside, and it was 3:45 a.m.

Who is calling this late at night?

He brushed his fingers through his hair, making it stand up. He realized it was not his usual cell phone but the burner phone. Only two persons had that number: Noah and Andrew.

Something must have happened, he thought.

"Hello?" he answered with a groggy voice. He rubbed his face with his hands to wake up.

"Hello Otis, I identified two more men meeting in that Restaurant Nevskij," Noah said.

"A new meeting?" Otis asked, surprised. He had not thought there would be another meeting this soon.

"Yes, same place. Same limousines," Noah explained excitedly. "Only this time, there were five of them. One less than the last time."

Otis rose in his bed, leaned on his elbow, and pressed the phone tighter to his ear so that he would not miss Noah's news. "Okay, tell me which one you recognized?"

"The one with the Basilisk tattoo is Sergei Stolyar. He is a rich Russian banker. A billionaire," Noah replied, pleased.

"Nice. Russian billionaires in clandestine meetings," Otis murmured.

"The next one is interesting. The man with Hydra tattoo is Orel Andruchenko. I'll send you his file, but you might know him from your time in Russia."

"I remember him now. I met him a couple of times at state dinners. He was a shark among sharks. I mean, he was ruthless and capable of anything," Otis frowned as he tried to remember the facts of the files he had read previously about this man. He had seen him in the news. He didn't remember if he had met him face to face.

"Read the file I just sent you. You'll find it interesting," Noah replied.

"Orel Andruchenko is most likely the leader of the group. He usually did not sit in the back row. He was always in the front when something major happened," Otis said.

"I'll try to recognize the other participant we have not been able to identify yet," Noah said. "His tattoo was not from mythology, but the Cyborg character, a superhero with special cybernetic enhancements, superhuman stamina, and flight capabilities. DC Comics introduced Cyborg as part of the Justice League in 2011," he added.

"Interesting. Why Cyborg?" Otis murmured more to himself than to Noah. "Why a character from an American graphic novel?"

"I have the DNA results you forwarded me. I have checked them against the federal and international databases. I have to double-check them. Something does not make sense," Noah commented.

"Why?" Otis raised his eyebrows in surprise. Noah had never said he had to double-check any of his work before. He had always been one hundred percent correct in everything.

"Something is off. I can't explain it yet. I must double-check," Noah replied vaguely.

"Okay. I'll wait for your call." Then Otis remembered something else. "Can you check the video from the Essex County Airport in Fairfield, New Jersey, from around noon to three p.m.? It's the day of the crash. I want to know if any of the same guys from these secret meetings were at the same time Zach's helicopter was being prepared for the flight. Maybe you can also check their video feed to see if any of the Werewolves were there."

"Sure, I'll do that tomorrow morning. Good night," Noah replied and hung up.

After Noah's call, Otis stared into the darkness of his room for a long time.

49

St. Petersburg

11. a.m. (GMT+3), The Troll Factory

An inconspicuous four-flour granite building stood on the corner of a busy Ulitsa Savuškina. It had lights on around the clock, every day of the week. The three lower-level windows were shaded, and the light shone through the shades all night, but the top-level windows had no shades. That's where the management of the troll factory had their rooms, took orders, and cared for their important visitors.

Unmarked cars were parked in front of the building, and beefy-looking armed guards with long trench coats patrolled around the house and in the doorways.

The Russian government buildings were always heavily guarded and protected. No one was allowed to enter the house without an entrance pass.

As the clock struck nine in the morning, a daily ritual unfolded within the workplace: the changing of the shifts. Approximately forty individuals who had diligently worked through the night filed out of the building, marking the end of their nocturnal duties. Simultaneously, a cohort of around fifty day-shift workers made their entrance, ready to assume their roles and tackle the day's challenges. This synchronized transition not only symbolized the relentless continuity of operations but also encapsulated the ebb and flow of the workforce, a dynamic rhythm that characterized the daily life within the organization.

It was almost noon in St. Petersburg when Hydra called the troll factory and its program manager.

"Do you know who I am?" Hydra asked. He made the call right after the Septem-group meeting. It was still nighttime in the United States.

St. Petersburg was eight hours ahead of Washington, D.C., but it did not matter because Hydra knew the troll factory worked around the clock. He could call anytime, any day of the week, and he would get someone to answer the phone.

"Yes, you are the ones from across the ocean. We have been ordered to follow your requests if you have any," Program Manager Anatoly Sokov replied. He was an overweight, Lincoln-bearded man with round glasses and a wrinkled white long-sleeve shirt and jeans.

"We requested your help before. It was a couple of years ago. Do you remember?" Hydra asked. He did not want to go into details on the phone.

"Yes, I do. Advertising and marketing, if I remember correctly," Anatoly Sokov replied. A casual reply was better than the truth.

"Yes, that's correct. We need you to do it again the next week," Hydra replied.

"Can we discuss some details first?" Anatoly asked and pulled out a notepad to write down.

"Yes, you know the facts. We need international marketing to start immediately promoting our products and services," Hydra explained. It was all in codes that they had agreed to before. Marketing meant opening social media accounts internationally; advertising was a code for starting discussions on certain topics. This time the phrase 'products and services' meant the actual Russian-made products and services. These products had restrictions now, but the Septem group hoped they could soon export everything without any sanctions.

The last occasion on which Anatoly's services were enlisted took place prior to the preceding presidential election, a pivotal moment in the political trajectory of the United States. During that time, trolls under Anatoly's strategic guidance generated a stream of favorable comments aimed at bolstering the public image of Andrew Burr, who was then a senator contemplating a presidential run. The memory of this orchestrated campaign lingered vividly in the minds of both Hydra and Anatoly, as they deftly manipulated the digital landscape to cultivate interest and garner support, ultimately influencing the course of the election and propelling Andrew Burr into the esteemed position of the current President of the United States. This historical collaboration between Hydra and Anatoly served as a testament to their proficiency in the art of information warfare, leaving an indelible mark on the political landscape.

Hydra and Anatoly had a long-term successful relationship. Hydra had participated in the management of the troll factories as well as the creation and setting of them up. He had personally selected all the different managers in the various troll factory locations.

"I understand. We are starting the marketing plan right now. Thank you for your interest in our services," Anatoly Sokov replied politely while jotting down some notes in his notepad.

"That's all for now. Let's hope the marketing works as well as last time," Hydra replied and hung up.

After the call, Program Manager Anatoly Sokov leaned back on his chair and turned to look outside his window. It showed Ulitsa Savuškina. The opposite side of Savuškina Street looked just like three- and four-flour businesses with no storefronts. Many buildings in that area were occupied and owned by the Russian government. They did not want to advertise their existence and what they were doing. A few trees were planted along the road, and the branches still had some snow on them. Dirty piles of snow were gathered along the sidewalks. It was still winter in Russia. This winter had not been as snowy as the previous ones, but the wind was cold and strong, blowing from Siberia and chilled to the bone when you went outside.

Anatoly Sokov got up and went to the tall gray file cabinet in his room. He wanted to see the notes from their previous meeting. He had only handwritten notes because nothing was recorded of these top-secret government orders. He pulled out the top drawer and browsed through the folders until he found what he was looking for: the file from the last time. It had a code name Dvoynik, the Doppelganger. He pulled it out and took it back to his desk.

He sat down and pushed back his round glasses before reading his notes. He remembered Orel Andruchenko. He was a tall man with sharp, pale blue eyes and a lean, toned body. Orel had an officer's physique hidden under the expensive tailor-made suit. He had come unannounced to meet him, but the guards had let him come upstairs because they knew him. Everyone in the government knew him. He had both power and money, and he had the ear of Russia's president. This man, Orel Andruchenko, needed no introduction. He came and said what he wanted and explained the timeline for this task. He didn't negotiate. He didn't expect any deviations from his requests. If you didn't do what he asked, you were history. Anatoly knew that. The memory of that meeting was now clear in his mind. Orel's voice was unforgettable, a sharp, piercing, commanding voice. The same voice he heard today on the phone.

On the most recent occasion, Orel issued a directive to Anatoly, tasking him with assembling a formidable team of ten highly skilled trolls for a specific mission. These trolls were not just any run-of-the-mill operatives; they were required to possess a mastery of US English, with a diverse range of linguistic abilities that included various accents such as Mexican, African American, and regional dialects from different parts of the United States.

Furthermore, Anatoly faced the challenge of not only identifying but also recruiting or hiring trolls who met these stringent criteria. The mission entrusted to this eclectic group was nothing short of intricate: they were to toil tirelessly around the clock. Their primary objective was to establish a presence on multiple online social media platforms and websites, strategically disseminating certain opinions while concurrently discrediting specific political figures and viewpoints. In essence, this elaborate operation required a sophisticated and adaptable team capable of influencing public discourse through a multifaceted approach across the digital landscape.

In other words, the trolls were to create a positive environment for political change in the United States. This was not all he wanted. He wanted the trolls to call the radio shows, present themselves as concerned U.S.

citizens, and talk about certain political topics. Not all of this happened immediately. Anatoly remembered that Orel had hinted that this project would last several years and some of these political topics would be provided to Anatoly later. It was the most detailed and longest project Anatoly had participated in. He considered the plan to be both a marketing plan and a social media strategy plan. It was part of the hybrid war Russia had launched against its enemies.

Anatoly's trolls were also encouraged to support demonstrations in the United States against the current government. He was told ahead of time that some of the trolls would have to influence the universities and colleges. Anatoly had asked how, and Orel Andruchenko, Hydra, had told him that his trolls could befriend students on campus or influence the students online to demonstrate and disrespect the current government leaders. And that's exactly what had happened, Anatoly remembered.

Orel had explained all of this to him in one session. It was a brilliant plan. He had considered the students. The chosen ones to represent young voters, blue-collar voters like the farmers and the factory workers, white-collar voters, or voters from the unhappy southern border states who did not like illegal drug and human trafficking. They should also include the rich and famous, Hollywood's cream of the crop.

Anatoly remembered how that man had presented him with a plan to reach all these voters and how to make them more favorable to the political changes they wanted. He also learned who Russia wanted to be the next president of the United States. It was Andrew Burr.

Anatoly remembered asking this man if the chosen presidential candidate was pro-Russian, but the other man laughed dryly and replied, "No, just the opposite. He is Mr. red-white-and-blue in person. He is a true American patriot. He is as American as can be, and that's the greatness of this plan, to degrade someone who genuinely believes in American values but is forced to work for our values."

And so, he was. President Andrew Burr was as American as the apple pie. He never said anything pro-Russian during his presidential candidacy. He never presented any opinions reflecting any pro-Russian opinions because he had none. He was a true American in his heart. He was the perfect scapegoat.

The trolls created the environment for a change with online postings, radio show calls, and organizing demonstrations all over the United States. They had a candidate they wanted to promote to be the next president, Andrew Burr.

Andrew was a long-term senator, and he was good and well-liked. When he was approached by his party representatives to become the presidential candidate, he first refused, but the pressure did not stop, and eventually, he accepted the candidacy.

Orel had expressed his concerns about what would happen if Andrew Burr did not win to Anatoly. They needed him to win because otherwise, they would have to wait for his son or his son-in-law to run. They had only these three choices. One of them had to be the president.

Orel had not explained this comment or given him a reason.

"Why does it have to be Andrew Burr or one of his relatives?" Anatoly had asked, and Orel had replied, "If I tell you, I'll have to kill you. It's the most secret project within the government." Anatoly had seen the ice and the determination in his eyes. The man was not joking. He was serious.

Anatoly never asked that question again. He did not want to die.

And now the same man had called and wanted more online pressure and pro-Russia comments on social media. He would do it, no questions asked.

50

Andrew

"The United Nations General Assembly meeting is being held in New York City the day after tomorrow, and we have heard that several EU leaders are supporting the continuance of existing sanctions against Russia but also suggesting that there should be more travel bans and business sanctions for Russian citizens to the U.S. and the European Union. The Russian currency is plummeting. The ruble is currently worth less than five cents," the morning news reporter announced and added, "The president of the United States has previously agreed to support all the suggested additional bans and sanctions."

Andrew Burr sighed and turned the television volume down. He had to plan his shocking announcement to the U.N. General Assembly and discuss it with the Chief of Staff and the Secretary of State. *What can I say when they ask why? I just don't have any reasonable excuse to reverse my previous decisions*, Andrew thought.

He picked up his phone and made two calls: one to his secretary, Esme. "Good morning, Esme. Can you please contact John? Check if he can take some of my daily meetings this week," Andrew said and referred to his Vice President John Rossi. He added, "I'm not quite up to my tasks now. You know because of Zachary," Andrew didn't finish his last sentence. Esme could draw her own conclusions.

Esme replied. "Good morning, Mr. President. Yes, I will contact the Vice President and ask him to take over some meetings and reschedule the ones on your calendar for this week. Anything else I can do for you today, Sir?"

"Yes. I need to have an urgent meeting with the Vice President, the Chief of Staff, the Secretary of State, and the U.S. ambassador to the United Nations. Can you ask them to come to the Oval Office this morning?" Andrew requested.

"Yes, Mr. President. I will call them right now and set up a meeting," Esme replied efficiently.

Second, Andrew Burr called Otis with his burner phone. "Anything new? I'm running out of time," he asked briskly when Otis answered the phone.

"Good morning, Mr. President. My friend managed to identify some of the participants in that clandestine meeting. We can safely assume that they were all involved in this kidnapping scheme," Otis replied.

"Good, good. Some progress," Andrew replied, relieved.

"My next stop is Essex County Airport in Fairfield, New Jersey, where Zachary and Dan boarded the helicopter," Otis said.

"Do you think you can find something there?" Andrew asked.

"It's possible that somebody might have seen something. Law enforcement did not check the airport facilities because the crash did not happen there. They did not interview any possible witnesses because they didn't know about the kidnapping," Otis replied.

"That's true. I hope you can find out something. Good luck." Andrew hung up and stared in front of him at the empty wall. Finally, Otis had made some progress.

He had no solid proof yet, but if the Russian government was behind the kidnapping, then this was an unconventional method of warfare. Their goal was probably to destroy the U.S. government inside and to enable Russia to conquer Eastern Europe and possibly other areas without U.S. interference. If they had the president of the United States in their pocket and doing as they requested, they would not have any major resistance, except the European Union, to oppose its expansion goals. However, everyone who followed global politics knew that the European Union was not a strong opponent due to its diverse countries and their different interests. The European Union could not even decide whether to keep an army of its own. He had to admit that the Russians had craftily worked on their plan and executed it.

He had less than 48 hours to prepare and practice his speech. He could not ask anyone else to do it because he could not let anyone know what he was going to say. He had always found that oral practice was essential before any public presentation. The words he would use, his tone in his presentation, and how he would gesture with his hands or keep them still. He felt like an actor in his dress rehearsal, running his memorized lines backstage before the performance.

51

At The Casino

At Golden Coastal Casino, a good-looking elderly gentleman checked in. His three-piece gray shade suit was the latest fashion from Milan. He looked like a wealthy businessman from Europe. He walked briskly to the front desk and commandingly told the clerk, "Good afternoon. I would like to check in. I have a reservation with the name Sergei Stolyar." He pulled out his wallet and platinum credit card and handed them to the clerk.

Sergei placed his travel bag beside him on the floor. He did not plan to stay for long, but it had to look as if he was a legitimate guest.

The clerk was a young lady in her twenties dressed in the casino's outfit with a dark skirt and vest, white blouse, and red bowtie. She was used to foreign dignitaries as well as the newly rich, so she didn't mind being bossed around. She quickly tapped the keyboard and checked the reservations. "Good afternoon, Sir. Let me just confirm your reservation and get you your keycard." The front desk clerk located Sergei's reservation and printed out the form and the keycard. "Here you are, Mr. Stolyar."

She swiped Sergei's credit card and then handed it back to him. Sergei placed his card back in his wallet.

"Is there anything else we can do for you today?" the clerk asked, smiling pleasantly.

"Yes, there is." Sergei, who was Basilisk in the Septem group, replied. "I would like to know if Estelle Thorne has arrived yet. I was supposed to meet her here."

The clerk at the front desk was helpful. "Let me check. Just a minute, Sir." She turned towards the computer and typed in her name. It took her only a minute to find out the information his guest had asked for. She smiled again and replied with a professional and polite smile. "Yes, she has. Her room number is 231. If you like, I can arrange for you to stay next door with her. It is available."

"That would be excellent. Thank you." Sergei nodded, pleased, and waited for the receptionist to change the room to the one next to Estelle's.

Sergei picked up his travel bag and walked towards the lobby. He smoothed his dark hair with grey and white hairs. He waited in front of the elevators for his turn, and when it arrived, he glanced around but didn't see anything out of the ordinary. Normal casino guests walked or sat in the lobby or visited the shops.

No visible security personnel, he thought. He entered the elevator and pressed the second-floor button, which was the floor where he and Estelle had their hotel rooms.

Sergei was in the casino to execute his order to take care of Estelle. He understood how crucial his task was.

Otis Thorne was trouble. The Septem group needed to get Otis out of the equation. The president relied on Otis and his capabilities to save his son.

When the elevator stopped on the right floor, Sergei stepped out and glanced around to locate her room 231 and then his room 233. The odd numbers were on the same side, so their rooms were next to each other, which was good. Exactly how he wanted.

He opened the hotel room's door and glanced around. It had a large queen-size bed, air conditioning, and an additional work area with internet access. A large walk-in closet with a safe was also added to the room. He opened the bathroom door, and the hotel had a large marble bathroom with thick white towels and white bathrobes for guests. He walked across the room and tossed his coat on the bed. *Nice, I'd like to come here again for a nice long weekend,* Sergei thought as he sat on the chair by the work area.

52

At the Airport

O tis woke up early the next morning. It was the day before the United Nations General Assembly would be held in New York. He hoped he could find new clues about how Zachary and Dan were kidnapped at the airport because he was the only one besides the president who knew Zachary had been kidnapped before the crash flight. The airport should have some footage of the whole area and the private helicopters leaving the airport.

Even if the helicopter crash was orchestrated beforehand, doppelganger-Dan, who was found at the crash site and the helicopter pilot, must have flown from the same route as the original flight plan, or that's what

Otis assumed. The pilot must have left the helicopter before the crash or managed to get out unharmed because his body was not found at the crash site.

The FBI, the Secret Service, and the Transportation Security Administration would have noticed if the helicopter had changed its route. Because of the members of the first family in the helicopter, the kidnappers must have known that there would be more eyes on the case than in any other accident in this country, Otis thought. Besides, the Director of the FBI had not mentioned any change in the flight route when compared to the original flight plan when he visited Andrew. He would have told Andrew if that was the case.

The sun was just breaking over the horizon when Otis stepped outside his apartment building in Georgetown. He pulled his parka tighter around him and fumbled his car keys in his pocket. He was deep in his thoughts when he opened his car and sat inside. He considered one more time if there was anything else he might have overlooked.

After considering the choices for a moment, he decided that the airport was the obvious next step. He started his car and drove towards Dulles Airport. He had left early to beat the worst of the morning rush, but the roads were still busy, especially going towards the airport. He checked the rearview mirror as he waited out the next red traffic light. He did not see any familiar vehicles, no motorcycles. When the traffic light changed, he continued and took the exit towards the airport. He kept his eyes on the rearview mirror to see if anybody made sudden moves to follow him. He did not notice anything suspicious. He drove to the short-term parking, got his parking ticket, and walked to the domestic flight terminal after parking. He heard the intercom repeating the security messages, "Don't leave your bags unattended. Please, contact airport security if you see a suspicious bag." This was all due to 9/11 and the escalating terrorist attacks all over the world. *With all the security at the airports, the kidnappers still managed to kidnap a member of the First Family. What went wrong?* Otis wondered.

Otis was right in suspecting that someone might be following him. This time the follower was better hiding himself amidst the heavy traffic. A lone Werewolf biker stopped outside the airport and his eyes followed Otis when Otis entered the terminal for national flights.

The biker made a quick call to his superior to check what he was supposed to do now. He got orders to stay where he was because if Otis had parked in the short-term parking, he would have returned to the same airport and picked up his car.

Otis had booked a flight the previous night online and had his ticket on his cell phone. He did not have any luggage or handbag, so he was able to proceed without further delays to the TSA checkpoint.

After landing at the Essex County Airport, and passing the TSA security checkpoint, Otis walked directly towards the pilot lounge.

Otis knew that Zachary and Dan did not use commercial flights.

He wanted to talk to someone in the pilot lounge, an employee, or another frequent flyer using private helicopters or planes at the airport. The pilot lounge was where the pilots took a break from the noise and the humdrum of the airport. It was also the place where Otis expected to find some pilots taking a break, checking out, and amending their flight release paperwork before heading out to their planes.

Otis got lucky because when he approached the lounge, the door opened, and a cleaning woman came out and held the door open for him, he did not need a keycard to access the lounge. He entered the lounge and smelled fresh coffee. There were a couple of white, round tables with metal chairs and recliners to watch television. The windows were shaded. It was early morning, and the lounge should have had more pilots, but this time just two pilots were resting and watching the news. He walked toward them and asked, "Excuse me, but could I ask you a couple of questions?"

When they turned their attention towards him, the other pilot said shortly, "If you're a reporter, you're not supposed to be here. This is just for the employees and the pilots." He turned away and continued watching the news.

"I'm not a reporter. I work for the president of the United States," Otis replied and showed them the letter he had received from the White House. "You can call that number and confirm my identity." Otis knew that the president had instructed his secretary to answer questions regarding his position as an advisor and to ask anyone calling to assist Otis.

The other pilot assessed Otis from top to toe and finally decided, "I think I will do that." He picked up his cell phone, dialed the number, and asked, "Whom am I talking to?"

"The White House?" he asked. "I have a man here. He has a letter from the president..." He was interrupted and listened to what the other person said on the other end before saying, "Yes, ma'am. Thank you so much. Have a nice day." He hung up, looked at Otis, and said, "I guess you are who you said you were. They confirmed your identity and that you work for the president."

The pilot leaned forward and looked Otis directly in the eyes. "What do you want to know?" he asked courteously. The confirmation call had piqued his interest.

Otis asked, "Did you happen to be here three days ago?"

"Yes, I was here. I flew a couple of times a week here and back to Albany," one of the pilots replied. "That was the day when the helicopter crash happened, wasn't it?"

"Yes, that's why I ask," Otis considered what he should say for a moment. He could say he was investigating airport security due to the recent helicopter crash or tell the truth. Otis chose the latter. "The president is a friend of mine, and he just wants to know the details of that day when his son and son-in-law boarded the helicopter here. It is devastating to know something like that can happen, and he wants to ensure there was no foul play."

"I had just arrived with my plane. I saw two vehicles, a black SUV and a sedan arriving and parking in front of the helipad area over there." He pointed towards the windows showing the view of the airport. "I recognized the president's son and the son-in-law. I have seen their pictures in the newspapers and the news. I've seen them here maybe five times before this last one."

Otis thought he had gotten lucky because this pilot had recognized them and seemed to be a dependable witness.

The pilot hesitated before continuing. "After I got here, I glanced outside. And the SUV was still parked there, with two motorcycles parked behind it. I mean right behind it, like bumper to bike's tire. Then I saw three men walking out of the hangar. It looked as if two of them were half carrying the middleman to the car. Two other men came after them and rode away on motorcycles. The sedan left right after that."

"Did you see the helicopter take off?" Otis asked.

"Now that you mention it, I didn't."

"Could you recognize any of the guys?" Otis hoped that the pilot would because that would help his case.

"No, I don't think so. I just mostly paid attention to Harley-Davidson motorcycles and their drivers because they were not the usual sight here. They wore black leather outfits with helmets. I know it sounds crazy, but the helmets were original, with spikes and horns. The one guy mounting the motorcycle was wearing regular clothes. I mean, not black leather pants or anything like that. It looked like a business suit to me. I could not see his face because of the helmet."

Otis thanked him and took down his information just in case he needed it again. He said, "Thank you so much. I will tell Mr. President how helpful you were. I'm sure he will want to personally thank you."

The pilot beamed at him. "I'm glad I could help."

Otis had done what he had to do there. He was ready to go back. He got the contact information of both pilots just in case he needed to call them and ask more questions.

He headed back to the domestic flight's desk and checked for the next flight to Dulles. He saw it leaving in an hour. He used his phone to buy a ticket and then returned to the TSA security checkpoint to fly back to Washington, D.C.

53

The Werewolf

When Otis exited Dulles Airport, he noticed a motorcycle parked close to his car. He knew that each member of the Werewolves motorcycle gang had a different means of showing his love for their club with the imaginary designed helmets and airbrush-painted bike tanks. A fiery wolf with bloody teeth had been painted on this particular Harley-Davidson Heritage Softail motorcycle.

Werewolves! They are following me. I didn't notice him when I left. It seems that he stayed behind waiting for me to come back, Otis thought, frowning. The Russian motorcycle club had also come to this country with their bikes. *This paintwork was not done recently. It looks older and has some scrapes on the paint job,* Otis realized. It showed preplanning. He had not seen any member of the Werewolves gang at the Essex County Airport in Fairfield in New Jersey, so he assumed they didn't know what he had done there or where he had gone.

Otis got into his car, started it, and headed out of the airport parking lot. He glanced at his rearview mirror and adjusted it to see the row of cars behind his vehicle. He saw the driver of the motorcycle mount his bike and then drive after him. The driver wore a helmet shaped like an alien head from a sci-fi film.

That Werewolf is shadowing me, Otis thought when he saw the helmet. *If I can capture this driver, I could have a direct link to the kidnappers.*

Otis made a call with his burner phone, first to the president, and second, to Noah.

"Mr. President, can you arrange for a couple of your Secret Service guys to assist me with an arrest?" Otis asked.

"Sure. I can send a Secret Service team to meet you after George Washington Memorial Pkwy when you take the exit to E St NW to W Executive Ave NW," Andrew confirmed.

"Excellent!" Then Otis explained what had happened and who was following him, adding, "This guy might be our first lead to find the kidnappers."

Two Secret Service agents waited in an unmarked sedan by the roadside near the exit to W St NW. They charged toward the motorcycle when they saw Otis's vehicle and the motorcycle after him. They blocked the road behind the driver of the sedan, and Otis blocked the front of the road. It looked as if the Werewolf considered driving off the road through the remaining snow piles on the roadside, but then reconsidered it and turned off his engine. The Secret Service agents came out of their vehicle and apprehended the driver. They took him with them and left his motorcycle on the roadside. Otis followed them to the White House.

The president was waiting impatiently, pacing in the living room of his private quarters when they arrived as a precaution if someone inside the White House was working for Russians.

"Your Secret Service team has the guy who was following me. He knows something about this kidnapping. We need to question him immediately," Otis said when he greeted the president.

Andrew Burr turned to the two agents who had assisted in apprehending the motorcycle gang member and said, "What I'm about to tell you will not leave this room. Is this clear?"

The team leader said, "Yes, Sir."

"It involves my son. He is not dead. He has been kidnapped. This gang member who followed Otis here is part of the group who kidnapped my son. I want information from him." Andrew looked stern as he explained the facts.

The Secret Service team leader looked surprised, "Zachary is not dead?" It was more of a question than a statement.

"He's alive for now," Otis replied sternly. "I'm trying to find him before anything happens to him."

That was a good enough reason for the Secret Service to detain the driver. "Yes, Sir," the lead agent said, stone-faced, and escorted the motorcycle driver to a room where they could interview him.

Otis knew that the Secret Service agents could interrogate and arrest people without warrants if a person committed an offense or a crime against the United States or the First Family.

He informed the president of what he had learned so far at the airport.

"What happened to Dan?" Andrew Burr asked, frowning.

"I don't know. Maybe they took Dan through a different door or waited with him inside the hangar. Maybe this pilot did not see another car parked on the other side of the hangar," Otis replied. Missing Dan had bothered him, too. He had no answer to that puzzle yet.

"Eyewitnesses are not always so sure what they see. Maybe this pilot just missed Dan," Otis replied. "I'll contact Noah and ask him to check out the satellite aerial footage. Maybe we can find out something more."

"I think the FBI has done that, and they have not found anything," Andrew replied.

"They don't know that Zachary was taken before the crash. That makes a big difference," Otis said, dialing Noah's number. When he answered, Otis asked about the satellite images of the airport on the day of the helicopter crash.

"I'll just have to find the right satellite and the right time," Noah replied.

"Just focus on the time around noon to three p.m. I want some images – if you can find them – images of a black SUV leaving the helicopter area with two motorcycles. I want to know where they go, and in what direction. We know Zachary was in that SUV: Also, I want to know if any other vehicles left that place any time after that."

"Sure. Let me access that data right away. I'll call you when I have something for you."

"Thanks," Otis said and hung up.

After ten minutes, Noah called back. "I have sent the images to your phone and in your email."

Otis scrutinized the attachment on his phone sent by Noah. The visuals comprised aerial snapshots encompassing the airport, the helicopter hangar vicinity, and the surrounding roads, all captured during the pivotal moments of the kidnapping. Seeking a more detailed analysis, Otis requisitioned a laptop from the president's staff, transferring the images to a larger screen. The expanded view allowed him to zoom in, revealing the distinct features of the SUV, the sedan, and the motorcycles – conspicuously absent of any other vehicles.

With an investigative fervor, he meticulously examined the footage chronologically, from the instance when Dan and Zachary entered the hangar to the purported time of the crash. Oddly, there was no trace of any other vehicles exiting the hangar during that time frame. Puzzled, Otis pondered the whereabouts of Dan, a lingering question that added an extra layer of complexity to the unfolding mystery.

A suspicion formed in his mind: If Dan was not in the hangar at the airport, then he had to be one of the guys in the SUV, in the sedan, or driving the motorcycles. Otis remembered the pilot described that one biker wore a "normal outfit, not all black clothes."

Was Dan involved in the kidnapping? Maybe, if Dan was already the doppelganger, the switch had been made before the crash, Otis thought. That would make sense. The doppelganger looked exactly like Dan.

Otis asked, "Did you or Irene notice any changes in Dan's behavior before the crash?"

"Dan? He seemed to be a bit stressed. But normal, I guess," Andrew replied.

"Next time when you speak with the doppelganger at the hospital, can you ask what has happened to Dan?" Otis asked. "Tell the doppelganger that you want to speak with Dan."

"I will." Andrew agreed. He could not and would not forget his son-in-law. Inside, he felt a pang of guilt. He had not pushed the doppelganger to tell him about Dan...

54

At The White House

Otis and Andrew followed the Secret Service agents to the interrogation room. The Secret Service agents escorted the gang member behind the gate's security station, down a long stairwell, along a windowless, underground passage, and into an interrogation room: a grey cement-walled cell with a simple table, two metal chairs, hanging light with one light bulb. One of the agents had a briefcase with him with chemicals that would make the prisoner talk.

Otis had suggested using the truth serum to get the required information from the gang member, and thus, the Secret Service agent had taken the briefcase with him. However, the interrogation technique had not been decided yet.

One of the Secret Service agents pushed the gang member to sit on the chair and handcuffed his wrists to the chair. The other one made sure that the prisoner did not have a chance to attack and escape.

Otis and Andrew remained by the doorway. They leaned on the wall and watched the agents working.

One of the agents asked, "Do you want the video on or off?"

Otis looked at Andrew, who nodded and said, "We better videotape this one. We might need it for evidence later."

Otis whispered into his ear, "Are you sure? You know it might also incriminate you?"

"We better have it on tape. We can keep the tape. We don't have to leave it here," Andrew replied.

"How do you want to proceed?" one of the Secret Service agents asked. "Chemical interrogation will be faster." He pointed at the briefcase with the chemicals they could use. "We can also tire him by using normal interrogation techniques, Mr. President," he added, waiting for the reply.

"We don't have much time. We don't know when this guy needs to report back to his superior," Otis reminded the president, who nodded. "We don't have time to use any softer interrogation methods. Besides, a motorcycle gang member would not respond to a talk or physical threat or pain. They were tough criminals, and most gang members had spent time in Russian prisons."

Andrew considered his words, then commanded, "Let's try the truth serum."

Otis knew there were no real truth serums in the markets, but the sodium thiopental made the subject disoriented and loosened his tongue. It would be best to use it now because they had no time to waste. A downside of this serum was that the subject usually had warm feelings towards the interrogators. Thus, they did not see any reason to lie, and they might even want to please the interrogators by telling what they wanted to know.

Otis was sure the Werewolves were given orders to report back to Dentist, their leader. They needed answers before the other Werewolves noticed that one of them was missing. He did not know how often the members reported back.

The Secret Service agent opened the briefcase he had brought with him. It contained a syringe and a bottle of liquid truth serum. He inserted the syringe into the bottle and filled it one-quarter full of liquid. He tapped the syringe so there were no air bubbles, then jammed the needle in the gang member's arm and squeezed the plunger. He pushed the plunger to the bottom, exerting pressure on the fluid to exit the nozzle and sending the liquid to its destination. The prisoner flexed his muscles as if trying to break free, but he could not get off the chair where he was handcuffed. When the liquid entered the gang member's vein, the agent closed the syringe back in his briefcase. He would dispose of the syringe later.

"Now, we'll just have to wait," the agent said, turning to face Otis and the president. This was a highly unlikely task for the Secret Service, but because the president had asked and his son was kidnapped by this prisoner and his group, they were ready to do this.

"For how long?" Andrew asked.

"Fifteen minutes, I guess," the agent replied and leaned against the wall beside the other agent and watched the gang member.

After ten minutes, the prisoner's head started lulling, he started giggling, and his eyelids were drooping. The agents looked at each other and nodded. The prisoner was ready.

The agents approached the gang member, slapped his cheeks gently, and asked, "Are you awake?"

"What's your name?"

"Alien," the gang member replied.

"That's not a name," the other agent replied.

"It's my gang's name. I'm a soldier. I'm a member of the Werewolves. Everybody calls me Alien."

When the interrogation continued, the gang member revealed some new information.

Alien said that some Russian oligarchs were part of the kidnapping plot. He did not know their names, just code names: Hydra, Basilisk, Hippogriff, and Phoenix. He was not sure if there were more participants. Those were just the names he knew. "The group called themselves the Septem group," Alien said groggily.

"The Septem group?" Otis repeated. He had learned Latin enough to know the numbers; Septem meant seven. Did this group have seven members? They knew only of five: those Alien had just mentioned and then Dentist, his gang leader.

"Yes, the Septem group," Alien confirmed. "The operation is called Pobeda." Alien's head lolled against his chest; his eyes were half closed.

"Pobeda, meaning the victory?" Otis asked. He knew enough Russian after having worked there for several years.

"Yes, victory," Alien replied.

He also told them their gang leader, Ivan Komar, the infamous Dentist, was in the United States. Otis already knew that.

"Who are the other two members of the group?" Otis asked. "You only mentioned five members of Septem."

"I don't know," Alien replied groggily.

"How did all of you enter this country?" Otis asked.

"We had diplomat passports. All our weapons came with the diplomat post," Alien said.

Of course, Otis thought. That made sense. Nobody would check the diplomat's luggage. Easy way to transport guns here. Then he realized that they were interrogating a Russian diplomat. He wondered if the president and the Secret Service agents realized that.

Andrew pulled Otis away from the prisoner and whispered, "The diplomatic passports! That means that the Russian government is behind this." Andrew had balled his hands into fists. He looked ready to punch somebody.

"Not just the Russian government. The oligarchs and the Werewolves allied in this plot with the Russian government. They are all involved in this kidnapping," Otis said.

"Yes, you're right. They would not all do what the president and the government want," Andrew said. He opened his fists and stretched his fingers open. He was calming down.

"I wonder if they have other demands than lifting the travel bans and undoing the economic sanctions. I can understand that their businesses have taken a hit since the economic sanctions started and when we froze their assets, but this is quite an elaborate plan: to blackmail the president of the United States and kidnap his son," Otis said quietly to Andrew.

"I'm sure the doppelganger will let us know soon," Andrew replied grimly. "Why did they use the Werewolves? Why are these criminals involved?"

"They are just hired guns, I think. They are in this plot for the money, if I guessed right," Otis replied, although he couldn't be sure of it. Dentist, the leader of the gang, had enough money and connections. He might be in for other reasons.

"I can ask the Secret Service to keep this gang member here for at least 72 hours. These agents already knew from the FBI that something was planned against me and my son. They will not argue against it. I need to inform the FBI, too," Andrew said.

"Give me some time to find Zachary first. Don't call the FBI yet." Otis replied. He was worried that if they contacted the FBI now, Zachary would end up dead. Besides, the FBI would not want to hear that they had interrogated someone with diplomatic status.

After the interrogation ended, the biker was left in the cell the Secret Service provided for their prisoner. Otis walked back to the private quarters with the president.

"He did not have the location of your son. He has not seen the place where they keep him. Otherwise, he would have told us," Otis commented on the results of the interrogation.

"We don't have much time. The United Nations General Assembly will be tomorrow," the president replied. He sounded defeated.

"I know. I must check the aerial views to see if I can find out anything else," Otis replied, consoling.

"I need to inform the U.S. Ambassador of my plans to revoke the sanctions. I cannot just let her hear the news without telling her the reason. Also, I must tell the Secretary of State," Andrew said, and his shoulders slumped as if the weight of the world was heavy on his shoulders.

"I know. It will be difficult to explain this," Otis replied.

"The United States has always been against terrorism. We have refused to pay the ransom and submit to terrorists' demands. Now I'm going to do exactly that!" Andrew shook his head in disbelief.

"Other presidents have secretly given up to terrorism and paid their ransom. Obama did so," Otis reminded him.

"I know," Andrew replied. "I'm concerned about their additional demands. I have no idea what they could be. I'm just worried that they will continue asking all kinds of favors from me as long as they have Zachary and Dan."

"Don't worry. We will get Zachary and Dan back," Otis assured. He sighed as he had no idea if his words were true. No one had heard from Dan since the crash. The doppelganger at the hospital would be the only one who knew where the real Dan was.

55

Septem

Dentist had planned to have a quiet lunch in a private room at Restaurant Nevskij. He had ordered his men to report every other hour. One of them, Alien, was late with his reports. He had last reported at Dulles airport to inform that Otis had flown back and had taken his car. Alien said he was tailing Otis, and that was the last time anyone had heard of him.

Alien is either dead or captured, Dentist thought. He looked grim as he balled his hands into fists and hit the table before him.

He had to inform the leader of the Septem group. A call to Hydra was not something he was looking forward to.

He didn't want to tell him they might have lost one man or failed following Otis. He pulled out the tablet he carried and started a video call.

Hydra answered almost immediately. He knew something was wrong when Dentist called without a previously agreed appointment time.

"What is it?" Hydra asked. His eyes were icy.

No small talk, Dentist thought. *Directly to the business. Keep the calls short.*

Dentist explained what had happened and offered his explanations for why Alien had not reported back. There were not many solutions, and he had considered all of them. So, he said, "Otis could have spotted Alien and confronted him. That could mean that Alien is either dead or captured. There's no other reason why he would not call and report."

Hydra's face stayed emotionless; only his eyes flickered with anger.

"Do you think he will talk if he is captured?" Hydra asked, keeping his voice calm.

"No, not even with violence," Dentist assured.

"But the Americans can use the truth serum." Hydra countered. "We can't let that happen."

"I realize that," Dentist replied. He had accepted the fact that one of his men was lost in this operation.

"I will contact Nachtkrapp. He needs to take action. The police didn't arrest Alien, so he is not in jail. He must be somewhere else. Most likely in some place where the president and Otis have access," Hydra said, ending the call.

Nachtkrapp had just returned home from the White House when he heard the tablet in his briefcase beeping announcing an incoming call. *No one usually called to it this time*, he thought. He left his jacket on the sofa in the living room and rushed to sit down. He opened his briefcase, put his tablet on the table, and opened it. A call from Hydra!

The Septem group agreed to contact only in emergency situations between the Nevskij meetings, he thought. *Something is wrong.*

Nachtkrapp answered the call without the video, "Please, wait." He opened his briefcase, took out his il dottore -bird mask, and put it on before turning on the video camera.

"What is it?" he asked Hydra. Nachtkrapp's voice sounded unnatural because of the voice-altering app he used on his tablet.

"We have an urgent task for you," Hydra started.

This is not good, Nachtkrapp thought. "What is it?"

"Alien, one of the Werewolves, is missing. He followed Otis Thorne to the airport and waited for him there. When Otis returned, Alien reportedly followed him from the airport. No one has heard from him since," Hydra explained.

"And you expect he is either killed or caught. What do you want me to do?" Nachtkrapp asked.

"You will have to check the White House quarters where the Secret Service has their lock-up cells. He might be there. He cannot be in police custody because the president does not want anyone to know his son has been kidnapped. We can't allow him to talk. He could reveal some details of our group and this operation. He can identify Dentist and maybe a couple more of our group members," Hydra explained.

Nachtkrapp paled under his mask. "I'm not a killer." When he joined this group, he had never assumed he would have to kill anyone.

"You might have to become one," Hydra replied coldly. "Our group is more important than a life of a gang member."

"I can understand that," Nachtkrapp replied bitterly. "But why can't I just try to free him if he is being held there?"

"You would expose yourself. We can't afford that," Hydra replied and added, "There are cameras everywhere. It's the White House. You know that as well as I do. It would be impossible to free him without getting caught on the video."

"What can I do? I can't shoot him in the cell if they have surveillance cameras. That would expose me too!" Nachtkrapp sounded desperate.

"You will use poison," Hydra replied calmly. "I have something for you that will work: nicotine," Hydra added.

"Nicotine? Will it kill him?" Nachtkrapp asked.

"Yes, high amounts of nicotine will kill. I'll send you enough to kill five people. It will kill Alien if you find him and if he is imprisoned at the White House."

"Okay, but how can I get it to him?"

"The food at Restaurant Nevskij is praised for being the best in town. Nobody will question you if you order takeaway dinner from their kitchen. The poison will be hidden in the food delivery container," Hydra explained.

"What if I can't find Alien?" Nachtkrapp asked, secretly hoping that would be true.

"Then we have to assume he is dead, or Otis Thorne has taken him and hidden him somewhere else," Hydra replied.

"Okay, I will contact you when I know more," Nachtkrapp said, ending the video call. He took off his il dottore mask and placed it on the table with the tablet. He usually kept the mask and the tablet with him 24/7. He did not want to miss any calls from the Septem group relating to Operation Pobeda. He got up and paced impatiently in his living room.

How can I take someone's life? I've never killed anyone! I hope that nicotine is as effective as Hydra promised because it will ruin my life if I'm caught, he thought.

56

Nachtkrapp

Nachtkrapp had not been able to sleep and had tossed and turned all night. He received the dinner from Restaurant Nevskij later that same evening. With the extra ingredient from Hydra, he guessed as he glanced inside the bag. There was a dinner, but also an extra package containing the deadly poison capsule.

Nachtkrapp, the White House's mole, went to work as usual. He started his day normally, greeting everyone in the hallway and chatting with the secretaries while picking up his first cup of coffee of the day. When he returned to his office, he closed the door behind him. He tried to remember the route to the Secret Service holding area where they kept the arrested persons. He had only seen it once when he was on a tour around the White House. He did not remember much about it except that there were always a couple of Secret Service agents guarding the area if there were prisoners.

He was sure the president would not have involved the whole Secret Service in this. Only a couple of agents were aware of the kidnapping of Andrew's son, he believed. Probably the ones closest to the president.

Nachtkrapp picked up his phone and called the desk, asking, "Hello, I might have lost my credit card yesterday at my meeting with the president. Do you know which agents were in his detail yesterday evening? I would like to know if they have found my card."

He listened to what the desk replied. "Thank you. Do you know if they are on duty today and where to find them?" He waited for the answer, and when he got it, he thanked the desk and ended the call.

The two agents were on duty today. They were assigned to a special task by the president yesterday. The desk had said they were in the interrogation room beneath the White House. He knew where it was, but the agents would be suspicious if he went there without a plan.

He took a sip of the coffee mug on his table and formed an idea in his head. Nicotine was odorless and tasteless poison. He could pour the poison into the coffee thermos and take it to the interrogation area.

He went to the kitchen and filled in a thermos with hot coffee. He took the thermos and some plastic cups with him and headed towards the underground tunnel leading to the interrogation room. He knew the cameras were not monitoring the narrow passage to the interrogation. He would be safe if he did not go inside the interrogation room.

His pulse jumped when he got closer to the area where he believed the agents were. His mouth felt dry. He swallowed. He had to calm down and not look suspicious. He took a few deep breaths before approaching the holding area, where he saw the two agents sitting in front of the interrogation room. They looked up when he approached.

"I just brought you some coffee. The president said you would be here. I know about the prisoner," the mole said. He was a familiar face in the White House and belonged to the president's closest circle. The agents did not even suspect him to be an enemy.

"Oh, thanks. The coffee is needed. We've been up all night," one of the agents said and held out his cup.

The mole poured some coffee into his cup and then into the other agent's cup too.

"Should I also give some coffee to the prisoner? He needs something to drink, I assume."

"Sure, let's get a cup, and I will give it to him," the other agent replied, getting up from his chair. He waited for the mole to pour some coffee into a plastic cup, then took it from him. He opened the heavy metal door and went inside with the cup. The mole heard the agent say, "Here's some coffee for you. Hope you like it."

The agent exited the cell and returned to the table.

The mole smiled and was ready to go. "I will leave you this coffee and cups. Have a nice day."

The mole planned to return after an hour to collect the coffee thermos. He had to get it back because it might have his fingerprints.

An hour went by excruciatingly slowly. The mole kept looking at his watch, and it was going as slow as a snail.

When the mole walked back to the interrogation room, he saw the two agents had fallen from their seats to the floor, curled up and unmoving. He checked their pulse.

No pulse. *They drank enough coffee laced with nicotine and died,* he thought, pleased.

He stepped by the interrogation room's door and looked inside through a peephole.

The prisoner was Alien, the missing Werewolf gang member. He had fallen off the bed to the floor. *Dead too,* the mole thought. His task was done. He had succeeded.

He turned towards the table and picked up the coffee thermos and the used coffee cups with him. He did not have to take the last cup from the interrogation room because he had not left any fingerprints on that cup. After all, the dead agent had taken it to the prisoner.

He had been worried that just one cup of coffee wouldn't be enough to kill Alien, but maybe the agents had given him another cup later. The poison would not have killed immediately. *They probably had headaches and nausea first,* he thought. If they drank some more coffee, they would have gotten more severe symptoms and died soon after that.

He made sure no one saw him exiting the underground passage and hurried back to the kitchen, rinsed the coffee thermos, and threw away the plastic cups.

He returned to his room, took out his tablet, and made a video call to Hydra. He blocked his image so Hydra would not see his face and used the voice-altering program to make his voice unrecognizable.

When Hydra answered, he said shortly, "It's done," and ended the call immediately. He didn't want to talk with the members of the Septem group longer than needed. He knew all the calls were monitored. He hoped his laptop was not, but if it was, then the shorter call was better.

When the call was done, Nachtkrapp noticed that he was sweating. He had been nervous about doing what he had been asked to do but kept calm and got it done. He looked down at his hands, which were shaking. He pressed them against the tabletop to calm them down and took a few deep breaths to steady his nerves. Next, he sat with his eyes closed for a few more minutes. When he thought he was back to normal, he stood up, walked to his closet, picked up a clean shirt, and tossed his old one in the closet. After changing the shirt, he felt refreshed. He had to look impeccable for the rest of the day. *Time to start the daily tasks*, he thought as he sat down by his desk again.

57

Otis and Andrew

The President of the United States received a call later that same afternoon.

"Mr. President," the caller was the Head of Security at the White House, "we have some bad news. Two Secret Service agents and the prisoner in the interrogation area are dead."

"How did it happen?" Andrew Burr was shocked. How could anyone get inside the White House and kill two agents and the prisoner?

"The two agents did not return to their post after their scheduled task. We started looking for them and found them lying on the floor dead in front of the cell down there," the Head of Security replied.

"What was the cause of death?" Andrew Burr asked. This was bad news!

"We can't be sure. It seems like they ingested some poison. There were no external marks, no violence. We didn't find any clues about how the poison was delivered to them. We'll have to wait for the autopsy to find out what killed them," the Head of Security replied. "This is, of course, our priority. If there is a lethal poison in the building, we have to find out how it got here and ensure you and your family are not at any risk," he added.

"Keep me in the loop. " I want to know who did this and how," Andrew said, ending the call.

He called Otis and left him a message about the deaths.

Otis was at class, but he listened to his messages when he returned to his office.

Otis cursed when he heard the news of the killed prisoner. He was sure there would be no trace or videos of who had caused the death of the gang member. *This secret group is efficient and lethal,* he thought. *These kidnappers are not ordinary kidnappers. They planned this high-level kidnapping and blackmail for a long time. They had someone inside the White House, a mole, to make sure they would know what was going on there. This last incident just proved it,* Otis thought.

One more thing had bothered him. When he visited the airport, the security was tight like in other national airports. He knew that the security checks had leaks, and quite a lot of hidden guns and explosives could go through the TSA checkpoints according to the blind tests conducted by the U.S. government. But still, he could not believe that no airport security personnel had not witnessed the kidnapping at the helipad area.

He picked up his phone and called Noah. "Noah, can you check who of the security personnel on duty at the Essex County Airport the day of the crash? Was there anything unusual?"

"Sure, let me check," Noah replied. Otis could almost imagine Noah hunching over the keyboard, his fingers flying over the keys, typing commands, and finding answers. It took less than a minute for Noah to come back with a response.

"It seems that one employee, Derek Smith, was in an accident that morning. He was hospitalized with broken bones, but his name was on the list of workers that day. Also, another worker called in sick. Jack Brewer. He was later found dead at home with his whole family. The police report suspected a robbery gone bad."

"Derek was in the hospital but also working the same day," Otis repeated. "That's not possible."

"Someone else was there instead of him assisting in the kidnapping," Noah concluded.

"Yeah, that's how they did it," Otis said in deep thought. This had just confirmed his previous concerns. This was a well-planned operation. These kidnappers did not hesitate. They were ready to kill for their cause. The slaughter of the whole Brewster family just proved it. "Thanks, Noah," Otis said and hung up.

58

The Casino Kidnapping

E stelle had decided to visit the spa first, then try a couple of slot machines before going to roulette and blackjack tables. The casino's slot machine area was busy that day. She was feeling lonely and wished she had someone to talk to. She considered calling Otis but decided not to.

Otis might be busy with the case, she thought.

She sat down to play with the slot machines; the seat next to her was empty. It did not take long before somebody came there. When the waitress came around and asked if she could bring anything, Estelle turned to give her order and was interrupted by a man's voice, "Yes, please, I would like to have a martini." His voice was rough with a slight foreign accent. Estelle turned to see who had interrupted her and saw a man around her age sitting beside her.

"Pardon, I must apologize. Ladies first," the gentleman said, gesturing for the waitress to take Estelle's order and flashing an irresistibly flirty smile at Estelle.

Estelle smiled coyly, batting her eyelashes. The man had light gray eyes, a neat, perfectly trimmed goatee, a bit of grey in his hair, and an impeccable coal-gray three-piece suit, which looked expensive. The pleats on his pants were razor-sharp.

A wealthy gentleman. Estelle assessed the man sitting next to her and told the waitress, "I'll have just a glass of sparkling water, thank you."

The waitress disappeared with their orders.

Estelle glanced at the man next to her. He still stared at her with a smile.

The man said, "I'll have to apologize again. I was rude to interrupt you and order before you. I just get so immersed in the game. I know it is not an excuse."

"That's all right," Estelle replied, turning on her seat and facing the slot machine again. She had not realized the man was not done with her until she heard his voice again: "I insist that you'll let me buy you dinner tonight." And when Estelle glanced at him, surprised, the man added, "Unless you have some other plans..." His cool gray eyes looked directly at Estelle, waiting for an answer.

"No, I don't. I would like to dine with you," Estelle replied, smiling.

"Is seven o'clock good?" the man asked.

"Yes, that's fine," Estelle replied.

"I will meet you in the lobby."

The man's phone rang, and he excused himself and walked away.

Estelle played the slot machine for a while, waiting for him to return, but he did not.

He must have received an important business call, Estelle thought. She realized she did not even know his name, and she hadn't told him her name either.

She got bored playing with the slots and went back to her room. She hoped he wouldn't cancel the dinner date. She had no idea she had met one of the oligarchs responsible for kidnapping the president's son.

Estelle had all afternoon to get ready for her date. She picked a few outfits and tried them on, but she did not like any of them, so she decided to go downstairs and check out the clothing stores. Estelle wanted to look irresistible tonight. An hour later, she returned to her room with shopping bags. She knew she had overdone it, but there had been several dresses she liked, and because she couldn't decide which was the best, she picked up two of them. Estelle also bought gorgeous high-heeled shoes in the same store, and when she headed out of the dress store, she noticed a haute couture bag store with a sale going on. After taking a shower, Estelle tried the new dresses again. She had picked a red and black one. She chose the black dress with tiny sparkles on the hem and neck for dinner. It had three-quarter-length sleeves and ruffles on the wrists.

Estelle took the elevator downstairs at seven p.m. When the elevator door slid open, she saw the man from the slot machine waiting for her in the lobby. She smiled and walked toward him.

"Good evening," she greeted him.

The man reached for her hand, kissed it, and held her hand in his when he said, "Good evening. I must be lucky because I have found the most beautiful woman to dine with me tonight."

The touch of this man's lips on Estelle's hand made her tingle all over.

"Thank you." Estelle blushed. "I don't even know your name," she added.

"My name is Sergei," the handsome stranger replied.

He is not Stan. Just a kiss on a hand, just a dinner, she reassured herself.

"Sergei," Estelle said adoringly. A Slavic name. A romantic name, she thought. "My name is Estelle. Nice to meet you." She fluttered her eyelashes at him and gave him a flirtatious smile.

Estelle looked up, and her eyes rested on him. He moved a little bit closer, not letting her pull her hand away. She could feel the tension in her body, the rapid heartbeat, her shortened breathing, and she thought, *Why not take this one chance, however dangerous, stupid, and unwise?* Estelle knew her son would not approve of her meeting someone like this again, not when he had just placed her here to be safe.

Sergei offered her his arm, and they walked toward the restaurant. They had a nice dinner and seemed to find topics to discuss without any awkward silence. Sergei ordered them venison and vegetables and the tomato-mozzarella bites and gorgonzola crescents for appetizers. The red wine was, of course, the most expensive one the restaurant had to offer. Estelle was pleased, and when the dessert came, a rustic black cherry tart with a dessert liquor, she was swooning over this new man in her life. *A wealthy man with good taste,* she thought. *Perfect for me!*

After dinner, when they took the elevator up, Sergei slid his hand behind Estelle's back. Estelle felt the warmth of his hand on her lower back and turned toward him. Her back was to the elevator door as the elevator stopped, and she heard the elevator door slide open. Two Werewolves entered. First, Estelle didn't see who had come in, but then she turned her head a bit to view the new guests and frowned as the two men didn't look like anyone she had seen at the casino. Estelle didn't have time to react. She felt someone press a chloroform handkerchief over her mouth, and she passed out.

Sergei, who was Basilisk of the Septem group, was fast in his moves and pressed the elevator to stop, then the P-button to descend to the parking level.

Estelle was unconscious, and the two Werewolves held her up between them. They supported her by the waist dragging her between them to the dark sedan waiting in the parking hall and placed her in the back seat with one of the Werewolves.

Basilisk went to sit in the front beside the other Werewolf, and they drove away. They did not hurry because they did not want to alert anyone. They were just like any normal guests leaving the parking lot.

"Did you leave the message to Otis Thorne?" Basilisk asked his driver, the Werewolf called Warboy. Like the other soldiers of the gang, his name was stitched in front of his vest with his rank, the lieutenant.

Warboy nodded and replied, "Yes, Goosebump is delivering the message to his campus residence as we speak." Goosebump, one of the gang members, was known for being one of the most psychotic and uncontrollable members of the Werewolves. He joked that he liked to give other people goosebumps, and that's how he had received his nickname.

Basilisk had asked more seasoned gang members to assist in Estelle's second kidnapping and requested a thorough briefing of who they were and their names. He liked to know with whom he was dealing. Basilisk had read how he had gotten his nickname. Warboy had fought in the war in Ukraine.

They decided to take Estelle to the same place they were keeping Zachary.

Basilisk wanted to be sure that Otis could not follow them.

"We need to check if this woman has a surveillance device before we get closer to the hideout," Basilisk suggested to the Werewolf member, Crusher, who sat in the back seat with Estelle.

Crusher nodded, grabbed her purse, opened it, and ransacked it.

"Here it is." He showed a tiny GPS locator and a microchip.

"Crush it and throw it out," Basilisk ordered, and the Werewolf rolled down the window, bent the small device between his forefinger and his thumb, broke it into two pieces threw the pieces out on the road, and rolled the window back up.

"Done," Crusher replied.

59

Otis

When Otis left the White House, he tried to call his mother's cell phone.

He let the phone ring for a long time.

No answer.

He tried again.

Still no answer.

He frowned. He had made sure his mother knew how important it was to answer when he called. She knew the dangers after Stan.

She might be playing cards and didn't hear the phone ringing or did not want to be interrupted in the middle of the game, he thought. However, he couldn't shake off the bad feeling he had.

Next, Otis contacted the hotel's reception, and when they answered, he asked, "Can you please call Mrs. Estelle Thorne's room?"

Estelle's room number didn't answer either.

A worry line deepened on Otis's forehead. Something was wrong. His mother wasn't in her room and wasn't answering her cell phone. Otis tried to convince himself she was shopping or playing slots, but he had a gut feeling something was terribly wrong.

She could be in the spa. She likes all kinds of mud treatments, facial masks, and massages, Otis thought. He tried to call the hotel's spa area to see if she had a reservation, but the hotel replied that she was not there. *She could be gambling in a casino. She would not hear her phone ringing with the slot machine's noise.* It was just a hopeful thought.

Otis went to his computer and checked her GPS tracker. Since his spy years, he had ensured his mother always had a GPS wherever she went. Estelle had one in her purse and one on her watch. Otis had made sure she had two because he knew how lethally serious these kidnappers were. The previous kidnapping attempt by Estelle's ex-boyfriend Stan had proven it.

This time Estelle's watch GPS showed she was in the hotel room, but Otis knew she wasn't there because she hadn't answered the phone. The purse's GPS showed his mother was moving away from the casino. Otis felt the hairs on his arm stand up. *She was supposed to stay at the casino until the kidnapping case was resolved,* he thought. Otis watched the GPS. He wanted to find out where she was heading, but the GPS dot disappeared from the screen after a short while. A lost signal! His mother would not know how to disable the GPS tracking unless it was an accident. And she certainly would not throw it away. He was now sure someone had taken his mother away from the hotel.

It must be the same group again. They must have searched her and destroyed the device, Otis thought.

Otis checked the location where the GPS signal had gotten lost: Arlington, VA. It was not far from the restaurant where the covert Russian meetings happened. He drove towards King Street and saw that Restaurant Nevskij was still open. It closed at midnight. Otis drove around the corner and saw the back alley where the delivery vans were parked. He felt his heart beat faster when he saw two motorcycles and a black sedan parked there. *This has to be the place where they brought my mother!*

Otis called Noah and asked, "Can you run these license plates for me?" He quickly read the three license plates to Noah.

He heard Noah's keyboard clicking when he typed fast, and then Noah said, "They are rentals, all three of them, and they belong to Blackline Limousine Rental Company owned by Maksim Liskin."

"Liskin is dead. Someone else is behind his business deals. I would guess it is one of the six guys who met at the restaurant," Otis concluded. He ended the call and decided to wait and see if the motorcycle drivers would lead him to the kidnappers' hideout. While waiting in the car, Otis reviewed the satellite aerial footage of the day of the crash that Noah had provided him. He saw the motorcycles going towards downtown Arlington. After a while, there was too much traffic, and it was difficult to follow them. He ran a hand through his hair. *It's possible the Septem group keeps their victims in this restaurant,* he thought.

60

Following the Kidnappers

O tis waited for two hours before the motorcycle drivers returned. The other driver had a porcupine-looking helmet, and the other had a helmet featuring a bull's skull with horns. They stood by their motorcycles, smoking, and talking, obviously waiting for the driver of the black sedan to join them. Otis could not see their faces to recognize if they were the same as in the airport arrival pictures Noah had sent him.

When the driver of the black sedan passed him and walked towards his vehicle, he saw his profile.

He could be one of the men in the secret meeting, Otis thought, but he could not be sure.

The cold wind forced the guy to pull up his scarf and his collar, and thus Otis did not have a clear view of his face. The driver of the sedan went to his vehicle and started it. The motorcycle drivers waited for the sedan to lead the way. When the motorcycles and the sedan passed Otis, he started his car and drove after them. He did not want them to notice him, so he tried to stay two cars behind the sedan as they headed to I-395 N. After twenty minutes of driving and tailing the sedan and the motorcycles, Otis called Noah and asked him to track down his location.

"Can you track me? I'm on I-395 N following two of the motorcycles."

"Sure," Noah replied. Otis heard a few clicks. "Just a minute. There, I have an overview of the traffic. I see the two motorcycles and your car a little bit behind them."

"How do you do that?"

"Easy. I have a GPS tracker on your phone," Noah said, chuckling.

"Thanks, pal," Otis said.

He had no idea Noah had a tracker on him. He guessed Noah had done it right after their first meeting. It would make sense. Noah was the genius considering the obvious and not-so-obvious problems ahead. He would have figured out the need for the GPS tracker.

"They are heading towards the center," Noah said, following the small dot on the map representing Otis's car.

"I hope they will lead me to where they keep my mother and Zachary," Otis said.

"Keep your phone line on in case you lose them and need directions," Noah replied.

The motorcycle drivers must have spotted their tail and decided to get rid of it because when they passed the Smithsonian buildings, they suddenly speeded up, drove on the sidewalk, and went on. Otis could not follow them.

"I lost them. They must have either seen me, or they are being careful," Otis reported back to Noah and parked in the nearest parking lot near the Smithsonian. He was disappointed because he had not been able to follow them, but he kept his emotions intact and voice calm.

"I can try to get something from the traffic cameras, but it will take some time. Two motorcycles are not that uncommon in the evening. It might be hard to follow them."

"Noah, can you check if the Russians own other buildings in this area? "

"Sure. Just give me a minute." Otis heard the tapping sound of the keyboard, and in half a minute, Noah was back. "Yes, the Russians own several properties in Washington, D.C., including hotels, restaurants, office buildings, and construction sites. Do you want all the Russian-owned buildings, or do you want to limit them to just these participants? The list is shorter if we stick to the buildings and businesses owned by these meeting participants, but we can't be sure if they are the only ones. There could be more Russians involved in the kidnapping."

Otis considered what to do next. "Let's check the buildings and businesses owned by the meeting participants. They want a tight circle of trust in this kind of a high-level operation."

"Okay. I can send them to you right now," Noah replied, adding, "You can view the list on your phone."

"Thanks, Noah. I'll contact you when I have something else."

Otis was sure he could not go through all the places by himself. He would need some help. Whom could he trust? No one was in the White House because he was sure there was a mole.

61

Otis

After the futile chase, Otis returned to his apartment. He parked in his normal slot in front of the apartment building where both he and Deena lived. He didn't see any light on Deena's, so he thought she must still be working. He felt a bit disappointed because he had wanted to talk to her.

He checked his mailbox and found a brown envelope with just his name written on top of it. He pulled out a handkerchief from his pocket and used it to hold the envelope in his left hand. He did not want to leave any more fingerprints on the envelope. He carried it inside and placed it on his desk while he got a pair of gloves. He opened the envelope carefully. Inside the envelope were a picture of his mother and a handwritten note stating the following:

"We have your mother.

Stop interfering with our business!

She will be okay if the president will do as we've asked."

Otis clenched his jaws as he re-read the message, trying to find any clues in the wording or the sentences. Nothing!

The note was probably too short for any kind of analysis, but he could take it to Noah. Maybe Noah could discover something about the note, ink, and the writer. Also, the envelope or the note might have some fingerprints.

He called Noah, and when he answered, Otis said, "Noah, I just got a note saying my mother has been kidnapped. I will bring you the note, envelope, and picture. Maybe we can find out where they are keeping he r."

"Okay, I'll wait for you," Noah replied.

Otis left immediately and took the envelope with its content with him. He walked briskly to his car and drove away from the parking lot. While driving, he kept checking the rearview mirror making sure no one was following him to Noah. He didn't want his friend to be compromised. He didn't see any motorcycles behind him, so after circling a bit, he took a direct route to Noah's house. When he got there, he parked in front of it. He didn't have to ring a doorbell or anything because Noah and his robodog Elmo were outside waiting for him.

Otis pulled out the note and the envelope from his pocket. "Here it is. This was left in my mailbox while I was gone."

"Let me get some gloves on," Noah replied. He let Otis in and closed the door behind them. He walked towards a desk in the hallway, opened the top drawer, and pulled out a pair of thin cotton gloves from a box. "Okay, let me have them now."

Otis handed him the note and the envelope.

Noah took the envelope first and handed it to Elmo. "Sniff."

Elmo did as he was told and sniffed the envelope.

"What are you doing?" Otis asked, puzzled. He'd never seen a robodog in action before. He had no idea what this robot could do.

"Elmo has an electronic nose that gives him the ability to smell. It's more accurate than what humans have. It mimics the level of the real dogs and bees." Noah turned the envelope around and let Elmo sniff the envelope on the other side. "Elmo's olfactory system uses chemical sensors to function as nostrils. He is like a real dog with a nose and a sense of smell." Elmo looked ready and turned his head towards the computers.

"What is he doing now?" Otis asked curiously.

"He is transmitting the data via wireless network to my computer. The computer analyses the data and the source of the scent if there is any," Noah explained.

Otis looked impressed.

"Let me do the same with the letter," Noah said, carefully pulling out the letter and holding it in front of Elmo's nose. He waited half a minute and turned the letter around, so Elmo could also have a better sniff of the other side of the paper.

"Let's go and see if Elmo picked up anything," Noah said. He took the letter and the envelope to his computer desk. He sat by his desk, inserted the letter in a scanner, and scanned it into his computer.

"I want to see if I can analyze the handwriting, too," he explained.

Otis sat beside him and waited patiently.

He saw some charts and numbers flashing on the screen, color charts, and spikes in charts indicating levels of ingredients in the analyzed material.

"What do you have there?" Otis asked, trying to read the charts.

"Most of the data is what you would find in any paper and envelope analyzed. However, here, see this one?" Noah pointed out one spike in the chart and explained, "This indicates a scent of garlic. The next one is the scent of rutabaga, and the next one is beetroot. Most of these scent spikes are food. The last one here," he pointed at one of the spikes and said, "This is a fungus, normal to basements or cellars, usually found in older brick buildings."

"The letter and the envelope were held or written in the basement of a restaurant. Is that what you're saying?" Otis asked.

"Yes, it looks like it. We should look for an older building with a cellar or basement. The scents of food can travel from floor to floor. It would explain the different scents," Noah replied.

"That would help narrow down the search area," Otis said. "Good. We can start with the Russian-owned older buildings and buildings converted to restaurants."

"Let me update your list limiting the buildings to restaurants and older buildings," Noah said, tapping his keyboard and sending a file to Otis's cell phone.

"Let's look at the letter," Noah said more to himself than to Otis. "I want to compare the handwriting to the known sources of handwritten notes by Russian oligarchs and criminals. Maybe we will get a hit."

"And looks like we did," Otis said when he saw a 95% match appearing on the screen.

"Let's see who," Noah said and tapped the keyboard.

"One of the guys in the meeting, Dentist."

"The leader of the Werewolves," Otis muttered. This just confirmed that Estelle and Zachary were held hostage by the same kidnappers.

"Thank you, Noah, again," Otis said, patting his friend on the shoulder.

Otis said, "I'll go to the casino tomorrow morning to see if I can get any surveillance pictures of who and how they kidnapped my mother. The casino was supposed to be a well-guarded place. I'll come here after that. You'll have better tools to analyze the surveillance pics if I can get them."

"Okay, I'll wait for the videos." Noah walked him to the door and watched him get in his car and drive away.

The evening had turned chilly. Otis turned the heat on to the maximum while heading towards Georgetown to his residence. Otis drove home thinking about what his next tasks would be tomorrow morning. He considered calling the president tonight and letting him know about the new twist in the case but decided it could wait. He would have more information after visiting the casino tomorrow morning.

62

At the Casino

It was a chilly morning, and Otis was shivering when he started his car and headed to the casino. The night temperatures were low, but it was already warmer during the daytime as the days got longer in the spring.

The tall, twenty-three-floor casino-hotel building was easy to spot even from far away. The sun hit the windows, making the whole building shine and sparkle in the early morning sunshine.

Otis parked in front of the casino, gave his keys to the valet and walked inside the hotel. At the reception desk, he glanced around and got the attention of the young receptionist. "Good morning. Can I speak with the hotel security?"

The young receptionist signaled the man beside her, and he approached Otis, "Is there something wrong?"

Otis read his nametag, "Steven, Manager."

"This gentleman would like to speak with the hotel security," the young receptionist explained quickly.

The manager reassessed Otis, who was leaning casually on the front desk. He saw a steely look and an appearance that assured him this was no joke. This man would not ask for security for any silly reason.

"Would you please come to my office, and we can discuss this in private?" Steven offered.

"Yes, sure." Otis nodded. Privacy was exactly what he wanted in this case.

Otis walked after Steven around the corner, and Steven headed towards the room that said "Office." He opened the door with his keycard and held the door open for Otis.

Otis entered a spacious office with a large desk, two guest chairs, and several file cabinets against the wall. He walked towards the closest chair and sat down. The manager walked behind his desk and asked with a friendly smile, "Now, what can we do for you, Mr.?"

"Thorne. Otis Thorne." Otis handed out his letter from the president's office and waited for the manager to read it. Steven's face turned serious. He looked up and asked, "What can we do for you, Mr. Thorne?"

Otis leaned back on his chair and kept his steely eyes on the manager when he replied, "My mother stayed here in your hotel. Last night she was kidnapped. I received a note from the kidnappers. I would like to see the security discs from the elevator, her floor, then the lobby or the parking area. I want to see who has her."

Steven frowned. "Are you sure it is not a hoax? Maybe somebody's prank?"

"I already tried to call her room. She is not there," Otis replied. He pulled out the kidnapper's note from his pocket and handed it to Steven. "Read this."

Steven read through the note and nodded. "I see. This seems real. Let me call our Head of Security. He can help you." From that moment on, the manager was very cooperative and dialed his security officer. "Carlos, can you come here to my office?"

When Carlos arrived, Otis showed him the president's letter. Carlos viewed it and asked, "I'll have to verify this. Will you excuse me?" Carlos was a big, burly man with a slight Mexican accent.

"Of course, take your time," Otis replied.

The head of security called the president's office. After the phone call ended, Carlos was ready to show the security tapes to Otis.

Carlos took Otis to the casino's surveillance center, situated in the same hallway as the office. Carlos opened the door with his keycard, and they went inside. Carlos sat down and tapped in the date, the time to pull up the video they were interested in. Otis sat down beside him. He stared keenly at the screen showing his mother's floor. He saw his mother exiting her room around seven p.m. and went to the elevator. When she had left the floor, Otis said, "Show the lobby."

Carlos was ahead of him, already tapping the keyboard to pull up the requested video. They watched the video showing Estelle greeting an elderly gentleman and going to the restaurant together. The next video clip showed Estelle dining with the same man.

Otis asked for a printed copy of Estelle's new friend.

Carlos forwarded the video after dinner, and they watched the couple enter the elevator. Next, they viewed the video of Estelle's floor, but she never showed up in the video after that. The elevator didn't stop on her floor.

"Where did they go?" Otis asked.

"Not to her floor," Carlos said, frowning.

"Can you check the parking hall?" Otis asked because he knew Estelle was grabbed and taken away. The kidnappers had to have a car in the hotel's parking hall.

"There they are," Carlos said, pointing at the garage video. They watched as two men and the dinner guest escorted Estelle out of the elevator. She looked unconscious because the two gang members were half carrying her to the parked cars.

The Werewolves, Otis thought.

The unconscious Estelle was assisted into the back seat, then the sedan drove away.

Carlos turned to Otis and said apologetically, "It seems that your mother was abducted after she entered the elevator but before she went back to her hotel room." The head of security sighed. "We've never had a case like this before. Have you contacted the police?"

Otis shook his head. "No, not yet. I will try to find the kidnappers myself."

After leaving the casino with copies of the surveillance videos and printed photos of the kidnappers, Otis called Noah. "I have some video images for you to analyze."

With the light traffic, it took him about half an hour to get to Noah's residence from the casino. He parked in front of his house, opened the gate, and walked towards the door. He heard a metallic barking and looked to his right: Elmo. Noah's robot dog approached him. looking at him intensely.

I hope Elmo remembers me, Otis thought. He stopped and waited for Elmo to come closer and sniff him. Elmo seemed to recall Otis because he backed away a few steps, then barked a few more times and sat down, his tail twitching from side to side.

"Is that a welcome bark?" Otis asked, taking a few steps towards the door. Elmo followed him. Otis looked at him and said, "It looks like you know me because you let me approach the door."

When he stepped onto the first step, Noah opened the door. "Hello, Otis."

"How did you know I was on your steps?"

Noah grinned. "I see everything through Elmo's eye cameras."

"Oh, I see." Of course, Noah had been watching him. He had probably watched his car on the traffic surveillance cameras and followed his trip from the casino to here.

Otis sat by the lazy chair near the big screens in the living room, pulled out a flash drive with the surveillance videos from the casino and the images of kidnappers, and handed them to Noah. When Noah sat by the computer and plugged in the flash drive. Otis assessed him. He looked good, even excited. *Maybe this kidnapping case has given him a welcomed distraction from new technology innovations,* Otis thought.

Noah pushed his shoulder-length hair behind his ears and then viewed the data from the flash drive. His three small diamond studs on his ear lobe sparkled when the light hit them. He wore a black Batman T-shirt today with white skinny jeans.

He looks like a teenager, Otis thought and smiled.

"That's the guy who kidnapped my mother," Otis commented when the video showed the image of an elderly man and asked, "Is this one of the guys at the covert meeting?"

Noah nodded. "Yes, he had Basilisk tattooed inside his wrist. His name is Sergei Stolyar."

"Can you check his businesses here in the Washington D.C. area? Offices, buildings, warehouses? Anything that would allow him to keep one or two prisoners without alerting any neighbors or law enforcement."

"Yes, sure. I have a list of buildings owned by all these men participating in these meetings. The only problem is that the list contains hundreds of buildings in different

states. I don't think you want to go over each one of them."
Noah handed him a two-page printout of the buildings
and addresses.

Otis took the document and glanced at the list. It was
too long for him to go through by himself. He needed help.

When they said goodbyes, Noah looked sad and lonely.

Otis decided to keep in touch with Noah more often.
He should not be alone with his robots.

Noah needs normal contacts, he thought, and then
grinned. He was not a normal contact himself: He was a
friend of the president of the United States investigating
his son's kidnapping. He was not "normal" in any sense of
the word.

His face turned solemn when he realized he had
probably put Noah in danger if the kidnappers ever found
out Noah knew about them. But with all the technology,
Otis knew Noah was not defenseless. His house was like a
fortress with all the security in place. He was probably safe
there. He would not let any stranger inside.

63

Estelle

E stelle woke up alone in a musky-smelling room. A little bit of light came through under the doorway. A single lightbulb was lit in the middle of the ceiling, but it left the corners of the room dark.

She moaned and tried to view her surroundings. *A basement? What was she doing there?*

This is not the casino or my hotel room, Estelle thought, worried. *Where am I? Why am I here?* She couldn't move her arms. They were tied behind the back of the chair. *Who has tied me up?*

Her last memory was of a casino: a nice dinner with a gentleman, some glasses of wine, and they headed towards the elevator. *What happened after I got into the elevator?* She frowned and tried to remember the details.

Two men came into the elevator while we were there. Something stung me in the elevator, she recalled. *I must have passed out. I don't remember getting out of the elevator or going to my room.*

She tried to move but couldn't move much because her hands and ankles were tied with plastic strips.

She had a throbbing headache. A slight head movement created a shooting, sharp pain behind her eyes and the base of her head. She cringed and closed her eyes again.

"Is anyone here?" Estelle called. She had a hard time getting any sound out. Her throat felt like sandpaper.

"You are our prisoner," a familiar voice replied behind her.

"Where am I?" she croaked.

Basilisk stepped closer and came to stand in front of her so she could see her.

That's the charming man I had dinner with last night, Estelle realized. *Sergei!*

Basilisk saw a recognition flash in Estelle's eyes before they changed to surprise and anger. "Sergei? Is that you? What are you doing?" Estelle asked furiously.

Sergei, a kidnapper? Otis will be so angry when he finds out, she thought, trying to pull her hands off the plastic ties behind her back, but it was futile.

Sergei stood close and viewed her. "Estelle, listen to me. You'll be fine. We need to make sure that your son Otis doesn't get involved in the kidnapping. You're our leverage."

Estelle scoffed. "Otis does not obey you. He'll find me."

Sergei picked a phone from his pocket, dialed a number, and pressed the speaker so they both could hear the ringing sound and then Estelle heard a familiar voice replying, "Hello, Mom? Is that you?"

Sergei held the phone close to Estelle's ear and ordered, "Tell him."

When Estelle did not reply, Sergei repeated the command. "Talk to your son."

"No! Never!" she protested and shook her head fiercely, causing her headache to flare up again.

Estelle and Sergei heard Otis asking, "Mom, what's going on?" He had recognized her voice.

Sergei shrugged. He hung up and put the phone back in his pocket. "I'll be back. You'll have time to consider your situation while I'm gone," Sergei said, turning off the light and leaving Estelle alone in the dark basement.

After some time had passed, two Werewolves entered the room, grabbed Estelle with her chair, and carried her to another room. She had been in a storage area, but now she was carried through a kitchen to a narrow passage to another room.

A speakeasy, a liquor smuggler's hideout from the Prohibition Era. Clever hiding place.

It won't be easy to find this hole, Estelle thought, depressed.

The Werewolves placed her in the middle of the room, still tied to the chair, and left her there.

64

Otis

Otis was back at his office at the university campus and staring at the pile of student essays to grade; His thoughts went to the call he had received from his mother's cell phone. He had recognized Estelle's voice in the background, and then Otis heard a stranger with a Russian accent demanding his mother to talk to Otis. He was sure it was one of the kidnappers talking. Estelle didn't want to obey them. Otis had understood that much.

The good news was that she was alive. They wanted his mother to talk to him. That was great because if they wanted to communicate with him, the kidnappers would likely want him to stop the investigation of the president's son and force him to stay away from the president.

Luckily, Otis had only one lecture that day at the university. Concentrating on the daily work was hard when he knew he was needed elsewhere.

He had already prepared his lecture but needed to review the material before entering the auditorium. He took the pile of essays and put them aside. He could do those later. Then he glanced at the lecture paper in front of him: Today's topic was the rise of populism in Europe and the Russian influence and their support of the populist parties in Europe.

His phone chirped, and he pulled it out and checked the message.

Noah has sent him a list of possible Russian locations where the kidnappers could keep Zachary and Estelle. They were all older buildings.

Noah sent another message saying that he had removed some locations from the list but only the ones that did not seem possible in his opinion. He had considered the area of the locations and the neighbors and eliminated the ones in wealthy areas with tight security and those with close next-door neighbors. In those areas, he believed the residents would alert the police if some motorcycle gang members appeared loitering where they didn't seem to belong. The kidnappers would not want that.

Noah is correct, Otis thought. *He made my job easier by reducing the number of locations.*

Otis knew he needed help to check out the addresses. He considered the Secret Service, but he discarded the idea because he could not be sure if they were compromised or if the information would leak to the mole in the White House. He knew the mole existed because someone had leaked the prisoner's location information, and then killed him and the guarding agents.

Otis had a few old friends at the Metropolitan Police. They were trustworthy, and he'd known them for years. They would not compromise the search. He could contact them and ask them to help, but he would have to tell them everything about the president's son. They would have to promise not to tell anyone about Zachary being alive.

It was a difficult decision because he didn't want too many people to know what was going on. The president's situation was difficult. Otis was still unsure what Andrew would do if Otis could not find Zachary before the United Nations' next meeting. He knew Andrew loved his son, but would he give up his son for his country? Probably not.

There wasn't much time. *Let it be enough,* he prayed silently. He didn't want Andrew to make a wrong decision and destroy his career.

He read Noah's location list one more time. This was the last chance. If he didn't find Zachary and Estelle in these places, then it was all over. The president would have to decide between his country and saving his son's life.

Everything goes to shit if I fail, Otis thought, leaning back in his chair. So much depended on his success in the next few hours.

65

The Prisoners

"Have you talked to my dad? Is he going to do what you asked?" Zachary asked. There was too much at stake now. He was worried.

The Werewolves guarding him just looked at him but did not answer.

What if my father chooses his career and his country instead of me? What would they do to me? Kill me? Most likely, he thought gloomily, and his heart pounded heavily in his chest with fear.

One of his guards brought Zachary a paper cup of coffee, small orange juice, and a paper bag with a breakfast sandwich, burrito, hash brown, muffin, and fries. *Breakfast,* Zachary thought. *I hope it's not my last one.*

Zachary's guards untied his wrist ties and let him stretch his arms and legs. His belly was growling loudly. He did not remember when he had eaten last time. He did not even know what time it was. He wolfed down the sandwich and the hash brown as fast as he could and drank his orange juice. He realized that if he ate fast, then he would be tied back to the chair. He wanted to stay free for a bit longer, so he slowed his pace and ate the rest of the breakfast unhurried, enjoying the food.

"Where is Dan?" Zachary asked. He had not seen his sister's husband since the kidnapping at the airport. "Is he alive?" Did you kill him?"

No reply.

Zachary looked at their faces, but they did not reveal anything.

After Zachary finished eating, his kidnappers tied him up again and returned to sit by the door.

Zachary did not know what was going on in the outside world. He had no idea what the kidnappers had asked from his father. He had read about previous kidnappings in the news, like the famous Lindbergh baby kidnapping. He knew that kidnappers usually wanted money. They could also have some political demands, like in the abductions in the continent of Africa when terrorists had taken Americans and kept them captured in exchange for prisoners or money, but he didn't know what these men wanted.

He turned his head to the door when he heard the hinges screech and some clattering sounds as it opened.

Two Werewolves carried an elderly woman tied up in a chair inside and set her chair next to Zachary.

Zachary knew who she was. They used to be neighbors before his father became a president.

"Zachary?" Estelle asked, surprised. "Otis and your father have been looking for you," she whispered. "That's why I am here. They want to stop my son."

Zachary and Estelle did not know that all that they said was recorded.

The mole in the White House had supervised the kidnapping and monitored every aspect of it. He frowned when he heard Estelle's words. "Otis...We need to get rid of him," he murmured to himself. *Why haven't the Werewolves taken care of this problem*, he thought angrily. Otis could destroy all their efforts if he discovered anything else about Operation Pobeda.

The Mole hoped that capturing Estelle would help to stop Otis and give them time to negotiate with the president and get what they wanted. He had met Otis a few times and did not believe he would let his mother die in vain. This was now the second time his mother had been captured. The first effort had been futile. The operatives had botched the whole abduction by not checking Estelle before taking her into the restaurant Troika. He hoped this time the operatives had been more careful. He knew Basilisk himself had been part of the abduction at the casino, so that was a good sign. *The group takes Otis seriously,* he thought.

66

The President

9:00 a.m. (EST), the White House, Oval Office

The president had asked to speak with the Secretary of State, Kristian Richter, and his United Nations Ambassador, Janet Wiggins. When they arrived at the Oval Office, he asked them to sit down. It was better that they were sitting because he was going to drop a bomb. He knew he was going to destroy his career and reputation with this speech he was going to give today.

Andrew didn't want to do this, but he had no choice. He couldn't let his son die.

He had waited for the last moment to reveal his plan, hoping he would not have to do this, and that Otis would have found out something by now, but he had not heard from him for the past hour or two. He had to go along with the blackmail to save his son.

Otis's progress has been steady but not fast enough, Andrew thought grimly. *I know he is right. I can't be sure that they will let Zachary go after this. They will have more demands, but I can buy him some more time with this announcement.*

"About my speech at the United Nations General Assembly today," Andrew started, looking at both of his visitors. "I will announce the United States will undo all the sanctions against Russia and release all the frozen assets of the Russians here in our country."

Secretary of State Kristian Richter was a fifty-year-old man with a twenty-year government career behind him, and he knew something was wrong when the president announced his plans. He jumped up from the couch. "But... You can't do that." His tone hovered on the border between suspicion and surprise.

Ambassador Janet Wiggins stared at Andrew with her mouth open and shook her head as if in disbelief at what she had just heard. She was a heavyset woman in her late sixties with greying, short blond hair.

Janet raised herself from the couch, holding her handbag tightly, looking adamant, then paused for a moment to collect herself before answering too harshly. "Mr. President, you can't possibly mean that."

"Please, please listen to me." Andrew raised his hands to calm them down and pointed towards the couch. He waited for them to sit down before he continued. "I mentioned this because you will get some heat because of my speech. However, it's my speech and my view of the global future. That's all. You can go now."

Both of his visitors were shocked. They glanced at each other and slowly stood up and left the room. This was completely different from what had been agreed to as the policy in this country. Andrew had never even hinted at wanting to loosen the sanctions before.

Andrew had not given them time to argue back or to oppose. Secretary of the State Kristian Richter and Ambassador Janet Wiggins stopped behind the closed door of his office and then looked at each other.

"What can we do?" Kristian Richter asked.

"Not much. If he is going to give this speech, we will have to accommodate his request. I wish I knew what was going on. He could not have changed his mind this fast, overnight. He was adamant that the sanctions must stay in place. He would never voluntarily take a position to remove them." Janet brushed her blond hair off her face and corrected her glasses.

"What if he is being blackmailed?" Kristian asked.

"No, I don't think that is possible. He is the president of the United States. Who could get close enough to find something to extort him?" Janet smiled. The idea seemed ridiculous.

"I don't know," Kristian replied and frowned. "Should we ask the Vice President if he knows what is going on?"

"Let's just pretend to play along and get our responses ready and be prepared for the media storm," Janet replied.

"Sure, we can always say 'no comment,'" Kristian replied to her, half-laughing.

It's going to be a shit storm after the United Nations meeting, Kristian thought. He decided to inform Press Secretary Brad Buchanan because he would face the fallout at the next press conference.

67

Brad Buchanan

P ress Secretary Brad Buchanan sat in his tiny room in the White House. The press secretary's tasks in the White House were still about the same as it was over fifty years ago in the 1970s when Richard Nixon was the president.

The press secretary made sure to formulate and deliver the president's ideas, arguments, and progress of his promises while he was still a presidential candidate to the American people and the rest of the world. Brad Buchanan already had some major tv-channel reporters calling him trying to get a head start on major breaking news. Brad was used to it. He usually just replied to all the questions,

"Wait for the briefing" or "no comments." Today he had a couple of reporters from the major news channels in his room asking questions about the president and the loss of his son and if it had affected his views of domestic and foreign terrorism.

Sometimes, Brad agreed to give some initial information to these news reporters, but not today. He was anxious because he knew the president had asked Secretary of State Kristian Richter and United Nations Ambassador Janet Wiggins to the Oval Office. He had vaguely told Brad that he wanted to discuss the speech he would give at the United Nations General Assembly.

When Brad Buchanan saw the Secretary of the State Kristian Richter appear by the doorway, he asked the reporters, "Gentlemen, can you please leave me now? I have a meeting with the Secretary of the State."

After the reporters left the room, the room fell quiet. Kristian walked in and closed the door behind him. Kristian sat down in one of the wooden chairs in front of Brad's desk and crossed his right leg over the left one. He looked directly into Brad's eyes and asked, "Brad, did you know what the president had in mind when he asked us there today?" He tried to read Brad's facial impressions when he said that.

"No, I just heard about the meeting," Brad paused and squinted his eyes as if to assess why the Secretary of the State asked that. "Why? Is there something I should know before the press briefing? I have his initial speech and topics he was going to discuss, but I have not received the final speech yet."

"You usually comment on his speeches and the drafts," Kristian replied.

"Yes, I do, but not this time. I saw the draft version some weeks ago. I don't know if he has added anything to it," Brad replied, looking surprised. He leaned forward and asked, "What happened this morning?"

Kristian looked downwards and brushed lint off the knee of his pants before answering. "He is going to tell the whole world that the United States will undo all the sanctions against Russia and release all the frozen assets of the Russians here in our country."

Brad stared at him, speechless. He swallowed once. "Shit!"

"Yes, that's the gist of it." Kristian sighed.

"I can't say 'no comment' on a policy change like that. That's breaking news," Brad stated.

"Yeah, it is. It's different than all the policies agreed within the party and the congress," Kristian agreed.

"What made him change his mind?" Brad asked.

"I don't know." Kristian sighed and raised his shoulders. "It was a surprise to us when we heard it this morning."

"I can see the headlines tomorrow: A rogue president on the loose," Brad muttered, adding, "or the president – the frenemy of the United States of America."

"Yeah, those are the nicest comments they will say. I would go straight to the point: Is the president committing treason or not?" Kristian remarked.

"I did not think about that. You're right. The treason might come up too," Brad replied.

"Well, I leave you to deal with the aftermath. The speech is about to happen in an hour." Kristian got up and left the room.

Brad leaned back in his chair.

This new speech will turn the press briefing into chaos. Should I suggest to the reporters that there will be no live coverage of the briefing? Brad considered. *On the other hand, live coverage would be interesting. It would show the American people the kind of circus a breaking news announcement can cause. I should probably invite only the major tv-channels. I can limit the exposure of my briefing to just them,* he thought. *I can also ask them to limit their questions to two to save time.*

Brad reached to grab his phone and called his secretary to contact the major channels with the basic rules and an invitation to a special briefing right after the United Nations General Assembly. He knew that the message would alert the channels that something big was going to happen. Brad could spin the news the way he wanted and answer only specific questions. But he was not sure what to answer yet. He knew that this news would make his career and how his time at the White House would be remembered. The briefing would also define the tone the major news channels would take on. He could make this the turning point of President Andrew Burr's career. He could also make the Russian sanctions look too harsh and get them some sympathy points.

Brad sighed. This job was harder than he had ever thought. It was like a game of chess: Always consider the next move, the next question, and then the follow-up question the press would ask.

I can't be seen as uncertain or unable to answer, he thought.

This will make my role more visible in the White House. I must make myself available day and night for the press, he thought and leaned back.

His secretary contacted and informed him that she had scheduled the meeting with the major news outlets.

Now, it was time to get ready for the briefing, and he called the president and left him a message to contact him about the United Nations speech.

68

The Speech

Nachtkrapp had stashed his tablet computer and his il dottore -mask in a bottom drawer of his work desk at the White House just for the specific occasions if he had to contact Hydra or any other members of Operation Pobeda. He kept the drawer locked so that no one else had access to them during the workdays. He carried both the tablet and the mask with him from home to work and back in his briefcase. He had to be able to report sudden updates and receive reports from the Septem group.

Nobody at the White House had seen the tattoo on the inside of his right wrist. He usually wore long-sleeved shirts and had also concealed the tattoo with thick skin-colored makeup. Now he wiped off the makeup before making the call to Hydra. When Hydra answered, he showed the tattoo on his wrist before he said anything. They had agreed on this procedure because they did not want anyone else to pretend to be part of their group: a tattoo identification first, then the sound identification, and then finally the face identification, except Nachtkrapp, whose face was always covered with the il dottore or the Plague Doctor mask making him look ghoulish and scary because the mask covered half of his face with an exaggerated bird beak nose and small, round holes for the eyes.

"I just got the news that Andrew Burr will accept our terms and announce to the whole world that the United States will undo all the sanctions against Russia. All the Russian-owned, frozen assets will be released, and the relationship with Russia will be stabilized." Nachtkrapp had a hard time hiding his excitement at the good news.

"Excellent. I will let the others know," Hydra replied, ending the call. He sat back, and his sharp eyes considered whom to call next. *Perhaps Basilisk*, he thought. *He was instrumental in capturing Estelle at the Casino. He deserves to know that the plan worked, and the president has surrendered. We own the president of the United States now, and we can ask anything we want.*

At one p.m. (EST), President Andrew Burr addressed the United Nations General Assembly for the second time during his presidency. In his short speech, he focused on Russian relations.

"Mr. Secretary General, ambassadors, and distinguished delegates welcome to New York. It is a profound honor to stand here as a representative of this great nation to address all of you. Let me recount the progress that we've made this past year." Andrew Burr looked around the room and saw many familiar faces listening and nodding, some smiling, some looking stern. He wondered how they all would react when they heard what he had to say. He leaned his hands against the podium, looked around the room, and saw some participants listening to the translator devices eagerly and some whispering to their neighbors or even looking bored. "Fortunately, the United States has done very well since the last Election Day last November eight. From the depths of the high unemployment and the financial crisis, we coordinated our efforts toward economic growth. Unemployment is at its lowest level in eighteen years."

He paused, then continued to the hard part of his speech, "As we see the growth in our nation, we want to hold out a hand to our new friend, Russia. For the benefit of global markets, we are urging all the nations here to drop all the economic sanctions against Russia, just like we will do." Andrew Burr exemplified this with his hands symbolically raising his right hand when he talked about the United States and his left hand when he talked about Russia. He wanted to separate the two countries as they were divided by different ideas and goals by symbolically using his hands to put distance between these two countries, former rivals, and enemies, but now coming together with this new proposal.

He saw the surprise in the audience and heard some quick comments, but he gestured for them all to calm down as he continued. "As a goodwill gesture, we will also vote against continuing the economic sanctions against Russia. We want all the frozen assets to be returned to Russian businesses and to lift all the travel bans against Russian nationals in the United States. I urge everyone to consider the enormous potential of the Russian people and their natural resources. We now live in a time of extraordinary opportunity: we can forgive and look forward to a new future – together."

Andrew Burr saw confusion and even anger in the faces of his audience. He knew this was not easy to accept. He did not want to do this, but it was to save Zachary.

"The success of the United Nations depends upon the independent strength of its members. To overcome the threats of the present and to achieve the promise of the future, we must begin with forgiveness. Our success depends on a coalition of strong and independent nations that embrace their sovereignty. Our goal is harmony and friendship, not conflict. This is what I believe: that all of us can be co-workers in the global economy. Our governments and the United Nations should reflect this indisputable truth. Thank you very much."

A deep silence fell in the room after the speech.

No applause.

The Russian Ambassador stood up and started clapping his hands slowly and loudly. The sound of his clapping echoed in the otherwise silent room.

Andrew Burr stepped down from the podium and hurried outside. He did not want to stay and answer any questions or hear any comments. That was not the speech he wanted to give.

Inside the Beast, his Presidential vehicle, he buried his face in his hands. It was done. The doppelganger and the kidnappers had gotten what they wanted. He just hoped it was the only thing he had to do to save Zachary.

The media exploded with the shocking announcement. It was just the opposite of what the president had talked about before.

Janet Wiggins, United Nations Ambassador of the United States, was asked the same question, and she could only reply that it was quite a recent decision. She would not comment if the views presented by the president today were the views of the whole party. She knew that Andrew Burr had decided based on his personal opinions, but she did not know the reasoning behind the speech.

Janet could not express her opinion that the president was in shock because he just lost his son, and she was sure it had contributed to this speech.

When Andrew returned to the White House, he went directly to his bedroom and removed his overcoat and tie. His last task as a president was done for a while. The vice president would take charge of the daily meetings and decisions until he "recovered from the loss of his son."

Andrew decided to call Otis. He should know that he had done what the kidnappers had asked. He should hear it from him and not from the news. When Otis replied, he said, "Otis, I just gave the speech at the United

Nations. I did what the kidnappers asked. It's going to be a shit storm. I don't know how long I can continue in my office. I know some members of Congress representing the opposition will want my head, and they will argue that I'm working for the foreign government and demand a special investigation in this matter."

"Okay, I understand. Thank you for letting me know. I know this was a difficult decision, but you wanted me to have more time to find Zachary, and I'm grateful for that," Otis replied and added, "I have some leads on the locations where the Russians might keep Zachary and Estelle. I plan to check them out today. I'll talk to you later."

69

The Troll Factory

10. p.m. (GMT+3), The Troll Factory, St. Petersburg, Russia

The troll factory was quiet. Most of the employees participating in the newest trolling had left home. Only the program manager had stayed behind. He sat in his room on the top level of the building and waited for an important call. It could mean life or death if the results of the recent trolling scheme did not please the client.

Program Manager Anatoly Sokov reviewed the social media sites assessing how his troll team had succeeded in manipulating the major media sites. He straightened his round glasses to be able to focus on reading better. He had a habit of adjusting his glasses several times a day because they kept falling, and he had to push them back up his nose.

The online analysis proved that the trolls had posted dozens of positive comments on President Burr's speech at the United Nations General Assembly. They listed several benefits of having good trade relations with Russia.

Moreover, the trolls had participated in several radio broadcasts pretending to be normal American middle-class, blue-collar workers concerned about global peace and expressing their views that having good trade relations with a superpower like Russia was important. Overall, the pressure to stabilize the trade with Russia seemed to gain a foothold in the media.

Anatoly Sokov was relieved that their trolling efforts worked. He leaned back on his chair and waited for a call from Hydra. He knew Hydra would call to learn about the results.

Anatoly sighed. He had worried that no amount of trolling would make any difference, but together with President Burr's speech, they had changed the general opinion.

Anatoly rubbed his Lincoln beard with his right hand in deep thought.

Who would have known that the president of the United States would change his opinion of the Russian sanctions so completely? It was just the opposite of what President Burr had previously had in his political agenda, Sokov considered.

Anatoly knew he could not say anything to anyone about what he suspected. He just hoped to stay alive after Hydra's next call. He was not stupid. He knew what he had done was part of a top-secret operation, and if he said or even hinted anything about it to anyone, he would be as good as dead.

It was almost midnight in St. Petersburg when Hydra finally called.

"Do you know who I am?" Hydra asked.

"Yes, you are the ones from across the ocean. I have your results ready," Program Manager Anatoly Sokov replied. He listed the online websites and opinions posted, the positive feedback, and the percentage of viewers with the same or supporting opinion.

"That sounds good," Hydra said. "It seems that you have succeeded in your marketing program. I think we can use your resources next time, too." Hydra ended the call asking Anatoly to congratulate his team.

Anatoly Sokov sighed in relief. He felt a bead of sweat run down his forehead. He wiped it off with his sleeve.

Until next time, Anatoly thought. He hoped it would not be any time soon.

Anatoly Sokov took the notes he had written down of the recent online results and walked to the file cabinet, unlocked it, and opened the drawer. He browsed the files and finally found the one he was looking for, the file for Operation Pobeda, and placed the new document inside the folder and closed the drawer. He locked the cabinet. He didn't want anyone to find out what they were doing and to whom.

His task was done. He was ready to go home.

70

Restaurant Nevskij

The temperature had fallen, and it was almost freezing. The streetlights gave their pale shine to King Street when the limousines arrived at Restaurant Nevskij. The evening rain had turned to hail and sleet. The weather was unrelenting, whipped into a rage by uncommonly strong winds.

Hydra stared through the car window from the back seat of the limousine. It was time for a new meeting with the other group members. This was a victory meeting because of the latest news of the United Nations meeting.

This weather is perfect, he thought. Nobody would be out walking or driving in this sleet. *Television channels claim that it's the greenhouse effect. Better for us.* Hydra smiled. *Our secret meeting will be private and without witnesses.*

Hydra observed his driver parking the vehicle in front of the restaurant. He waited for the doorman to come to greet him with the umbrella. He showed his wrist tattoo to the doorman, who nodded. Hydra adjusted his white silk shirt sleeve to cover his tattoo again, then stepped out into the storm. He wore a simple-looking gray suit with a pair of tasseled black loafers and looked like one of the hundreds of Washington lobbyists, except his eyes were sharp and cold like the arctic ice. He was not a sheep in a herd; he was the wolf among sheep.

The doorman had difficulty holding the umbrella as the wind was so strong that it tried to blow it over. They walked rapidly to the front door. The doorman let Hydra inside and then greeted the next passenger in the following limousine. The limousines arrived in an orderly fashion, one at a time. Each one waited until the previous one had driven away before approaching and parking in front of the restaurant.

The thick blue curtains were drawn over the windows so no one would see inside the restaurant. Just like before, one large wooden table was placed in the center of the room. The flower arrangements of white and purple tulips with the dark green wavy leaves of bird's-nest fern were arranged around the dining room.

The table was set for seven, and like before, one seat was empty. Nachtkrapp participated via video. He had already made contact and was waiting online for the others to arrive and sit at the table. Nachtkrapp had his usual black il dottore -bird mask on covering his face.

Besides the restaurant tablet computers, each participant had another similar tablet computer at home for emergency contact use only.

This time the preset tablet computers included video footage of the United Nations General Assembly and Andrew Burr's speech. The live video was of their prisoner, Zachary, and his Werewolf guards. Estelle was of no importance now because Andrew Burr had accepted their terms.

Hydra started the meeting by going directly into the business. "You all have probably heard the speech and the comments. If someone has not, they can download it and review it on the tablet." He looked around to see if anyone wanted to view it, but everyone seemed ready to continue the meeting. "The next demand concerns NATO and its command-and-control centers in Eastern Europe with the

Patriot missiles and the NATO troops." Hydra paused and looked around the table. He saw serious men dedicated to their mission. "We demand that NATO will withdraw all its troops and dismantle its command-and-control centers with all the Patriot missiles within the next month. Any comments?" He looked around the table.

"Is one month a reasonable time?" Hippogriff asked.

"No, probably not. The negotiations with NATO countries will take longer, but America can withdraw their soldiers and missiles," Hydra replied. "The other NATO countries won't have a credible presence in Eastern Europe. Besides, they can't create a balance of power against Russia without NATO forces."

"Can our first request be the removal of the Patriot missile system? That missile system blocks all kinds of air threats, from ballistic missiles to drones. We need to get those removed as soon as possible. After the command-and-control centers are dismantled, we can deal with the troops." Phoenix argued.

"You suggest proposing a specific timeline and a step-by-step process to remove the unwanted troops and missiles. We might have to settle for that eventually. First, we need to tell them exactly what our demands are," Hydra concluded. "Do we all agree?"

Hydra glanced around the table and saw his coconspirators all nodding. No one argued against his thoughts.

"We have one more thing left to do tonight. We can give the green light to our Postmaster to contact the president and give him our new demands," Hydra said.

Postmaster referred to Dan Wheeler's doppelganger, their contact person and the president's son-in-law at the hospital.

Hydra stood up, pressed his hands against the table, and said goodbye in Russia, "Do svidaniya!"

His words echoed in the room, and the other participants repeated goodbyes.

Hydra left first. He put on his light-brown camel coat and hung his multicolored silk scarf around his neck. When the doorman opened the front door, Hydra noticed it had stopped raining, although the wind was still strong. The streets were covered with a thin layer of white snow, and it shined in the front lights of the waiting limousine. Hydra walked to his limousine without glancing back. The members of this group would exit the same way as they arrived, one at a time.

Cyborg was the next one to leave. He picked up his black parka by the doorway. He peeked through the glass outside to see if the weather had gotten any better. He did not like the stormy weather, but it looked as if the worst of the storm had passed. It looked almost calm outside.

Cyborg was a tall man, cadaverously skinny, with eyes sharp and deep in his oblong skull. He had a high forehead, and his hairline was receding. He was not strikingly handsome, but he possessed charisma very few were blessed with, a gift well-honed during his long, successful career. His skinny appearance hid the fact that he was all muscle with no fat. He had always appreciated his body and what he had inherited from his birth parents. He wore a long winter coat over his plain light blue sweater and dark pants. He was not dressed in a business suit like most of the other participants.

Werewolf left the restaurant next. He wore his usual black and worn-out leather jacket, black turtleneck, and black leather pants. He looked tough, rebellious, and dangerous. He hadn't come with his motorcycle, but a limousine like the others. That was their deal.

Phoenix waited for Werewolf's limousine to leave and then hurried towards his vehicle. He wore an impeccable black overcoat, a dark suit with a white silk shirt, and a fuchsia-colored tie. He appeared fit for his age, closer to his forties, with short, dark hair. His mocha skin looked healthy in the streetlight as he entered the limousine.

Basilisk and Hippogriff were the last ones to leave the meeting. They could have passed as any other Washington area businessmen with their expensive latest fashion overcoats. The loose, long overcoats gave them an air of mystery. Their silhouettes vanished in their luxury limousines like two spies in shadows.

After the last guest had left, the doorman turned off the lights, locked the front door, and left the restaurant by walking towards the corner and then disappeared into the night. None of the members of Operation Pobeda nor the doorman knew they had been observed silently by the surveillance cameras across the street.

Noah was up and recording. He had got six faces for facial recognition. He already knew some of them.

71

Otis

A ringing cell phone was not one of Otis's favorite ways to wake up to a new morning. He glanced towards the window. It was still pitch-black outside. He turned his head towards his nightstand, pressed the light button, and squeezed his eyelids tight when the bright light almost blinded him for a few seconds. When his eyes adjusted to the light, he viewed his alarm clock. It was barely 5 a.m. He checked the screen of his cell phone and saw it was Noah calling. He rubbed his face and eyes before answering with a question, "What's up?"

"Otis, I got great news. I got all six participants. They were all there last night at the Restaurant Nevskij," Noah chattered excitedly. "I identified the sixth participant! He's the last one we could not identify before. I managed to get a view of his face on the restaurant's glass door. Then I ran some facial recognition programs against the national and federal databases and found him."

"Who is he?" Otis asked, wide awake now, turning to sit on the edge of the bed.

"That's the weird thing." Noah sounded hesitant as if he did not want to reveal his findings. "He is not a Russian. He is an American and was born in Boston. I found his driver's license."

"An American? Do you have his name?" Otis asked.

"Yeah, his name is Joe Steel," Noah replied.

"Did you find anything else about him?" Otis asked. His heart raced faster. This was a breakthrough.

"He studied at Harvard," Noah said. "And guess what he studied?" Noah didn't wait for Otis to answer but answered himself: "Medicine."

"Harvard and Boston again," Otis muttered. "Just like Zachary and Dan," Otis said in deep thought. "There must be a connection between them and the Russians. Can you dig deeper? I want to know everything about his family, his life, and his work."

"Sure," Noah replied and continued, "I'll also send you the last footage of the secret meeting. I got them entering the building. The weather was abysmal, sleet, rain, and strong wind, and the doorman greeted them by the limousines, but I got their faces when they left the meeting."

After the call, Otis was too awake to go back to sleep.

Why would an American work with or for Russians? Why would someone betray his own country? Is Joe Steel a spy? Otis wondered. He got up and walked toward the kitchen to get a cup of black coffee. He needed some caffeine now to figure out this puzzle called Joe Steel. *That name, Joe Steel, sounds so normal, plain. What is so special about him?*

He turned the light on above the kitchen counter, poured some water into his coffee machine, and added a scoop of vanilla-flavored coffee. He enjoyed flavored coffee. He always had several different flavored coffees in his kitchen cabinet. He had read about a recent study that adding some vanilla and cinnamon to your morning coffee can have even health benefits, like lowering your cholesterol and improving your brain function.

This morning I could use some improvement in my brain function, he thought.

He considered what he would like to eat for breakfast. *A turkey sandwich would be good,* he thought. He made his sandwich while waiting for the coffee to drip. While eating his early morning breakfast, his brains were working in high gear.

Was Joe Steel blackmailed by the Russians? No, that's not the case because it looks like he was equal in the meetings. He had the limousine like the others, he had the tattoo, and there was no sign that anyone had forced him to join the meeting. He was in on it, but why?

He took a yellow paper pad in front of him and started scribbling the names and the professions of the Septem-group participants. He reviewed the information Noah had sent him to make sure his information was correct.

Alexei Petrov, Phoenix, had made his money with metal, coal, and natural gas.

Orel Andruchenko, Hydra, was close to Russia's previous and current President. He was the previous President Putin's close advisor in reorganizing the intelligence agencies in Russia. He was a billionaire and made his fortune by investing in energy and oil. He was the one with political connections to the top levels of the Russian government.

Boris Kryukov, Hippogriff, owned rental car companies and restaurants in Russia and the United States. He had made a fortune in the media business. He owned both the restaurants Nevskij and Troika.

Ivan Komar, Werewolf, had connections with the mob, a known criminal. He was the leader of the Werewolves motorcycle gang and a close friend of both Putin and Ruskin.

Sergei Stolyar, Basilisk, owned the largest private bank in Russia.

And then we have Joe Steel, Cyborg, an American who studied medicine at Harvard. The same university where Zachary and Dan had studied. Did they know each other? Otis drew a circle around him. He had to ask Andrew Burr if he recognized the name Joe Steel.

Otis drummed his pen against the table. The different professions... He knew there was something in that.

He turned and poured some more coffee into his cup. He circled the professions on his list: The two first ones had gotten their fortune in natural resources. Hydra also had political connections. The next one owned rental car companies and restaurants. Then the mob connection, the criminal element. The last two were finance and medicine. All from the different fields of business. It was like a cross-section of society from crimes to administration. What worried him most was that the participants were not any minor league candidates, but they were millionaires and billionaires and owned financial institutions, media, and natural resources. They had money to finance anything. With their media connections, they could affect global news by feeding fake news.

The field of medicine did not fit the picture. Not yet. Joe Steel? He drew a question mark after his name. Why him? What was so special about him to let him be equal in the billionaire meeting?

Maybe Doppelganger-Dan was the answer. *Joe Steel could have something to do with creating the doppelganger*, he thought.

He picked up his phone and called Noah. "Hey, can you check up on Joe Steel? I need his specialization. Did he specialize in plastic surgery?"

"It will take me some time to find that information in the Harvard databases. I'll call you back when I have it. Okay?" Noah replied.

"Thanks," Otis replied and hung up. He had another cup of coffee and decided to wake up Andrew. He picked up his phone again and called him.

The president did not seem to be having a good night either because he answered after the first ring.

"Good morning, Andrew. I come bearing news. Firstly, my mother was abducted last night, and it seems highly likely that she's been taken to the same location where your son is being held captive. Secondly, in light of these ominous developments, I've made the decision to reach out to some of my former associates at the Metropolitan Police Department. I've enlisted their support to aid me in investigating these Russian-owned buildings. Navigating such a complex situation alone is impractical, especially considering the potential presence of armed adversaries. I deemed it necessary to bolster my efforts with additional firepower, and the assistance of my contacts from the police department ensures a more comprehensive and secure approach."

There was a short pause before Andrew replied, "Estelle? Kidnapped? A family member in the hands of kidnappers is hell. I'm so sorry. I know you got involved because of me."

"Andrew, please, this is not your fault. It's the Russian kidnappers who did this. We'll get through this ordeal together and get both my mother and your son home safe." Otis tried to sound firm and assuring. Otis had to tell that because he did not want to tell Andrew what had passed in his mind: There is no guarantee that we will ever see them alive again. He could not and would not tell that to Andrew. Hope was all Andrew had.

72

The New Demands

President Andrew Burr was having his breakfast in the family dining room in the White House's private quarters when he got a call on his private cell phone. He squinted at the screen to find out who had tried to contact him. He frowned when he saw it was the hospital's number. There was only one person who would call him from there. *Doppelganger-Dan!* He cursed in his mind.

He put down his fork and knife and pushed his plate with blueberry pancakes aside. He closed his eyes, took a deep breath to calm his voice, and answered the phone, "Good morning, Dan."

"Good morning, Mr. President," the loathed voice of Doppelganger-Dan replied.

Andrew almost shivered. He felt like he was holding a live rattlesnake by the tale.

"I hope you slept well after the United Nations General Assembly, Mr. President. I have the new orders for you."

"How many demands do you have?" Andrew asked, agonized, holding his cell phone so tightly that his knuckles turned white.

"I think you should visit me today," Doppelganger-Dan said, adding, "We can never be sure if someone is listening to our conversation."

Andrew swallowed and said, "I'll be there shortly." He hung up. He placed his phone back in his pocket and pushed his chair backward. He had lost his appetite. He felt as if the weight of the world was put on his shoulders. He knew that this new extortion was just another nail in his coffin. His political career would be over.

It took only thirty minutes for Andrew to get to the hospital. He asked his Secret Service detail to wait outside while he was in Dan's hospital room. Andrew tried to act nonchalant and cool when he entered the room. He did not want to give Dan the pleasure of seeing him worried.

Dan tried to assess Andrew's mood when he entered the room but did not see any emotion.

The president stopped a few feet away from the bed and asked, "Tell me about these new demands."

No small talk, just straight to the point, Dan thought. That's fine. He sat up on the edge of the bed, pulled on his robe, and closed it in front of him.

"Mr. President, first, I just want to congratulate you on your excellent speech at the United Nations General Assembly. I enjoyed it very much, and so did my partners." Dan watched Andrew's face first pale and then turn reddish. He had hit the sore spot. *The president is furious,* he thought. *He does not like being a puppet on a string.* Dan smiled coyly.

"The next demand concerns NATO and its command-and-control centers in Eastern Europe with the Patriot missiles and the NATO troops. We demand that NATO withdraw all its troops and dismantle its command-and-control centers with all the Patriot missiles within the next month. Any comments?" Doppelganger-Dan looked up and saw Andrew's shocked face.

"Are you serious? I can't do that." Andrew shook his head. What they asked was just impossible to do. He could not suggest that.

"Think about it," Dan said calmly. "NATO was established after WWII to protect Western Europe from a Soviet attack. NATO's military structure was directed towards that understandable and clear goal. Which was to protect the European countries' sovereignty and peace. The European countries were considered a geographical risk, and any new war in an area with different interests and separate governments would be a potential risk. Especially after WWII, the Soviet invasion was a real threat in the minds of world political leaders. Therefore, it was decided that the United States' military strength was needed in Europe to support the countries, and together they could defer any Soviet attack." Dan paused, then added, "As you see, it is not so far-fetched to reconsider NATO's existence. NATO's purpose ceased to exist when the Soviet Union collapsed. It needs to be dismantled like the Soviet Union."

Andrew stared towards the floor. He did not want the doppelganger to read what he was thinking at that moment. He realized that the doppelganger was not stupid. He had his facts correct, but it was risky to suggest dismantling NATO and withdrawing all military support from the European countries. The European Union did not have its military. Instead, it relied on NATO's forces. The individual countries had limited military but would not match NATO's troops or the Russian army.

Andrew knew that the Russians did not appreciate having U.S. missiles and troops in their backyard. He did not want to give in to these demands, and he knew he had to act agreeable, and therefore, he replied, "NATO is an alliance, and you must negotiate with the other partners. I cannot withdraw the United States from NATO immediately because we have contracts that require certain finance, military actions, troops, and cooperation from all NATO members. In 1991, when the Soviet Union was dissolved, NATO included more Eastern European countries, the former Soviet satellite states, in this alliance because we wanted them to be part of the Western defense system."

Andrew glanced at Doppelganger-Dan to see what he thought about his response. Dan looked expressionless, and Andrew decided to continue cautiously, "We can always argue that the NATO alliance should be renegotiated. Also, we can claim that the individual countries or the European Union should establish their military defense and army. The United States should have considered the primary objectives in Europe before accepting new partners in the NATO alliance. We tried to assist Russia's post-Cold War development toward democracy and capitalism. We could claim that the United States should have decided what was more important: to assist in Russia's development or to support these former Eastern Bloc countries. We tried to create strong footholds in these Eastern European countries, but Russia had a hard time accepting the former Cold War enemy so close to its borders. We could not succeed in both objectives."

"I see you do agree: the NATO alliance can be renegotiated," Doppelganger-Dan replied, flashing a quick smile. "Our timeline is one month. You'll have to start the negotiations immediately."

Andrew shook his head. "I can suggest having an additional NATO meeting, but that will not change the contracts with the alliance. Joining or resigning from NATO is an act of state, which means that it requires the Senate's decision. I can't do it alone. "

"Start the process. I'm sure we can negotiate an appropriate timeline," Doppelganger-Dan replied.

"I still want to talk with my son. I want to know that my son is still alive and my son-in-law, too," Andrew requested.

"Zachary is alive. I will ask him to call you," Doppelganger-Dan assured. He did not look in his eyes when he said that.

Andrew noticed that he did not mention his son-in-law. He had a gut feeling that something was wrong.

The doppelganger did not tell me everything. He is hiding something, Andrew thought.

"And Dan?" Andrew pressed.

The doppelganger did not reply to his question. He just shrugged his shoulders. "Now you know our demands. I will try to get Zachary on the phone soon."

Andrew realized that the real Dan might be dead. *The kidnappers would have said something, or would they?* Andrew wondered. *What if the kidnapping had gone wrong, and the doppelganger and the real Dan had been in the same place same time? It would have been a catastrophe for whoever had organized this kidnapping and blackmailing. How can I tell Irene that her husband might be dead?* Andrew worried.

"I'll see what I can do with this new NATO demand. I hope it is the last one." Andrew got up from his chair and brushed his coat lapels. He turned away to leave the room when he heard Doppelganger-Dan's voice behind him.

"No, I'm afraid this is not the last demand. We have another one," Doppelganger-Dan replied, looking smug.

Andrew felt his blood run cold. He turned around slowly and asked, "More demands? What are they? When do you plan to tell me those new demands?"

"Not right now. You have this NATO objective to deal with. I'll get back to you tomorrow," Doppelganger-Dan replied. "Besides, nobody considers it strange if you visit your son-in-law at the hospital every day. It's good for your public image: showing empathy and caring for your family, and all that."

"I'll be back tomorrow. But I want to hear from Zachary before our next meeting," Andrew replied, leaving the room feeling light-headed and nauseous. He leaned against the hospital wall for a moment. His knees felt weak. He brushed his hand over his face and tried to collect his thoughts. He saw his security detail waiting for him and straightened his posture, looking ahead sternly. He was still the president. He would act like one. He would not show any weakness.

Andrew walked towards his security detail and headed towards the elevators. His security detail phoned his vehicle and made sure it was waiting for him downstairs when they exited the elevator.

Andrew walked towards the car, and his driver held the back door open for him. He sat down and watched the busy sidewalks, the pedestrians, the streetlight turning from red to green through the window. Andrew saw all that, but his brain was not registering any of it. He had other, more important things on his mind. He knew he would not be able to sleep tonight. He had to prepare an initial proposal for the doppelganger to review.

Maybe it would be enough to show goodwill instead of doing anything that would risk the relationships in the NATO alliance, Andrew thought. *I will never get the Senate to accept resigning the NATO and withdrawing all our troops and missiles from Europe. Somebody in Congress will start asking questions about my recent actions and claim that they are against the best interest of this country and our allies. What if these Russian kidnappers just go on and on forever? I can't stop them. They can ask whatever they want. I will still try to do my best to save my son. Can I be sure that my son will not die when this is all over? Should I tell someone in the White House or my security advisors? If I do, I will be removed from my position, and the Vice President will be sworn in. It will be Zachary's death sentence. I can't do that. I hope Otis finds Zachary before I go forward with any of these new demands. Regardless of what happens, I will probably be prosecuted as a traitor after this whole thing is over,* he thought.

73

Andrew

The United Nations General Assembly meeting and President Andrew Burr's speech had created an uproar on both sides of the aisle in Congress. The press was eager to hear more about this new political direction and what caused the lenience towards Russia. Some congressmen demanded that Andrew should step down. Some from his own party suggested that his speech was due to the stress and loss of his son.

Nobody knew what was going on and why the president had done what he had done. Andrew couldn't explain it.

Vice President John Rossi had asked for a briefing with the president. He had already taken all the presidential duties except the United Nations speech.

The president and the VP sat in the Oval Office and went through the schedule. Secretary of the State Kristian Richter and Chief of Staff Lawrence Conklin were also present, sitting on one of the two corduroy sofas in the Oval Office.

Esme, the president's secretary, had brought them some coffee and served it in white porcelain cups.

"Thank you for arranging this meeting so fast, Mr. President," Vice President John Rossi said, sipping his coffee.

"We need to address the topics you raised in your United Nations speech yesterday," Vice President John Rossi started carefully. He didn't want to sound too pushy or anger the president.

"Oh, yes, sure, let's discuss that," Andrew sounded absent-minded. His thoughts were still on the latest Russian demands, and he tried to figure out how to fit NATO into the discussion.

"Mr. President, could you please explain your speech?" Secretary of the State Kristian Richter asked. He did not want to beat around the bush. "Was it because of your son?"

"I want our two countries to get along. The world economy would benefit if we cooperated. If we normalize the relationship between our country and Russia, we can make considerable progress in trade deals and imports. Russia's currency ruble would get stronger, giving Russians more power to buy Western products." Andrew's reply was basic economics.

"Congress has to approve this change in our politics. We need to explain this change with more detailed evaluation and statistics," Vice President John Rossi replied.

"Yes, you're right," Secretary of State Kristian Richter said. "We have to make a statement and explain the change in the politics to the public and the Congress."

"I apologize for my sudden change of mind and for expressing my personal opinions to the United Nations. "I'm sure you can address the nation and explain my speech as a friendly handshake to Russia," Andrew said, trying to calm down his Cabinet members. He saw that Kristian was upset and felt he had been ignored.

The vice president wrote a note in his notebook and glanced toward Kristian. "I'm sure Kristian and I can figure out something."

Kristian looked like he wanted to continue this topic, but Andrew switched the subject.

"I would also like to discuss NATO and our military role in that alliance. It's quite an expensive arrangement. I think the NATO alliance should be renegotiated. NATO's structure and organization have remained the same for decades. We have just accepted more partners," Andrew explained.

"That's true, but we had not planned to make any changes with NATO this term," Vice President John Rossi replied, carefully placing the White House porcelain cup on its saucer.

"You are absolutely right. I just wanted to mention that. We should look at it sometime," Andrew replied.

As those were the topics they had agreed to discuss, and Andrew had given his answers, they wrapped up the meeting.

An aide appeared to escort Secretary of State Kristian Richter and Vice President Rossi to the Rose Garden. A news conference was going to be held soon to announce that Vice President John Rossi would be replacing Andrew Burr in public events and meetings for an unspecified period so that Andrew could recuperate from the loss of his son. John Rossi did not plan to address the United Nations speech. He would have to avoid questions about that topic or talk around the topic without specifically stating any facts.

Andrew walked back to the private quarters. He was out of the daily politics. He sat down in front of the television and surfed through the different channels.

Most news channels covered his speech at the United Nations General Assembly. There were several interviews with the members of Congress, some of them appraised him for his visionary speech encouraging peace in the world, and some demanded he resign and accused him of being a traitor and working for a foreign government.

His private cell phone chirped. A caller ID showed it came from his son's number.

"Dad? They said I can call you," Zachary said. He sounded out of breath, scared.

"Zachary! Are you all right?" Andrew asked, worried.

"Yes, I think so. Please, do what they ask. I don't want to die. They keep me in this basement—"

The call was interrupted.

Andrew heard a slapping sound, and his son cried in pain. He realized that the kidnapper had slapped his son in the face to shut him up.

Next, Andrew heard a foreign-accented voice telling his son, "No places. No clues. Just tell him what we asked you to say."

Zachary came back on the phone and said, "Dad? Are you there?"

"Yes. I will do what they ask. Tell them not to hurt you," Andrew replied.

"There is a woman here. You know her, too. Estelle Thorne," Zachary said.

"I know. Otis's mother was abducted too. Is she all right?" Andrew asked.

"Yes, she looks all right. They just brought her here. They wanted me to tell you that she is here with me," Zachary said.

The phone was taken away, and Andrew heard a strange voice telling him, "You know the demands. Do as you are told, and you will see your son one day. Tell Otis to back away. Her mother is here with us. If he wants her back alive, he should do what we told you."

The call ended abruptly.

Andrew sighed. He had had no time to ask how Dan was. Still no sign of him, no word if he is all right. He doubted he would hear from him again. He was not with Zachary and Estelle. He was probably dead. It would be hard to tell that to Irene. He could not tell her now because she had to act normally because of the doppelganger. Andrew called Otis and let him know about Zachary and Estelle and that they were being kept together in the same place.

74

The Strange DNA Results

While the president was having a meeting at the White House, Otis was at his apartment viewing the aerial photos of the airport and the surveillance camera photos of the casino kidnapping again. He had to find some clues in the photos: where the kidnappers were going, where they were hiding, or just something else. Otis's phone rang, and it interrupted his thought process. He glanced at his phone, saw Noah's name on the screen, and answered.

"Hello, I've got some news for you," Noah said. "Joe Steel is not a plastic surgeon but a genetic engineer. He has authored several research articles about human genes and how to manipulate them to remove hereditary diseases and even give the child the desired look like blond hair and blue eyes."

"A genetic engineer? How does that fit into the picture? Otis murmured. "How does he fit with this Septem group and the Russians? Why is he involved in the kidnapping? I would understand if he were the plastic surgeon who had operated Doppelganger-Dan."

"There is something else you need to know," Noah commented and paused. He wasn't sure how to tell Otis this. It was too strange to be true, and yet it was. "I have double-checked the DNA analysis you gave. The result is weird. I can send you the analysis, but you won't believe it."

"Why do you say that?" Otis frowned.

"Are you sure you took the test correctly?" Noah answered with a question.

"Yes, I'm sure. I took it myself," Otis replied.

"And nobody manipulated it?" Noah asked.

"No, absolutely not," Otis replied. "You have both Deena's test results and the original vial with the blood.

You can recheck one more time if you think that's necessary. I took two samples to make sure that I would have a backup just in case something went wrong."

"I know. I checked both samples of the blood and the DNA. I don't doubt Deena's results. That's not the problem," Noah replied.

"Then what is it? Did you get a match in the federal databases?" Otis asked.

"Yes, sort of a match," Noah said. "I just can't believe it is correct."

"What is it? What's wrong?" Otis asked.

"I got the match in the CIA databases. " Your DNA seems to be from the Soviet Union," Noah said.

"Yes, that's probably likely. This doppelganger has both Russian and Jewish genetic profiles. I already knew that. Why do you think there is a problem?" Otis asked.

"No, not just from Russia, but from the era of the Soviet Union specifically," Noah corrected. He let his words sink in

.

Otis realized his mistake. The timeline: The Soviet Union ceased to exist in 1991, and the DNA had to be earlier than that. But how could that be? Doppelganger-Dan looked like a twenty-five-year-old man. If he had been in the Soviet Union before 1991, his sample should have been taken as a baby. Even if that were the case, and if the DNA had been taken when he was just a newborn, he would be over thirty years old. The CIA did not take DNA samples from babies. Noah was right. Something was wrong.

"CIA does not have baby files. He is too young to be in the CIA files. That's the problem," Otis replied cautiously.

"Well, that, too. But that's not the only thing," Noah replied.

"What is it? Spill it out," Otis demanded.

"The result seems impossible," Noah said. "I've double-checked it more than once. I get the same result. My analyses don't lie. The same DNA belonged to Joseph Stalin. I mean the same, 100% same. He is Joseph Stalin. Because nobody can have the same DNA unless you are a monozygotic, identical twin originated from the same egg. How could you have a blood sample like that?"

"I don't know. It's not an old blood sample. It's from a guy who looks like the president's son-in-law, Dan Wheeler. He looks like he is about twenty-five years old. I don't know who he is," Otis explained. "I don't understand this. Did you say you double-check your results?"

"I have rechecked it twice. I can do it one more time, but it won't change the result." Noah waited to let the information sink in.

"Yes, please. Do it one more time. If the result changes, call me back," Otis replied and hung up. He did not believe it would change. Noah was always meticulous in his research. He had never been wrong when he presented the results.

Otis leaned back in his chair, put his hands behind his head, and stared at the white ceiling. *What on earth is going on?* he wondered. *I've got Joseph Stalin in the hospital or someone who has his DNA. Someone who is not his son because then the DNA would be different. Stalin did not a have twin in the record. Even if he had, that twin would be over one hundred years old now. He was born in 1878. An identical twin is impossible,* Otis concluded his thought.

How can the doppelganger have the same DNA as Stalin? Could the CIA's database be corrupted or tampered with? Perhaps somebody had switched the DNA... No, that's too far-fetched, he thought. But somehow, the doppelganger's DNA matched Stalin's DNA in the CIA's database.

Otis turned his head towards his desk and saw what he had just written down: Joe Steel, genetic engineering. *That's how he fits into this group. He has made Stalin's clone,* Otis realized. *Only a clone can have the same DNA. How is it possible? Human cloning is illegal. Besides, I have not heard that anyone has succeeded in it,* Otis thought.

Stalin died in 1953. How did he get the genes for cloning? Cloning technology was not that advanced in 1953. How would any scientist know how to extract and store human cells properly for future use? I need to get more information about this Joe Steel, he thought. *He has to be the key to all this. The name Joe Steel is too plain and simple. It sounds like a fake name.*

Otis called Noah back and asked him to find out everything about Joe Steel, his background, his parents, his relatives, anything. There had to be a link between him and Stalin.

This was the weirdest case he had ever worked on, and yet, if what he suspected was true, then this was more science fiction than a normal blackmail and kidnapping case.

75

Otis

O tis's next step was to contact his old friends at
the Metropolitan Police Department (MPD).
Since the kidnapping case was extremely sensitive, he
decided to first meet them in person and ask for their
assistance. He did not know how far this Septem
group's power could reach and who their contacts
were. If they had done any deeper background checks,
Septem might know who his friends were. Otis could
not be sure whom he could trust. He was sure his
old MPD friends were above suspicion because their
nature was more to follow and uphold the law instead
of working for a foreign entity like Russia.

The capital city and the president were significant targets for any terrorists, and that's why Washington, D.C. was the most policed city in the United States of America, considering the number of policemen per person living in the area. The MPD was divided into several different divisions and bureaus. His friends, Inspector James Morris and Lieutenant Joaquin Hernandez worked in the Joint Strategic & Tactical Analysis Command Center, Sergeant Carl Spiegel and Officer First Class Tom Braga in Special Operations Divisions in the Homeland Security Bureau, and Inspectors Harry Vernon and Robert Fink in the Investigative Services Bureau of the Metropolitan Police Department. Even if they were from different bureaus, they knew each other and often met and socialized after work.

It was no wonder that Otis knew members of the MPD. His path had crossed with the police several times when he had followed someone or had needed more information on his work with the agency. Even though his specialty was Eastern European politics, he had started his career in Washington, D.C., with basic surveillance tasks with the FBI and then moved to the CIA. Eventually, he was assigned to embassies in Eastern Europe and Russia for different cover roles.

Otis and his MPD friends had agreed to meet at lunch, around noon, at Dick's Diner.

At lunchtime, Otis had a hard time finding a parking place and ended up parking two blocks shy of his destination and walking to the chosen restaurant in the bitter wind. It was one of those spring days when the sun felt warm, but when the wind hit you, it chilled you to the bone.

Otis pulled up his parka zipper, tightened his gray cashmere scarf around his neck, and pushed his hands deep into his pockets. He saw the other passers-by bundled up in thick winter coats and scarves just like he was. After ten minutes of fast-paced walking, he saw the sign of the lunch restaurant, Dick's Diner, in front of him.

He noticed a couple of police patrol cars parked in front of the restaurant. He stopped and looked through the front window and saw several policemen eating burgers and fries. The diner was a popular lunch place for many on the force because it had reasonable pricing, tasty food, and fast service. They even had donuts and muffins for dessert.

Otis opened the door and caught the familiar scents of onions and meat frying and freshly brewed coffee. His belly reminded him with a loud rumble that he had not eaten since early that morning, right after Noah's call. Even if the name of the restaurant claimed it was a diner, it was more like a deli with a counter for ordering or eating and a few tables in the dining room. It allowed the customers to pick up their takeaway orders if they had no time to eat lunch there. The place also had a couple of waitresses to deliver the orders if the customers did not pick them up at the front counter.

At this time of the day, the restaurant was busy. Otis was pleased that the restaurant was almost full because the sounds of the customers chatting at the nearby tables would cover whatever he had to say to his friends. The customers were a mix of locals with on-duty police officers.

Otis looked around. He was sure that his friends had reserved their tables earlier that morning to make sure they would get the ones they wanted. He saw them sitting at two tables at the back of the diner. Their tables were perfect for observing the customers coming in and leaving. The seating also hindered any outsider from listening in on their discussions. He waved at his friends by the doorway and headed through the diner towards them.

Otis heard a waitress calling the orders to the kitchen. He both smelled and heard the sizzle of the steak and bacon on a hot grill.

When Otis reached his friends' tables, he pulled out a chair, sat down, and greeted everyone. His friends had already ordered, and he quickly glanced at the laminated menu on the table: the basic American fast-food choices mixed with some Mexican dishes.

Otis waved at the waitress and ordered a bacon-cheese hamburger with fries and a coke. He thought to stick with the greasy food because he could not be sure when he would get his next meal.

"What's up?" Tom Braga asked and leaned forward toward Otis and held out his hand. Tom was from the Special Operations Division in the Homeland Security Bureau.

Otis shook his hand with a wide smile. "Nothing much. Busy as hell. Need your help, though," he replied.

Tom Braga was a scruffy-looking, seasoned police officer. His wrinkled shirt, stained pants, and uncombed hair were just a cover for a sharp mind and cautious behavior.

Otis looked around the table. These were all his old friends, men he had known for years. He was sure he could trust them, and more importantly, he was sure they were not involved in the kidnapping operation. It was more than he could say about the White House staff.

Otis pulled the president's document from his pocket and showed it to his friends. Each of them read it and silently passed it to the next one. When the document had gone around the table, and Otis got it back, he folded it neatly and put it back in his pocket. He looked around the table and saw stern and scrutinizing looks.

"Now you've all read the document. I have a business proposition for you. I need your help in a case involving the president and his son," Otis started, speaking quietly.

"His son? Are you talking about his dead son?" Joaquin asked. Lieutenant Joaquin Hernandez worked in the Joint Strategic & Tactical Analysis Command Center. He was the youngest one in the group. He had olive-colored skin and dark hair. He forked through his steak as if it was his enemy.

"Zachary is not dead," Otis replied.

First, Otis saw the surprised looks, then disbelief in his friends' eyes. A brief silence followed. Otis saw his friends mull the news over.

"That helicopter accident has been thoroughly investigated. Even the Feds checked the site and interviewed the eyewitnesses. There's nothing more we can do," James Morris argued.

Inspector James Morris was from the same department as Joaquin. He was a bald man in his fifties. It looked like he was trying to watch his figures or blood cholesterol levels because he had only ordered a bowl of chili with two slices of bread. The chili's scent was a mixture of beans with pepper and hamburger. James seemed to enjoy his chili because he was wiping the remains with his bread slices.

Otis looked around the restaurant to make sure that no one was observing or stalking him when he revealed the kidnapping. "The Russians used Zachary's kidnapping to blackmail the president." He saw his friends' eyes change from surprise to anger.

The waitress brought in Otis's order, and they all waited until she had left before commenting on what Otis had just revealed to them.

Otis grabbed his hamburger with both hands and sunk his teeth into it. He was so hungry, and his mouth savored the taste of hamburger, bacon, salad, onion, pickles, and sauce.

"You got to be kidding!" Harry Vernon commented and slammed his hand on the table. Inspector Harry Vernon worked in the Investigative Services Bureau of the Metropolitan Police Department. "I have not seen anything in our intelligence analyses or internal reports."

"I have the images of the kidnappers. They have been identified. Believe me, they are Russians, or most of them," Otis added between the bites.

Robert Fink had been quiet, but now he decided to speak his opinion. He worked in the same department as Vernon. "It explains the speech President Burr gave at the United Nations the other day. He is being extorted. He had to present himself as pro-Russian to save his son."

"Yes, you're right. He had no choice," Otis said.

"Russians!" Joaquin mumbled, crumpling his napkin into a small ball and throwing it on the table.

"And that's not all. They also kidnapped my mother," Otis added and told them about the first attempt of kidnapping and then the second one at the casino.

"Why did they go after her?" Joaquin asked.

Otis shrugged. "Because I'm not married, and I don't have any children. She is the closest relative I have. They anticipated that the president would ask me to help him because of our long relationship," Otis told his friends. "You might or might not know, but the Burr family lived next door to us, and we grew up together."

"Those bastards!" James mumbled, referring to the kidnappers. He had put aside his empty chili bowl and moved on to coffee in a white cup and a glazed doughnut on a white plate.

"What do you want us to do?" Carl Spiegel asked. He had snow-white hair and was just a couple of years short of the mandatory retiring age. He sipped his coffee and viewed Otis over the rim of the cup.

Otis saw all his friends' eyes glued on him. He put aside his plate, having finished his burger and fries. He wiped his mouth and then inhaled, assessing his friends. *They are the best for this job,* he thought. "It might be dangerous. It is off the books, on your own time. We can't tell anyone what we are doing or why we are doing it. Are you in or out?"

His friends viewed each other and then nodded.

"In," Carl replied for all.

"Let's order some more coffee here. I need to fill you in on my plan," Otis said, waving to the waitress who took their order. When she left, he explained Noah's role and what he had found out about the kidnappers.

After the waitress had brought more coffee, he continued, "I need help to comb through the Russian-owned buildings in the city. Zachary was ordered to tell me that Estelle was there with him. He managed to tell his father that he is kept in a basement or in a place that looks like a basement, maybe a cellar. That's a clue. Noah, my friend, analyzed the paper they left me, and there were traces of fungus and food which indicated that the place is an older building and may be connected to a restaurant. Another clue is the kidnappers: we know they are Russians. We also know that Werewolf bikers are involved. We can expect to find their bikes and their soldiers near the place where they are keeping the hostages."

"Werewolves!" Inspector James Morris pondered, "Are they the Russian motorcycle gang with the tattoos and crazy helmets?"

"Yes, the same group," Otis confirmed. He wiped out his hands on a paper napkin before he pulled out some photos of the airport TSA checkpoint and showed them. They saw the leather pants and vests.

"They might be using the embassy, too. We can't go there," Carl commented.

"I don't believe they are," Otis began and continued, "Russia wouldn't want officially to be involved in a kidnapping of the president's son. Unofficially, the Russian government is involved and supporting this Septem group. It would not look kosher if the motorcycle gang stayed in the embassy. They are hiding somewhere else. They want to separate the government and this operation for plausible deniability." Otis paused, then said, "The Werewolves have been watching and following me. I don't think they followed me here. We would have seen them. We better leave this place separately. I don't want them to know I have asked you to help me."

"How do you want us to proceed?" Carl inquired. Sergeant Carl Spiegel worked in Special Operations Divisions in the Homeland Security Bureau.

"You better decide yourselves. I have a list of buildings here." Otis pulled out a list from his pocket and shared it. "They are mostly warehouses, restaurants, and some other business locations. It should not take you more than a couple of hours to go through these addresses. The kidnappers shouldn't see me around because they know what I look like. I don't want to alert the kidnappers before we are ready to rescue Zachary and my mother."

"If we see the Werewolves hanging around a building, we'll call you," James Morris said. He glanced at the list and added, "I think we can concentrate on the warehouses and old warehouse buildings turned into restaurants because you said Zachary mentioned a cellar."

"We'll find them. Don't worry," Carl said.

"I sure hope so." Otis sighed. He was left to pay the bill, and the others left in groups of two. After paying, he waited a few minutes, then got up and walked to the door.

Otis observed the customers at the restaurants. No one seemed interested in him or following him to the door. He pulled his parka zipper up, pushed his hands deep in his pockets, and headed towards his parked car. When he returned to his car and got inside, he pulled out his burner phone and checked the messages.

There was a message from Noah, and instead of listening to the message and checking the attachment file, Otis decided to call him.

"I just sent you a file with the data of Joe Steel and the results of the DNA analysis. You need to read them. I think you must talk to the president, too," Noah said. "I checked the data several times. The result is correct. There is no doubt about it. It's unbelievable, but you must believe me when I tell you it is all true."

"Okay, I'll check the email and contact Andrew," Otis said. He read his email through his cell phone and viewed the attached file. He stared at the screen for a long time, trying to digest the data. He just could not believe it. He did not want to believe it.

No wonder Noah had said it was unbelievable. It was. No one would believe it.

76

At the Hospital

1 P.M. (EST), George Washington University Hospital

President Burr decided it was time to hear the next kidnapper's demands. When he arrived at the hospital, he went directly to the elevator and pressed the button on the third floor, where the doppelganger's room was. When the elevator door opened, the Secret Service team checked out the elevator first, and then the president was allowed to enter the elevator. The elevator stopped on the second floor, and a couple of the nurses got in. The Secret Service agents were standing in front of the president and watching everyone who entered the elevator.

Andrew kept his eyes on the floor lights, and when the third floor's number lit and the elevator door opened, the agents stepped outside the elevator first, and then they let President Burr get out. He headed towards room 314, where the doppelganger was. He requested the Secret Service agents to wait outside in the hallway because he wanted to enter alone and talk to the traitor alone with no witnesses.

When Andrew knocked at the door and entered the room, Doppelganger-Dan was awake and lifted his head to see who had come in. The president's ice-cold stare would have made any lesser man shiver, but Doppelganger-Dan only smiled and did not seem to care.

Doppelganger-Dan noticed that Andrew looked as if he had not slept since the previous visit. He had black circles under his eyes and looked older than in his usual press photos.

President Burr stopped beside the bed. He stood straight-backed for a moment, then pulled a chair and sat down. He pulled out a folded document from his front pocket. "I have a draft of the NATO proposal we discussed yesterday." When Doppelganger-Dan reached for the paper, the president put it back in his pocket and said, "We had an agreement. I had a call from Zachary. I did not hear anything from my son-in-law."

"Oh, the call... yes, I remember we talked about that. If you had not asked your friend Otis to meddle in our business, we would not have had to kidnap his mother," Doppelganger-Dan snapped.

"May I remind you that you tried to kidnap her the same time you kidnapped my son? You failed the first time. He was not involved before you made the first attempt," President Burr replied.

"Yes, I had forgotten about that." Doppelganger-Dan cursed in his mind. The president's memory was better than his, even without a good-night-sleep. He had completely forgotten the first failed abduction attempt.

"You promised to tell me about my son-in-law!" Andrew almost spat the words from his mouth. He got up and was ready to leave. "Is he dead or alive?"

"I'm only authorized to tell you about the next demands. Do you want to hear them or not?" Doppelganger-Dan said. He could not reveal anything else to President Burr, not without Hydra's approval.

Andrew did not say a word. He just waited, standing by the bed.

Doppelganger-Dan angled his head. "We need some extra funding. A special program would be excellent, to support human cloning and using unborn babies as sources of new organs."

"That's illegal!" Andrew Burr replied, horrified. "Human Cloning Prohibition Act of 2001 specifically prohibits any person or entity from knowingly performing or attempting to perform human cloning or even participating in human cloning attempts. I was one of the first members of the Senate to vote against it."

"It's 2022. What you thought two decades ago, in 2001, is ancient history. You must understand the benefits of cloning to prolong life and to grow spare parts of the human body when needed. It's what we need. Your ethical opinions won't matter."

Andrew swallowed hard and felt bitter bile rising from his stomach. His acid reflux was acting up again because of the extra stress and sleepless nights. He had voted against cloning. He was adamant in his decision to not support human cloning.

"We also suggest that you need to start considering the class society in a more capitalistic way. We must let the wealthier and more educated people have better chances in longer and healthier lives, don't you think?" Dan asked.

"You need to understand that if the scientists manage to perfect the cloning technique, it will clear the path to human genetic modification. We could erase some genetic diseases before babies are born. Scientists could track down the genetic diseases in parents' DNA and then replace the bad cells with healthier ones once in embryos."

"All the cloning technologies are extremely expensive because they cannot be automated. Besides, I don't understand how and where the scientist would find the volunteers to try cloning. They would have to be real women participating in the actual cloning experiment. I don't think the first experimental subjects would be from rich families or their babies. They would not allow it. I don't quite understand your reasoning behind the cloning and why you would like me to support it," Andrew said, frowning. He had not expected this to be the next demand. Cloning seemed to be too mindboggling an idea for the kidnappers. It just did not make any sense: first, the economic pro-Russia demands, and now legislation changes for a pro-cloning proposal?

"Okay, let me explain how cloning would work in practice. We must use the poor, low-income females as the new body-part breeders. We will artificially inseminate them in a facility, and then use their unborn children as organ donors. We will also use them as the guinea pigs in fine-tuning the cloning techniques before we can offer it to the wealthier families who can pay for it," Doppelganger-Dan explained.

"I cannot do that," Andrew replied. "There is no way that the Congress will accept funding for such a cause." No one would accept that. He would essentially permit the use of the lower-class families as experimental subjects to benefit the wealthiest families. Not just wealth divided this country and its population, but ethnicity, too. This cloning proposal would allow rich families to use any lower-class families as subjects in their medical trials.

"I'm sure you can find a way to fund something secretly without telling so many details. Just think about the Pentagon's budget rip-offs: 640 dollars for a toilet seat, 74,000 dollars for ladders, and 7,600 dollars for a coffee maker. I'm sure you can be as innovative as the Pentagon in their budgeting," Doppelganger-Dan replied mockingly. "You don't exactly have to tell the specifics of the research."

"I'll get back to you," President Andrew Burr said. He calmly turned around and walked away. When he closed the door behind him, he took a deep breath. This sounded crazy. The kidnappers could not expect him to propose a pro-cloning amendment. He had to talk to Otis right away.

When Andrew returned to the White House private quarters, he pulled out his burner phone from his pocket. He saw that Otis had called. He listened to the message.

He returned his call immediately. "Otis, I've got some new demands from the kidnappers," Andrew said and then explained, "I don't understand why they want me to support the gene manipulation. They also want me to change the gene manipulation and cloning laws. These new demands don't seem related to the previous demands."

"I have some news. It might help you to understand. We should talk," Otis replied.

"Can you come to my private quarters by three today?" Andrew Burr asked. He had already been on his way to the elevator and would be back at the White House soon.

"Sure. See you soon," Otis replied and ended the call.

He checked his watch. He had just enough time to drive to the White House.

77

The Clone

3 P.M White House, private quarters

A ndrew Burr greeted Otis when he entered the private quarters and took him directly to the library room. The large bookshelves were filled with criminal law books and expensive first-edition books, but you could also see some contemporary thrillers and historical novels.

The library walls were painted antique white, and there were a couple of side tables with green marble tops. The room had originally had a few Victorian-style armchairs and a sofa with gold and rose brocade fabric, but because the antique chair and the sofa had not been the most comfortable ones to sit and read, the first lady had ordered a couple of nice leather club chairs to replace the sofa.

"Do you want anything to drink or eat? Andrew asked, walking to the side table with a crystal bottle and glasses.

Otis shook his head and said, "Just coffee, thank you."

Andrew rang the bell, and when the maid came in, he told her to bring in some coffee for both.

"I had lunch with my friends at the MPD. They will help to search the Russian-owned buildings here in the city," Otis mentioned to Andrew while he sat down.

"Excellent! I hope they can find the kidnapper's hiding place," Andrew replied.

Otis nodded. "They are efficient and will be thorough in their search."

"Doppelganger-Dan revealed their new demands today," Andrew said and frowned. "They request more funding for human cloning. I told them that it's against the law in this country." Andrew paused and said, "I can understand the economic requests and even their NATO requests. These sanctions and military establishments are directly threatening or harming Russia's economy and their border security, but why the human cloning?"

"I might know why. I found out who the last participant was in that clandestine meeting," Otis replied.

"Who?" Andrew asked, frowning. He had to wait for Otis's answer because they heard a knock on the door. The maid brought in coffee and scones and placed them on a small table in front of them. She poured the coffee into bone-white porcelain cups and then exited the room.

Otis and Andrew sipped the coffee quietly.

"You won't believe this what I'm about to tell you. First, I must tell you a bit about history, starting World War II," Otis began. "In 1941, Joseph Stalin's son was captured by the Russians, and he was taken into a prison camp."

"Stalin's son? Stalin was the dictator of Russia. Very cruel, if I remember correctly. He executed thousands of people," Andrew replied.

Otis replied, "Yes, that's correct. He served as General Secretary of the Central Committee of the Communist Party of the Soviet Union from 1922 to 1952."

"I don't understand the connection to our problems," Andrew said.

Otis said, "Let me explain." And then he continued his story. "It was assumed that Stalin's son Yakov died while trying to escape and was shot on the barbed wire fence surrounding the camp. Some sources said he was electrocuted in the fence, but these were just stories. None of them were true."

"And how is that related to the person we are dealing with now?" Andrew asked.

"The son survived. He changed his name to Jacob. He did not want to go back to Russia and live under his father's dictatorship. He had requested asylum from the Allies," Otis explained. "But before the Allies came and freed the prisoners, Stalin's son Jacob met Joseph Mengele, the Angel of Death, at the camp. He became his assistant in the revolutionary and inhuman medical experiments for 21 months while Mengele was operating and doing his research there."

Andrew placed his coffee cup carefully on the plate. His right hand was shaking a little bit. He tried hard not to show it, but he could not believe what he had heard.

Andrew shook his head. "Mengele used the prisoners as guinea pigs in his experiments," Andrew said with a hint of disgust in his voice.

"He was especially interested in genetics and studying identical twins," Otis replied. "Some of our current medical knowledge is based on the information found in his medical research notes. He did a lot of tests with poisons, high-altitude tests, and surgeries," Otis replied. "Back to Jacob: He had access to the Nazis' medical experiments at the prison camp and assisted in some of the experiments. He was especially interested in genetics, and he showed some skills in the field of medicine. Even Mengele appraised him as his apprentice. After the prison camp was dismantled, he applied to study medicine at the Medical University of Berlin. He married a Jewish woman after the war so that no one would suspect him of being a Nazi or a communist. First, they lived in Berlin while he studied. But when his wife got pregnant, they moved to the United States. The family changed their last name when they immigrated to the United States. It's not Stalin. Their new last name was translated from the original, and Stalin became Steel. Our intelligence services were grateful for the information Jacob Steel provided about his father, Stalin, and his closest circle. Jacob's son, Joe, was raised here in the Boston area. He was a genius in the field of genetics, even better than his father, Jacob."

"Are you telling me that the grandson of an ex-Russian dictator is living here in the United States and has learned his skills from his father, who studied under Mengele in the Nazi concentration camps?" Andrew Burr asked. He could not believe his ears.

"Yes, that's what I'm telling you. And this son, Joe Steel, is a genius in his field. His colleagues have appraised him of being a great instructor, a visionary, and probably a future Nobel prize winner."

"And he is here in the United States?" Andrew asked.

"Yes, he is living and teaching in Boston." Otis paused and waited if Andrew would make the connection.

"Zachary went to the university in Boston. Is that a coincidence or not?" Andrew commented.

"The same university, but a different discipline," Otis replied. "I don't know if they met."

"And Joe Steel knew about my son's kidnapping?" Andrew asked.

"Yes. It seems so. He was the sixth member of the meeting at Restaurant Nevskij. All the other members were Russian oligarchs," Otis paused and added, "He is the one with the Cyborg tattoo."

"Why would Joe Steel participate in the Russians' operation?" Andrew asked.

"I don't know for sure," Otis replied. "It is possible that his father, Jacob, had secretly worked for Russia all his life. Maybe he was never loyal to any other country than Russia. Maybe he transferred these feelings to his son, Joe."

"You mean Jacob was a spy in deep cover for decades? Is he a Russian mole? And his son too?" Andrew asked.

"That's one possibility. The other possibility is that Joe Steel has some ulterior motives. His motives might be personal." Otis took a scone from the plate and ate it.

"What do you think his motives are?" Andrew asked.

"Again, I can only guess. I asked Noah to dig deeper into the life and work of Joe Steel. He found out that he had been an avid advocate for human cloning and using the organs of the unborn babies as an acceptable method to have 'spare parts for humans'," Otis replied.

"I won't do anything to support human cloning," Andrew said steadfastly.

"You might have to pretend to do that if you want to see Zachary again," Otis warned. "And I want my mother back and alive, too," he added.

Andrew thought about the kidnapper's last demands and the news Otis had just told him.

Otis tried to decide how to tell the next shocking news, Andrew. There was no good way to tell the bad news.

"There is something else you need to know. It's related to the kidnappers' last demands," Otis started. "Remember the DNA test we took at the hospital?" He put down his coffee cup and looked sternly at Andrews.

"Yes, Doppelganger-Dan's blood and hair samples and his fingerprints," Andrew replied and asked, "Did you get the results?"

"Yes, and they are quite unbelievable. I don't know how you are going to react," Otis told him.

"Bad news?" Andrew asked.

"Yes, you could say that," Otis replied. *Worst possible,* he thought.

"If you put like that, I think I should have a drink first," Andrew Burr replied and walked to the side table, poured a glass of whiskey, and returned to his seat.

"As you know, Joe Steel and his father were both geniuses in genetics. Joe's father had learned his skills from Joseph Mengele. Even if we do not appreciate the way Mengele did his human tests, we must admit that his results and deductions were so advanced that even today, we base some of our current genetics research on his research. After stating that, I must admit that Mengele was not so far away from successfully removing and transplanting human body parts. He had done a lot of tests on the prisoners, all of whom died after his tests. Another area of study was genetics and cloning. Mengele was interested in duplicating the perfect Arian. He also wanted Nazi Germany to have a successor after their leader Adolph Hitler had died," Otis explained.

"I hope you're not trying to tell me that a little Adolph is living somewhere?" Andrew retorted.

"I don't know about that," Otis replied, smiling. Andrew sighed visibly.

Otis continued explaining, "Mengele worked with Jacob Stalin for less than two years. Mengele did not have time to finish his genetics and human cloning research, but Jacob, his assistant, Joe Steel's father, managed to clone a human."

"But not Adolph?" Andrew asked.

"No, not Adolph," Otis confirmed.

"Who did he clone?" Andrew was not sure if he wanted to know the answer.

"Joseph Stalin," Otis replied and finished his coffee. "I think Joe Steel used his father's cloning research to clone his grandfather, Joseph Stalin and succeeded in it."

"Is the clone like us: a normal human being?" Andrew asked.

"You tell me. You know him," Otis replied. He waited for the news to hit.

"How do I know him? How could I know a human clone?" Andrew asked, puzzled. "Who is he?" His brows drew together.

A silence fell between them. Otis did not know how to tell him. This was the most difficult task he had ever done because this was going to hurt his old friend. He sighed.

"Your son-in-law, Dan Wheeler." Otis dropped the bomb. The silence hung between the two men, like waiting for an explosion to happen. Otis hoped Andrew would say something, yell, pace, anything. The silence was more terrifying than anything else.

Otis watched as Andrew tried to get his thoughts around the idea that his son-in-law was Joseph Stalin's clone.

Andrew got up, walked to the side table, poured a glass of whiskey, and gulped it down like plain water. Then he returned to his seat.

"You mean Doppelganger-Dan. Are you sure?" Andrew said in a flat tone, not wanting to admit the truth presented to him.

"Yes, we took the DNA sample of your son-in-law while he was at the hospital. We thought he was a doppelganger, but it seems that he is not. He was pretending to be that, but he is Dan, according to his medical records," Otis explained.

"Are you telling me that my daughter is married to a clone?" Andrew whispered. His face had turned ash gray. He looked like he was going to throw up.

"Yes, we found a hit in the DNA databases. His DNA matched Joseph Stalin. We checked his fingerprints, and they matched Dan Wheeler. Dan's fingerprints do not have to match Stalin's fingerprints because clones don't have the same fingerprints as the original person had."

"But his name is Dan Wheeler. Not Steel or Stalin." Andrew tried to sit calmly, but Otis noticed his fingers moved restlessly on his knees.

"Yes, he was adopted by Wheelers when he was a baby. His adoptive parents knew he was a clone. I'm sure Joe Steel has been their 'family doctor' since little Dan was born. He must have wanted to follow up on how his clone grew up and if there were any medical or mental problems."

Andrew Burr shook his head, not wanting to believe it. "Dan – a Russian clone? I just can't believe it." His face was composed, his voice weak, and he met Otis's eyes without a blink.

"He is also a Russian spy because he works for the Russian kidnappers," Otis said.

Andrew nodded.

"Dan is a foreign agent operating on our soil and working against this country," Otis added.

"The clone has slithered into my closest circle like a snake and become part of my family. He has plotted against me and our government," Andrew murmured.

"Stalin once said, 'Everyone imposes his system as far as his army can reach,'" Otis replied.

"They did not need an army. They used their advanced medical knowledge and infiltrated us here on our turf," Andrew retorted.

"Yes, they did. But there is still time, and we can stop them." Otis got up and patted Andrew on the shoulder. He had not lied to him. They still had time, but not too much.

Otis let himself out and left Andrew alone in his thoughts. The biting cold wind chilled his fingers, and he shoved his hands deep into his pockets when he walked to his car. He stopped and turned around and viewed the White House. The lights shined through the windows, and he imagined how many people were busy working there. One of them was the Mole. He was somewhere there in that famous building, scheming and planning. He saw the Secret Service agents walking around the premises. They kept the building and premises safe but did not know their enemy was already inside.

Otis continued to his car and drove away. The streets were not busy, and it only took Otis about twenty minutes to get to his apartment. He opened his door and went inside. He fumbled the wall with his right hand, looking for the light switch when he suddenly felt a sharp pain on the back of his head. Sparklers of pain erupted inside his head, and his vision blurred. His body made a thud when it hit the floor and passed out.

78

The Mole

The mole of the White House had followed Otis. He knew about Otis's meeting with the president and wished he could have been a fly on the wall and listened to what they said. The mole had second thoughts about Estelle's kidnapping because it would tie Otis to the case and keep him motivated, but it might not stop him.

Otis had been deep in his thoughts and had not noticed a black sedan following him from the White House to his apartment. The sedan had stayed two or three cars behind him all the time.

The mole decided he had to find out what Otis knew about the Septem group. He was worried about his position. The mole knew he had used il dottore -mask and a voice-modifier app in all the video conferences with the Septem group. However, he realized that the other members might recognize his accent and the familiar words he used, even if they did not know his face or recognize his voice.

When they reached Otis's apartment building, the mole had waited for Otis to go in first and then let himself in the building and quietly followed Otis to his apartment door without Otis noticing him. When Otis turned his back, the mole hit him hard on the back of his head.

The mole stepped over Otis's body and entered the apartment leaving the door open. He did not plan to be there for a long time. He had a pencil flashlight with him that he used to look around the room. The hardwood floor creaked when he moved around the apartment. His breathing was fast. He was excited to search, but at the same time, he was scared he would be caught breaking in.

The mole checked out Otis's computer. It requested a password, and he cursed quietly. He looked around the area near the computer to see if Otis had written the password somewhere, but he could not find it. He had no time to figure out his password. He rummaged through the papers on the desk. Nothing there. Next, he went back to

Otis, searched his pockets, and found his two cell phones, but both asked for a passcode. *No use to me,* the mole thought.

The mole looked around and saw his briefcase. He went through the papers, mostly students' essays to be graded. Then he saw a small post-it note pushed into the side pocket of the briefcase. Otis had written on it: Blood type A positive, DNA heritage Jewish and Russian. He took the note with him. He knew what that was all about. Two persons had that background: Cyborg and Dan.

The mole had hoped to find out if Otis knew about him, but he could not find any notes or messages about that. He had no time to rummage through the desk drawers as he heard heels clicking in the hallway approaching the apartment.

Cursing his bad luck, the mole hid behind the door and saw a woman's shadow appear in the open doorway.

"Otis! Oh my, what happened?" She leaned over Otis and checked his pulse.

The mole stood behind the door, holding his breath, hoping she would not see him.

Otis moaned.

"I'll just go to the kitchen and get some cold water and a towel for your head," the woman said and hurried to the kitchen. When the mole saw the kitchen lights turned on, he quickly stepped from behind the door, passed Otis's body on the floor, and hurried away. The hallway's thick carpet dampened the sound of his steps.

Otis was still half-conscious and did not notice any movements.

Deena hurried back with a glass of water and a towel for Otis. She kneeled beside Otis. She had no idea she had just missed the mole. She pressed the cold, wet towel over Otis's forehead.

Otis opened his eyes and saw Deena. He tried to move, but his head felt like somebody had hit him with a sledgehammer. He cringed and closed his eyes tightly.

Deena bent over and felt the back of his head gently. "You have a bump the size of an egg," she said. "Did you slip and fall?"

"I remember opening my door, then something hit me from behind. That's all I remember." Otis sighed when Deena placed the cold towel over his head again.

"Drink some water," she said and held out the glass. Otis lifted his head warily, winced as the pain hit him again, and took a sip of water.

"It could have been a burglar," Deena said, but she did not believe it herself. The television and the DVD player were both there. *If the intruder did not take anything, then this attack was probably a personal attack, not a burglary*, Deena thought.

"I think this had something to do with the helicopter crash and the disappearance of the president's son," Otis replied and told Deena what he had found out so far about the kidnapping.

"That's why you needed the blood test," Deena stated the fact.

"Yes, but I didn't want to involve you. I don't want to put you in danger." Otis moved to a sitting position and rubbed the back of his head gently.

"Isn't that my decision? I'm already involved. I did the tests," Deena said.

"Yes, you're right," Otis agreed.

"Maybe you should come to my apartment tonight. Just in case the unwanted visitor comes back," Deena suggested.

Otis looked at her. Her eyes sparkled when she added, "You still owe me dinner, but I can make an omelet for you tonight if you haven't eaten yet."

"An omelet sounds good," Otis replied.

Deena helped him up. Otis leaned on the wall and checked his pockets. His cell phones and wallet were there. Nothing seemed to be missing.

"This could have been just a warning," Otis remarked, adding, "Maybe the Russians wanted to scare me to stay away from the president. Whoever it was, he did not want to kill me."

"Maybe, but let's just go now. You can ask the police to come and check your apartment if you like," Deena replied.

Otis shook his head. "No, better not. Nothing was taken." He stood up, locked his apartment door, and took his briefcase from the floor where it had fallen.

They walked across the hallway. Otis leaned on Deena's shoulder. Deena opened her apartment door, and they went in.

Inside, Otis glanced around. Deena's apartment had the same layout as his, but the two-bedroom apartment looked cozier and lived-in because of the paintings on the wall, the lush velvet couch with colorful pillows, and the little flowerpots on the windowsill.

"Sit down anywhere you want. I will just go to the kitchen and cook," Deena said while taking off her winter overcoat and boots.

"I think I will join you in the kitchen," Otis said. The back of his head still felt like someone was hammering it. Otis left his parka, briefcase, and shoes by the door and walked after Deena. He sat by a small kitchen table and stretched out his legs.

Deena took out the eggs, onion, and ham from the refrigerator. She cut the ham and onion into small slices and then cracked the eggs in the frying pan. She turned to Otis and said, "I hope you like onions and ham with your omelet because I don't have much else."

"Sounds good," Otis replied. *Feels like home*, he thought, watching Deena cooking.

When the omelet was ready, Deena folded two pieces on the plate, carried both plates to the table, placed one in front of Otis, and sat next to him.

Deena looked concerned, touched his arm, and asked, "How's your head?"

"Every time I move my head, I feel this splitting headache," Otis said, wincing, and gently touching the bump on the back of his skull.

"Do you want some pain medication?" Deena asked worriedly.

"Yes, please," Otis replied.

Deena disappeared to the bathroom and came back with a bottle of pills.

"Thank you." Otis took one and swallowed it with some water.

While they ate, Deena asked some questions about the kidnapping case. Otis answered as best as he could. "Now, you probably know as much as I know," Otis said, smiling.

Deena said, "I would like to meet your friend Noah. He sounds interesting."

Otis nodded. "Maybe someday."

They finished the dinner, and Deena carried the plates to the sink. When she turned, Otis was behind her. "Thank you for dinner," he said, wrapping his arms around her body.

Deena's eyes darkened as she looked into his eyes.

Otis leaned towards her and brushed his lips on hers.

"Otis," Deena whispered his name and her lips touched his lips gently.

Otis tightened his grip around her waist and leaned to kiss her again. *She smells like honey and sugar,* Otis thought, *and her lips are so soft.*

Deena's arms went around him, fingers diving into his hair. Her body pressed tightly against him, shivering as the kiss grew hotter. When Otis moved his head, he felt a sharp pain that made him almost pass out. His face turned ashen.

"I think I have to lie down," Otis said and let Deena help him to the bed. He turned towards Deena and traced a fingertip down her high cheekbones.

Deena smiled. "Get some sleep now. You'll feel better in the morning."

79

Otis and Deena

Otis woke up the next morning and cringed when he tried to move his head. The attack had given him a splitting headache, maybe a concussion. He put his right hand on the back of his head and felt the bump carefully. It was big, like the size of half a baseball. He saw Deena through the doorway. She was in the kitchen wearing just a morning robe. She looked ravishing with no makeup and uncombed hair. Otis wished he could see that view every morning when he woke up.

"Good morning," Deena said when she saw him sitting on the bed edge and holding the back of his head. She smoothed her morning robe in front of her with her hand.

Deena asked the obvious, "You've got a bad headache?"

Otis nodded. "Yes, the mother of all headaches."

Deena laughed lightly, went to a medicine cabinet, and brought a white pill to him with a glass of water. "Here, take this. It will help with the pain."

Otis took the pill and swallowed it with the water. "Thanks, I will need it. Busy day ahead."

"Not before you have a proper breakfast. I made bacon and eggs. And coffee, of course." Deena turned and went back to the kitchen.

"You're pampering me," Otis muttered, smiling. He got up carefully, trying not to move his head, and walked to the bathroom. He washed his face and looked at himself in the mirror. His face was pale with a five o'clock shadow. He ran a trembling finger over his chin. He had to go to his apartment to shave and brush his teeth, but he did not want to go there.

The pain medication helped because his headache seemed to fade away. He was ready to have some breakfast and then get back to work.

"I have one lecture today and then some papers to review. I did not have time to do that last night because of the attack. I'll be at the university most of the day, then I'll see my MPD friends tonight. We try to comb through the

Russian-owned buildings to find the hostages," Otis told Deena while sipping his second cup of coffee.

"Call me if you need any help," Deena replied. "I'll be in my lab today."

After breakfast, Otis went back to his apartment. He opened the door quietly and waited for any sounds or sudden movements but heard nothing. All his senses were alert, and his muscles tensed. He stepped in and glanced around. Everything looked normal.

Otis considered calling 911. It might be worth reporting the attack because the person might come back. The problem with reporting it was that the police would want to know why somebody would break into a professor's apartment and not take anything valuable. He decided to call one of his friends at the MPD, Harry Vernon. He could quietly investigate and make sure the MPD would patrol the apartment building more frequently.

Otis knew Harry well. It was early, so he would still have his second cup of coffee cooling in front of him. When Harry answered, Otis said, "It's me, Otis."

"Oh, good morning." Harry sounded surprised. He had not expected Otis to call him so soon after their meeting. They were supposed to search the Russian buildings before meeting him. "Is there something new?" Harry asked, wording carefully so that nobody spying on Otis's call would know what they were talking about.

Otis decided to reveal the problem on the phone. If the intruder was listening to his calls, he would know the police were involved. It would probably be safer for him and Deena.

"I had a burglary attempt last night at my apartment. I don't want to contact 911 or the campus police. Nothing was taken," Otis explained. "The intruder hit me on the back of my head. I passed out, but Deena found me. I think she might have scared the intruder away."

"Okay, I'll contact the neighborhood patrol and ask them to go by your house more frequently. I can explain that there has been some vandalism in your building," Harry said and jotted down some notes on the paper in front of him.

"Thanks. I'll see you soon." Otis ended the call.

When Otis finally got outside, the freezing mist lapped at his face. He pulled up the collar of his parka higher. He walked to his car. He looked around it and even under it. Nothing suspicious. He viewed the doorframes to see if any additional wires were attached or any signs of tampering. Nothing suspicious. No bomb, no tracking device. He opened the door and viewed the seat and even under the seat. Nothing. He had to check to be sure. The attack had made him cautious.

Otis realized he was the only witness to the blackmailing and the kidnapping. If he was out of the picture, the president had no one to turn to except the official channels. The president had the video of Zachary that the kidnappers sent him, but would that be enough? Probably not. It would not prove that Zachary was still alive. The kidnappers could have killed him after the video call.

My mother would likely be killed if she were no use to the kidnappers, Otis thought somberly. *I must find a way to save her and Zachary.*

Otis got in his car and drove north from his apartment building. He checked his mirrors to see if any cars made sudden movements and followed him. He did not see anything unusual. He turned to the right and then straight towards the university.

Otis had to adjust his speed to moderate instead of his usual fast speed because the streets felt slippery after the cold night, and the snowy mist reduced the visibility to almost zero.

The early morning traffic was thick, and the cars were packed almost bumper to bumper on the roads. Lots of cars honking and waiting for the traffic lights to change.

Otis was not in the mood for lecturing. He knew he had to do his job. Otherwise, he would have no job at the end of the semester. His mind was more occupied with this secretive group and the kidnapping than his daily lectures. Luckily, he knew his today's topic well: The collapse of the Soviet Union and its effects on the global economy.

He pulled into a parking lot in front of the building where his office was located. He checked his rearview mirror to see if anybody had followed him. He did not see any familiar-looking cars. He opened the door, and the cold mist hit his face chilling him to the bone. *Another spring day,* he thought grimly when he picked up his briefcase from the front seat of the car and hurried inside.

Otis checked the time. He had about an hour time to review his notes and get ready for the lecture. After that, he planned to review the students' papers before meeting his old MPD friends and see if they had any reports for him.

80

The Search

Otis's friends went around the list of buildings teamed in pairs: Inspector James Morris and Lieutenant Joaquin Hernandez started and took the blocks from Capitol Hill to the Smithsonian. Sergeant Carl Spiegel and Officer First Class Tom Braga searched the area in Southwest Waterfront, while Inspectors Harry Vernon and Robert Fink took the downtown area. They did not have any luck. They met back at the Ol' Irish Pub for a beer and exchanged news at five that same afternoon.

The freezing rain had stopped. The sky was grey like it was ready to rain when Otis approached the pub. When he opened the pub's door and entered, he saw his friends standing by the impressive mahogany back bar with pints of beer in front of them and one pint waiting for him.

The Kinnock family had owned and run the pub since the 1920s. During the Prohibition Era, the pub served only as a lunch place, but after that era ended, liquor and beer filled the shelves behind the old bar. The pub had kept a loyal customer base and was usually packed full every evening.

When Otis walked closer to the bar, he saw slumped shoulders. His mood got worse. *No luck,* he guessed as he noticed the drooping faces and no cheerfulness.

"You didn't find anything promising," Otis asked, stating the fact.

His friends shook their heads. "Nada. Zip."

"We still have places to check," Otis assured them. "Let's go sit over there." Otis took his pint and led his friends to a corner booth. Harry and Robert had to drag a couple of extra chairs to sit on at the end of the table.

"When I checked the airport photos, I saw the kidnappers heading towards downtown. Maybe they didn't stay there. It's possible they went first there and later moved the hostage to another location. As you know, Arlington has many Russian-owned places. I have a gut feeling that we will find them," Otis explained while he sipped his beer. He showed the aerial photos to his friends and Noah's list of buildings.

"It's not too late to check out some of these other Russian-owned buildings," Harry said, looking around to see if the others agreed. "Besides, we did not drink that much, just one beer," he added.

"Okay, let's go," Joaquin said and finished the glass in front of him. They gathered their coats and left the bar.

Otis and his MPD friends divided the rest of the Russian-owned buildings between them. Otis took the first part of the list with Inspector Harry Vernon and Lieutenant Joaquin Hernandez, and their list consisted of the first three buildings in the Arlington area. Inspector James Morris and Robert Fink had the next three buildings on the list Noah had created, and Carl Spiegel and Tom Braga had the rest.

They had excluded the addresses that did not seem to have any basements, like new office buildings, and decided to just drive by the older buildings with basements, including warehouses, hoping to see a possible location.

Otis believed that the hostages were held in an older building. There could not be any other renters because they would notice any suspicious behavior, like the hostages and their guards in the building.

Otis, Joaquin, and Harry had checked out two addresses on their list, and they had just one place left, a storage warehouse. When they got there, they saw a large brick warehouse with loading docks. It was close to Route 50, the Baltimore-Washington Parkway, and the Capital Beltway, and thus, served quick access to downtown Washington, D.C.

The area was surrounded by a metal fence and two guards inside the security booth by the gate. The guards came out of the booth when they heard a car approach and tried to see who was inside the approaching car, but the headlights blinded their view.

Otis changed glances with Harry and said, "This could be it. Those guards look more like bikers than security guards."

"Yeah, you're right. They are protecting the area as if there's something valuable inside," Harry replied.

They drove slowly closer along the fence towards the gate and assessed the guards. "They look like members of the Werewolves with black leather jackets and pants," Otis commented.

"Can you see the logo on their jackets?" Otis asked.

Harry shook his head, "No, they have not turned their back, and the front logos are too small to read this far away." Harry drove by the gate but didn't park there. Instead, he drove around the corner and parked. They got outside the car and waited for the guards to stop looking. When the guards did not have a clear view of the car, they relaxed and went back inside the booth.

"We should try to get inside and see what they are guarding, "Otis said. He knew it would be illegal entry, but they were not trying to make a case for a prosecutor.

"Do you see what kind of automatic rifles those guards have?" Harry asked. "We have to be prepared if we go in." He checked his Smith & Wesson semi-automatic 9mm gun. It held twelve rounds in the magazine, plus one racked in for a total of thirteen.

"Yes, you're right," Joaquin replied. He checked his .357 magnum revolver while Harry went to open the trunk and revealed their other weapons. Otis followed him and saw a loaded shotgun with an extended tube, an AR-15 carbine, extra ammunition boxes, and some extra revolvers inside the trunk. In addition to the revolvers and magazines, Harry carried two extra sets of handcuffs, a radio, a Taser a flashlight, and a baton in his trunk.

"Are you prepared for a war?" Otis chuckled.

"Just prepared for everything," Harry replied calmly. "Do you want Sig?"

"No, thanks. I have my Glock with me," Otis replied.

"Well, just in case..." Harry took out a Sig P226 9mm with 45 rounds, put it in his pocket, and took out his rifle.

"Ready?" Harry asked and looked at his friends.

They both nodded.

When they approached the gate, the guards did not even ask questions but aimed and shot toward them.

The guards had been suspicious of the slow drive-by, and they had been watching and waiting, Otis thought. He took cover behind a nearby car, parked by the fence near the gate, and saw Joaquin rolling on the ground, unharmed, trying to aim toward the shooters.

Harry was behind a trash can, shooting and covering Joaquin.

Otis strained to get a better view of the guards and their booth.

Joaquin hit the guard on the left, and the guard fell. The other guard turned, tried to run away, and kept shooting behind him while running and glancing behind his back. Harry managed to shoot him, hitting the guard on the right leg, and the injured guard collapsed on the ground.

Everything was over within minutes.

Otis got up behind the car and walked towards Joaquin, who brushed the dust off his clothes.

After Joaquin put his .357 magnum revolver back in its holster, he joined Harry, and they walked briskly towards the first fallen guard, followed by Otis.

The injured guard was hit in the hip. The red blood colored the ground under him. Harry took the guard's left hand and instructed, "Press here. The paramedics will come soon."

Harry approached the second guard and checked his leg. His wound was bursting blood at the same pace as his heartbeat.

Not good, Harry thought. *The bullet must have hit an artery.* He pulled off his belt tied the belt tightly above the wound, and said, "Keep this tight. Otherwise, you'll bleed out."

Joaquin dialed 911 and explained the situation to the dispatcher.

Otis walked towards the first wounded guard and straightened his jacket. On the front lapel, he saw the Werewolves logo and the member's name: Typhoon. He pointed that to Joaquin. He noted the logo, too, and nodded. They were members of the Russian motorcycle gang.

Otis hurried over to the second guard and checked his jacket. Same logo but a different name: Serpent.

"Do you want to wait for the patrol cars before we go in?" Otis asked.

"I think Joaquin can take care of the paramedics and patrol cars. We should take a quick look inside," Harry countered. He was interested in seeing what these Werewolves were guarding.

They entered the warehouse through a covered dock. Its door was closed but not locked.

They saw a row of crates. Some were opened, and in them, they saw machine guns. The other side had some plastic bags with white powder in them.

"Drugs and guns," Harry mumbled. They walked around the warehouse but didn't see any basement entrance or signs of the hostages.

These Werewolves were just running a criminal operation here, not kidnapping, Otis thought. This was not the right location. He balled his hands in fists. The night's operation was careening wildly off the course from finding Zachary and Estelle.

They walked back to the dock and went outside. Joaquin was still out there watching the two guards.

They heard distant emergency sirens.

The police patrol cars and the ambulances were approaching.

Harry walked to Joaquin and asked, "How do we explain this? We didn't have a search warrant."

"We can say that we got an anonymous tip that something was going on at this address. When we got there, the guards with the machine guns looked suspicious. When we went closer, they opened the fire," Joaquin suggested.

"Yes, that could work out," Harry agreed.

While they waited for the patrol cars and the ambulances to arrive, Otis received a call from James Morris.

"Otis, I think we have found the right place." James gave him the address. "Carl and Tom are heading this way, too," he added.

"We'll be there as soon as we can. We got mixed up into something else here," Otis replied.

James had to be sure that he got the right place if he had already alerted Tom and Carl, Otis thought.

Otis quickly briefed Joaquin and Harry and said, "I'll go and wait in the car while you deal with this mess."

Within minutes, three patrol cars approached with sirens on, flashing red and blue lights. They screeched to a stop beside Harry and Joaquin. The sound of sirens and police radios echoed in the quiet warehouse yard.

Harry and Joaquin had their batches out and identified themselves to the officers, gave an oral debriefing, and brought them up to speed. The patrol officers on duty took over the drug warehouse, arrested, and Mirandized the two guards before they were taken away.

Finally, Otis and his friends were ready to leave for the new location James had given them.

81

The New Address

Otis told the new address to Harry, and Harry drove fast around the corner heading in that direction. The streets were busy, it was not that late, and many people were still driving home from work, shopping, or going out.

When they got near James's location, Otis glanced around. He saw a rundown block and a row of renovated business locations. The block used to have several businesses, including a shoemaker, a bakery, and a bookstore. Now, the red brick exterior of the buildings was partly peeled off and in need of repair. The street artists had painted their multicolor graffiti on the walls making it look like a colorful contemporary artwork.

The address James had given on the phone was at the end of the street. The building had the same red brick exterior as the others, but it did not have a visible business sign outside. Otis and his partners saw seven motorcycles parked on the building's left side.

This looks promising. More Werewolves. Maybe they are guarding something more valuable than just guns and drugs, Otis thought hopefully. He had a gut feeling that this was the right place.

And then they heard a sudden burst of gunfire.

When Otis and his MPD friends drove around the corner to see the other side of the building, they saw that the side was already renovated and had a working restaurant.

A restaurant! That's what they were looking for! Otis stopped and stared at the restaurant.

"I know this place. I've been here before," he said. His thoughts were racing through his mind. Could he have been this blind? Could both Zachary and Estelle be here? He had not considered that. He saw that Harry and Joaquin were waiting for his explanation.

"This is the same place where the Septem group held its meetings," Otis explained, adding, "Restaurant Nevskij!" He had not realized that the restaurant was on this block. He had always driven along King Street to get there. Otis continued, "I didn't believe they would keep Zachary and Estelle here. It's such a busy place. This restaurant is one of the most popular ones in this area."

Harry parked the sedan closer to the corner.

Joaquin checked his .357 magnum revolver. He had not shot too many rounds at the guards in the warehouse.

"Hiding in a public, popular place, right under our noses," Harry said. He checked his weapon and ammunition. He was ready to go.

A stream of images swirled in Otis's mind: the images of the Septem group's clandestine meetings. Next, his thoughts circled back to the kidnappings. *This is the meeting place. Why would Estelle and Zachary be here? It would be too obvious. Either it was smart or thoughtless. Unless they were sure the hostages would not be found even if we located the restaurant building where they met. What if Zachary had escaped? The kidnappers would have lost a valuable restaurant property because Zachary could have identified it as the place where they kept him. Besides, this restaurant had too many customers. What if one of the customers had discovered Zachary? They would have recognized him as a member of the First Family. No, this place was too popular and too obvious. They can't be here,* Otis thought.

They ran towards the restaurant's entrance and followed the sound of the gunfire.

Otis assessed their situation as his former CIA training kicked in. He saw unmarked sedans parked by the curbside. Those were his friends' vehicles.

Otis noticed a crowd of bystanders watching the scene at a distance. He hoped none of them would come closer until the gunfire stopped. He did not want any shooting victims. He also saw faces and figures in the windows, customers may be, and hoped they would stay put, not panic, and run outside.

Otis realized that if Zachary and his mother were inside, they were in danger. They might get shot! Frantic, he moved behind one car, then ran behind another, and found his MPD friend James crouched behind the next car's open door.

"James!" Otis called him.

James quickly nodded at him, noting that Otis, Tom, and Joaquin had arrived, and returned his eyes toward the building and the gunfire. Otis ran ducking low to James, crouched beside him, and asked, "What happened?"

James kept his eyes on the building when answering, "The Werewolves saw us. A couple of their soldiers were outside keeping watch. I think either they identified us as police officers or someone watching inside recognized us. I don't know. Suddenly, we were under fire."

"We found their warehouse with their stash of drugs and machine guns. Maybe they had a surveillance camera inside or outside the warehouse, and someone alerted these guys here. The guards in our location were members of the Werewolves," Otis explained.

"That would explain it. We couldn't figure out why and how they were able to identify us. Your explanation makes sense," James said through gritted teeth. "Now, we are stuck here."

"Are the hostages inside? Are they safe?" Otis asked, worrying for his mother and Zachary.

"We don't know yet. We have not been able to get close to check any basement areas."

Joaquin and Harry had followed Otis and positioned behind the next car.

Otis saw Robert Fink getting hit and collapse on the ground, blood pooling under him. He was two cars away from Otis. He calculated the risk of going there. He viewed the doorway. Two Werewolf soldiers were positioned there with machine guns.

Otis asked, "Can you give me cover? I'll try to run to Fink and see what I can do for him."

James, Joaquin, and Harry started a fierce shooting toward the doorway, and the two Werewolf soldiers backed away from the doorway. That's when Otis saw his chance to run to Fink. He tried to crouch low behind the parked vehicles to make sure there was a minimal target for the shooters to hit. Within seconds, he was beside Fink. He kneeled and checked his wound. He had been shot in the right shoulder, but another wound was slightly lower. Otis suspected the bullet had pierced the lung.

He picked up Fink's phone and called 911. "Officer wounded," he told the address and asked the 911 dispatcher to send paramedics. He did not mention that it was an injured police officer from the Metropolitan Police Department because Otis knew there would be some questions from the Arlington County Police Department regarding why the MPD officers were involved in a shootout in their area.

Otis put pressure on Fink's shoulder wound and put his coat under his head. There was not much anything else he could do until the paramedics arrived. "Just hang in there. You'll be fine," he told Fink.

Otis checked his surroundings and saw his friends Carl Spiegel and Tom Braga hiding behind the corner of the building.

They must have run there before the situation got too heated, Otis thought. They both seemed okay, except Tom did not seem to have ammunition left. Carl shot two rounds, and then Otis saw his Glock clicking empty. *They are stuck there now,* Otis thought.

Only two Werewolves were shooting at us, Otis assessed. They both wore black leather cutoff battle vests. The other had a dragon tattoo and was bald, and the other had a long shaggy beard and a spider tattoo.

If we could get one of them, then maybe the other one would surrender. Otis considered their chances.

Harry and Joaquin kept shooting at the two Werewolf soldiers. The spider-tattooed Werewolf soldier cried in pain and fell backward. The dragon-tattooed one paused and looked towards his comrade but then shot out a burst of quick shooting to make his enemies crouch in cover and quickly pulled his brother inside.

Otis could not see if the spider-tattooed man's wounds were serious.

He heard the distant emergency sirens. Maybe a couple of blocks away, he thought. The emergency vehicles' red and blue lights came into sight and colored the nearby buildings. The Arlington County Police Department arrived, and it only took a couple more minutes before he saw the ambulance turning around the corner and parking next to their vehicles.

Otis saw the official vehicles parked in front of the restaurant at odd angles. The ACPD police officers with bullet-proof Kevlar vests exited their patrol cars, ready to take down any resisting criminals. Otis waved at them to get their attention. One of the ACPD police officers approached him, a team leader, Otis suspected. Otis pulled out Robert Fink's batch to identify him as a police officer and pointed towards Tom Braga and Carl Spiegel and said, "They are MPD officers as well as those two behind that car over there," and he pointed behind him towards the corner where Harry and Joaquin were holed up and shooting.

"Why is MPD in a shootout in our area?" the ACPD team leader asked, looking solemn. Otis knew that no love was lost between the different police departments if anyone stepped over their assigned districts and service areas and was not informed about it by their superiors in proper channels. The ACPD team leader looked upset, ready to start a turf war. Otis heard a static noise on his radio. The team leader put his hand over his radio, ready to pick it up to call for more backup if needed.

"We looked for the president's son," Otis replied, quickly explaining the kidnapping.

The ADP team leader's face turned serious.

Otis noted that and continued, "We did not know these Werewolf gang members were here. They started shooting at us right away. They must have either expected us or been informed that we were coming. Earlier tonight, we stumbled into their drug and weapon warehouse. The warehouse guards could have alerted these members here," Otis clarified. "This was not an official MPD case. These officers were all here on their own time."

"We'll clear this all up later," the ACP team leader added, "First, we need to get the customers out of the restaurant and get the rest of the shooters inside the restaurant to surrender."

The ACPD officers gathered behind Otis, and the paramedics checked Fink's condition and ran to get stretchers.

"There is only one shooter inside the restaurant now. He is one of the Werewolves. He has a dragon tattoo. He is a bald, tall guy. We got the other one with a shaggy beard and a spider tattoo," Otis quickly described what had happened. "The spider-tattooed soldier took a bullet. I don't know if he is wounded or dead. His colleague pulled him inside. He was bleeding."

Joaquin ran closer to Harry and introduced himself to the ACP team leader. "The Werewolf soldiers are quiet now. Maybe you can go in and check the situation."

The ACPD team leader took out a megaphone and called, "Please, put down your guns. We are coming in."

A few seconds went by, and then they saw a machine gun thrown through the doorway.

They heard a thud as the machine gun hit the pavement.

"I surrender," a thick Russian accent called out. "Don't shoot! I'm coming out."

"Okay, come out. No guns. Keep your hands above your head," the ACP team leader shouted back. He gestured to his team to be ready.

They saw the bald Werewolf soldier appear in the doorway and walk slowly toward the ACPD officers. But without warning, he suddenly pulled out a gun from behind his back, aimed it toward the ACP officers, and started shooting.

A deafening burst of gunfire filled the air.

The Werewolf shooter had no chance. The police officers gunned him down in seconds. The officers ran towards him and kicked the gun away from his body.

The shooter was barely alive. He coughed blood a couple of times, then his body went limp, and he died on the scene.

The ACP officers rushed inside.

The restaurant customers were terrified. Some were crying, some were screaming, and some running toward the police officers.

The ACP officers had to ask the customers to stay put until they had checked the building and made sure it was safe for the customers to leave. They would also need to give their witness statements and contact information.

The ACPD team leader returned to the doorway and waved at Otis. "You can come in now."

Otis entered the restaurant, followed by his MPD friends.

Otis and his friends spotted the spider-tattooed Werewolf crumpled on the floor by the doorway. A pool of dark red blood surrounded him, and the blood had soaked into the restaurant's carpet.

Otis knew just by looking at him that he was dead as a doornail because his lifeless eyes stared up at the ceiling.

The paramedics went to him to check his life signs just to confirm he was dead. He was wounded in his stomach on the right side and had bled out on the floor. When he passed the body, Otis smelled the distinct sickeningly sweet, metallic scent of blood.

Otis looked around: bullet holes peppered the walls, and the flower vases were broken. The blood stains were splattered on the floors and counters and colored the entrance red.

It will take some time before Restaurant Nevskij would be back on the list of the most popular fine dining restaurants in this area, Otis thought while viewing the damages.

The ACPD team leader let the MPD officers pass by but stopped Otis and asked, "Do you have any credentials? What is this business about the president's son? The news reported that he is missing and assumed to be dead, and now you are claiming that he is not. I want some explanation before you mess up my crime scene. I know these MPD officers are out of their precinct, but they know the protocol here. My boss will talk with their boss to clarify why they are here." He paused, looking Otis sternly in the eyes, and asked, "I don't know anything about you. Who are you?"

Otis pulled the president's note out of his pocket and showed it to him.

The ACP team leader read it and frowned. "Are you a spy or something?"

"Or something," Otis replied. "We are looking for two hostages: Zachary and my mother. MPD officers were helping me to comb through the Russian-owned buildings. This was one of them."

"That would explain the shooting. These Russians tried to protect this place," the ACPD team leader concluded.

"We will look around to see if we can find the hostages if that's okay with you," Otis replied.

"Sure," the ACPD team leader said. "We can help. Our guys are just combing through the upstairs."

Otis looked up to the second floor and saw ACPD police officers on top of the stairs, going room by room, checking out the rooms in pairs. Soon they came downstairs, and one of the police officers said, "Nothing there. It was empty. All employees are either in the restaurant dining room or in the kitchen." The team leader first pointed to the dining room and said, "Let's check those areas."

Otis said, "We can check the basement level or wine cellar while you do that." Seeing the suspicious look on the face of the ACPD team leader, he quickly added, "We won't mess up your crime scene. We just want to find my mother and the president's son if they being are kept here."

The team leader nodded in agreement. "Okay," he said. "We already checked the kitchen. It was empty."

Otis went to the kitchen and saw a wooden door half open. He walked to it and saw a spiraling, narrow stairway leading downstairs. Joaquin, Harry, and Tom came and joined him. Joaquin tried the light switch by the doorway, but the stairs remained dark. The light did not turn on.

Harry took out his flashlight from his pocket and turned it on. The flashlight beam bounced on the walls and then returned, lighting the steps.

Harry and Joaquin descended the stairs as stealthily as possible. They were narrow and made of stone, with only one rail on the right side of the wall.

Old buildings, Otis thought, suppressing a shiver. He felt the familiar adrenaline rush caused by fear, his heart started racing faster, and the hair on his neck stood up. He had to remind himself that he was safe. He knew his fear was irrational, caused by narrow spaces and feeling trapped.

He had been diagnosed with cleithrophobia, the fear of being trapped, when he was in his teens. It was triggered when he fell into a tight borewell on the ground when he was about twelve years old. He had been playing hide and seek with his friends in an old, abandoned mansion and had run ahead, looking back to see if anyone was following him, and then he had fallen into the well. It had taken several hours before he was rescued. His friends had not seen where he had disappeared to because the well had muted his calls for help.

The doctors had told him that this phobia is different from claustrophobia, being afraid of small spaces. Also, they explained to him that a person can suffer both phobias, claustrophobia, and cleithrophobia simultaneously.

The specific focus of this cleithrophobia was being trapped, locked in, or otherwise unable to leave. This phobia was triggered by a lack of escape, not the space itself. That's why Otis was always aware of his surroundings and made sure he was able to find an escape route. He did not want to have any panic attacks.

Otis looked back, and behind him, he heard the ACPD officers and saw their shadows moving in the brightly lit kitchen. In front of him, he saw Joaquin and Harry descending using the flashlights, tracking down the steps. Their heavy steps echoed in the stairway.

Otis's heart and breathing calmed down. He was ready to follow his partners.

82

Restaurant Nevskij

It was dark. Harry fumbled on the right side of the wall, trying to find the light switch. He found it and turned on the lights in the basement.

The dim lights flickered, casting an intermittent glow in the basement, leaving the corners dark.

Restaurant Nevskij's basement was more like a wine cellar with bottles in rows on the wall. There were some crates on the floor. The air was cool and musty.

Otis and his MPD friends looked around, but they could not see any other doors leading to any other rooms. The wine cellar was empty.

"Nothing here," Harry said, voicing his disappointment.

"Maybe there is another room," Otis replied. "Let's go back to the kitchen."

They returned to the kitchen. The kitchen had bright red lights that almost felt blinding after the dimly lit basement.

They looked around but saw only the refrigerator, two large freezer doors, prep tables, and rows of pots and pans on the stoves and grills. They found no other doors except the one leading to the hallway and the restaurant dining room.

A dead end, Otis thought, frustrated. His eyes probed around, trying to find something he had missed. *Nothing here,* he thought. Yet, he had a feeling he had missed something.

The ACPD team leader walked into the kitchen, saw their long faces, and said, "You didn't find the hostages."

Harry shook his head. "Nothing in the basement. It was just a wine cellar with bottles."

Otis stopped, turned towards Tom Braga, and asked, "Why did those two Werewolf soldiers shoot at us? "They were waiting for us, that's for sure," Otis said, adding,

"Why shoot at us if there's nothing here? We did not find anything here."

Otis was puzzled. He glanced at his friends and saw that Tom had an idea. *The old hound dog smells a trace*, he thought, pleased. He knew there had to be something somewhere in this building, a lead or a clue.

"We have missed something," Tom replied. He started looking around the kitchen area with refreshed eyes.

Otis stood still and stared at the large freezers. Two freezers. It wasn't too suspicious of fine dining restaurants. However, there was something off in these. He walked to the freezers and put his hand flat on the doors. One was cool, but the other was warm, at room temperature.

Joaquin, Tom, James, and Harry gathered behind him.

"Did you find something?" Harry asked.

"Check out these doors. One is cold, one is not." The others put their hands on the door to check the temperature.

Harry said, "Yeah, you're right. Something is wrong. Let's check this one out."

He pulled the handle of the warm refrigerator, and it opened with screeching hinges. Not a real refrigerator at all, they realized. The door revealed a secret passage. Harry lit his flashlight and turned the beam into the darkness of the narrow passage. He could not see the end of the passage where he stood.

"I'll be damned!" Tom cursed.

"Probably a speakeasy from the Prohibition time." Joaquin hissed through his teeth.

This was a clever hiding place. No one would suspect a freezer door to be an entrance to a secret passage leading to a hidden room, Otis thought. The Russians must have found the passage and used it for their own sinister purposes.

"We have to go and check where this passage leads," Harry said.

Otis took a deep breath to calm down. He had to remind himself again that he was safe. There was a way out. He could always walk the same way back. He did not want his cleithrophobia to cause a panic attack, not now when Zachary and his mother were close. At least, he hoped they were close. He couldn't be sure of it.

Crouching, as the passage was not high enough for a taller man to walk through unbent, Joaquin led their way.

The Russians must have renovated the passage because it had new LED lights along the brick walls. The cement floor was clean. The scents from the kitchen behind them – onions, grilled chicken – lingered in the air. Otis heard the shuffling of footsteps and his friends' breathing ahead and behind him. Otherwise, the passage seemed to be soundproof and quiet.

At the end of the passage, there was a massive-looking, old wooden door. The door had a small window with a wooden window cover.

They could not see inside what was on the other side of the door as it had a large padlock on a chain. The lock was placed there to keep something or someone inside.

They stayed quiet because they did not want to alert anyone if the Werewolves were guarding someone inside.

"What do we do now?" Joaquin whispered, mouthing the words. They might have found what they were looking for.

"Let's find out if there's anyone in there," Otis whispered.

Harry moved to the right side of the door and pointed to the others to do the same. The passage was too narrow to take cover if shooting started again.

"MPD! Open the door!" Harry yelled.

No answer.

"MPD! Open the door!" he repeated. "Is anyone there?"

"Yes, we are here." They heard a weak, muffled voice replying. "We can't open the door. We are tied up."

We, Otis thought. It had to be Estelle and Zachary!

"We have to get this padlock open!" Otis urged.

"Let's go and find a pair of pliers," Joaquin suggested. "Maybe we can cut that chain."

"Those two Werewolf soldiers probably had the key, but we did not go through their pockets," Tom Braga commented.

"It's too late to check that. They are on their way to the morgue," Otis replied.

"I'll go back and look for a tool," Tom said. He was the last one entering the passage. After a few minutes, Tom returned with a hammer and pliers. "Let's try with these."

The ACPD team leader followed him. "We can call for a locksmith if the door does not open with those tools," he said, adding, "Too bad we did not check the two guys before they were taken away."

"We didn't know what to look for," Otis replied.

Within minutes of using the pliers, they got the chain broken. Harry pulled the padlock and chain away, dropped them on the floor, and opened the door.

A whiff of warmer air came through the door.

At least they were not freezing here, Otis thought and rushed inside.

83

The Rescue

*T*his *must have been a successful speakeasy during Probation. It was not easy to find*, Otis thought and looked around. The room looked like a basement or a storage room, just like Zachary mentioned during one of his calls. Otis quickly surveyed the room, making sure no other guards were hiding anywhere. He wanted to make sure that the captives had not missed anyone or anything.

Otis noted the brick walls and the dim-hanging light bulbs. It was no longer a bar for illicit liquor-selling purposes.

The Russians must have found this place by accident and converted it to a storage room for their illegal drugs or weapons, Otis assumed.

Otis's eyes met the two tied-up hostages sitting on the wooden chairs.

Estelle's eyes filled with tears of happiness when she saw Otis.

Zachary and Estelle both looked unharmed.

Finally, they would get away from their prison.

Otis rushed to his mother and hugged her. "It's all right, mom. I'm here. The ambulance will take you both to the hospital. I'll meet you there. I must call Andrew first."

Next, Otis turned to Zach and said, "You're safe now. Your father will meet you at George Washington University Hospital. Don't talk to anyone about this kidnapping until you speak with your father. Okay?"

Zachary nodded. He understood that his father had to discuss it with him first because of the kidnapping and the related Russian extortion.

The MPD and the ACPD officers gathered around Otis and the hostages. Otis heard somebody calling for paramedics.

The ACPD team leader came to stand beside Otis and nodded at Zachary. "That's Zachary, the president's son who was supposed to be dead."

"Yes, he is. Don't let the press know about him yet. His father should hear the good news first," Otis replied and continued saying, "The other one is my mother."

The ACPD team leader replied, "Thank God we found them both alive. This could have turned ugly easily if the kidnappers had positioned more armed men here." He turned to walk away but then returned, "As a personal favor and to make my report easier, could you please brief me with all the details of this kidnapping case before the press hears about it?"

"Yes, sure. I can do that right after this call." Otis called President Andrew Burr to let him know that the hostages were found and to report what else had happened during that night. Andrew Burr sat with his Vice President John Rossi. He was discussing visiting some of the European Union countries and the political speeches the president had planned to give in Berlin and Brussels.

When Andrew's burner phone buzzed, he quickly picked up his phone and answered. It was unusual for him to interrupt his work-related meetings with the Vice President, but this time he did that.

"Otis, do you have any news?" Andrew asked.

"Mr. President, we found Zachary and Estelle. They are both all right. The paramedics took both to George Washington University Hospital."

Otis heard a sigh of relief on the phone and said, "Zachary looked fine. The paramedics wanted to take them to a hospital to be checked out just to be sure. I told Zachary not to speak with anyone about the kidnapping until he speaks with you. "

"Thank you, Otis," Andrew said.

After taking Otis's call, Vice President John Rossi saw how Andrew's stressed appearance changed to immediate relief.

Good news, John thought. He had been worried for the president after the helicopter crash. President Burr had acted rashly and unpredictably and had not discussed his decisions and speeches with his advisors.

John Rossi had noticed that Andrew Burr had seemingly aged after the crash. He had dark circles under his eyes as if he had not slept well for days, and his eyes looked sunken deep in his skull. He looked twenty years older than before, and he was hunched over like an elderly man. His shirt had a stain on the front, and his trousers were wrinkled.

Andrew placed his phone on the table in front of him. He looked at John Rossi and said, "I received really good news. Zachary is alive. I must tell you..." He had no time to finish his sentence because he felt a sharp, shooting pain radiating from his chest to his left side. He almost collapsed, but John Rossi called for help, and the Secret Service agents ran to assist the president, grabbed him by the elbows, and put him to rest on a couch.

One of the Secret Service agents was already on the phone calling the White House doctor. After explaining the president's symptoms on the phone, the doctor told them to transport him immediately to the hospital. He was probably having a heart attack. "The medical office of the White House was well equipped, but the president might need a specialist to check up on him in case they must do surgery," the White House doctor explained to the agent on the phone.

John Rossi stood there looking at his old friend. He did not know what to do or say. He was puzzled by his last words that Zachary was alive. How could that be possible?

Andrew held his right hand over his left arm. His face had turned greyish, his skin was clammy, his eyes were closed, and he seemed to have difficulty breathing.

The Secret Service agents rushed and carried the president to a helicopter on a stretcher, and he was transported to George Washington University Hospital.

The presidents were usually treated in a military hospital close to Washington, D.C., either Bethesda or Walter Reed AMC, but the White House doctor had decided to take Andrew Burr to the same hospital where both Dan Wheeler was currently treated. It would be simpler to protect the First Family if they were all in one location.

The Secret Service agents had called ahead to the hospital and said that a cardiac victim needed immediate assistance. The paramedics waited for the president with the gurney on top of the hospital. When the helicopter landed on the helipad, they rushed to meet the helicopter and assisted the president to the gurney and inside the hospital.

John Rossi contacted the First Lady, who was in Florida. She said she would be coming back to Washington, D.C., soon. Next, he let Andrew's daughter, Irene, know about the incident. "Your father is in the hospital. The same where Dan is being treated. He had a heart attack. I'm on my way to the hospital."

"Oh, my God," Irene uttered. "I must go there immediately." She had a call waiting, and when she answered, it was Otis calling. Irene interrupted him, saying, "My father had a heart attack. He was taken to George Washington University Hospital. Meet me there." She hung up, grabbed her coat and purse, and rushed out of her townhouse. When she got to the hospital, her father was already in surgery. Irene stayed in the waiting room to hear the results of the surgery.

Otis knew that Andrew had been under enormous stress, and when he heard that Zachary was alive and well, it hit him hard. Otis felt guilty. He should have gone and told Andrew in person.

84

At the Hospital

George Washington University Hospital

O tis drove to the hospital when he saw that the paramedics had taken Estelle and Zachary into the ambulance. He followed them to the hospital.

The Secret Service agents guarded the whole floor where they kept the president and Dan. Zachary and Estelle would also be treated at the hospital and have a room on the same floor. The MPD had already contacted the Secret Service and informed them that the president's son was on his way to the hospital.

Irene was outside in the hallway with Vice President John Rossi when Otis stepped out of the elevator, saw them, and walked to greet them.

"Mr. Vice President," Otis said shook his hand, and turned to face Irene. "Irene, how are you?"

Irene smiled tiredly. "Otis, I'm fine. Thank you for coming." She extended her hand to shake his hand.

"How is your father?" Otis asked.

Irene's eyes filled with tears. "Not good, I'm afraid. He is still in surgery. We are waiting for the doctors to come and tell us how it went."

"I have something to tell you. It's going to be a shock." Otis was not sure how to tell them, but he knew he had to tell them what he and Noah had discovered. They both needed to know.

He took Irene's hand, led her to sit on the chair, and then said, "As you might know now, your brother, Zachary is alive, and he is being treated in this hospital too. He is okay," Otis said and added, "Irene, please don't tell Dan about Zachary," Otis warned. "I'll explain everything l ater."

Vice President John Rossi was up to speed immediately. "That's what the call was about. You told Andrew about his son, and he got a heart attack."

"Yes, I'm afraid that's what happened," Otis replied, looking guilty.

Irene looked surprised, then raised her hand to cover her mouth. Her hand was shaking. "Zachary is alive? He is here?"

"Yes, he is alive and here," Otis repeated.

Irene's brows drew together. "How is it possible that he is alive? Everyone thought he was dead."

Irene was not stupid. She realized she had missed some information.

Otis considered telling her the whole truth but then decided that a half-truth was better now. "Zachary was kidnapped by an international group. Some of them were criminals. They tried to extort your father. That's all I can tell you now."

Irene nodded, looking puzzled.

Otis had not told Irene what the kidnappers had wanted. He was sure Irene would ask that next. He did not want to go into the gory details.

"Go find your brother. " I need to talk with the vice president about the helicopter crash and everything else," Otis said, taking a few steps toward Andrew's hospital room.

Irene nodded. "I will bring Zachary to see his father," she said, turning around and walking fast toward the hallway's end.

Otis extended his hand towards Andrew's empty hospital room and asked Vice President John Rossi. "Please, can I bother you for a moment, Mr. Vice President?"

Vice President John Rossi nodded and followed him into the empty room already prepared for the president.

Otis explained to John Rossi briefly what had happened since the helicopter crash, the Septem group, Operation Pobeda, Zachary Burr's kidnapping, and the extortion.

John Rossi listened to the conversation quietly, but when Otis got into the Russian demands, he burst out, "That explains the United Nations General Assembly speech. Andrew had to do that!"

"To save Zachary," Otis concluded. "He had no choice. The Septem group had planned the kidnapping so close to the United Nations meeting that I did not have time to find Zachary."

Otis told about the other demands that the Septem group had given to the president. The last one requiring the legalization of human cloning made John Rossi frown and ask, "Why would they want that? All the other demands are related to the frozen Russian assets or to improve their political and global position in the world, but that last demand... it does not make any sense."

"It does when you hear the rest of the story," Otis said gravely. He had considered keeping the doppelganger's real identity safe, and so far, he had referred to him as the doppelganger, but John had to know the truth to understand.

"We did DNA and blood analysis of the doppelganger. He's a clone," Otis explained.

"That's the reason the group wanted human cloning to be legalized," John said, but then he realized that Otis had held back some information. He almost feared to ask. "Whose clone is he?"

"He is Joseph Stalin's clone. Stalin's grandson created him," Otis replied. "The clone, Dan, worked for the Septem group. He was part of their operation, a useful tool in their game. I don't believe he is the official member of the group. The White House mole is the seventh, the unidentified member of the group."

He saw the shock on John's face.

Andrew's son-in-law was Stalin's clone.

Joseph Stalin, the dictator of Russia, was a ruthless leader who killed millions but was also a brilliant politician.

The Russians had played their cards well. If the Septem group had succeeded, the Russian world dominancy would have been on its way, John thought. The son-in-law was well known in political circles and the capital city. He was predicted to be the next presidential candidate after Andrew's term. The United States would have had a clone of the former Russian dictator as their president. John Rossi paled when he thought about the possibility of the Russian clone holding the highest position in the country.

"What a nightmare. No wonder Andrew had a heart attack," Vice President John Rossi sighed.

"My question is, what happens next?" Otis asked.

"I need time to think about this. I have taken over the president's tasks now. I would assume a Congressional hearing will determine what will happen to President Andrew Burr. You'll probably have to testify. You can always make a deal with the FBI to tell everything you know about the kidnappings and the extortion," John Rossi replied.

Otis said, "Do you believe there will be treason charges?" He was curious because he had done some research on that topic, and he knew that the penalty would include imprisonment without the possibility of parole, fines, and even the death penalty.

"Yes, I would assume so because of the Russian collusion. The opposition always wants reasons to impeach the president in power," John Rossi explained.

Otis nodded. "I will contact the Director of the FBI and make an appointment with him as soon as possible."

"Good," John Rossi said and was about to leave when Otis said, "There's one more thing: What about the Russian mole in the White House? I don't know who he is."

John Rossi raised his eyebrows and said, "That's problematic. I can't trust anyone except you." Vice President Rossi patted Otis friendly on the shoulder.

"And some of my friends in the Metropolitan Police Department," Otis added. "They helped search the Russian-owned buildings."

"Yes, sure," John Rossi replied. "Do you have any plan to find out who this Russian mole is and how to capture him?"

"I have some ideas on how to proceed," Otis replied. After leaving the vice president, he called the FBI and asked for an appointment with the Director of the FBI, informing him that it was about the kidnapping of the president's son.

Director of the FBI E. Thomas Ruckert, E.T., called him back almost immediately. "I want you to come here as soon as possible. How about ten tomorrow morning? We need to go over this kidnapping and whatever information you have about it."

"I will see you tomorrow at ten," Otis confirmed. "I'll bring with me another person. His name is Noah S. Pye. He assisted me in this case."

"Okay, I'll see you both tomorrow morning." E.T. ended the call.

Otis called Noah and told him about the FBI meeting. "We will ask for immunity of all charges," Otis said. "We won't talk before we get that. This case is so big that we need to make sure we won't be railroaded."

The next call was to Deena. "It's over. Tomorrow night, you'll have your dinner and the whole story."

He heard Deena laugh at the other end of the line. "Where do you want to dine?" she asked.

"Not in any Russian restaurant," Otis replied, laughing.

85

The Mole

8:00 p.m. (EST), Press Briefing Room, the White House

"President Burr has been taken into the hospital due to a heart attack. We don't know his condition yet." Brad Buchanan informed the news reporters at the White House Press Room. "The vice president has stepped in and has taken over his tasks for now." Brad Buchanan wore an immaculate grey suit, revealing his wide shoulders and thin waist. His wealthy New England family background showed in his posture, his speech, and his choice of words.

The media representatives raised their hands and shouted out questions over each other.

"What hospital is he in?"

"Is he undergoing surgery?"

"What is the prognosis?"

"How long will he be away from the presidential duties?"

"Is he coming back?"

The reporters shouted questions to Brad Buchanan. He held up his hands to calm down the reporters and said, "I don't have anything else to tell you. We'll inform you when we have more news about President Burr's condition, and how serious it is. Pray for him and his family."

Brad left the podium and heard the reporters behind him talking to each other and calling their news desks.

The White House mole was worried. He picked up a phone, made a call, waited for three rings, and then hung up. That was the agreed safety procedure. Now he had to wait for his co-conspirator to call back on a secured phone line. He had time to start his voice-altering app on his phone. He did not care to use the video call and his mask.

Within minutes the mole received a call from an anonymous number. He replied, "I have some news."

Hydra replied, "We also have news, but it isn't good. You go first."

"The president is in the hospital due to a heart attack. The vice president has taken over his duties."

The mole heard the Hydra curse in Russian. "More bad news."

"More? What do you mean?" the mole asked. He had not expected that comment from Hydra.

Hydra replied, "We lost the hostages today. The police searched the restaurant and found the speakeasy room."

The mole's complexion noticeably paled as he responded, "I was completely unaware. My focus has been consumed by media matters and monitoring the president's status." He hesitated, contemplating another query before voicing it, "What will become of our group and Operation Pobeda?"

"We failed. We need to make sure we survive. We have to clean up this mess. We can't leave any incriminating evidence behind that could lead law enforcement to us. We are still an anonymous group working behind the scenes. I hope we stay that way. We must live and try again. The rest of the group will leave this country tonight. I mean Hippogriff, Phoenix, Basilisk, Dentist, and his Werewolves or what's left of them. I was packing when you called. We will have one more meeting online in an hour. We will have to decide what to do with the clone." Hydra didn't wait for the mole to reply. He hung up.

The mole put the phone back in his pocket, turned his chair towards the window, and stared outside.

Everything they had planned had failed. The mole considered his options: to run or to stay. He had not been in the meetings. President Burr and the police would not know anything about him. He might be safe even if the rest of the group might be exposed. The only one who knew who he was, was Hydra, and he was leaving the country.

86

The Last Meeting

The Septem group had a secret video conference online. They could not meet at the Restaurant Nevskij. They had heard about the police raid, and the media reports of the shootout at the restaurant were all over the news.

"This is the last meeting of this group," Hydra started, "at least for now," he added. He had not given up all hope to return and finish what they started. He was not sure how much Otis and his allies knew. "We know that the Restaurant Nevskij was razed by the local law enforcement officers, and the two captives were released. We don't know if the FBI was involved. Our Werewolf guards are dead. We only have the news reports of the scene." Hydra paused and let the news sink in before continuing, "The hostages are currently at George Washington University Hospital being checked out. The president of the United States had a heart attack or something similar." Hydra ended his report and looked at the serious-looking faces on the computer screen.

"Is President Burr going to die?" Basilisk asked.

"I don't know. We need to wait for the results after the surgery. There's no news yet. I know why you ask. He was the person we invested in. We don't have a plan for the successor, who is going to be Vice President John Rossi. Operation Pobeda was created for the incumbent, President Andrew Burr. We don't have a contingency plan for the next in line."

"How much do they know?" Cyborg asked, looking worried. His work was in jeopardy. He was an American citizen colluding with the Russians. It would not be so easy for him to just leave everything behind. Besides, his life's research was also at stake.

"I don't know. We better prepare for the worst." When Hydra said that, the severity of the situation hit the other participants. Most of them had already packed and were ready to go, except Cyborg and Nachtkrapp.

"My work and my life are here!" Cyborg cried out. "What about my research? My clones? My facility and equipment? I can't just leave everything behind." He was mostly concerned about his research facility with his cloning technologies and the knowledge of where the rest of the created clones were. His research facility included the DNA from different sources, not just Stalin's.

"It's your choice. I advise you to leave. You'll have no future here if the president or Otis Thorne finds out about you and your other clones," Hydra said coldly.

"How would they know our identity?" Basilisk asked calmly. When Cyborg heard his cool voice, he settled back down and seemed to pull himself back together. "We have not told anyone outside this group who we are or even the name of our group. Our captives did not know. It is safe to assume that they don't know about us."

"They know about you," Hydra added.

The other participants fell silent. They only saw each other on the screen, but they could feel the tension building between Basilisk and Hydra.

"What do you mean?" Basilisk asked, alarmed.

"You were the one who took Estelle. Do you think Otis Thorne has not accessed the surveillance tapes from the casino? He has seen your face. He'll find out who you are." Hydra's voice was calm, and his eyes icy. He watched Basilisk's face pale as he swallowed a few times.

"I... I did not think about that," Basilisk replied quietly.

"Everyone else is safe then, except Basilisk?" Cyborg asked, hope shining in his eyes.

"Maybe. We can't be sure of that," Hydra replied. "I don't see how they would know about us. We have been careful." He paused and continued saying, "Dan is compromised. He was the key to this operation. We can't leave him alive. You know what to do, Cyborg." Hydra gave an order to Cyborg, who looked reluctant. "Are you asking me to terminate him?" Cyborg wanted the confirmation.

"Yes, I want you to terminate him so that no one would suspect anything," Hydra instructed. His eyes were like sharp daggers boring into Cyborg's eyes.

Cyborg sighed and replied reluctantly, "Okay. I will terminate him. He was mine from the beginning. It is just poetic that I'll end his life, too." He knew there were others. This one was the first and the most important for Operation Pobeda, but not the only one.

"But after Dan is gone, there are no other loose ends," Nachtkrapp concluded with hope in his voice. He wanted to stay and continue his life like none of this had ever happened.

"That's correct. The news reported that our Werewolf guards were killed in the Restaurant Nevskij's shootout," Hydra confirmed.

They had all entered the country with diplomatic passports, and the local law enforcement could not touch them even if they found out about them or identified the group members. Even the Werewolves had diplomatic passports. They were untouchable.

Only Nachtkrapp and Cyborg are not diplomats. Their lives are here. They could be in danger, Hydra thought. *The Septem group would sacrifice them if necessary.*

87

At the Hospital

"President Burr had several blockages in his arteries. We had to do an emergency open-heart surgery on your father," the doctor told Irene after the surgery.

Irene lifted her right hand over her face, and her eyes filled with tears.

"Is he all right?" Zachary asked.

"He had a stroke and a heart attack. His left side was paralyzed when he arrived here. We have started treatment for that but we will have to wait and see how he recovers. He got here fast, but it will take time for him to heal. We can't be sure how much damage had happened before we got him to the surgery," the doctor replied. He looked tired after being in the surgery room for hours.

"He had a stroke and a heart attack simultaneously?" Irene asked.

"Yes, I'm afraid so. Sometimes that happens. A stroke happens when blood flow to any area of the brain is cut off and the brain cells are deprived of oxygen. This will also lead to the paralysis your dad exhibits now. He has lost muscle control which explains the paralysis, and he might suffer memory loss too," the doctor explained to them. "Don't give up hope. The surgery went well."

Irene looked relieved. She leaned against the wall, her hand on her chest.

"Can we see him?" Zachary asked.

"He is still under anesthesia. When he wakes up, we'll transport him to his hospital room," the doctor replied. "I will also inform the White House doctor of the situation."

"If he had a stroke and his left side is paralyzed, can he serve as a president after that?" Irene asked after the doctor had left the room.

"I don't know. I don't believe so. I think the vice president will be sworn in and serve the rest of the term," Zachary said.

When Otis parked his car in front of the hospital the next morning, the sky was cerulean blue, and the sun was shining. *Not a cloud in the sky*, he thought. He knew he still had some storm clouds ahead in his future, not to mention the president's fate, but he hoped they would be solved soon.

First, Otis went to the gift shop and bought two "Get Well Soon" balloons, one for Andrew and one for his mother, and a bouquet of tulips for his mother. Then he took the elevator up to the floor where his mother, Estelle, and Zachary were. They had separate rooms near Dan and Andrew.

Otis had not visited Dan since Restaurant Nevskij's shootout and rescue operation. The Secret Service agents were guarding the whole floor.

Dan could not escape. His time was running out.

When Otis entered the floor, he saw his mother talking to a handsome doctor, maybe ten years younger than she was.

Otis saw her tilting her head and brushing her hair with her left hand.

She's flirting, Otis observed, surprised.

She will be safe here with all the Secret Service agents buzzing around, safer than at home, Otis thought. He felt like a third wheel watching her mother and the doctor chatting. He realized that her mother wanted to continue her flirtation with the doctor.

"I'll see you later. I'll have to see Zachary," Otis said, turning towards Zachary's hospital room. He waited for the Secret Service agents to check their guest list.

Otis looked back to see his mother smiling and touching the doctor's arm with his right hand.

She looks like a cougar stalking her prey. She is not going to settle down, not even after this kidnapping, Otis thought, smiling and shaking his head in disbelief.

The Secret Service agents granted him access. Otis knocked on the door before entering Zachary's hospital room. He was sitting on the bed, and his sister, Irene, was there with him. Zachary looked pale but healthy. They both smiled when they saw Otis coming in.

Irene ran towards him and hugged him. "Thank you so much for saving my brother."

"You're welcome, but it was not just me. You need to thank the MPD and the ACPD police officers, too," Otis replied.

"You did all the searching. I know that. I saw my father with you so many times. You both knew Zachary was alive, didn't you?" Irene insisted.

"Yes, we knew Zachary was kidnapped. We were not sure for how long he would stay alive, so we couldn't tell anyone," Otis said. He twirled the balloon stick in his hand and looked around where he could put it. He saw some other balloons with some flowerpots on the windowsill. He walked there and put his balloon with them. He pulled out a chair and sat beside Irene next to the hospital bed.

"Zachary," Otis started, "Can you please tell me anything you heard or saw when you were kidnapped? Did you hear any names?"

Zachary shook his head. "No, I did not hear any names except my father's when these bikers wanted me to call him."

"Did you ever hear them mention a group called the Septem?" Otis asked.

Zachary shook his head and furrowed his eyebrows. "No, I've never heard of that name before."

"Think about the moment when you were kidnapped. Tell me about it," Otis asked.

"Dan and I arrived at the airport. We got out of the car and walked towards the hangar. We got inside the hangar, then someone came behind me and put something over my mouth. I passed out. I don't remember much about that," Zachary explained.

"Did you see what happened to Dan?" Otis continued questioning Zachary.

"No, I didn't. I asked about Dan when I woke up. He was not there with me," Zachary replied.

"Dan was brought here after the crash," Irene said. "I don't understand how he never told me about the kidnapping. He must have seen it. He let us believe that you were killed in the crash. He never said you could be alive."

Irene realizes that Dan's story about the helicopter crash was a lie, Otis thought.

"Don't worry about it, Irene. Your brother and your father need you now," Otis said. "The FBI will interview Dan today."

"Okay, I'll be here with Zachary and my dad," Irene replied.

"I'm going to see Andrew now. It was great talking to you both." Otis got up from the chair and walked towards the door.

The Secret Service agents recognized Otis when he approached the president's hospital room. They nodded and greeted him, allowing him to enter.

Otis took a deep breath. He did not know what to expect to see. He remembered Andrew as a strong, healthy man. He had heard that Andrew's left side was paralyzed.

Otis pushed the door open and saw Andrew lying on the hospital bed. He looked pale. His eyes were closed, but when Otis got closer, he opened his eyes. The left side of his face sagged slightly, and his left eyelid drooped, making his eye look half closed. His left hand was straight on his side. Otis suspected that his left hand was also paralyzed.

Andrew had an EKG beside the bed monitoring his heart and an IV hanging by his bed.

Otis heard the steady beeping of the machines. He stopped, looked around, and pulled one chair closer and sat by the bedside.

"Good morning, Mr. President."

"Call me Andrew," Andrew replied. His speech was slurred because his facial muscles on the left side did not work, but his mind was alert.

Otis smiled encouragingly.

He'll heal. He's a fighter, Otis thought and said, "We rescued Zachary and Estelle. Both are here at the hospital being checked out. They look good."

Otis saw the relief on Andrew's face.

Andrew needed some stress relief. The last days had been too hard for him, Otis thought.

"Thank God," Andrew managed to say. He had difficulty speaking and trying to pronounce words. "I want to see my son."

"Irene will bring him here soon," Otis replied.

"Did you tell Irene?" Andrew asked, looking worried.

"You mean about the blackmail and her husband?" Otis completed Andrew's question. He understood without saying.

Andrew tried to raise himself to a more sitting position, but he could not do that because only his right arm worked. He leaned back on his pillows. He shook his head.

"Tell me," Andrew asked.

The EKG beeped a bit faster, and Otis glanced toward the machine to make sure Andrew was not having another heart attack. Everything looked normal on the screen, just a little bit of elevated heart rate.

Otis turned his gaze to Andrew. "No, I didn't tell Irene. I don't know how to tell her about her husband. I don't think she would believe me."

"Irene needs to know," Andrew said with difficulty. "Tell her the truth." He had a hard time forming the words.

"I can't tell her that her husband is a clone," Otis said. "I can tell her that the investigation of the kidnapping and the crash is still ongoing." He knew it would not be long before he or someone else would have to tell Irene the whole truth. Irene will have a lot to deal with.

"I know I must tell her before the FBI arrests Dan," Otis replied.

"Good," Andrew said with difficulty.

"I will let you rest now. We can talk about this later. I have a meeting with E.T. at the FBI headquarters in twenty minutes."

"You'll tell him?" Andrew asked.

"Yes, I have to disclose the whole kidnapping case," Otis replied.

Andrew sighed. His presidency would end soon. They both knew it.

88

At the FBI Headquarters

FBI Headquarters, 935 Pennsylvania Avenue, NW, Washington, D.C

The J. Edgar Hoover Building is a low-rise concrete, light-gray colored office building located at 935 Pennsylvania Avenue NW in Washington, D.C.

Otis had agreed to meet Noah in front of FBI Headquarters. Noah was already there waiting for him with a heavy-looking shoulder bag when he arrived. Otis assumed he had the dossier of this kidnapping case with him.

When they entered the hall, they first went through the metal detectors. A young brown-haired secretary in a black suit, a white blouse, and black pumps waited for them by the front desk. She shook their hands and then told their names to the front desk. Ready-made Visitors' badges were handed to them. They signed them and attached them to their lapels, and then the secretary led them to the elevators and pressed the top floor button.

The Director of the FBI, E. Thomas Ruckert (E.T.), was waiting in the conference room accompanied by Special Agent Luis Rochas and his partner, Nat Griffin.

E.T. introduced them, informing Otis and Noah that these two agents were investigating the helicopter crash. Otis and Noah shook their hands and then sat down across the table in front of the agents.

E.T. sat at the end of the table as a chairman.

Rochas leaned forward and said, "If we are all ready, then let's start the recording," he reached out to press the recording button on the recorder in the middle of the table.

Otis placed his hand over the recorder and said, "Let's talk first. Off the record, okay?"

Special Agent Rochas's eyes snapped back up to Otis's eyes. He looked surprised.

Otis met Rochas's gaze steadily and then turned his head towards E.T., who nodded, approving it. "Sure, let's do that. We're not in a hurry."

"Okay," Rochas said leaned back on his chair, and stared at Otis in the eyes.

If you want to intimidate me, that's not working, Otis thought and almost smiled. I've been in tougher interrogation and interview situations than this. Otis stared back at Rochas, who finally lowered his gaze and started fiddling with the pen on the table in front of him.

Otis turned to E.T. and went on, regaining his composure, "First, we need to discuss the immunity agreements for both of us."

E.T. stared at him for a moment before replying, "You know this involves national security at the highest level?"

"Yes, I do know that. I also know that there was no other choice. We had to do what we did without contacting you or any other agencies because we did not know who was involved and how deep the conspiracy went."

E.T. sighed. "Okay, put the tape back on."

Agent Rochas reached for the tape and pressed the button.

"We agree that both Otis Thorne and Noah S. Pye will have immunity agreements. They'll now brief us on everything they know about Zachary Burr's kidnapping and Russian involvement. Additionally, we will request a non-disclosure agreement from both. Agreed?" E.T. looked around the table, and everyone said, "Agreed."

"And how about President Burr?" Otis asked, "What will happen to him?"

"It's not my decision. We can only make a recommendation based on this discussion. It's up to the Congress hearing what will happen." He pointed towards the recording, and Rochas turned it off.

"Unofficially, off the record, I'd say that due to his severe health problems, he won't be able to serve his term, and the vice president will take over permanently. It's not certain if Andrew Burr will ever recover from his heart attack, but I doubt that Congress will indict him, and even if it would happen, the next president would likely pardon him due to the circumstances."

E.T. nodded to Rochas, who reached out and pressed the record back on.

"Okay, let me tell you how this started and what I know," Otis said and started his account of what had happened since the helicopter crash. He explained how one of the airport employees, Derek, was in the hospital in a hit-and-run accident, and the other one, Jack Brewer, and his family were murdered, and the murder was disguised as breaking and entering.

The Russians had used their identities to enter the secured airport area.

The agents made notes to check up on that while Otis continued his story. They interrupted Otis's story the first time when Otis mentioned the Werewolf soldier following him and being arrested by the Secret Service agents.

"Is he still under arrest?" Special Agent Griffin asked.

"No, he was poisoned," Otis replied. "He's dead, and so are the two Secret Service agents guarding him."

"Was it the mole in the White House?" E.T. asked.

"Yes, I assume so," Otis said. "I don't know what poison was used or how it was administered. I'm sure you can get more information if you contact the head of Security at the White House."

"We'll do that," E.T. replied, and the agents wrote the task down in their notepads. The FBI needed to know if there were any loopholes in the security of the White House.

The agents interrupted Otis a couple more times when he continued his report. E.T. listened to him until he had finished his statement.

Noah had the photos of the participants coming out of Restaurant Nevskij and the aerial images from the airport area with him. He handed them over to the agents.

They each viewed the photos. "Do you have the names?" E.T. asked.

"Yes, I wrote the names behind the photos," Noah replied.

"How certain are you of the identification of these men?" E.T. asked.

"One hundred percent," Noah replied.

E.T. turned around the photos and read the names. Then he handed them to Special Agent Rochas, who immediately made notes in his notepad. They knew they could not arrest the men with diplomatic protection, but they could ask the White House to expel these men from the United States.

"This whole story is quite unbelievable. The Russians had an operation on our soil: Operation Pobeda. They had an organized group called Septem to orchestrate all the tasks in the operation. The most incredible part is the doppelganger; the clone of Joseph is Stalin," E.T. repeated and shook his head. "Are you sure about that?"

"Indeed, and we possess both the DNA evidence and his comprehensive blood analysis to substantiate it," Noah affirmed. Extracting a document from his backpack, he extended the findings to the agents.

"And he's the president's son-in-law," E.T. summarized. "How the hell are we going to keep this from the press?" He shook his head in disbelief. "Why Stalin?" he asked.

"Noah might have an answer," Otis said and turned to Noah and asked, "Show the images you dug online from the Russian newspapers. Noah did as he was told; he opened the shoulder bag he had with him, pulled out a dossier, showed some articles and images, and explained, "These are the images of 2015 to 2018 of the Werewolves in Germany. They rode to Berlin for the MC rallies marking the anniversary of the end of World War II. They displayed red flags with portraits of Stalin and shouted World War II-era Red Army oath: For the Motherland! For Stalin!"

Noah showed more images of the Werewolves' visit to Poland and Germany. In Poland, they had visited Russia's memorial to Polish WWII prisoners of war slaughtered in the Katyn massacre in 1940.

"Next year, in Berlin, they rode to the Soviet War Memorial (Tiergarten), a WWII memorial to honor the fallen soldiers of the Soviet Armed Forces in the Battle of Berlin in April and May 1945," Noah explained and handed the images to E.T. to view, and then continued, "Stalin is considered the winner of WWII, defeating the Nazis and the fascism, and boosting the Soviet Union's economy."

"He executed over one million people!" E.T. exclaimed.

"He was a strong, iron-clad leader. At Russia's current political climate, the people look for a strong leader, a true patriot," Otis replied. "The memory of the gulags, the Russian labor camps, and the millions executed are swept under the rug because they can be considered as taking care of the non-patriots, the rebels, and the terrorists colluding with the enemies of the state."

"That explains it," E.T. replied. "Stalin's clone would create a new, strong leader like the original one was. If this clone had continued his political career, he might have even become our president."

"What are you going to do with the clone?" Otis asked. "Are there any laws for human clones?"

"Do any of our laws consider a clone a human being?" E.T. asked. It was just a rhetorical question. "Is this clone just a weird result of scientific research? Does a clone have any rights?" He sighed. "I know there is going to be a series of questions to be answered concerning the human clone. One important question is, is the president's daughter legally married if she is married to a clone." He shook his head. "This is a mess."

"I might have a suggestion," Otis said. He had also thought about the same questions. "When you capture the creator of this clone, you could place Joe Steel and his clone in a supermax prison in an undisclosed location. I don't mean Guantanamo Bay, but a distant place, far away from the prying public eye, like the new one in Northwest of Alaska."

"How do you know about that?" Special Agent Rochas asked.

E.T. waved his hand and said, "You know because of your previous work in the agency. That is a good idea. We can also ask him to work for us. His clone proves that he's ahead of any research we're currently aware of."

"He's also an American working with the Russians," Special Agent Rochas reminded. "He's guilty of treason and probably also terrorism. We can't just take him and ask him to work for us."

"Worse criminals have been pardoned, for example, the Nazi scientists. We don't know if he would agree to work for us. He might refuse. He might also get away before we capture him," E.T. replied.

"Joe Steel won't be able to get away. The Russians have diplomatic passports, but he doesn't. He won't be able to cross the border by plane or boat," Special Agent Griffin assured. "We can send his images to all the borders and TSA checkpoints."

"He might be interested in cooperation and sharing his research if his only future is the supermax prison," Otis replied.

"You're right. He'd prefer research instead of life in prison," E.T. agreed.

Otis looked around the table. Everyone looked tired after the interview. "If that's all you need, we'd like to go now."

"How about the Russian mole in the White House? You mentioned him, but you didn't provide any proof of who he is," Special Agent Griffin asked.

"I know he's someone in the president's closest circle. Someone who knew the flight schedule. Someone who knew about me and that I had meetings with the president. I don't know his identity yet, but I have an idea how to find him," Otis said.

"Tell us," Special Agent Griffin said.

"The only thing I'm certain is that the mole has kept in touch with the group and Dan Wheeler, the clone, in the hospital. Did you apprehend any cell phones in Restaurant Nevskij?"

"Yes, we did from the dead Werewolf members," Griffin replied.

"Did you check the numbers they had called?"

Griffin nodded. "Yes, but that was a dead end."

"I hoped there would have been a call to the White House," Otis said, looking disappointed. "Anyhow, that was my idea."

"Any other ideas?" Rochas asked.

"Yes, we can check the hospital phone records. He didn't have his cell phone at the hospital. The president specifically requested that so we could monitor his calls. He used the hospital landline phone. We knew he was the Russian contact, the Postmaster. We had to keep tabs on him. It was easy as long as he stayed at the hospital and was using only one phone."

"Let's check it right now," Special Agent Griffin said. He called someone and asked him to get the account of the calls Dan had made or received. It did not take long before he received a callback. He took down some notes before ending the call. "The received calls were mostly from unknown numbers except for two numbers he'd called. They belonged to the president and the other to Press Secretary Brad Buchanan."

"Nothing there," E.T. concluded. "We still don't know who the mole in the White House is."

Otis was disappointed. He had a feeling that he had missed some information now, some important minor detail.

"What'll happen next?" Otis asked.

"We'll arrest Dan," Special Agent Griffin replied.

"I better come with you. I need to tell Irene about her husband and what's going on. She needs me to tell her about Dan, not a stranger," Otis said.

"I'll come with you," Noah said.

When Otis looked surprised, he added, "I've never seen or met a real human clone."

"We need to find the clone maker, Joe Steel," Special Agent Rochas said. "He's an American. I doubt that the Russian embassy will allow him to hide there."

"I don't know how organized this Septem group is, but I know they are not careless, and they have money. You should be prepared that they will try to cut off any loose ends, like the clone," Otis warned.

Before Otis had time to finish his sentence, Special Agent Rochas was on the phone calling the hospital.

They all knew that the Secret Service was there guarding each room where the members of the First Family were.

"Don't let anyone enter Dan Wheeler's room before we get there." Otis heard Special Agent Rochas telling the Secret Service agent on the phone.

"You should give him the description of Joe Steel," Otis said, pointing to his photo on the table. "He might present himself as a doctor, which he is. He must be arrested if seen there. He might try to assassinate Dan."

Luis Rochas grabbed the photo and said to the Secret Service agent on the phone, "I will scan you a picture of a man we suspect might be an assassin. Arrest him if you see him there." He opened his scan app on his cell phone, scanned Joe Steel's photo, and sent it to the Secret Service agent.

"Dan is the only one who can reveal the whole plot to us and tell exactly who was involved," Otis added. "It's important that he's kept alive."

"Do you think he knows who the White House mole is?" E.T. asked.

"I don't know. He might know, but he might not tell us. He might try to make a deal," Otis replied.

89

The Arrest

When the six FBI agents entered the hospital with their windbreaker costumes identifying their agency, the patients and the hospital employees stopped and stared at them, hustled together, whispering to each other, and some even took videos with their cell phones. Everyone knew by now that the president's son-in-law, Dan Wheeler, was at the hospital. Not everyone knew that the president's son, Zachary, was also at the same hospital.

The Secret Service agents were in front of Dan's hospital room. When the FBI agents marched towards the door, one of the Secret Service agents stopped them and whispered, "We got him. He's inside."

"You got the suspect, Joe Steel?" Special Agent Rochas asked, stopping next to the Secret Service agents.

"Yes, we did. He came here just after your call. He was dressed like a doctor and tried to enter the room. We recognized him from his photo and arrested him. He is being guarded in the next room," the Secret Service agent pointed towards the next room from Dan's hospital room.

"Great," Rochas said and pointed towards the next room, and two FBI agents went inside that one. Soon they came out with Joe Steel in handcuffs.

Otis was curious and stared at the arrested man. Joe Steel, aka Cyborg, was the one who had created the first human clone. He was a genius.

Joe Steel looked like a normal guy. He had a high forehead, and his hairline was receding. He was a tall man with sharp, penetrating eyes. He glanced towards Otis and obviously recognized him. Joe stopped in front of Otis when the agents walked by and said, "You're Otis Thorne. Just one man took down our operation Pobeda. You won this battle, but not the war."

"What war?" Otis asked.

"The war for global dominance," Joe Steel replied haughtily. "You know the war was, first of all, a financial one. Our group wanted to seize back the Russian fortune in the frozen bank accounts. We also had a secondary goal, a decolonial one, that is, we wanted to weaken the global domination of the United States of America, freeing the countries from being dependent on the United States and its military and monetary power."

The two FBI agents pulled Cyborg with them, and they walked away from Otis. Special Agents Rochas and Griffin stayed behind. They had also heard the conversation between Cyborg and Otis, and Otis knew they would report it back to their director.

Joe Steel was probably right, Otis thought. *Even if we, the United States of America, have won this battle, more battles will come.*

Otis and Noah waited in the hallway, watching Special Agents Griffin and Rochas enter Dan's hospital room, bring Dan with them, and take him to the elevators.

Noah looked at Dan curiously and said, "He looks like a real human. I could never tell he was a clone."

Irene came out of Zachary's hospital room and rushed towards the elevator, but the FBI agents did not allow her to go with them. She turned and saw Otis standing with Noah.

Irene ran to Otis and pleaded, "Otis, please, help me. They have arrested Dan. Why? What's happening? They did not want to tell me anything."

"Let's go back to Dan's room, and I'll explain everything," Otis said, leading her inside the hospital room and asking, "Please, sit down. We have a lot to talk about."

Irene did as she was told.

"This is Noah S. Pye," Otis introduced Noah to Irene. "He helped me to find Zachary."

Irene nodded and begged, "Please, tell me about Dan." Her eyes were wide and filled with fear. "The FBI agents told me Dan will be charged with treason. How is that possible? He has not done anything!"

"He has done more than you think," Noah said.

"What do you mean?" Irene turned to Noah.

"It's better if Otis explains," Noah mumbled.

"Your father asked me to tell you, but It's difficult," Otis started. "He committed treason because the FBI can prove that he conspired with the Russians and participated in the kidnapping of your brother, Zachary."

"That's not true. " Dan was in the helicopter with Zachary," Irene said, shaking her head.

Otis took Irene's hands in his and looked her straight in the eyes. "No, he was not. He was behind the kidnapping.

It was a fake crash. He helped the Russians to kidnap Zachary at the airport."

"But why?" Irene asked with tears in her eyes.

"Dan has always worked for the Russians," Otis said. He turned to Noah for support. Noah looked at Otis and said, "Just tell her the truth. She must know."

"The truth? What truth?" Irene asked, turning her eyes from Noah to Otis. She pulled her hands away from Otis's grip.

"Your husband was a clone," Noah dropped the bomb. "Stalin's clone... You remember Stalin, the Russian ex-dictator?"

Irene gasped and put her hand over her mouth. A dead silence fell over the room.

"You are joking," Irene said after a long silence. She tried to get up to leave, but Otis gently placed his hand on her shoulder and pushed her back on the chair. "You need to listen to us. It's all true. He is a clone. Dan was designed and created by an American scientist who is Stalin's grandson," Otis explained and continued, "I don't know if you are legally married to Dan. I don't know what rights Dan has because he's a scientific experiment, not a real human being. We don't have laws for his kind. I'm not sure what'll happen to him. He committed treason, but can he be charged with the crime? I don't know. One thing is for sure: he'll be incarcerated for the rest of his life."

Irene stared at Otis and then turned her eyes to Noah. "You are serious. This is not a joke."

Noah nodded.

"But if he's a clone, then this must have been planned years ago," Irene said.

Otis nodded. "Yes, cloning was an ongoing experiment that started during WWII in the concentration camp where Stalin's son met the famous Doctor Mengele. I don't know when the idea of cloning Stalin emerged, but we know that it must have been a long process. There must have been several failures before the successful clone was born. They must have planned your marriage with him to get closer to the president and Zachary."

"Years of planning," Irene said quietly. "He never loved me. It was all just part of the plan."

"We don't know if the clone has emotions like we do. We don't know anything about clones," Otis replied.

"I don't know what to think," Irene said. "I need to see my father," she added. She stood up and said, "Thank you for telling me everything."

Otis looked at her when she exited the room. She was brave-looking, even if her whole world had just collapsed.

He looked at Noah and said, "I don't know what to say to help her. She'll have a lot of media pressure when this is all over. The FBI can't keep the clone a secret."

"Maybe they can," Noah said. "They've kept bigger secrets for decades. They can file and stamp this case as a top secret for the next fifty years if they decide that's best for the nation. I think in this case, they will do whatever they can not to let the world know how the Russians manipulated the First Family."

"You're probably right," Otis said.

Identifying the mole was still a problem, and Otis was sure he had missed something he had heard or seen during the last hours.

Otis asked, "Can we still go through Dan's phone records one more time? We missed something at the FBI meeting."

"The received calls were mostly from unknown numbers besides the two numbers that he had also called," Noah repeated the information they had gotten from the FBI.

"How about the numbers Dan called?" Otis asked.

"They belonged to the president and the other to Press Secretary Brad Buchanan."

"Can you do a background analysis of Brad Buchanan?" Otis asked. He knew that Zachary, Dan, and Brad had been friends for a long time. But was there something else behind that friendship?

"Yes, sure. Just wait a minute," Noah replied. Otis saw him pulling out his tablet from his shoulder bag and saw his finger fly on the keyboard, and a quiet tapping sound filled the room.

He heard Noah mumbling, "A confidential file. That's interesting."

It took a couple of minutes before Noah replied. "Did you know that Brad was adopted?"

"No, I didn't know," Otis replied. The whole White House staff had to go through a security clearance process, including Brad Buchanan, but an adoption might not have raised any red flags.

"The adoption file was marked confidential. Guess where he was adopted from?" Noah asked.

"Don't tell me... Russia?" Otis replied. A cold shiver went up his spine. He should have thought of that before. Zachary, Brad, and Dan had been called the three musketeers at the college. He should have known. He should have guessed that Brad was part of Operation Pobeda. This whole operation had been planned years ago when they had befriended Zachary at the college. This was a long-term plan; only the goals and the demands changed depending on the current needs of the Russian leaders. The Russian government had waited for the perfect opportunity to execute their clandestine operation and use their most valuable assets, the clone, and the mole.

"Yes, Russia. We've apprehended him—the mole inside the White House," Noah declared, closing his tablet and returning it to his bag.

Otis picked up his phone and dialed E.T. When E.T. picked up, Otis conveyed, "We've identified the mole. It's Brad."

"Thank you for the heads-up. Do you have evidence?" inquired E.T.

"Noah has it, and he'll forward it to you. It's circumstantial but should suffice for the time being. Your next step is to apprehend him and secure a confession," Otis responded.

"We'll handle that," E.T. assured.

90

The Cleanup

After the last call, E.T. checked out the information Noah had provided about Brad. Then E.T. called Otis back and asked Otis to join him and come to see the arrest himself. They stood side by side in the hallway of the White House and watched as the Russian mole, Press Secretary Brad Buchanan, was escorted away, guarded by the FBI agents. His hands were handcuffed behind his back.

Otis stopped them. "Would you please wait? I want to check something."

The FBI agents hesitated and looked at E.T., who stood beside Otis.

E.T. nodded and said, "This will just take a moment."

Otis stepped behind Brad, grabbed Brad's hands, and turned his right wrist upwards, showing the tattoo to E.T. "Here is the additional proof," Otis said.

E.T. glanced at the tattoo and said, "What is it? Some sort of a bird?"

"Nachtkrapp is a night raven that terrorizes people and brings death to those who look at it," Brad explained through gritted teeth.

"I've never heard of it," E.T. replied, "I don't know much about mythological creatures."

Otis explained, "The mole, Brad Buchanan, never revealed his past as one of the children Russia's government had sent to the United States of America. He never lost his ties to his old home country, Russia, and secretly worked his way up in the food chain. He went to the right colleges and befriended the right friends: Zachary, the future president's son, the president's daughter, and her husband."

E.T. shook his head in disbelief. "How is all this even possible?" E.T asked. "He was the Press Secretary. He was a close friend to Zachary and Irene."

"We were all just pawns in this chess game," Otis replied. There was nothing else to add. He turned around and walked outside.

Later that evening, at Otis's apartment, Otis had invited Deena to have a luxurious dinner with him. Otis had taken Deena to 1789 Restaurant at 36th Street.

They had both ordered Striped Bass with caper-tomato broth and sorbet with a glass of Brachetto D'Acqui wine for dessert. Deena had suggested that they go back to her apartment and check for the latest news because the Director of the FBI, E.T. Ruckert, was supposed to be a guest on the late evening news. So, they did that.

At Deena's apartment, she took out a bottle of white wine, and they sat on the couch waiting for the news broadcast to start.

An NBC anchor appeared. He looked to be in his fifties, upright and compelling. He wore a gray suit with a red tie.

Otis turned up the volume, leaned back on the couch, and put his hand over Deena's shoulder.

Time to see how E.T. spins this tale, Otis thought. He can't tell the truth to the public, not the whole truth. It would be a risk to national security, especially the Mole in the White House.

Otis raised a glass of white wine to his mouth and took a sip. He glanced sideways at Deena and saw her cradle her wine glass with two hands, seemingly anxious to see the broadcast.

"We are joined now by the Director of the FBI, E. Thomas Ruckert," the anchor said with a solemn face, "who has come here to share with us the latest news of what has happened in the White House." He turned towards E.T. Ruckert and said, "Welcome, Director Ruckert."

Otis turned up the volume.

"Please, call me E.T.," Director E.T. Ruckert replied. His shiny jet-black hair was neatly brushed backward. His eyes were bright, like two charcoal buttons, and his olive skin was accentuated with the crisp white shirt and red-blue tie he wore to the interview.

"I'm sure all our viewers would like to know what happened. Let me just play back the scene taken earlier from the helicopter crash that we now know was a fake crash to cover up Zachary Burr's kidnapping."

They played archival footage of a scene showing police patrol cars, FBI agents, and ambulances searching for the crash site.

The news anchor continued, "This was taken at George Washington University Hospital yesterday. Zachary Burr is walking out, obviously not harmed. Can you please tell us exactly what happened between the fake crash and when you discovered Zachary was alive?"

E.T. cleared his throat and began, "Thank you for inviting me here. I'd be happy to tell you. Obviously, I can't reveal all the details yet because our investigative teams are still working on it," he replied and continued, "We heard from an informant that a hit was planned against the president of the United States. That was around the time the helicopter crashed. We informed President Burr about the potential risk. After the helicopter crash, we tried to locate the eyewitnesses, but we were unable to find anyone. We believed then that the crash was a coverup. We started investigating, and we found out that a Russian criminal motorcycle gang had entered this country. We had the local police departments look for signs of the motorcycle gangs, and they found two locations: the other one was a storage facility for illegal drugs and weapons, and the other one was a restaurant where we found Zachary Burr alive and well. Zachary was held captive for ransom, but the ransom did not happen." Otis noticed the white lie: there was never a ransom.

The FBI had decided not to say anything about the blackmail, Otis thought.

The news anchor interjected, "Was there a shootout by the restaurant?"

"Yes, two members of the Russian gang were killed in the shootout before law enforcement was able to enter the building."

"This was in front of Restaurant Nevskij?" the news anchor chimed in, staring earnestly at the camera.

"Yes, that was the name of the restaurant," E.T. agreed.

"President Burr had a heart attack," the news anchor started, "We can assume that it was because of the news of his son's rescue operation?"

"Yes, that's right. When President Burr received the call that his son was alive and well, he had a heart attack," E.T. concurred.

"And this was also the reason why President Burr decided to resign, and Vice President Joh Rossi has his inauguration tomorrow," the anchor summarized.

"Yes, that's correct," E.T. replied.

Otis looked thoughtful. That was not the whole truth, but it seemed to be enough for the media.

"Two other persons were arrested after this: Dan Wheeler, President Burr's son-in-law, and Brad Buchanan,

White House Press Secretary. Can you tell us more about these arrests?" The news anchor asked.

E.T. cleared his throat and stared directly at the television camera. "Their arrests are a different matter. We are still investigating their involvement in an information leak within the White House. However, I can tell you that it seems they have given some highly classified, top-secret information to foreign country operatives, information that can damage our national defense."

Otis had a difficult time hiding his smile.

Deena picked up her wine glass, and as she brought it to her lips, gazed up at Otis over the rim.

Deena knew the real story. Otis had filled her in.

"Can you say anything more specific about their arrest?" The news anchor asked, trying to press E.T. to reveal more details.

"As I told you before, the investigation is still ongoing, and I can't tell you more because we are still doing our duty," E.T. replied, smiling at the camera. "All I can tell you is that our national security is secured, and all the Americans can sleep well tonight."

Otis listened, amazed at how deftly E.T. walked a thin line and revealed part of the truth but not the whole truth. He was sure Noah was listening to the news too.

91

The Concluding Meeting

The Oval Office, a week after the Mole was arrested

"The Werewolves were used as a foreign force battalion within the United States to assist in a revolutionary extortion coup to control and influence the executive office. They were disguised as a normal motorcycle gang like the Hells Angels, but their goals were designed high-up in the Russian Government and assisted by the Ministry of State Security (MGB). Their goal was to ensure the frozen Russian assets were restored and the Russian government to regain more power in the global political arena," Director of the FBI E. Thomas Ruckert, E.T., explained to the newly elected President of the United States, John Rossi, and the representatives of the other national agencies including the directors of the CIA and NSA. He gave them a file of Operation Pobeda.

Andrew Burr had resigned and was still in the hospital, being rehabilitated after the paralysis. President Rossi's inauguration had been just the day before this meeting.

E.T. adjusted his red tie and scanned the faces sitting around him for a reaction. The silence hung in the air like the suspended moment before a bomb explosion hit the ground. This information was explosive.

Everyone in the room knew it. They had listened to E.T.'s report with mixed feelings. Some of the audience looked aghast, some angry, and some just surprised.

The men had coffee served on white porcelain cups, but hardly anyone had touched their coffee when they had heard the topic of the classified meeting.

"We can't tell any of this to the press," E.T. said, looking around the room to confirm his conclusion. President Rossi was the first one to speak up. "We can file it as confidential for the next fifty years," President Rossi suggested. He saw nods of agreement around him.

"What about President Andrew Burr?" Roscoe Heller, Director of the CIA, asked. "He has committed treason based on the evidence we just heard."

President Rossi looked at him sternly and replied, "Considering his health, and that he barely survived the heart attack and the stroke that left his left side of the body paralyzed and that he can barely form words, I don't think any Congress or court will find him guilty. And even if they would, I would pardon him. No one could have done anything differently if they had been in his shoes. The Russian Mole made it impossible for him to confess to anyone, and he couldn't know who to trust inside the White House or in any of the agencies."

"And the clone?" Roscoe Heller asked.

"We have transported him to a black site facility in Northwest of Alaska, a familiar facility to you, I suppose, because your officials use it, too," E.T. said. "Joe Steel has agreed to continue his research under our surveillance. We'll receive valuable information about human cloning techniques. He'll have a research area to work. The clone will be monitored and studied for the rest of his life. He is a scientific experiment and nothing more."

"And Burr's family?" Roscoe Heller asked.

"Zachary shows no signs of post-traumatic syndromes following the kidnapping. He's already back at work. Additionally, his sister has annulled her marriage to Dan. It seemed the most straightforward resolution since the legal status of a union with a human clone remains uncertain, given the absence of specific laws pertaining to clones."

"And Otis Thorne and Noah S. Pye?" President Rossi asked. He knew E.T. had asked Estelle Thorne, Irene, and Zachary to sign the confidentiality agreement.

"They are back doing what they did before this operation. Otis and his mother are personal friends of the Burr family, and they won't tell their secrets to the press," E.T. replied.

"Could you tell us more about the members of the Septem group?" Gordon Frost, the Director of the NSA, asked.

"Of course," E.T. replied with a single nod and began, "The Russians, namely Sergei Stolyar, Alexei Petrov, Boris Kryukov, Ivan Komar, and Orel Andruchenko, who participated in Operation Pobeda have been expelled from this country. They called themselves the Septem, the seven: five Russians and two Americans, namely Brad Buchanan, aka the White House mole, and Joe Steel were the members. Their photos are included in the file each of you has in front of you. The clone, Dan, was not a real member of the group but a useful research experiment. The Russian oligarchs have already left our country," E.T. explained. "We have also announced the freeze of their assets, including the closure of their warehouses, businesses, and restaurants in the United States. Since these five oligarchs used diplomatic passports, we concluded that the state was aware of this attack if not directly involved in planning it; therefore, we suggest that the United States should suspend bilateral relations with Russ ia."

Roscoe Heller, the Director of the CIA, asked, "Should we expel Russian diplomats who have been identified as undeclared intelligence officers? We could also freeze the Russian state's assets," he added.

"We have just the diplomatic passports to prove that these oligarchs cooperated with the state, but other than that, we can't prove that the state knew what was going on," E.T., the Director of the FBI, replied.

"Okay, we let the sanctions be as they are and concentrate on these oligarchs who were directly involved in planning and executing this operation," Heller said.

"I guess we have wrapped this case," President Rossi added, "I have issued an executive order that provides additional authority for responding to a hostile foreign activity that seeks to interfere with or undermine our judicial or governmental processes and institutions. We're all alarmed by Russia's actions and need to find a way to secure our highest positions in the government."

"What was Russia's reaction?" Gordon Frost, the Director of the NSA, asked and sipped coffee from his cup. He was dressed in a dark suit with a crisp white shirt and a blue tie.

President Rossi turned to face him and replied, "A spokesman for President Vladislav Ruskin in Moscow said that Russia regretted the new sanctions against their oligarchs and would consider retaliatory measures."

"That's their standard reply," Roscoe Heller scoffed, tapping his fist on the tabletop. "These Russia's actions are almost a declaration of a war."

"We don't need to go to war with Russia. We just won a battle, and it has had its casualties: Andrew Burr lost his presidency, his health, his son-in-law, and some close friends of his family. Let's not forget that. This is not just politics. Real persons, their lives and careers were destroyed and changed forever," President Rossi replied stiffly. He had no intention of starting a war during his term in office. Then he continued, "Let's keep an eye on the Russians from now on. I want all your agencies to check through your employees and the White House staff to ensure no Russian moles are left."

President Rossi stood up and said, "Russia's threats to the United States' national security and its global existence are imminent and present. Even if the enemy was Russia this time, the next time, it could be another hostile country or a terrorist group."

CODE NAMES

HYDRA
OREL ANDRUCHENKO

CYBORG
JOE STEEL

WEREWOLF
IVAN KOMAR   DENTIST

BASILISK
SERGEI STOLYAR

PHOENIX
ALEKSEI PETROV

NACHTKRAPP
BRAD BUCHANAN   PRESS SECRETARY

HIPPOGRIFF
BORIS KRYUKOV

92

Moscow

The Kremlin, Moscow, 9 a.m. (GMT+3)

T he Mil Mi-8 medium twin-turbine helicopter landed on the Kremlin's helipad, and a familiar figure exited the helicopter. Two helipads were built in 2013 and located in the Kremlin's Taynitsky, the Secret Garden, at the southeast corner of the Kremlin.

A familiar form of the current Russian president appeared from the helicopter. President Vladislav Ruskin crouched as he walked away from the helicopter pad and was flanked by two officers in military uniforms.

Both Vladislav Ruskin and his predecessor Vladimir Putin had used choppers to travel on official business because Moscow's traffic was a nightmare. Long official motorcades would add to the traffic jam, and nobody wanted that. The police would block the roads, and the normal drivers would have to wait for the official motorcade to pass.

Before entering the Kremlin fortress, President Ruskin glanced around and admired the golden domes and the crenelated walls surrounding the Kremlin area. The Kremlin was a conglomeration of a fortress, palace, church, and arsenals, filled with ornate towers built by different czars in the 1400s to 1700s. There were still snowbanks and bare branches in Taynitsky Garden, but the garden had glorious flower banks of tulips in the summertime, and the air would be filled with sweet floral scents.

President Ruskin's Cashmere topcoat billowed behind him in the wind when he marched to the heavily guarded doorway and entered the building. Under the topcoat, he wore a custom-tailored gray business suit made by the latest Italian fashion gurus. He had a white silk shirt and a woven silk tie in shades of burgundy.

He walked along the dim passages until he arrived in a meeting room where the remaining members of the Septem group were waiting for him, namely: Hydra,

Hippogriff, Dentist, Basilisk, and Phoenix. Everyone else except Dentist wore dark business suits. Dentist wore his leather MC cutoff and leather pants. They sat around the large mahogany table and waited for President Ruskin to arrive. They exchanged nervous glances, but nobody said anything. They knew all the meeting rooms were recorded inside the Kremlin. It was better to sit quietly and still, not showing any nervousness or fear.

When the president entered the room, the group stood up.

He sat down, motioned to the chairs around the table with his right hand, and said, "Please, sit down. Explain what happened." His last words were directed to the man sitting on his right side, Hydra.

The atmosphere in the room was tense.

"We failed. Operation Pobeda was exposed," Hydra started. He looked uncomfortable, and beads of sweat had formed on his forehead. He took a white handkerchief from his pocket and quickly patted his forehead before he continued, "We lost Cyborg and Nachtkrapp. They are both alive."

"Should we do something about that?" President Ruskin asked, raising his eyebrows. The failure of this multimillion-dollar operation was not what he had expected or wanted.

"The Americans probably offer Nachtkrapp to us in exchange for some American officials and citizens we hold in our prisons," Hydra replied. He didn't believe President Ruskin would be interested in saving the life of the former mole, Brad Buchanan.

"Do we want him here?" President Ruskin asked.

"He has good Intel from inside the U.S. government and the White House. He knows the officials currently in power and the politicians that can be in power after the next election," Hydra replied cautiously.

"Get on with it then, make the exchange," President Replied, impatiently drumming the table with his fingers.

Hydra elaborated, "Cyborg has been incarcerated in a prison in Alaska. Retrieving him poses considerable challenges, as the Americans are unlikely to willingly surrender both him and his clone, Dan Wheeler. Their intention is to scrutinize the clone and possibly enlist Cyborg to continue his research under their watchful eye."

Curious, President Ruskin inquired, "What about the other clones? What has become of them?"

"We've reached an understanding with Cyborg; he will maintain the facade that only one clone, Dan Wheeler, was successful. The Americans remain unaware of the existence of the other clones. This leaves us with the option to leverage them as needed," Hydra replied.

"Good, good." President Ruskin looked thoughtful and said, "Is his research completely out of our reach?"

"No, not exactly. there's another one who knows everything." He did not reveal who this one was, but continued adding, "He had an apprentice. Cyborg has meticulously written down his cloning research experiments. I'm sure his apprentice can follow his notes," Hydra replied, relieved that the discussion had headed in this direction instead of finding the guilty ones to blame for the failure.

"In conclusion, we managed to start the discussion in the United Nations General Assembly to withdraw all the sanctions. We managed to overthrow the elected president of the United States and replace him with his vice president. We were successful in causing suspicion and chaos within the American government. We successfully used the troll factory in creating fake news," President Ruskin paused and said, "Operation Pobeda was not a complete failure." He stood up and said, "Thank you, gentlemen, for your effort. The motherland will need your services again soon."

The remaining members of the Septem group got up and watched President Ruskin exiting the meeting room. The short meeting was over, and they had kept their lives. The atmosphere in the room got lighter, relieved.

On his way out, President Ruskin smiled to himself and thought: Our world behind the scenes is shrouded in secrecy. This was just the beginning. We'll find a way to try again.

Praise for the Series

"**A** riveting political thriller: President Andrew Burr's son has been kidnapped and soon finds himself being blackmailed. Quickly learning there is no one else in the White House he can trust, he turns to the only person he feels he can trust--former CIA operative Otis Thorne. Jones' narrative strikes the right note as it starts off with a gripping scene and never lets up. The author's writing style reminds me of Tom Clancy. If political intrigue, secret organizations, treachery at every turn, and emotional stakes are your jam, this book is for you."

"Amazing Story! This story is non-stop action and wonders from the first page through the last! Who would have thought that Cloned people would be anywhere than in a science fiction movie? The way that Otis Thorne works through what is happening to the how to fix what is happening, is truly Amazing! I am so glad that he is on our side! Thank you, Arla Jones, for a wonderful story, that may or may not be fiction."

"Keeps you guessing: This story made me love mystery/thrillers again. Arla Jones clearly knows her stuff and uses that knowledge to lead you through a world of shock and awe. I never give spoilers in my reviews, and her blurb tells you enough that if you like this kind of thing, or hey, even if you don't, read this book. You will NOT be disappointed. I haven't read a thriller in a long time because they were all the same. This one will not be the only one I read from this author. Great story!"

"Great Story Concept:The plot of this book caught my interest. It was the storyline and characters that kept me reading. The concept isn't new, but the presentation is original and modern.I enjoyed the various perspectives. The author's choice to give the tale from various character POVs helped bring it alive. However, I felt Noah was truly the protagonist instead of Otis. Overall, I felt this was entertaining. I think you'll enjoy this thriller."

"What a bug problem! This book will stay with me for a long time, and then some more! Thinking this is high-tech with the hidden away testing, and then wondering if this was a created pandemic disease, but when the truth is out, it is very sinister. How could anyone from any country think that was a 'good idea'? Hatred and greed at its worst, is what I think! This was a very fast-paced book, that is made for more mature readers, who love a terrifying thriller! Thank you, Arla Jones, for an excellent story, that I hope never comes true."□

Otis Thorne Series

Otis Thorne series includes the following books:

- Fathers and Sons
- Black Dust
- The Facility
- Death Walks in Washington D.C.

About the Author

Born in the land of saunas and snowy winters, Author Arla Jones has embarked on a literary journey that spans continents.

Now living in the United States, she infuses storytelling with the European aspects and the diverse tapestry of American life, creating fiction that is as unique as her own life's journey.

Also By The Author

The Otis Thorne Thriller series

Fathers and Sons

Black Dust

The Facility

Death Walks in Washington D.C.

The Lost Tomb -series

The Lost Tomb

Venomous Dunes

The Lost Oasis of Love

Mummy Returns

Jaxon Axis -series (Dystopian, Sci-Fi)

Jaxon Axis and the First Crime

Jaxon Axis and the Ice Age

The Starbound Orphans Series (YA/Sci-Fi-thriller)

Starbound Orphans

Starbound Journey

Starbound Hearts

The Kingdom series (YA/fantasy)

Wings of Sea

Wings of War

Wings and Fins

Wings of Shadows (coming soon)

Fairytales Retold (YA)

Snow in Paris

Monster Girlfriend Chronicles (YA, Teen love, Monster love, LGBTQ)

The Spring Break with my Monster Girlfriend
The Summer of MoNsters
Christmas with my Monster Girlfriend
The Portal of Monsters (coming soon)

The Ackley Family Saga (historical romance)

Lord Ackley's Choice
A Rose So Red
Court of Kisses

Romance Short stories

Snowbound Strangers (contemporary romance)

Home for Christmas (romantasy)

Westerns

The Lady and The Stubborn Rancher

The Lady and The Robber Baron

Bury My Dreams

The Ashburn -series (the paranormal investigators)

On Death's Door

Finders Keepers

The Snowman

The Cupid and the Elf -series

Love Trap

Naughty Elf

Ghost Stories

Cursed Banshee

Don't Go There

The Boy Called Pink

Bloody Shamrock

The Wonderland Executioner Series

The Red Queen Executioner

Crimson Tide – series (Horror, Scifi/thriller)

Dead Reef, Blood Tide

Dead Reef, Rise (coming soon)

Cold Blood, Scales of Tomorrow (prequel, coming soon)

Sci-Fi

The Host

Dead Reef, Blood Tide

Dead Reef, Dark Tide

Romantasy, Paranormal Romance

Grimhilde

Circus Hearts

Beauty is the Beast

The Minotaur series

Minotaur's Muse

Minotaur's Curse

Ariadne's Revenge

A Titanic Paranormal Novel

Chasing Death

Middle Grade / Children's books

Attack Of the Iguana

Evil Elves

Attack On the North Pole

Krampus Escapes

Krampus: The Christmas Troublemaker

The Underground Cat Academy

Three Ghost Brothers (by A. T. Sorsa)

Ayla Jones (Dark/Gothic/Paranormal romance, Romantasy)

Donder – the Claus Club series

The Night Riders

The Dragon Prophecy Series

No Way But Down

Dragon Unleashed

The Bloodlines Series

Bloodlines of Revolution

Bobbie Robins Contemporary thrillers

Samantha Raven Trilogy:

I'll Be Your Shadow

I'll Never Let You Go

I'll Be Back

Anthologies:

The Tales of Howloween

Find a full list of my stories:

https://beacons.ai/arlajonesbooks

And a scannable qr code:

Made in United States
North Haven, CT
31 October 2025